WILD & SWEET

RHENNA MORGAN

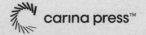
carina press™

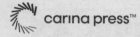

carina press™

ISBN-13: 978-1-335-01267-8

Recycling programs
for this product may
not exist in your area.

Wild & Sweet

This edition published by arrangement with Harlequin Books S.A.

® and TM are trademarks of the publisher. Trademarks indicated with
® are registered in the United States Patent and Trademark Office, the
Canadian Intellectual Property Office and in other countries.

www.CarinaPress.com

Printed in U.S.A.

This one's for the underdogs. The misfits, the wallflowers or those too shy to step out of the shadows. I see you, and I think you're *beautiful*.

WILD &
SWEET

Chapter One

Friday nights were such an irony. With no social life, Gabrielle Parker could stay up as late as she wanted and sleep to obscene hours the next day, but there was never anything worth burning the midnight oil to watch. On the bright side, she'd logged a few more hours of overtime at the garage. Fixing clunker engines that should have been scrapped years ago might not compare to a hot date, but one more paycheck and that computer she'd been saving for was a done deal.

She dodged a nasty pothole on the dark country road and steered her custom '71 Chevy C-10 truck into her tiny subdivision. God, she loved where she lived. Big yards, a beautiful lake not more than three hundred feet beyond her backyard, no fences, and down-to-earth people. Dallas and its suburbs might be caught up in everything new and flashy, but Elk Run clung to its sixties and seventies charm. In fact, it was the only neighborhood in Rockwall or around Lake Ray Hubbard that hadn't sold out. There sure wasn't any waterfront property left. In the past ten years, all the land around the lake had either been gobbled up by big conglomerates for their huge money-making enterprises, or fancy, schmancy neighborhoods lined with jaw-dropping McMansions.

Rounding the wide curve at the end of the one-street

edition, her headlights swept her single-story, ranch-style home. The simple rectangle layout with its shallow, gray asphalt roof and buttery-yellow siding probably wouldn't appeal to other people her age, but she wouldn't trade it for anything. She could do without the empty driveway, though. Her brother's missing car was no surprise. After all, Danny had a thriving social life, but in the two years since their dad had died and left them the house they grew up in, she still hadn't gotten used to coming home without Pop's car being in the third empty space.

She slammed the shifter into Park, killed the engine and snatched her purse off the bench seat. Maybe Danny being out on the town was a good thing. No older brother meant no one giving her grief over her movie selection. She could *Pretty Woman* it up all night and no one would be the wiser. Or maybe tonight she'd splurge and give *Troy* a go. Hard to say no to Brad Pitt in his heyday.

Two steps past the gleaming indigo hood of her truck, she stopped dead in her tracks. Mrs. Wallaby's porch light wasn't on. She could have sworn she'd left it on this morning when she fed her vacationing neighbor's cat, but then she'd also been running thirty minutes late for work and hadn't had her first cup of coffee. With that combination, she was lucky she'd made it to the garage with jeans on.

Keys jingling in the otherwise quiet spring night, Gabe cut across the three-quarter-acre lot to her neighbor's house. Now was as good of a time as any to pick up the mail and make sure Astrid had enough to eat. The sky was deep sapphire velvet with not one cloud to mar it. People in the city didn't have a clue what they were missing on a night like this. Fancy skylines and close conveniences might be nice every now and then, but no way would she trade it for the starry goodness overhead.

She thumbed through Mrs. Wallaby's mail on her way to the front stoop, sorting out the weekend sale circulars and bills. Unlocking and opening the front door, she flipped the hallway light on, let the storm door swing shut behind her, and ambled through the short entry.

"Astrid?"

She'd made it halfway through the living room before the darkness registered. In the corner, the lamp she definitely remembered flipping on before she'd left this morning sat dark on the end table next to the couch. And where the heck was Astrid? The only time she no-showed at mealtime was when strangers came to visit.

The fine hairs on the back of her neck and arms lifted and a shudder trickled down her spine. The house was pure quiet. No breeze, no settling creaks, or humming from the air conditioner. Just dark. Eerie, too-quiet dark.

She dropped the mail on the coffee table and slid her phone out of her jeans pocket. No reason to freak out. Mrs. Wallaby probably just sent one of her grandkids out to check on the house and they'd accidentally trapped Astrid in a bedroom. It sure wouldn't be the first time the skitzy cat had found herself in such a bind.

Punching the main button on her phone for a quick check-in with her neighbor, the home screen flashed a blinding white. Before she could blink her eyes back into focus, quick-moving, heavy footsteps pounded from the hallway behind her and a bulky, shadowed form lumbered toward where she stood. For one freeze-frame moment, his remarkable gaze locked onto hers, spotlighted by the phone's soft glow. Before she could dodge out of the way, he shoved her hard to one side. Her boot snagged on the coffee table, and the right side of her torso slammed crosswise against the marble top.

Son of a freaking gun. That hurt.

The screen door slammed, and the rumbling echo of her crash course with Mrs. Wallaby's anvil-sturdy furniture still resonated through the house, but no more footsteps. And thank God for that, because her side felt like it had gone head-to-head with an engine block. Rather like a stubbed toe times ten thousand while some unseen force squeezed her lungs in a vise grip.

She pushed to her back and yelped into the darkness. Okay, so moving wasn't a super bright idea. Neither was breathing. But staying here was even higher on the stupid scale. Yeah, the house was quiet now, but only an idiot hung around in the dark after a run-in with a thug, and she was definitely not an idiot.

Bracing her ribs with one arm, she sucked in a very limited breath and forced herself upright. An ugly grunt croaked up the back of her throat and a cold sweat broke out across her forehead and neck. For about five seconds, she wasn't even sure staying vertical was a maintainable goal. If she couldn't see with her own eyes that Mrs. Wallaby's table was still whole and hearty post-tumble, she'd have sworn a sliver of the marble had broken off and buried itself between her ribs.

She shook her head and clamped tighter to her phone. She staggered to the sliding glass door that led to the backyard just in case the shady linebacker was still out front and flipped the lock. Putting her weight into opening the door, she tottered out into the night as fast as her protesting ribs would tolerate and dialed 911.

Two hours since Zeke Dugan had walked away from his last trauma case, and he still couldn't unwind. After three twelve-hour emergency shifts in a row, his body might be on board with a direct trip home and a whole lot of shut-eye, but his psyche was still jonesed up from blood, guts and gunshot wounds.

Punching the locks on his Z28, he strode to the private rear entrance of Trevor's new bar, The Den. Not a snowball's chance in hell he'd have brought his custom '69 hot rod to Deep Ellum if he'd had to park it out front, but safe in the private back lot with Beckett's security cameras overhead, only an idiot would mess with his baby.

The crowd's low and happy rumble hit the second he pulled the door wide. Barely nine o'clock on a Friday night and the place was already packed, which went to prove that Jace and Axel weren't the only two Haven brothers who could launch an entertainment venue. Any businessman who could draw the Deep Ellum crowd before eleven or midnight was a genius.

Zeke chin-lifted to the little brunette bartender he'd referred from his own days slogging drinks while he worked through med school. "Hey, Vicky. Guys busy?"

"Only if you call Trevor gloating over his full house with Jace and Axel busy." She motioned to the adjacent room through the wide arch, never breaking stride on the order she was working. "They're laying down roots in their usual booth. You want a Bohemia Weiss?"

"Yep. No hurry."

She grinned. "You sure? You look like you need a shot of something with more punch."

Oh, hell no. "You forget my Mr. Hyde side?"

Her smile died, and this time she nearly fumbled a shot glass. Of course she hadn't forgotten. Zeke's hair-trigger temper had intervened in the form of unforgiving fists and zero conscience when a bunch of frat boys thought it was a good idea to not take no for an answer where she was concerned. It was a wonder he hadn't gone to jail. But then again, that was the night he'd met Jace and Axel. If it weren't for them heading off the cops, he'd still be tending bar, but with a record, instead of living his dream as a trauma doc.

Her expression softened, understanding and grateful all at once. "I haven't seen that side of you in years, but if it's high-end Brazilian beer you want, then that's what you'll get."

"Appreciate it." He ambled to the opposite side of the bar, weaving through the forest of square tables and laughing patrons. Trev had wanted a place where people could hang out as regulars but with a trendy vibe. He'd absolutely nailed it. Rock music and movie memorabilia from the past forty years adorned exposed red brick and ivory mortar walls, but the bar along the back had literally been flown in from Kilkenny, Ireland. If a Hard Rock bar got it on with an Old-World Irish pub, The Den would be their out-of-control offspring.

Crossing into the second room, the whole atmosphere shifted. Tiny white lights like the ones that went on Christmas trees were strategically placed on the ceiling so they didn't look strategically placed, and every seating area had its own style. Sixties to ultramodern, tables or booths, it didn't matter. Every spot gave a nod to a different trend.

Not surprisingly, more of the women hung out in this room, which was also why the brotherhood had its own reserved spot in the back. No one sat there but brothers or those they'd claimed for their own. Ever.

Jace, Axel and Trevor all marked his arrival about three steps into the room and offered everything from a raised beer to shit-eating grins in the way of greeting. The tension he'd been carrying around all night seeped out of him. This was what he needed. If anyone could help him get to the bottom of whatever was eating him, it was his brothers.

He jogged up the three steps to the raised, semienclosed space and rounded the table for a chair with primo viewing. "No Viv tonight?" he said to Jace.

Jace finished off his Scotch and slid the empty out where their waitress could see he needed a fresh one. "Got a gig she's working tonight. Some of Trev's old buddies."

Axel snickered. "Not thinkin' managing a male dance review falls under your new wife's definition of *hardship*."

"Whoa," Zeke said to Trevor. "Been a while since you've been in touch with your old crew." In fact, Trev studiously avoided all reminders of his brief stint shucking clothes for drooling women.

Trevor raised his beer and eyeballed Jace over the rim. "I'm actually surprised Jace didn't put up a fuss when I told Viv what the guys needed. They might not go full monty onstage, but backstage it's a damned free-for-all."

Jace stretched one arm along the back of the vacant chair next to him and smirked. "So long as they don't touch and I'm the one burning off the sexual frustration after, I don't care if they drop trou the second she walks in the back door. Besides, Viv worked up is a thing of beauty."

"Ach, Christ," Axel said. "There he goes again. Rubbin' his good fortune in everyone's face."

Their waitress sauntered up the steps, hips swinging and long, uber—platinum blonde hair hanging loose to her shoulders. The impact would have been a knockout if the smile on her face didn't feel so calculated. "Vicky sent your refreshes. Scotch for Axel and Jace, Bud for Trevor, and Bohemia Weiss for Zeke."

Impressive. Zeke didn't recognize the woman so she had to be fairly new. Either Vicky had prepped her good before sending her in with refreshes, or she was a woman with drive. The question was whether the drive was healthy ambition or geared toward snagging a sugar daddy.

Trevor finished off his beer and slid it to the waitress. "Thanks, Lannie. Don't worry about us for a while. If we need you, we'll flag you down."

So she was after a sugar daddy. Too bad. Good help willing to learn and grow in a place like this would be a godsend to Trevor with all his success.

"You sure?" she said. "I don't mind checking back."

"We're good, darlin'." Pure calm, cool Trevor. With the life he'd been born into, the guy made it a point never to lose his head for fear of leveling justice via his fists.

Disappointment penetrated those vibrant, but all too worldly green eyes of hers a second before she spun and sashayed down the steps.

"She's a persistent lass," Axel said.

Trev pushed back on the hind legs of his chair and rested the butt of his beer bottle on his thigh. "A little too much for my taste. Never seen a woman scope out and target customers with big cash to spend faster than Lannie."

"You sure she's not a plant?" Jace said. "Never know who might be out for info."

Trevor shrugged and took a swig of his beer. "Knox ran a check. Wouldn't hurt to have him take another go, though."

"Where the hell are he and Beckett anyway?" Zeke said. "I thought they were coming out tonight?"

"Knox is knee-deep in some hacking case. Beckett

had a last-minute call from some socialite out in Fort Worth in need of a security detail," Jace said.

Axel snickered and sipped his Scotch. "Bloody bastard never could say no to a pretty face."

"More like a pretty paycheck," Trevor said. "Beck said she's got good long-term client potential with low risk."

"Damn. I wanted to hear how Danny was doing with Beckett's crew." Zeke had been the one to introduce Danny Parker to the brothers almost two years ago. If things kept going the way they were, he was all but one vote away from being the next addition to the family.

"Not a bad word to be heard," Axel said. "Beckett says the man's taken to security and protection like an adolescent boy to *Playboy.*"

Not surprising. Danny's future had damned near gone to hell in a handbasket his senior year in college, breaking into high-end homes and stealing what he needed for a blossoming drug habit. According to Danny, it was his dad and a serious come-to-Jesus one-on-one that had knocked some sense into the young kid. "Knox ever finish the deeper dive on Danny's background?"

"Not much more than what we uncovered when you first brought him in," Axel said. "Always worked at the same body shop. No major changes in relationships. His mom's still stacking up minor drug offenses, though how the hell she's dodging them I'll never figure out."

"She a looker?" Trevor asked.

"Haven't seen a picture, but Knox has," Jace said. "Said she doesn't look a thing like Danny, but probably held her own about twenty years ago."

Zeke turned his bottle on the tabletop, widening the circle of condensation around it. "She going to be a problem?"

"Don't think so," Jace said. "Knox found trails where

Danny's given her money, but no evidence it's more than him making sure she keeps her distance. From what we can tell, there is absolutely no love lost between mom and the rest of the clan."

"He's got a sister, right?" Trevor said.

Jace nodded. "Yep. Gabrielle."

"Gabe." All heads shifted to Zeke. "He calls her Gabe. Says all the guys do."

"You met the lass?"

Zeke shook his head. "No. Been by there a few times and have seen her truck out in the drive, but she's always locked up in the bedroom when I'm there. Got a sweet ride. Another one of Danny's custom jobs, a '71 Chevy C-10 with a highboy conversion."

"A woman with a custom truck." Trevor shook his head and knocked back more of his beer.

"Not surprising really, if you think about it," Zeke said. "She grew up with men. Danny said their dad kicked her mom out when Gabe was little. Add to that, she works with men all day as a mechanic. Danny says she's a really good one, too."

Jace planted an elbow on the table and ran his thumb through the beard along his jawline. "Well, she must spend a lot of time there, because she hasn't got much of a social life. Knox said she didn't have one damned social media account active. No records. No tickets. Hell, all he could find in the way of pictures was her driver's license. For a twenty-four-year-old in today's world, she's an anomaly."

"Any idea how we find out more about her?" Zeke said.

Trevor tipped his head to the wide arch that fed in from the main room. "We could just ask him."

Sure enough, Danny ambled into the room hand in

hand with a tiny little brunette with supershort hair and a biker vibe. His customary wool skully was in place, this one navy blue instead of his usual gray or black. His black hair hung way past his shoulders. Blended with his dark skin, most people chalked him up as Native American on first glance, but given what Danny had shared about his dad, Zeke guessed his ancestry ran closer to India.

"I don't know." Zeke tapped the side of his beer with his thumb. "Any time Gabe's come up in conversation, he's gotten tight-lipped. I get the feeling he's sensitive where she's concerned."

"Protective." Axel twisted enough to get a better view of Danny, now introducing himself to his lady's friends. "Not a bad characteristic in my book."

As if he felt the four sets of eyes on him, Danny turned and locked gazes with the rest of them.

Jace waved him over.

Danny gawked, obviously surprised by the summons. Considering no one but brothers, Viv or the moms ever sat at their table, the shock was understandable. Even the women around Danny seemed a bit stunned.

Still, he didn't hesitate. If Jace's invite made him uneasy, he didn't show it, making his way through the casual sitting areas like he traversed the path every day.

Before he hit the top stair, Zeke stood and held out his hand. "Hey, man. Didn't expect to see you here tonight."

Danny clasped his outstretched palm. "Didn't exactly plan on it, but…" He motioned over his shoulder where the brunette still waited with her friends. "Sometimes you go where goodness leads, yeah?"

He shook hands with the guys and took a chair with his back facing the crowd. Not a bad move considering how many curious eyes were pinned on him. Trevor dove in first, making small talk and asking about Danny's gigs with Beckett.

Axel leaned in and rested his forearm on the table. "You thinkin' Beck's line of work is something you might be interested in long-term? Or are you more interested in building your custom work?"

Danny's eyes widened. "Hadn't really thought that far ahead. Can't really pull custom work alone. Not without a bigger pipeline."

"If Zeke's ride is any indication, you got a serious gift." Jace dipped his chin. "If it's something you enjoy doing, then you should do it."

A ringtone sounded and Danny grimaced. He slid his phone out of his back pocket, checked the home screen, and frowned. For about two seconds, it looked like he'd answer it, but he sent the call to voice mail instead and set the phone face up on the table. "Sorry."

Before anyone could answer, the phone lit up again.

"This ain't a job interview," Jace said. "You need to take the call, take it. That seat won't combust while you're gone."

Danny picked up the phone, scanned the men at the table, and stood. "Yeah, it's my sister. Give me a minute."

As soon as he hit the bottom step, Jace mirrored Axel opposite him and crossed his arms on the table. His gravelly voice was only loud enough those at the table could hear. "Well, that could prove a timely opening."

"Timely, or altogether wrong." Zeke jerked his head to where Danny was standing not fifteen feet away. Danny's stare was hard and locked on some distant spot against the far wall, one hand planted on his hip and tension radiating off him hotter than a late-August afternoon in Texas. "Whatever she wants, it doesn't look good."

Zeke had no more finished his sentence than Danny

hustled back up to the table. "Hey, guys. I hate to do this, but—"

"There a problem?" Jace said.

"You could say that. My sister's hurt. Had some asshole tackle her while she was checking on a neighbor's house."

The buzz Zeke had fought to unplug since he'd walked out of Baylor's level-one trauma center ratcheted back into top gear. "Hurt how?"

Danny shook his head. "I don't know. Not bad enough she couldn't call me herself, but bad enough I could hear paramedics in the background givin' her shit for not taking treatment."

"It's bad enough she called paramedics?" Zeke said.

"Not her. The cops. Sounds like she walked in on a break-in next door." He met each man's eyes one at a time, but did it with an urgency that said he'd put his sister's needs before his own without a backward glance. "I gotta go."

Zeke stood. "We'll take my car. I got my stuff in the back."

"Man, I can't ask you to do that. It's all the way out in Rockwall."

Rounding the table, Zeke slapped Danny on the back. "I know where you live. My ride was practically reborn in your garage, remember?"

"Ah, the legendary birthing place of badass hot rods and our fearless doc in action." Axel stood and chin-lifted to Jace. "This I gotta see. You in?"

Jace threw back the rest of his Scotch, plunked the tumbler on the table, and followed his lead. "I hear Rockwall's a happening place on the weekends. Can't miss this."

Trevor grinned and rose slow from his chair. "Have

a feeling I'm gonna regret missing this, but I got a business to run. Y'all have fun."

Danny stood rooted in place, his gaze shuttling between the three of them.

Axel motioned him down the stairs. "Your sister needs you, and we're following you two. Get a move on."

God, the look on Danny's face was priceless, the lingering worry for his sister mingled with the disbelief he had not one, but three men at his back when he needed it. Zeke slapped him on the shoulder and jerked his head toward the back parking lot. "You heard the man. Let's do this."

Chapter Two

Just over the I-30 bridge, Zeke downshifted and took the first exit on the far side of Lake Ray Hubbard.

The engine protested the unwelcome yank on its reins with a throaty growl and startled Danny out his silent study of the passing scenery. "Sorry, man. I should have been giving directions."

"Might have only been to your place a few times, but it's kind of hard to forget." The subdivision was basically just one long street lined with small, old-school craftsman—and ranch-style homes that looked as good now as they had thirty or forty years ago. Even better were the huge yards and scenic views. Just driving into the neighborhood was like entering a utopian time warp. "So tell me what we're walking into."

"Don't know much," Danny said. "Just know Gabe went to check on one of the neighbor's houses and got knocked around by someone who'd broken in. She called the cops, then me."

"You catch anything the paramedics said to her?"

"Couldn't hear them over her growlin' at them to stay the hell away from her."

Yelling was good. It was when people were too out of it to give a shit, or couldn't talk at all that spelled trouble. "She say where she got banged up?"

"Nope, but she's not too talkative. Not in situations like this. Tends to clam up." Danny rested his elbow on the passenger door and shoved his skull cap back an inch. "She sounded like she hurt, though. Kind of like she was holding her breath. If you knew Gabe, you'd know that means it's probably bad."

"When you say she tends to clam up, what's that mean?"

For a second or two, Zeke thought Danny had zoned on him again, his gaze locked on the businesses and homes streaming by outside. "She doesn't do so good with people. One-on-one she's okay once she gets to know you. It's the getting to know you part that's tough. She comes off a little rough. Standoffish. Most people figure she's a bitch."

"Is she?"

Danny twisted to make eye contact. "Gabe? Ah, hell no. She's about as sweet as you'll ever find. She just locks up around strangers. People think it's because she wants nothing to do with 'em, but the truth is, she can't cope."

"She's an introvert?"

Danny shrugged and straightened in his seat. "We thought that was the deal at first. Or that she was really shy. Then some shit went down in middle school and high school. Dad took her to a shrink, and he said she had some kind of anxiety thing. Something to do with social settings."

"Social Anxiety Disorder?"

"Yeah, that sounds right."

Well, that explained why Knox couldn't find a social footprint for her. "The doc give her anything for the diagnosis? Any meds to help her out?"

"He offered, but she wouldn't take 'em. Said she didn't want drugs controlling her."

Man, he hated hearing things like that. It wasn't an uncommon response, but it was damned unfortunate considering the right scrip could open up a whole new world for people like her. "You don't talk about her much. What's she like?"

Danny huffed out a near silent chuckle. "Like I said. Sweet. Got a great eye for art. Takes care of the whole damned neighborhood like they're her blood." He opened his mouth, closed it, and frowned.

"What? Her having a heart and taking care of the people around her sounds like a good thing."

Danny shook his head. "Taking care of the neighbors isn't the bad part. What sucks is they're the only friends she's got."

"How's that bad?"

"Because there's not one of them under the age of sixty-five. She's twenty-four years old. Most women her age are on the phone, ringing up their girlfriends non-stop, and out chasing men. Gabe's got no girlfriends. Only had two boyfriends I know of, and those lasted about a week each."

Now that was intriguing, especially considering how Danny had no problem jumping into social situations and making friends with even the nastiest personalities. "You think something happened to trigger it? Something in school maybe?"

"I don't know. Maybe. She tried to fit in with the girls at school a few times, but none stuck. The last time I heard her mention people from school, she was twelve. Came home in tears and wouldn't go to school for two days after that. Dad didn't have a clue what the hell to do, so he bought her a camera. She's been wrapped up with her art ever since."

"Photography?"

"Sort of. More like graphic art, but she takes the pictures and then makes them into something else. You have to see it to understand."

Rounding a wide curve in the old road, the Camaro's headlights swept the painted Elk Run subdivision sign up ahead. Unlike the fancy rock and ironwork entrances that marked the high-end neighborhoods farther down, Elk Run's reminded Zeke of public campsites and state boundary lines alongside the highway. They'd barely made the turn into the neighborhood before the blue-and-red flashing lights from the cruisers and ambulance ahead slashed through the Camaro's interior.

"Damn." Danny leaned forward a little in his seat. "She didn't tell me it was this bad."

"Probably looks worse than it is." Zeke paralleled against the curb closest to the ambulance, and the headlights from Jace's Silverado slid into the spot behind them. "Why don't you head on in to check on Gabe, and I'll see what the paramedics know. I'll meet you inside."

He'd barely got his car out of gear before Danny jumped out, rounded the hood and jogged to the house's main entrance. After grabbing his gear from the trunk, Zeke met up with the two-man ambulance crew before they could get their rig in Reverse. "Gabrielle ever accept treatment?"

"Sorry, man. We can't talk treatment without a release."

"Right. Let me put this a different way. I'm a doc and a friend of the family. How did she present?"

The driver glanced over at his partner, who promptly shrugged as if to say he didn't have a clue. He looked back at Zeke. "You taking responsibility?"

"Absolutely."

The guy huffed and rubbed the top of his head. "She's

a stubborn one. Never did let us do an assessment, but given the way she's holding her torso and the shallow breaths, I'd say she's got contusions and cracked or broken ribs."

"Anything else? Focus? Dizziness? Pupils?"

"Looked okay as far as we could tell. Hung around as long as our boss would let us, but if she's not up for help, we've got no reason to stay."

Zeke nodded to them both, waved, and stepped back so they could back out. "Thanks. Appreciate it."

Jace and Axel strolled up on either side of him, but it was Jace who spoke. "What's our play on this?"

"If we're as close to bringing Danny in as I think we are, then I vote we treat him like we would a brother."

Axel grinned, slid one hand in his designer slacks and moseyed toward the cluster of cops gathered in front of the house. "Take control it is, then."

Jace chuckled and prowled alongside him. For about a millisecond, Zeke pitied Rockwall's finest. The founding members of the Haven Brotherhood were notorious for sending the best of law enforcement on a merry dance. In under five minutes, they'd have this crew eating out of their hands.

Zeke jogged up the steps to the front stoop where a uniformed rookie stood watch. Before the kid could put up much of an argument, Zeke slid through the open front door and into the main living room. Two steps in, he froze.

The woman beside Danny had her head down, her hair obscuring her face, but the differences between them even without her facial features showing were night and day. Where Danny was even with Zeke at six foot three, Gabe couldn't be much over five foot. And she was tiny.

A honey-blond faerie hidden behind a deceptively rough exterior of faded jeans, flannel shirt and steel-toed boots.

Danny's escalating voice punched through Zeke's dumbfounded haze. "What the fuck do you mean there's nothing you can do? She's hurt. She gave you a description. Find the motherfucker and make his ass pay."

Before the cop could consider putting the cuffs on his belt to good use, Zeke stepped in. "Hey, Danny. How about you let me see how your sister's doing?" He offered his hand to the cop on Gabe's other side, opened his mouth to speak, and damned near swallowed his tongue.

Oh, yeah. Gabe was a living breathing faerie, complete with pale blue eyes, a heart-shaped face and pouty, full lips. No man could look at her mouth and not crave at least a taste.

"I'm Dr. Dugan." He forced his attention away from Gabe and focused on the irritated cop. "I'm a friend of the family. I think if we can make sure Gabe's okay, everybody's stress level might even out. You got everything you need from her for now?"

The cop shook the hand offered and nodded, more than a little relief dancing behind his tired eyes. "What we don't have now, we can follow up on tomorrow." He cast a curt glare Danny's direction then a tight smile at Gabe. "You think of anything else, don't hesitate to use the number I gave you."

If she heard anything the cop said, or noted his swift departure, she didn't show it, keeping her gaze locked on Zeke. Her breaths were definitely shallow, and not once had she loosened the arm she had wrapped around her torso. The other arm she kept tucked tight to her side. The light in the room wasn't much, but her pupils looked normal.

She inched behind Danny and sucked in a short, sharp gasp. "I'm fine."

God, she was cute. Kind of like a cornered, feral kitten who couldn't decide whether to bolt for the closest hiding spot or come out clawing. Even glaring daggers at him it was all he could do to hold back a chuckle. "That's what the paramedics said you told them, too. The problem is, your brother's about to go vigilante on a bunch of guys with badges because he's worried about you. He'd probably let that shit go a whole lot faster if someone who actually knew what they were talking about made that call."

"For the love of God, Gabe," Danny said. "Zeke's a trauma doc. He drove all the way out here, so just let him check you out."

The arm she held wrapped around her torso tightened and, while it was a subtle move, she flinched. Not a good sign if such a minute shift caused her pain.

"Give me five minutes," he said. "You might be right and just have a strain. If that's the case, you can give Danny a hard time for making a fuss."

She bit her lower lip, and his gut tensed as sure as he'd taken a physical punch.

Funny. Under normal circumstances, he could outwait the most stubborn patient, but standing there in front of her, an almost lethal tension burned through his muscles. Like his whole damned life teetered on the tip of a fiber-optic point and could topple into hell or float to heaven depending on how she answered.

Her gaze shuttled from Danny to Zeke. "Five minutes."

Wow, Danny hadn't overexaggerated. People really could get the wrong impression from his sister's hard exterior, but the fear behind her eyes said the limit was more about what she could tolerate when it came to strangers.

"Five minutes," he agreed. He could have done it in three, but he'd take the extra bonus. Then he'd figure out how to make the leap from stranger to someone worthy of coaxing the wild and sweet kitten from her corner.

Gabe was out of her ever lovin' mind. Saying she could make it five minutes around Danny's friend without coming off like a complete idiot was like saying she could tap dance for ten thousand people. If he'd been some average, ordinary Joe, *maybe* she could have pulled it off, but this guy—this doctor—was too beautiful for words. Olive skin, storm-gray eyes and dark chocolate hair cut in one of those short *GQ*-model styles that was just long enough a woman could run her fingers through it.

Or hang on for dear life while he kissed her with those killer lips.

Danny prowled to the wide window that spanned the front of the living room. They were down to just one cop car now, but the red-and-blue lights on top of it still strobed for all they were worth. "I'll go follow up on Mrs. Wallaby's house. Make sure she's locked up."

"No." She twisted to stop him, and a sharp jolt pierced straight through her chest. Scrunching her eyes, she held her breath and prayed the pain would ebb a little faster than it had the last two times she'd made such an ill-advised move. She wasn't stupid. Whatever injury she'd earned was way worse than anything else she'd had before, and if she hadn't seen the whopping ambulance bill Mr. Decker down the street had earned after his heart attack, she might have let the paramedics take a look.

Big, strong hands curled around her shoulders. Not Danny's, though. She opened her eyes and got a load of

Zeke's up close and personal goodness. Talk about effective pain relief. Her whole damned body purred on idle, soaking in everything about him, stabbing pains be damned. You couldn't really say he had a beard. More like well-trimmed morning stubble that accented a strong square jawline. His nose made her think of marauding Vikings, but up close his lips made her full-on stupid.

Zeke loosened his grip on her shoulders and smoothed his big hands to her upper arms. "Steady now?"

Steady was debatable, but she wasn't thinking about the ache anymore. More like 100 percent focused on the warmth of his touch through her soft flannel button-down. "Yeah."

"Good." He locked gazes with Danny over her shoulder. "How about you stick with us for right now? Axel and Jace have things out there under control."

"Yeah, man. Absolutely. Whatever she needs."

Zeke studied her a second longer, released his hold on her arms, and jerked his head toward the bedrooms down the hall behind him. "How about we check you where we don't run the risk of an audience?"

He turned and led the way before she could muster any kind of argument. Careful not to jar her torso, she followed him down the hallway, Danny close beside her with a sturdy hand at her back. The stage fright sensation that came with strangers wasn't surprising after battling it for years, but her response to Zeke was different. Even Jimmy Franklin in high school didn't have this kind of impact on her, and he'd muddled her mind enough to talk her into giving up her virginity in the backseat of his mother's Honda.

Zeke Dugan was a whole different beast. Everything about him was bold and powerful. Even the way he walked commanded attention. For a doc, he was pretty dressed down, his faded Levi's molding lean hips and grip-worthy backside. His pale blue T-shirt was simple, too, but stretched across his torso in a way that promised lean, defined muscles underneath. Everything about him exuded confidence. A man comfortable taking control even in unfamiliar surroundings.

Without his powerful scrutiny bearing down on her, her thoughts boomeranged back to Zeke's comment and the shitty committee that inevitably piped up with any unknown or stressful situation stomped up to their pulpit.

You don't know this man.

Unknown equals unsafe.

Too many people, all of them looking at you.

Judging you.

She tried to ignore the surging chorus and muttered to Danny, "Who're Axel and Jace? I don't want them in Mrs. Wallaby's house."

"They're friends." Danny kept his easy stride. "Good people. If Mrs. Wallaby was here, she'd have Axel set up with chocolate cake inside of five minutes, so let it go."

Easy for him to say. He wasn't the one her neighbor had entrusted with her house, and she couldn't afford to let one of the few people she could actually talk to down. For years, Mrs. Wallaby had been the closest thing to a mother she'd had.

Instead of taking a left to Danny's room, Zeke stepped into hers, flipped on her light, and stood to one side of the door. He motioned her toward the bed. "You want to sit or stand?"

"Stand," she said. Then tacked on an awkward, "Please." Yep. No way was she getting anywhere near a bed with this guy. She couldn't even manage decent manners, let alone conversation, and he wasn't even in touching distance yet. And was that a foreign accent?

At first she'd thought he sounded like someone from the East Coast, but for a second there, his words had an almost Latin lilt to them.

"Not a problem." He shut the door like he was in a physician's exam room instead of surrounded by her very private haven. "Danny, can you get the blinds?"

He's only here as a favor to your brother.

No man like this guy would ever be interested in you anyway.

If you let him look too close, he'll see the real you.

Before she could panic and bolt, he was in front of her, the expression on his face all business. His long strong fingers cupped the sides of her face along her jawline and guided her head side to side, then front to back as if checking mobility. "Danny said you fell?"

She tried to mute the negative thoughts in her head and nodded, though his firm grip didn't allow for much. "Whoever it was pushed me over."

"You landed on the floor?"

"No, on the coffee table."

"That thing?" Danny said. "I've seen cinder blocks with more give."

The quip drew a grin from Zeke and the lightheadedness Gabe had struggled with grew a whole lot more pronounced.

"Pretty sturdy stuff, huh?" He checked her eyes. "Did you hit your head?"

"I don't think so."

"No loss of consciousness?"

"No."

"Dizziness?"

"Does not being able to breathe count?"

It came out huskier than she'd intended, and she blanked her face to try and cover it.

Instead of garnering distance with her disaffected expression as she had when she'd used it in high school, Zeke nailed her with a blisteringly hot smile. Her heart jolted hard enough to give her shrieking ribs a run for their money. "Yeah, that counts."

"Okay, then dizzy." See? Not so bad. She'd answered his questions and only came across as a borderline bitch. Not too bad considering the circumstances. Until he reached for the unbuttoned edges of her flannel shirt and edged it off her shoulders.

Gabe jerked away and gasped at the sudden movement, tightening her arm around her chest.

Zeke froze, but kept his hold on her shirt. His voice was low and calm. Professional and soothing. "I need to see, *gatinha*. Danny's here. You're safe."

God, she was an idiot. Of course, it wasn't personal. He was a doctor and did this kind of crap every day. Heck, she'd probably never see him again after tonight anyway. She nodded and focused on the far wall. Colors from her latest art projects tucked into her many photo boards blurred together. Soft pink flowers, bold blue skies and sage-green grass. "It's Gabe, not *gatinha*."

"I know what your name is." Even without looking, she could hear the smile in his voice.

"Then who's *gatinha*?" The soft flannel skimmed over her shoulders and down her arms, leaving tiny goose bumps in its wake. The fabric *swooshed* in an airy heap to the bed behind her.

"Not a who. A what. You see if you can figure it out while I check your ribs." He urged her to drop the arm she still had wrapped around her middle and lifted the hem of her tank. The cotton tickled her bare flesh on the way up, and his breath drifted light and teasing across her belly as he crouched beside her.

She tried to block him out, to imagine she was some-place else, but his scent was all around her. Not over-powering cologne like some men favored, but a barely there hint of something summery and warm. Like a re-ally high-priced body wash with a seriously powerful, yet sensual undercurrent.

He pressed in one particular spot on her side, and she hissed. "This where you made impact?"

Despite the painful contact, her cheeks burned as though someone had taken a blow torch to them and her heart fluttered in an out-of-control beat. "I think so."

"You'll have some pretty bruises for sure." He straight-ened and stood perpendicular to her injured side, placing one hand over her sternum and the other directly opposite on her spine. "I'm going to push my hands together, and I want you to show me where it hurts, okay?"

She nodded, almost eager for something to take her mind off all the other sensations battering through her. In all of a second, she changed her mind, the slow pres-sure between his hands sending a brutal stab through her chest. She pointed to where it hurt. "Here."

Instantly, he let go and stepped back, reaching for the high-end messenger bag he'd brought with him. The stethoscope he pulled free sent a wave of relief through her. This routine she was familiar with. With the ear tips in place, he stepped in close and placed the flat disc above her heart. "Just breathe normal."

Yeah, like anything in her life had been normal for the past hour. Breathing had been a crapshoot since she'd landed on the coffee table. Next to him, it was twice as hard.

He shifted and slid the disc under the back of her tank. "Take a deep breath."

She shook her head. "It hurts."

His hand at her shoulder squeezed in a comforting grip. "Just do your best."

Her best wasn't much and sent a fresh wave of discomfort coursing through her torso.

Stepping back, he dropped the stethoscope around his neck, trailed his gaze along her shoulders and arms, and frowned. "You cold?"

More like strung out on sensory overload and in desperate need of a beer. "A little."

He snatched her flannel off the bed and held it out so she could slide it on without too much torque on her ribs. When he'd helped guide the edges up and over her shoulders, he turned her to face the end of the bed, sat on the edge so he was on eye level with her, and loosely clasped his hands between his wide legs. "I'm about ninety-nine percent sure you've got two, maybe three, cracked ribs. If that's the case, treatment is minimal and easy for you to handle on your own. The problem is, I'm worried about your breathing. Broken ribs on their own aren't a huge issue, but if they puncture a lung it can cause problems fast."

Danny edged in closer to her and smoothed his hand down her back. "How do we know if that's a problem?"

"I need an X-ray."

"No hospitals." She scowled up at Danny beside her. "I just got my bills paid off, and I'm not racking up more if I can take care of it on my own."

"I said you could take care of the ribs on your own," Zeke said. "Lungs are a whole different matter. We're talking the difference between you having a few weeks of rough sleep, versus you not waking up." He zeroed in on Danny. "She needs an X-ray."

Danny stepped back and motioned to the door. "Okay, let's go."

"No."

"Gabe, don't be a dumb ass," Danny said. "It's an X-ray, not a fucking transplant."

"Yeah, well, the last time we walked into a hospital, Dad never came back out." She clamped her lips up tight and averted her face. Great. Now she was a loon and a wimp.

Warmth and the delicious pressure of Zeke's fingers encircled her wrist. "What if I told you there's a place I can take you and it won't cost you a dime? A standalone place without a ton of people."

"Like an urgent care?"

"Sort of, but without all the crowds. We'll take X-rays, see what the damage is, and go from there. But trust me, lungs are not something you want to mess with. Better to play it safe."

A firm, but polite knock sounded on the door. Danny opened it but kept one hand on the knob, only leaving a two-foot gap between the edge and the jamb. Her brother's Goliath frame blocked whoever was on the other side. "Hey, Jace."

A deep rumbling voice issued from the hallway. "Everyone's pulling out. Beckett's got a crew coming by to do their own check of Wallaby's house."

"Who's Beckett?" She shifted closer to Danny so she could put a face with the voice.

Danny stepped away at the same time, revealing yet another seriously hot guy with one hand propped on the door frame. So this was Jace. She'd heard Danny mention the name a time or two, but never imagined he'd look like this. He wasn't *GQ* hot like Zeke. More like old-school rock-star hot, complete with shoulder-length dark hair and a full beard/mustache combination. She'd bet he had at least one custom Harley lined up in his garage to go with his faded jeans and well-worn leather jacket. He even had the dirty growling voice and the wicked, all too assessing stare to go with the image. "How you holdin' up, sugar?"

Gabe ducked her head, her sturdy boots the visual equivalent of a lifeline.

"Best guess is two or three cracked ribs," Zeke answered for her, "but I need X-rays to rule out pneumothorax."

Quiet stretched in the tiny room. Even without looking up, she had a good feeling there was a lot of silent macho man eyeballing going on.

Zeke broke it with a firm, "I want to take her to Sanctuary."

That got her attention. She looked up in time to see Jace's grin flatline.

Jace studied her, considered Danny for another second, then focused on Zeke. "You sure?"

"What's Sanctuary?" she asked.

Zeke stayed focused on Jace. "Not safe to let it go without checking and she's not comfortable in a public place."

Funny how he'd zeroed in on the real stickler instead of the cost aspect of her not wanting medical treatment. The care and concern probably should have been a comfort, but the fact that he'd figured out what a freak she was only made her feel two more shades of stupid. "I'm fine."

Jace pulled a toothpick from his pocket, tucked it under his tongue, and scanned Gabe head to toe. "Sugar, if my brother's willing to put his ass out there and take you to Sanctuary, then I doubt the word *fine* is anywhere in his diagnosis." He dipped his head toward Zeke, an unspoken and indefinable meaning behind the look so intense it sent a shiver dancing down her spine. He turned and sauntered down the hallway. "Let's huddle with Axel, and we'll head out."

Chapter Three

Only an industrial-grade exterior light marked Sanctuary's heavily secured, yet nondescript entrance, but Zeke could have navigated his way there in his sleep. From the outside, it was little more than a standalone warehouse nestled alongside a whole string of storage buildings. The inside was a whole different ballgame, one he and his brothers leveraged for a variety of favors when the right opportunities presented themselves.

He parked his hot rod just outside the main door, and Danny swung Gabe's truck in right beside him. Thankfully, Jace and Axel had agreed to let him handle the thing with Gabe solo. Neither of them were too thrilled with the fact he'd mentioned Sanctuary in front of Gabe, but once he'd reminded them how close Danny was to being family, they'd dropped their argument and headed back to work. It didn't hurt that Zeke had come up with the idea of playing the mini emergency facility off as a private medical care operation to cover what really went down inside.

Punching the automated locks Danny had added to the car, Zeke ambled to Gabe's truck and held the passenger door wide while Danny helped Gabe out of the raised cab. "The ride hurt too bad on the way over?"

Gabe didn't look at him, but shook her head. Understandable considering the night she'd had and the pain she wrestled.

"We'll get this over with as quick as we can, then Danny can pick you up some painkillers on the way home." He flipped the locks on the building's front door and deactivated the high-end security system inside the entrance. When Beck had insisted on the fingerprint scanner on top of the standard key code, Zeke had argued they were going overboard on precautions. Then Beck had pointed out the total cost of the assets hidden inside, and Zeke had conceded overkill might not be a bad deterrent. Especially considering the type of people he treated here.

He flipped the light switches and the rows of commercial fluorescents overhead hummed their eager greeting. Two emergency gurneys were centered on the industrial tile floor with focal lights mounted above them. Racks stocked with all the basic emergency gear he could ask for lined both side walls, while huge monitors and Knox's state-of-the-art computers were mounted along the front.

Danny paced to the center of the room and gaped at all the equipment. "Man, this is cool."

"Where are we?" Gabe didn't seem nearly as impressed, holding her spot by the door just as tightly as she kept that arm of hers coiled around her waist.

Zeke shrugged and fired up the main computers. "It's not as big of a deal as it looks. Just self-insurance taken to the extreme."

"Self-insurance." The way Gabe said it made it more of an openly skeptic statement of disbelief than a question.

"Yep. Some people would rather fork over cold hard cash for their own setup and guaranteed privacy. Not to mention, there's no wait time."

"And you know people like this?"

"I know a few." Most of them were men with a dirty background and zero interest in getting anywhere near a public facility with records and a friendliness for cops. Not to mention, they were usually plugged up with bullet holes or knife wounds when they came through Sanctuary's doors.

He motioned to the dark, isolated room off to one side. "Danny, do me a favor. Turn on the light in there and help Gabe have a seat."

The two shuffled off in the direction indicated while he dug through the cabinets in search of a hospital gown. He could have sworn he'd ordered some when they first tricked out the facility, but damned if he could find them now. Then again, modesty wasn't something he normally had to deal with behind these walls.

To hell with it. He gave up looking and headed in with Danny and Gabe. If her color was any indication, she needed pain relief and quiet a whole lot more than she needed standard protocol. One look at her, tense and obviously shaken as she perched on the edge of a metal chair, and the same protective impulse he'd battled when he'd touched her at her house roared full bore. "Okay, *gatinha*. I'm just going to snap some pictures, take a look at what's going on and we'll see if we can't get you home. But first, we've got a tactical hurdle to leap."

She frowned at him then glanced at Danny. "What kind of hurdle?"

He nodded in the general direction of her torso. "My machine doesn't play nice with metal. I might not be a woman, but even I know pretzeling into or out of a bra is a trick even without a broken rib. With one, it's going to be impossible. So who do you want to help you out of it? Danny, or me?"

In all of two seconds, her cheeks flamed a bold red and her already shallow breaths turned even threadier. "I can do it."

Zeke lifted a brow. "You willing to risk hurting yourself more in the process?"

Unlike Danny, who had an unbelievable poker face when he chose to use it, every thought and emotion Gabe processed burned bright and beautiful across her face. Embarrassment. Fear. Confusion and acceptance. It kind of made him want to see a whole lot of other expressions on her face. Like the fleeting glimpse of pleasure he'd caught when his fingertips first touched her skin.

"You won't look?" she said.

He fudged as much as he could. "I promise I'll give you all the privacy I can, but you've got to remember, this is an everyday thing for me."

She bit her lip and stared down at the floor. "Then I'd rather have you."

"Thank God," Danny said, twisting for the door and fiddling with his skully like he always did when he was antsy.

Zeke held out his hand and pulled Gabe to her feet. "Danny, why don't you wait in my office across the hall? It shouldn't take us more than five minutes once we get her situated."

Seemingly happy to have dodged an awkward moment with his little sister, Danny hightailed it out of the room and shut the door behind him.

Zeke stood behind Gabe and peeled her flannel shirt off her shoulders with as much indifference as possible. It was a hell of a lot harder the second time knowing what was hidden underneath. Unlike her brother, Gabe's skin was closer to cream, only a hint of golden goodness taking the edge off what could have made her seem pale.

And it was soft. Soft, taut and stretched over easy, lithe curves that made him want to touch her in ways that would make Danny shoot him on sight.

He eased the hem of her tank up.

Her hands closed over his, stopping him in his tracks.

"It's okay. I'm just lifting it enough you can slide your arms out. We'll get the bra off and get the tank back in place. The cotton will be fine for the X-rays."

For a few seconds all she did was stand there, locked in place. More than anything, he wanted to move in closer and give her comfort. Tactile, lingering comfort.

She swallowed so big, it looked like it hurt, then she nodded and released his hands. "Okay."

Moving as quickly as he dared, he lifted the shirt up, thankful for how the stretchy fabric allowed her to slip her arms out with minimum distress. He didn't give her time to process what came next, flipping the clasp on her bra.

Her gasp ricocheted through the room and made his dick twitch with a whole lot of ideas on how he could illicit the same sound.

God, he was an asshole. A patient was standing in front of him, hurting and mortified, and he was entertaining how many ways he could get his hands all over her. He slid the straps off her shoulders and tugged the tank back down so she could maneuver her arms back in. "See? All done."

Before she could answer, he strode around her, folding up her innocent white bra as he went, and laid it in the chair next to her purse. His mind conjured up a whole slew of images to go with that plain scrap of fabric, none of them decent or acceptable given the circumstances. He ground his teeth together and forced his thoughts back to the task at hand. "Okay, let's see what's going on with your ribs."

The process went relatively quick and easy. Or easy for him anyway. To her credit, she muscled through the difficult times when the shots required she lift her arms up and out of the way, but shook with fatigue by the time it was over. He guided her back to her chair and paused by the closed door. "You want help putting that back on, or can you handle freewheeling it on the way home?"

Another appealing flush rushed up her neck and she stuffed the bra deep in the hippy-style hobo bag. "I'm good."

Yeah, she was. Tough in a way that put most of his patients to shame. And yet, she was still the kind of soft and sweet you wanted to see curled up next to you. Definitely a feral kitten.

He opened the door and found Danny anchored on the other side, his arms crossed and his mouth pinched in a hard line. "You done?"

"Yep. Give me five and we'll know what's up."

Reality was more like three minutes, the result pretty much what he'd expected—two clean, nondisplaced fractures and no sign of damage to the lung. Good news for her as far as risk went, so long as she didn't push matters in the early healing process. He grabbed an Rx pad, powered down his computer and flipped the lights.

Gabe's semiwhispered words drifted into the intersecting hallway. "Don't you think it's weird he's got access to his own mini hospital?"

Zeke hesitated outside the X-ray room door.

"It's not a hospital, Gabe." Danny didn't seem as interested in hiding his commentary. His deep voice traveled crystal clear. "It's like an Urgent Care. You can find one of those on every damned corner anymore. And no, it's not weird. You know how rich people are. Enough money and connections and you don't have to wait or deal with the riffraff. So what if it helped you out this time?"

"It's just weird. How do you know those guys aren't into illegal things?"

"Trust me. The brothers are many things, but the one thing you can count on is them doing the right thing. Always."

"That's the other thing. Why do you keep calling them brothers?"

"Because they are."

"They don't look a thing alike. No way they're family."

"Blood ain't everything, Gabe. Let it go."

Danny wasn't wrong on that score. In the ten years he'd known Jace, Axel and the rest of the guys who came after, he'd had more of a family than he ever did growing up. Not that his parents didn't try, they were just usually too beat after trying to make a living to have much energy left for a little kid.

Gabe kept up with her arguments, her suspicious nature undoubtedly something he should be more concerned about, especially with Danny having one foot in the brotherhood. Instead, all he could focus on was her voice. Soft and sweet as a fluffy kitten even if she was talking ninety miles an hour. Which was kind of funny when he thought about how limited her words had been throughout the rest of her ordeal.

A shaky vulnerability crept into her voice. "What happens if they're not as good as you think they are and something happens to you? You're all I've got left."

"Jesus, I'm not in high school anymore, Gabe. I haven't done anything like that in years."

Well, not entirely true. Zeke knew damned good and

well Danny had done at least three sizable B&Es to pay off his dad's mortgage. But Gabe had gotten to keep the house she'd grown up in.

"I'm not Mom," Danny said. "I know you missed her growing up, but I'm not going anywhere. Not by choice or by accident. The brothers are just guys like me who found a way to make their mark on the world. They're helping me find my way."

"How? Doing what?"

Danny hesitated.

Zeke straightened off the wall he'd leaned into and rounded the entry. Keeping his head down, he scribbled out a prescription, hoping his preoccupation would cover the timing of his arrival. "Well, the good news is your lungs are solid. On the downside, you've got two fractured ribs."

"How do you treat that?" Danny said.

Zeke halted in front of the two of them and focused on Gabe. "Not much I can do. In the old days, they'd wrap the chest to alleviate the pain and support movement. Some folks still do, but I don't advise it. The most important thing you can do is take big, deep breaths several times a day. If I wrap your ribs it'll make deep breathing hard to do."

"What about work?" she said.

"Danny says you're a mechanic, right?"

She nodded.

"Yeah, engines aren't going to be on your short list for at least three to four weeks."

"I can't be off work for four weeks."

Danny squeezed her shoulder. "Mike's cool. He'll work you some kind of deal."

"If he doesn't, let me know," Zeke said. "My brothers have all kinds of businesses. I'd bet at least one of them needs some short-term help that wouldn't put too much strain on your ribs." He handed her the script. "These ought to help with pain until you can shift over to ibuprofen. For at least two or three nights, I want you to be sure and take them at night so your breathing stays steady while you sleep."

She carefully tugged the paper from between his fingers and scowled down at it. "You don't have drugs here?"

And there were those cute claws. Funny how all they did was make him want to provoke her a little more. "This is a medical facility. Not a pharmacy. Besides, uncontrolled narcotics are against the law. I've got a license to protect."

Talk about a complete load of shit. He had enough narcotics to cover all kinds of injuries locked up nice and tight in storage, but no way was he clueing her into that after what he'd overheard. He stepped back and motioned Danny to the door. "Why don't you get her home so she can rest? There's a twenty-four-hour pharmacy just up the street, and those should be pretty cheap generic."

Danny helped Gabe to her feet. "Aren't you coming?"

"Nope, gotta clean up and turn everything off." Reaching into his back pocket, he pulled out his billfold and snagged a business card. He handed it to Gabe. "If the pain gets worse or you're worried about anything at all, call me at that number. I don't sleep much so don't worry about what time it is."

Danny stretched out his hand. "Thanks, man. I can't tell you how much I appreciate you helping us out."

Zeke shook the hand offered and slapped Danny on the back. "Wasn't a problem. Happy I could help." He made it until Danny and Gabe reached the main door before he gave in to pure impulse. "Hey, *gatinha*."

She kept her torso ruler straight, but craned her neck toward him.

"Whether you call or not, I'm stopping by in a few days to check on you."

Gabe frowned.

Danny smiled huge and almost smacked Gabe on the shoulder, but stopped a few inches before he made contact. "See? Told you the brothers were awesome."

An unapologetic snort drifted back to him a second before the door shut, leaving him alone in the sterile room.

Awesome wasn't what he'd call it. Dancing into dangerous territory was more like it. But for the first time in months, that constant buzz beneath his skin was quiet, and he had a pretty good idea tangling with the little kitten was the cause.

Chapter Four

Gabe snapped the cover on her e-reader closed and tossed it on the bed beside her.

Toothless lazily opened his eyes and glared his displeasure with the disruption of his cat nap. Despite having a queen-size bed to stretch out on, her lazy feline had opted to cozy right up next to her uninjured side. The light from her bedside lamp reflected against his shiny black coat, and his emerald green gaze implied further movement would not be tolerated.

"Like you haven't had enough lazing with me the last five days." She braced her arms on either side of her and pushed upright, careful not to jar her torso.

Toothless gracefully leaped to the floor. He sashayed out the door, snapping his tail as angrily as his movie namesake.

"Show-off." Her dismount wasn't nearly as smooth, but it was a sight better than it had been her first day at home. At least Danny had been right about her boss, Mike. He'd agreed to let her work the garage desk for two or three weeks, but only if she agreed to take the first week off and give herself time to heal.

With pay.

Talk about small miracles.

She padded through the living room and into the

kitchen, flipping a few lights on along the way. Through the wide window over the kitchen sink, only a thin band of deep gold remained on the horizon, the sun having just disappeared. The view from her backyard was one of her favorites, especially when the lake was smooth like tonight and the brilliant colors were mirrored on its glossy surface.

She pulled a bottled water from the fridge, pried open the cap, and leaned against the counter. The microwave's digital clock glowed a neon-green 8:12 p.m. back at her. Too early to go to bed and too late to start anything new. She'd thought she'd never get bored with reading, watching movies, or tinkering with her art projects, but nearly a week with nothing to do sure proved that theory wrong.

She ambled to the living room and the picture window that overlooked her porch and the other two homes that lined her cul-de-sac. The streetlight reflected off the subtle metallic flecks in her truck's indigo paint. It wasn't as flashy as Danny's '69 Chevelle beside it, but it was everything she'd wanted. Classic, functional and fun with a hell of an engine under the hood. One she'd rebuilt and souped up herself.

Off to the side of the property, the lights inside their oversize detached garage glowed a soft buttery yellow. For the first time in months, Danny had shown up right after work and hit his own private haven to start work on a new custom job.

Her thoughts drifted back to the scary, take-control guys Danny had brought the night of Mrs. Wallaby's break-in. Or, more accurately, the hot doctor. If she had a nickel for every time he'd bebopped into her head the past few days, she wouldn't have to work for a solid month. The whole preoccupation was insane. She wasn't even sure she'd uttered a complete sentence in front of the guy.

If anything, he probably thought she was a basket case, and he sure wouldn't give a girl like her a second glance.

She was halfway across the driveway, the crisp bite of grass just waking up from winter's rest and the familiar algae scent of the lake filling her lungs, before she realized where she was headed. The closer she got, the stronger the strains of AC/DC grew. She opened the steel side door and let it bang shut louder than necessary so she didn't scare the bejesus out of Danny sneaking up on him. She rounded the tail end of the black '37 Ford Coupe and found the driver's door propped open with Danny stretched out across the bench seat, his head all but wedged under the dash. "You've got a long way to go on this one."

"Boy, that's no shit." Danny twisted enough to make eye contact. "'Sup, Sugar Bear?"

Ugh. The dreaded nickname of shame. All because her headstrong nine-year-old self had wanted nothing but Sugar Crisp cereal for breakfast, lunch and dinner for a solid two-week stretch. By the time she'd moved on to grilled cheese sandwiches, the name had stuck.

She thumbed the radio behind her down to background noise and leaned a hip against his workbench. "You going to be out here all night?"

"Only been at it two hours."

"I know, but I'm bored."

Danny's warm chuckle rolled out from the car's dirty, dilapidated interior. "Can't help you with that one. Got my hands full at the moment. The guy who hired me wants the job done in a month."

She snorted. "Maybe if you worked on it full time."

"Yeah, that's not going to happen. I told him I worked at my own pace. Took a little to convince him it was less about money and more about art." He glanced up at Gabe and grinned unrepentantly. "Wrangled a little extra incentive money, though."

"Well, that's a plus." At least he had something new and fresh to work on. She'd never realized how much her job balanced out her life. Every engine that ended up in her bay was a riddle to solve and fix. Some were tiny, and some were huge and made her absolutely nuts in the short term, but they all posed a challenge. The whole indolent-lifestyle thing sucked. "You've been busy a lot lately. The body shop backed up?"

Danny's back and forth with the ratchet paused for a second, then kicked in a notch faster. "I'm not working extra at the shop. Been picking up some new jobs. Learning new gigs."

"With those guys that were here last weekend—the doc and his friends?"

"Yep."

She smoothed her thumb along the workbench's rough edge. More than once, she'd wished she asked them more about themselves when she'd had the chance. Asking Danny had been a crapshoot. Most of the time he clammed up whenever conversation steered their direction. "Zeke said they had a lot of business. What do they do? I mean, besides the doc."

He shrugged. "They've all got their own gigs. Bars, restaurants, shipping, computers, security. One's even got a private-jet charter service."

"So, how do you fit in? With the jobs, I mean."

"They're teaching me stuff. Introducing me to people. Showing me how to run a business." He peeked out from under the dash. "I met the guy for this job through them."

So what happened if Danny found a whole different career?

You'll be alone.

No Dad.
No Danny.
Just like your mom all over again.

She shook her head, pushed the negative thoughts aside, and cleared her throat. "Are Axel and Jace the ones the doc works for? The ones with enough money to have their own clinic?"

"Jesus." Danny tossed the ratchet to the floorboard and sat up, pinning Gabe with an angry glare. "You're like a dog with a bone. No one can just be a good guy with you, can they? Not unless they're old and in a position where they can't hurt you."

"I didn't mean anything by it. I was just asking."

"Really? 'Cause it sure as shit sounded like you were trying to dig up dirt. Or, in your case, looking for reasons not to like them. That's what you do, right? Find reasons people can't be trusted and keep them at bay. Right?"

"It was just conversation."

"You want conversation? Okay, here's conversation. Zeke's a good guy. Reached out to me and offered me not just friendship, but a whole different perspective on life when my own friends couldn't be bothered to talk to me about anything except sports and chicks. He'd just worked a twelve-hour shift Friday when he dropped everything to help you. Axel and Jace had already put in a full week, too. But you? You looked at them like you couldn't bear to breathe the same air as them."

"No, I didn't."

"Really? You didn't even bother to tell Zeke thank you before we left."

She hung her head. Tears blurred her scuffed black boots and the oil-stained concrete beneath them, and a slow burn spread along the bridge of her nose. "I felt bad about that." Countless times, she'd replayed the whole night and wished she'd said more. Or at least smiled.

"Shit, Gabe." Rustling sounded from the car's interior, and the next thing she knew Danny was in front of her, his big fingers pinching her chin and urging her head up the same way her dad used to. "I'm sorry."

She shook her head, freeing her chin from Danny's grip and dashing the single tear that escaped with the back of her hand. "No, you're right. I could have been nicer. I should have been. I just…" *Wanted to get the heck away from everyone and hide in my room where I didn't feel like everyone was looking at me. Wanted to stop all the pessimistic gloom and doom in my head.*

"You know how hard it is for me around people. And my side really hurt."

"I get that. But you poking around and asking questions about my friends is more about you fortifying those walls of yours than any social hang-up. You don't trust. I get it. But not everyone is Mom. Not everyone is some quick-shot jock out to score a hot piece of ass."

She jerked as sure as someone had slapped her and her ribs barked a sharp reprimand. Bracing her side, she held her breath and waited for the throb to ebb. "I don't know what you're talking about," she eked out. "I don't know any quick-shot jocks."

"Come on, Gabe. I'm a guy. We can spot a man out to nail a chick in all of five seconds. You think I don't know that asshole in high school tagged you and ran?"

The blood rushed out of her face, and for a second she wasn't 100 percent sure she'd stay upright. As awkward moments went, the only thing that could have been worse was to superimpose her dad where Danny stood. "You didn't… You never said anything."

"How the fuck could I? Or Dad? You locked yourself

up in your damned room for days. Hell, it's a wonder Dad didn't string the bastard up by his nuts."

She paced a few steps away, completely at a loss for words. All this time she'd thought no one knew about her seriously bad lapse in judgment, and here they'd known the whole time.

"I don't blame you for being careful," Danny said. "A girl like you, sweet and always willing to look after the people you care about, you almost have to be. But the brothers? They might have their own way of doing things, but they do them in a way they're proud of. That they believe in. They take care of each other and the people they love, and they do it with a vengeance. Honest to God, I hope they're around a lot more. I hope they let me in their circle so I can learn from them and make my life better like they have. If that happens and you want to keep your distance when they're around, that's cool. Just do me a favor and try not to treat 'em like they're scum, because they're not. Not to me."

She swallowed and faced him, a whole storm of emotions she couldn't quite identify swirling inside her at one time. Surprise for sure, but a little jealousy, too. She'd give anything to have friends she could count on like she did Danny. Friends her own age. "I don't think I've heard you get that fired up about anything since Dad sold his part of the garage."

"Yeah, well. I save my speeches for when it counts." He stood there, patient and proud, his arms at his sides and his shoulders back, but vulnerability swam behind his dark eyes.

"I'm sorry I was rude," she said. "You're the last person I want to hurt. If they're around more, I'll try harder."

He grinned, his usual, playful self whipping back into place. Emotions were always that way for him. He moved with them the way the wind ebbed and flowed over the lake's surface, at one with what he felt instead of fighting against it. "I appreciate it."

"And I didn't mind breathing the same air as the doc."

"Uh-huh."

"Actually, I thought he was cute."

Danny's jaw slackened for a beat then he shook his head as though clearing an unwanted mental imagine. "Now, that's information I could do without."

She giggled and promptly winced, fighting back the rest of her laughter.

Danny lurched toward her as though he thought she might lose her balance and fall. "You okay?"

"Yeah, just better not to laugh. Or cough. Or sneeze. Or breathe." She waved him off and slowly straightened.

"You think Zeke's hot, huh?"

She rolled her eyes and paced to the Ford's back bumper, running her finger along the worn, dull finish. "Doesn't matter. He's a doc and I'm a mechanic. In what fucked up world would that ever work?"

"Their world is a lot different than the one you're used to. They make their own rules. Their own life. You might be surprised where a sweet mechanic might fit into it." He ambled up beside her and tweaked her nose. "And don't cut yourself short. You might've kept half the damned male population at bay through school, but that didn't mean they weren't prowlin' around looking for a way in."

"Whatever." Danny had always made claims like that. Her father, too, but she never believed them. How could she when her own mother had chosen a life without her? "You really knew about Jimmy Franklin?"

"Hell yeah, I knew. I also made it painful for him to take so much as a step after I figured out he wasn't coming back. Fucker probably had a few cracked ribs of his own to contend with." He winked at her. "Karma's a bitch, ain't she?"

For the first time all day, her boredom and the suspicious thoughts she'd wrestled rolled off her shoulders. She slipped her arms around Danny's waist and rested her forehead on his chest. "I love you."

"Love you, too, Sugar Bear." He kissed the top of her head, ruffled her hair like she was still two, and backed away. "Oh, speaking of the hot doc, he said he'd be out tomorrow to check on you."

"He did?" she squeaked.

Danny hesitated midway situating himself on the car's long bench seat and cranked his neck in her direction. The grin on his face said he'd caught the tell all too clearly. "Yeah, he did. And the more I think about it, the more I'm thinking there's a good chance I won't be here when he does."

Chapter Five

Zeke paralleled his ride outside Gabe and Danny's house and popped the shifter into Neutral, his gaze locked on the empty space next to Gabe's flirty blue truck in the driveway. No Danny, which meant no buffer between him and Gabe for his friendly house call. The way he figured it, he had a fifty-fifty shot things would either snap, crackle and pop the way they had when he'd helped her take off her bra, or he'd end up zigzagging a landmine-rich environment.

He grinned, killed the engine, and strolled up the drive. He'd take the risk. Hell, with as much headspace as their last interaction had taken up the past six days, it was a miracle he'd held off visiting this long. He jogged up the front steps, pulled the old-fashioned silver screen door wide, and knocked on the white painted-wood door.

A red brick wall surrounded the raised patio, and a two-person porch swing hung at the far end. Cozy. The kind of place you'd kick back, chat with neighbors and finish off a beer on a spring or fall night. Picturing Gabe there was all too easy. People might make her jumpy and bring out her sharp tongue, but underneath it he sensed a quiet grace.

The slats on white wood blinds shifted enough for

someone to peek out, and a second later the front door opened.

"Hey." Gabe stepped back and gave him room to enter, tucking one hand in her jeans pocket. The denim was seriously old and probably as soft as her white cotton tank. "Danny's not here yet. He said he'd be home in a bit."

She was barefoot. Why that made her about twenty times sexier than last time, he couldn't begin to describe. Maybe it was how dainty her feet were. Or the fact that her toenails weren't decorated in some fashionable color of the month. Whatever it was, he had a hell of a time trying not to ogle. The way her honey-blond hair hung loose around her face only made it worse. "How you doing, *gatinha*?"

She shut the door behind him and motioned him toward the kitchen. "I still don't know what that means."

"I told you to look it up."

"I tried, but I don't know how it's spelled."

He strolled behind her and set his messenger bag on the kitchen table. The stacked up pans in the sink and killer smells coming out of the oven made it clear she'd been cooking. Something with cheese and spice. "*G-A-T-I-N-H-A*."

He'd barely gotten the last letter out when a black cat darted out from behind the couch and down the hallway to Gabe's bedroom. "You and Danny have a cat?"

"*I* have a cat. His name is Toothless."

"From *How to Train Your Dragon*?"

Surprise widened her gaze, and her lips softened in an almost-there smile. "You know animated movies?"

"I work in an emergency room. You'd be surprised what a good animated show will do to distract tiny patients." He glanced down the hall. "Toothless isn't too much on people, is he?"

She tucked her hair behind one ear and ducked into the galley kitchen. "He's okay once he gets to know you."

Kind of like Toothless's owner, which only made him want to see what it would take to make her willing to hang around instead of running for cover.

"What is that anyway?" She turned on the water, picked up a pan, and started scrubbing.

"What's what?"

"The language you used. *Gatinha*. It sounds Spanish."

"Better be glad my *mamãe* didn't hear you say that. You'd be sucking on a bar of soap." He moseyed up to the counter beside her, grabbed the dishtowel lying off to one side, and waited for her to finish. "She and Dad are from Brazil, so we spoke almost nothing but Portuguese in my house."

She eyeballed the towel, then him, then went back to washing the pan. "Huh. It sounds like Spanish."

"A little, I guess."

She rinsed the pan and handed it over without meeting his eyes. "Your parents moved to Dallas from Brazil?"

Wait, what? How the heck did she think… "Oh, my folks don't live in Texas. They live in North Philly. I moved here for college. Got a scholarship to SMU."

A firm knock sounded on the front door.

Gabe frowned, shut the water off, and snatched the towel from his hands. "Give me a minute." A few seconds later, she opened the old wooden front door, and the late-evening sun slanted through the living room.

"Hi, there. You must be Mrs. Parker." Whoever the man was could've passed for a used-car ad announcer— questionable professionalism and high hype.

"*Miss* Parker. And I'm not interested in selling." Gabe tried to shut the door.

The man held up his hand to stop her. "Miss Parker.

Yes, I'm sorry about that. If you'd just give me a minute, I've got a client who's very interested in your home."

"Them and about twenty other people who've sent their folks in to talk with me." She planted one hand on her hip. "I appreciate what you're trying to do. I really do. But I'm not up for selling. Not now, not tomorrow, not ever."

Zeke prowled up behind her and laid one hand on her shoulder, his stare locked on the too-pushy salesman. "I think she's done."

Clearly, Pushy Dude hadn't planned on a man being home, because his forehead wrinkled up like a Shar-Pei. "Are you the man of the house?"

"I'm the man who's telling you she's not interested in talking." He gripped the door and started to shut it.

The man braced his hand on the wood and held out a business card. "Why don't you take this just in case you change your mind? My clients are very interested in making a very lucrative offer."

Zeke peered down at Gabe. "You want the card?"

"Nope."

"Didn't think so." Zeke glared at Pushy Dude. "She doesn't want it. Time for you to go."

Pushy Dude lowered his hand and opened his mouth to say something else.

"Say another word and I call the cops," Zeke said.

The threat worked, and Pushy Dude's mouth snapped shut.

Zeke closed the door, locked it and steered Gabe back to the kitchen. "That happen a lot?"

"More than you'd believe. Every Realtor says they've got clients looking for land on the lake. They wanna build big retirement homes. Ours being right on the point with a straight-on view of the lake makes for a prime target."

She dove back into washing the dishes, though her efforts were about ten times more vigorous than they were before.

Zeke held his silence, giving her the time to tame her emotions while the faucet filled the kitchen with the quiet drone of rushing water. If there was one thing he understood, it was anger. How fast it could light and how hard it was to put out. At least for him it was. Most of his dangerous days were behind him, but that didn't mean he didn't have a healthy appreciation for how fast his bad behaviors could snap back into place.

As soon as she rinsed the suds from the sink, she shut the water off, turned, and leaned a hip against the sink. "Thank you."

"You're welcome." Zeke laid the last pot aside and mirrored her pose. "You okay with me checking your ribs? We can wait until Danny's here, but I want to make sure you're healing right."

Something had happened in the silence. Putting his finger on what it was seemed about as vague as a foggy dream after waking up. Illusive and intangible, but it was there. A softening around her mouth and eyes. Caution mixed with curiosity.

She pushed away from the sink, wiped her hands nervously on her hips, and studied the floor as though checking for crumbs. "Where do you want me?"

Fuck, if that question didn't punch him square to the gut. The better query was where *didn't* he want her? And didn't that make him a class-A jackass. Danny was almost a brother, and here Zeke was drawing out a checklist for all the places he'd like to tag Danny's sister. "Wherever you're most comfortable."

Still keeping her gaze averted, she padded to the living room.

Not the location he would have picked, but at least the impersonal space might help him keep his thoughts in check. The blinds were opened only enough to let in the waning sunlight, so he strolled toward where she stood beside the couch.

Gabe glanced at the blue-gray chenille sofa. "Should I sit or stand?"

"Standing's good." He stopped just beside her, placed one hand on her sternum, and the other opposite it on her spine. "Same drill as before. I'll squeeze, you tell me where it hurts and how much."

She nodded her head and he pushed. "Here, but not as bad as before."

Good news for sure, and she'd taken a whole lot more pressure before she cried uncle. He dug his stethoscope out of his bag and put the ear tips into place. "How's your mobility? Moving around a little better?"

"For most things. Laying on my side sucks. So does sneezing or coughing, but I haven't taken the pain meds in three days."

"Good." Her heartbeat was more accelerated than he'd like to hear, but he'd chalk that up to a stranger being in her house than any health issue. He moved the disc to her back. "Take a deep breath for me."

She did, the expanse of her lungs almost triple where they'd been the night of her injury. "You've been doing the breathing exercises."

"You told me to." She took another long, slow inhalation, and he shifted to check the lower sounds in her lungs.

"Your lungs sound good." He pulled the tips out of his ears, draped the stethoscope around his neck, and shifted so he was between her and the couch. He sat on the edge. "Can you lift your arms up without too much pain?"

She lifted both in lieu of answering, but only as high as her shoulders and even that seemed uncomfortable.

"Hold 'em there just a second." He lifted her tank, halting so the hem ran parallel to the edge of her bra. "Oh, *gatinha*." Without so much as a blip from his conscience, he smoothed his fingertips up the side of her torso. Deep purple fanned out from the point of impact, fading into pale, ugly green. The rest of her belly was smooth and toned, her creamy skin soft and tempting, but the bruises played him. If he ever found the son of a bitch who'd done this to her, he'd give his anger free rein, an outcome that assured the bastard would be covered in much, much worse.

Gabe shivered and sucked in a tiny hiss.

Palming her uninjured side just above her hip, he steadied her and met her gaze. "You okay?"

"It's hard to breathe."

"With your arms up?"

"No, when you touch me."

He froze, the raw fear in her soft blue eyes pinning him in place. Not frantic fear. Her gaze was too steady for that, but her pupils were dilated. Goose bumps lifted across her skin, and while she might have claimed she couldn't breathe, her chest rose and fell in a heavy, passionate rhythm.

"I didn't mean to make you uncomfortable." He guided her arms back to her sides and smoothed her shirt back into place. Even with the bruise marring her smooth flesh, it was a damned shame to cover her up. He could spend hours touching her. Learning her. "You're safe with me. I didn't mean to make it awkward."

"It wasn't awkward. It was just…well, I didn't mean it bad." Her face flamed a bold red, and she took a step back, smoothing her hand down her stomach as though verifying everything was in its proper place. She stared at the coffee table and tucked her hands in her pockets. "I should apologize. I was rude the other night and never thanked you. I should have."

"I wasn't expecting a thank-you, and I was happy to do it." He paused a minute, practically willing her to look at him again. "Your brother's a good friend. Maybe you and I just got off on the wrong foot and need to give it another go."

She nodded and bit her lip.

Either her reaction had knocked her for a loop, or he'd read the situation wrong and she was afraid of him. Or, given the tremors shaking her hands, *terrified* would be a better word.

A car door slammed outside.

Gabe snapped to attention and winced, bracing one elbow close to her injured side. "That's Danny."

He tried to steady her, but before he could close the distance between them, she spun away and grabbed a covered casserole from the counter.

"I need to get some food over to Mr. Crawford." She'd nearly made it to the front door when Danny pushed it open.

"Hey, Sugar Bear. What's your hurry?"

She caught the screen door before it could close and nudged it wider with her elbow. "Dinner will be ready in thirty minutes."

Danny back-and-forthed his attention between Gabe trotting down the sidewalk and Zeke still shell-shocked near the couch. "What set her on fire?"

Zeke shrugged, but kept his eyes on Gabe through the window she padded down the street. Her blond hair swished around her shoulders with each step, and if the rough sidewalk bothered her bare feet, she didn't show it. Everything about her screamed innocent sensuality. "Not sure."

Well, now, that was a crock of shit. And if Danny had walked in about two minutes earlier, he'd know exactly what the problem was. He stuffed his stethoscope back in his bag and hoped like hell Danny wouldn't dig any further. "I'm headed over to the compound later. You wanna come by?" Since Danny wasn't a brother yet, an invite to the ranch they called Haven on the outskirts of town was a no-go, but anyone and everyone was welcome at the compound—a damn nice spread the brotherhood owned in one of Dallas's most elite neighborhoods—so long as they had an invite.

Danny shut the door and nudged the blinds to one side so he could get a better view of Gabe. "Sure. Anything on the agenda?"

"Jace found out everyone's got the night off, so it's poker night."

"Bad luck for you. You've got a shit poker face." He let the blinds slide back into place and ambled to the kitchen.

"Like I could sit still that long. I'll probably end up whipping Knox's ass at 'Call of Duty.'" He headed to the door. "Give me a call when you're headed out."

"Hold up." Danny slid his skull cap off his head and scratched his forehead. "Listen, man. I wanna apologize about Gabe. If she acts funny, it's just because being around new people is really hard for her. She's cautious—"

"You don't need to apologize. She was fine. Even chit-chatted before I checked her ribs." He motioned to the kitchen. "But if you're worried, you can bribe me with one of those casseroles the next time I come out. I don't know what that shit is, but it smells fantastic."

"Why wait 'til next time? Stay and have some now."

"Not so sure that's a wise move. Gabe actually said more than two words to me this time around. Me crashing dinner might jack up my progress. You don't surprise a woman with extra headcount and no warning. Even I know that."

Danny smiled huge and smacked Zeke on the back. "You don't get it. There's no such thing as surprising Gabe when it comes to dinner. She cooks for a damned army. That's why she feeds the whole neighborhood."

"But she just took a whole casserole to the guy down the street."

"Yeah, that's nothing. Check this out." He rambled into the kitchen, opened the oven door, and pulled out the top rack. "Now do you get what I mean?"

Boy, did he. Not one, but two big casserole dishes sat side-by-side, a thick layer of golden, bubbling cheese on top of each. "Man, that looks good."

"Tastes even better." He slid the rack back in place and shut the oven door. "So, you staying for dinner or what?"

It was tempting. So much so, he halfway wondered if that wasn't exactly why he should head out now and meet up with Danny later. Then again, it was a prime opportunity to learn more about Gabe and maybe rattle those walls of hers a little more.

The last rays of sun bathed the world outside in a rich gold, and the sidewalk Gabe had disappeared down stood empty. He could still picture her, though, hustling down the street way faster than she needed to. A woman running from something while trying not to show it.

"Yeah, man," he said. "I'll stay."

Gabe meandered through the quiet neighborhood, her pace heading back to her house about half what she'd used to deliver Mr. Crawford's casserole. Twenty-five minutes she'd been gone with a whole lot of inane, neighborly chatter in between, and she still couldn't shake her mortification. On its own, admitting to Zeke she couldn't breathe wouldn't have been so bad. Especially if she'd chalked it up to discomfort. But nooo. She had to open her lamebrain mouth and admit it was his touch that made her wonky.

Not exactly your smoothest move.

What he meant by "I didn't mean to make it awkward" was you're not his type.

You're a mechanic. He's a doctor. That combination will never happen.

The fresh deluge of thoughts pummeled through her head, casting fresh bruises against her already battered confidence. She shook them off and focused on the world around her.

Beneath her bare feet, the sidewalk still held a hint of warmth, but the air ghosting around her shoulders promised an early spring-chilled night. If it weren't so late in the evening, half the retired couples would be out on their porches, sipping sweet tea and waving at her as she made her way home, but by now most of them were settling onto their couches for their favorite Thursday television shows. She loved that about her neighborhood. The simplicity of it. The quietness and peace in an otherwise supercharged world.

Thank God, Danny had saved their home. The last thing she'd expected when the bank advised how far behind their dad was on payments was for Danny to step up and offer his savings so they could keep it. And he hadn't just paid off the back mortgage payments, but the remaining note.

Her easy strides slowed to a crawl. Her dad had died a little over two years ago, about the same time he'd said he met Zeke. Danny had said the cash came from savings earned on his custom jobs, but something about his claim never sat right.

You saw Zeke's clinic. Clearly his friends have lots of money.

Money that could lure Danny closer.

Away from you.

Upping her stride, Gabe checked her watch and hustled around the final curve to her house. She wouldn't listen to the negative thoughts. Not this time. Danny believed in his friends. Rehashing the past earned her nothing right now. Besides, in a few more minutes her casseroles would be done. Trusting Danny to take them out when the timer went off was always a gamble. The last time she'd assumed he would brave oven mitts, he'd turned off the ringing timer and promptly gotten sidetracked by sports replays.

The setting sun glinted off Zeke's cherry-red Camaro in front of her house and jolted her heart back to where it had been when she'd beelined out the front door. She paused and studied the street behind her. She'd already maxed out on Mr. Crawford's conversational skills. Mr. Yates's choice of programming always leaned toward the History Channel, which made her nod off. Mr. and Mrs. Malone had decent taste in shows, but it seemed kind of weird hanging with a married couple this late on a Thursday night.

Next to her house, Mrs. Wallaby's house sat empty. She could hide there until Zeke left. Of course, then her casseroles stood a strong chance of turning into mini bonfires.

"Not everyone is Mom."

Danny was right. Much as she hated to admit it, he'd plucked a nerve last night when he said she kept people at bay on purpose. No matter how much the idea of being around his friends scared her, or how much Zeke left her breathless, they were important to Danny.

She squared her shoulders and climbed the stairs. How hard could it be to sit and listen to them do their thing? Danny hadn't asked her to be anyone's best friend, just to be polite.

The living room was empty, but a draft whispered across her skin, the sound of low, masculine voices and the lake's scent mingled with it. Another step forward brought the kitchen and sliding glass door to the back patio into view. Sure enough, there they were. Danny kicked back in an Adirondack chair with his feet kicked up on the matching ottoman, beer in hand, and Zeke a mirror image beside him.

A bump and glide against her shins jarred her attention.

Meow.

"You waiting for me, handsome?" She crouched and accepted Toothless's greeting with a scratch behind his ears. He rubbed his cheek against her leg and offered up a deep, rumbling purr. "Well, at least someone doesn't think I'm a dork."

The metal-on-metal scrape of the screen door sounded just as the oven timer buzzed.

"Hey, Gabe." Danny glanced at the oven like he'd never heard the annoying ringer before then jerked his head toward Zeke. "Zeke's staying for dinner."

"Okay." She killed the timer and dug her oven mitts out of the drawer, thankful her response had come out somewhat even keel.

Danny ambled to the fridge behind her. "Zeke, you need a fresh one?"

"I'm good."

Making sure Danny had cleared out of her way first, she bent to open the oven door and jerked upright, fumbling the oven mitts as she pressed both hands to her sides. "Damn it."

Zeke shot forward, steadying her with his strong hands on each shoulder. "You okay?"

"Yeah. I just forgot to brace first."

His grin went a long way toward numbing the pain, the flutters it stirred low in her belly twice as powerful as the lingering jolt from her ribs. He stooped before she could fully enjoy the view, retrieved her oven mitts and pulled the casseroles out of the oven. "It looks great. Lasagna?"

"Healthy lasagna," Danny corrected, pulling out his chair at one end of the table. "Ever since Dad died, she's banned fast food. Says we need to eat clean, but swear to God, she makes the shit taste good."

Zeke eyeballed the two slabs of cheesy goodness. "That's healthy?"

Gabe nudged him to one side and set about cutting big portions. "It's low-fat mozzarella and turkey sausage, so the fat's a lot lower."

"Which means I can eat two helpings," Danny said.

Not moving from his spot beside her, Zeke took a pull of his beer and leaned one hip on the counter.

"You can sit. I'll bring you yours," she said.

"I'll wait for you."

Well, that was different. Nice, actually. Although, having an audience while she tried to get the ooey-gooey pieces on the plates without ruining the overall appearance was a little disconcerting. She handed a plate to him and picked up the other two.

Zeke stopped her with a gentle touch on her arm. "Where's your drink?"

"I'll grab a water from the fridge," she said. "Go. Sit. Dig in."

Instead of heading to the table, he set his own plate down on the countertop and opened the fridge.

She slid Danny's plate in front of him, pulled her usual chair out and eased into it, mindful this time of her ribs. The water bottle's plastic seal cracked behind her.

"Here you go." Zeke dropped into the seat opposite Danny.

"Thank you." At least she hoped she said it out loud. For the longest time, all she could do was stare at the opened bottle. No one ever did things like that for her.

She peeked up to find him staring at her.

Shit. Not staring at her, but waiting on her. Unlike Danny, who'd already gobbled half an oversize serving. She snapped into gear and picked up her fork.

On cue, Zeke did the same and cut into his lasagna, his focus on Danny. "Your dad had a heart attack, right?"

"Yep."

"Was it heart disease, or something else?"

The whole handsome, polite and thoughtful routine must have temporarily unplugged her anxieties, because the answer shot out of her mouth before she could analyze the action. "Cholesterol."

Was it her imagination? Or did he almost smile again? "He take meds for it?"

"Yeah," Danny answered, "but he didn't diet or exercise. Said he got enough of that at the garage, and he'd rather eat what he wanted and die happy."

Zeke chuckled at that and cut another bite. "You had yours tested?"

"Gabe did. Healthy as a horse, as always."

"How was yours?"

Now there was an opportunity she wasn't missing. "He wouldn't go."

Danny froze with a loaded forkful about four inches from his mouth. "There's not a damned thing wrong with me. And I'm eating all the healthy stuff, so it's all good."

"You know I could run the tests," Zeke said.

Danny shrugged and dug in for another bite. "No need for you to bother with that."

"I ever give you any indication you're a bother?"

Her whole life she'd trailed around behind her big brother, idolizing him and plotting his demise in equal turns, but never had she seen him so surprised. So openly vulnerable. He grabbed his napkin and wiped his mouth.

"Okay, so we'll run the tests," Zeke said, not waiting for Danny to say more. "Knowledge is everything. I'd think you'd know that after being around me and the guys this long."

"Yeah." Danny played it off as no big deal, but there was a raggedness to his voice that wrenched her heart. "Appreciate it."

So did she. Big time. Ever since her dad had died, she'd tried everything from bribes to blackmail to get the same agreement, yet here Zeke had gotten it in under sixty seconds. More than that, he seemed to truly care about her brother. Maybe there really was something to Zeke and his friends being different than most.

Zeke turned his focus on her. "Danny tells me you're an artist."

"He told you what?"

Zeke's gaze cut to Danny, then back to her. "That you're an artist. He said it's pretty cool. That you take your own pictures?"

Even though the room was cool and bright, her skin burned as though fifty spotlights with an extra ten degrees of heat were aimed on her at one time. She forced herself not to fidget and pulled in a slow, steady breath. She could do this. It was simple conversation with a man who'd been nice to her. "It's not really art. More like messing around on the computer."

"Knox would be all over that," he fired back and took another bite.

"Who's Knox?"

"One of my brothers. Total computer geek. Has a laptop within reach at all times. I'll have to introduce you two."

"Is he a real brother, or one of your friends?" How she managed the verbal volley, she couldn't imagine, but she almost hit her knees in gratitude when he smiled big enough to show a dimple.

"He's my brother by choice. I'm an only child."

See? Not so bad. She moved a bite of lasagna around on her plate and tucked her free hand under her thigh so he couldn't see how bad she was shaking. "How'd you meet him?"

"Jace and Axel. They were the ones you met the other night. Jace is the wild biker-looking guy and Axel's the cocky Scotsman. We've got a place in the center of town we hang out at called the compound. Knox should be there, and Danny said he's coming over. You can come too if you want. Hell, you might even score me points with Viv."

"Who's Viv?"

"Jace's wife. They just got married a few months ago. She'd probably like having another woman around. She's as cool as they come, but even she's gotta get tired of hearing us yack about sports and cars."

Gabe glanced back and forth between her brother and Zeke. "What's wrong with sports and cars?"

Zeke laughed, set his fork on his plate, and pushed it a few inches away. "Okay, so maybe you'll score more points with the guys than Viv."

"Might be a good idea, Sugar Bear. You haven't been out of the house much all week. And you'd like Viv. Nice. Down-to-earth. Easy to talk to."

The down-to-earth and nice part she didn't doubt. From what Zeke had shown of himself the past few days, everything Danny had said about him and his friends were true. Easy to talk to though? That was a stretch on a good day, no matter who was on the other end of the conversation.

Danny watched her, a wordless plea to play nice moving behind his dark eyes.

She *had* been bored the past week, and having more time around Zeke to fuel a jillion new fantasies was an added bonus. Assuming she could keep her shit together and not let her defensive coping skills out of the bag.

She tucked her hair behind her ear and ignored the fresh wave of panic blasting through her veins. "Okay, I'll go."

Chapter Six

Gabe white-knuckled the passenger's armrest in Danny's Chevelle and gaped up at the multi-million-dollar villa outside her tinted window. "I thought Zeke said the party was at a compound."

"It is. That's it." Danny killed the engine and leaned over the center console enough to peer through Gabe's window. "They've got another place on the outskirts of town called Haven. It's a big ranch, but only family goes there. This place ain't too bad, though, is it?"

"Danny, that's not a compound. A compound is a metal warehouse. Or an old armory. This place is where the governor should live."

"Nah." He straightened, smacked her on the shoulder, and popped his door open. "Don't let appearances fool you. The brothers might like nice digs, but they're as down-to-earth as you and me."

Danny unfolded himself from his seat, the leather groaning under his weight, but Gabe's muscles were too locked up to move.

A shadow moved across her window a second before her door swung open. Zeke rested one forearm on the window and braced his other hand on the car's roof. "Not thinking you'll have much fun if you don't get out of the car."

"I was just…" Scared shitless? Thinking of hot-wiring Danny's car and pulling a Mario Andretti back to her house? "I'm not so sure I'm dressed for a place like this."

"What?" He checked her over then glanced back at villa. "Oh, you mean the house. It's pretty, but I wouldn't base dress code on the outside. It's the people in it who count." He held out his hand. "Come on, *gatinha*. It'll be fine."

Easy for him to say. His dinner wasn't halfway up the back of his throat and threatening to spew all over someone's fancy entryway. She put her hand in his and carefully wedged her way out of the bucket seats.

Up ahead, Danny opened one of the huge double doors and marched in like he owned the place. So much for him being a helpful buffer.

Zeke shut her car door and lowered his voice. "Don't overthink this. There's no one here that will make you feel uncomfortable. I promise."

She swallowed to the extent her dry mouth would allow and met his steady gaze. "What makes you think I'm worried?"

"Well, for one, you haven't taken a solid breath since I opened the door. And second, a crowbar couldn't pry your hand from mine."

Shit.

She relaxed her grip and smoothed her shirt along her stomach. "Sorry. I don't do so good with new people."

"You've met Jace and Axel already." He splayed his hand across her lower back and urged her forward. "And you've gotten to know me a little. That's a start."

Before she could argue, he'd steered her up the beautiful rock-work entry and through the door Danny had left wide-open. To say the inside was breathtaking was a huge understatement. The entry alone looked like some-

thing from a Hollywood-insider magazine, complete with
a sweeping spiral staircase and wrought iron balusters. A
huge chandelier hung centered from a shallow dome accented with stone masonry moldings, its center painted
to mirror a spring sky with white puffy clouds. The foyer
floor was an intricate swirl of soft taupe and ivory marble, but beyond the huge archway opposite where she
stood, distressed wood floors in deep chocolate stretched
into what she'd guess was a formal living room.

"Don't get any ideas. A few of the rooms are overwhelming like this one, but you'll see most of the place is
more in line with a bachelor pad." He cupped her elbow
and steered her to the stairs. "I'll show you around later.
Let's head up to the game room first and see if they've
got everything set up."

Happy chatter spilled down the staircase. Most rumbled in rich baritones, but one feminine lilt mingled in
between, all of it punctuated by light, carefree laughter.
With each step her heart hammered harder, every nightmare scenario from high school replaying in her head
in high definition.

They rounded the corner and stepped into a whole
lot of unexpected. Where what she'd seen so far was re-
fined elegance, the game room was a bachelor's paradise.
The hardwoods she'd glimpsed downstairs were repeated
here, but the old-world Tuscan vibe was replaced with
clean contemporary angles and lots of toys. At one end
was a huge flat-screen TV with two smaller ones on either side and plush ivory leather recliners lined up like
movie-theater seats. At her end of the room was a foos-
ball table, a pinball machine, and a poker table to rival
Vegas. Around the latter sat a whole slew of people, her
brother already happily ensconced with beer in hand and
one foot propped in the empty chair next to him.

"'Bout time you got here, brother." The Scotsman she'd met last week was just pulling out his own chair. As appearances went, Axel was the poster child for non-conformity—long russet hair like a barbarian straight out of the Highlands dressed in designer pants and a crisp button-down to rival fashion's elite. He lifted his crystal tumbler and grinned at Gabe. "Though seein' the pretty lass on your arm makes the wait worth it."

Every head turned her way, curiosity etched on their faces. The conversation stopped.

Run.

Just turn around and go back out the way you came. Keep your distance.

Zeke's warm hand slipped beneath her hair and palmed her nape. "Jace, Axel, you remember Gabrielle from last week."

"You mean, Gabe," Danny added. "No one calls her Gabrielle."

"So this is Danny's sister." A blond Adonis to rival Brad Pitt in his younger ponytail days stood and moseyed their direction. From his scuffed brown cowboy boots and faded jeans, to his chambray button-down and rolled-up sleeves, he was the ultimate sexy cowboy personified. "Personally, I think Gabrielle's a lot better fit." He stopped right in front of her and held out his hand. "I'm Trevor."

"It's okay," Zeke said low enough it barely registered. "He's harmless, for the most part."

Gabe shook the hand he offered, hating how sweaty her palm was when their hands made contact.

"Danny, my man," Trevor said. "You've been holding out."

Zeke tugged her hand out of Trevor's. "She's been here

three minutes. How about you hold off hitting on her for another hour or two?"

"He's right. Give her some air." The woman with long dark wavy hair sitting next to Jace stood and rounded the poker table. She stepped in close and gave her one of those sideways half-hugs Gabe had never been able to figure out. "I'm Vivienne, but everyone calls me Viv. I'm Jace's wife." She steered Gabe toward the table, tearing her away from Zeke's steadying presence.

In the space of seconds, Gabe's throat constricted and her skin grew clammy. The shapes and colors of the room were still there, but only as hazy blobs. Vaguely, she registered Viv talking beside her, but it resonated with a cave-like echo. Even if Gabe could make out the words, she wasn't sure her mind could focus enough to wrangle a reply.

Zeke's voice registered. "Hey, Viv. How about you let me show Gabe what we've got stocked in the bar before we get her situated at the table?"

Thank God. His subtle scent coiled around her, clearing her overloaded senses with its warmth the way a vibrant sunrise scattered what remained of night's fog. His hands cupped her shoulders and the next thing she knew, her feet were moving one in front of the other. The chatter round the poker table resumed behind her and the long bar with its high barstools and mango pendant lights overhead came into focus.

One of the barstool seats pressed against the back of her thighs.

"Just slide back and rest." Zeke guided one of her hands to the bar's edge and curled her fingers around the black padded leather. "Keep your chin down for a minute and take slow deep breaths."

Her fingers trembled and shivers wriggled down her

back, spurred stronger as the room's coolness pushed the last of her anxiety away.

"Better?" Zeke sat on the barstool beside her, one elbow propped on the bar.

"I think so." Eyes closed, she blew a stream of air up toward her bangs and prayed the adrenaline surge would hurry up and work its way out of her system. "How bad was it?"

"Danny knew what was up. Maybe Jace, but everyone else just thought I was a hoarding bastard."

Well, that was a plus anyway. "You knew what was wrong, didn't you?"

"I've seen a few panic attacks, so yeah."

She opened her eyes and met his calm, steady stare. Where she'd been afraid to really look at him before, somehow it was easier now. Like her mind had accepted he'd seen the worst of her and figured it wouldn't matter what he saw going forward. "Danny told you, didn't he?"

"That you're not a fan of crowds?" He shrugged. "He might have mentioned something like that."

Which probably meant he knew a whole lot more than her being socially awkward. That alone said how much Danny trusted Zeke. Her brother might be the happy-go-lucky, fly-by-the-seat-of-your-pants type, but he knew how embarrassed she was of her issues. One thing family didn't do to one another was air dirty laundry, especially when said airing might cause a loved one pain.

She scanned the room, desperate for something to get the focus off what had nearly been a top-notch disaster with his friends. "I thought your friend Knox was supposed to be here."

"He and Beckett are on their way. Knox called when we were about ten minutes out. They ought to be here anytime." He stood and rounded the bar. "You want something to drink? Beer? Wine?"

"I think water might be the smarter choice."

He grinned and dug a water bottle out of the small stainless steel fridge.

"So all of these guys are your brothers?" she said.

"Brothers by choice, yeah."

"You know that sounds a little weird, right?"

"Not really." He cracked the seal on the lid, twisted it off, and set the bottle on the bar in front of her. "Life gives you what you need when you need it. If it hadn't been for Jace and Axel, my life could've gone a whole lot different."

A big booming voice rang out behind her. "Okay, my brothers. Prepare to lose your bankroll."

A man as tall as Danny and Zeke strolled into the room, his black hair trimmed tight enough it would almost pass military muster. While his gray T-shirt, jeans and boots were about as unremarkable as a wardrobe choice could get, the muscles underneath the T were oh-my-God eye-catching. It wasn't overdone like in one of those bodybuilding magazines, but it was still enough to make even the cockiest of bastards take a step back and reevaluate getting in the guy's face.

Beside him was what Gabe had always imagined a hot nerd would look like. Tousled dark blond hair, solid, but lean body, and sharp, aristocratic features.

The two waved at Zeke and Gabe and commenced much hand slapping and high fives with everyone at the table.

"And now you know Beckett and Knox," Zeke said from beside her. "Wanna guess which one's which?"

"I'll go with the smaller one being Knox."

Zeke urged her out of her chair and guffawed. "Don't

ever tell him you called him small. You'll wound his already battered geeky ego." He jerked his head toward the table. "You ready to try again?"

Not really. Watching from a distance was a whole lot easier than anything up close and personal.

"I'll be right there next to you," he said. "Danny, too."

She closed her eyes, wishing that maniac internal panic would just disappear for once. "I'll give it a try."

Jace was the first to notice them headed their direction. "Gabe, you gonna play?"

It was a simple question. Nothing difficult. All she had to do was answer and be polite. "I'm not sure I'd be any good at it."

Axel's gaze snapped to Danny. "Shite, you've never taught the lass to play cards? What kinda bloody brother are you?"

"I'll help her." Zeke pulled out a chair for her and jerked his thumb at Trevor. "Move the hell over. You can save your moves for later."

"What? So you can make a play?" Regardless, Trevor stood up, a small smile playing around the corners of his mouth. "And since when have you been able to sit still for poker?"

"Since about right now." He dug out his wallet, slid a stack of hundred dollar bills free, and tossed them toward Jace. "Gabe and I will play one hand for now."

Jace eyeballed Zeke, then Gabe, then Zeke again, and raised an eyebrow.

Zeke shrugged and settled in the chair next to Gabe.

All of a sudden it hit her. "Wait. You play with real money?"

Trevor hesitated in shuffling the deck. "Is there another way?"

Danny tossed over another wad of cash to fund his own pile.

Holy crap, no way could she do this. "I can't—"

"Sure you can." Axel slid a huge stack of chips across the green felt. "They're just stacks of plastic after all."

Trevor dealt the cards, each one sliding neatly in front of its target with laser precision.

This was insane. Certifiably insane. Beneath the table her leg, next to Zeke, took up a nervous jiggle.

Zeke picked up the cards with one hand and covered her hand on her bouncing thigh with his other. Instantly, her mounting tension cut in half and her leg stilled. He fanned the cards so she could see each one and frowned. "So what do you think you should do?"

"I have no idea. I told you I don't know how to play."

He tossed the cards into the middle and shoved her ante behind it. "We fold."

"You just want to give up?" She almost stood and took the chips back. "You don't want to lose all that money."

"It's a rotten hand," he said. "Better to go for it when you've got something to work with."

"Just like life, lass," Axel said. "Toss the shite and roll with the good."

And just like that, things settled into a steady, relaxed, but playful pace. Deal, assess, bet, and move on. She even found herself smiling at some of the banter tossed back and forth between them, especially when Viv managed to innocently put one of the men in their place.

Beckett scooped his winnings from the center. "Hey, Danny. I meant to tell you, my guys did a check of your neighbor's break-in. Whoever it was, was good. No prints. No signs of forced entry. Hell, I don't even think they took anything."

"What were you doing in Mrs. Wallaby's house?" It

just popped out, fueled by years of practice keeping any-one and everyone at a safe distance. Unfiltered and 100 percent the harsh tongue Danny had begged her to keep under lock and key.

The room went silent. Well, all except for Danny, who ducked his chin, rubbed the top of his head as though searching for his cap, and muttered under his breath, "Jesus, Gabe."

Jace cocked his head. "We thought you'd want to know more about what happened, so we had Beck run it down. Maybe we were wrong."

Now she'd done it. Danny, the man who'd always had her back even when she didn't think she needed protec-tion, wouldn't even look at her. Her heart fumbled in a string of unsuccessful attempts to beat. "I just thought the cops would handle all of that. I mean, that's what they do, right?"

"Did they?" Jace said.

"Hell no." Danny tossed his cards into the center of the table. "They haven't been back out once." He pinned Beckett with a hard man-to-man look. "I appreciate it. I know Mrs. Wallaby would, too."

"Yeah, well, she needs a better security system," Beckett said. "Or at least to use the one she's got. If she wants a new one, let me know and we'll hook her up at a discount."

"I doubt it'll get that far." Danny took a drink of his beer. "Gabe talked to her a few days after it happened and she seemed okay with everything, but if she's like the retired couples down the street, she'll probably sell out once she's back from Florida."

"I saw those two empty houses near the end of the block," Beckett said. "Those the ones you're talking about?"

Trevor dealt a fresh hand and Danny studied his cards. "Yep. No clue who the new owners are. No one's moved in."

Beckett frowned for all of two seconds, then shrugged. "Well, if she doesn't want us to do it, I could teach you how to install one for her. You could get the parts through my company at cost and pocket the rest for yourself."

"No shit?" Clearly the news was exciting for Danny, because not only did his eyes get good and wide, but Axel got a good look at his hand and grinned.

"Be a good thing to know," Beckett said. "You're already a natural in the field. Why not add the technical side to it?"

Whoa. Wait a minute. She opened her mouth to speak, but this time checked her delivery and managed to soften it about half a second before her question hit air. "What's he mean, in the field?"

Axel tossed two cards to Trevor. "Beckett runs a security company. Handles the wires and the muscle. Danny's been running point on a few security details."

"Security details?" she asked.

"Yep. Physical protection. Like a bodyguard." Beckett nodded and studied his cards. "He's got a good eye."

Bodyguards get shot.

Dead people don't come back.

Danny's all you've got.

She forced a smiled. Or at least she thought it was a smile. On the inside it felt more like a warped grimace. Danny was happy. People were giving him kudos for doing a good job. And they seemed like good people. Friendly and down-to-earth just like Zeke had said.

She rotated her bottle of water in the little circle meant for beverages and swiped a bead of moisture off the label. The topic shifted to something else, something about a new client for Knox and cyberattacks. She needed a break. Fresh air and time to level out. She waited until Viv glanced her way and asked directions to the restroom.

Viv hopped up and guided her to a beautiful half bath down the hall. As soon as the door shut behind her, Gabe locked it and darted for the ornate lavatory with its gold filigree cabinet accents and granite top. She splashed cool water on her face and focused on steadying her breath.

Have you looked at this house? Really looked at it?

They're professionals. Educated. Smart.

You're a mechanic. You're a social freak.

You don't fit in here. Not with them.

Not with anyone.

She shook her head and dried her face. Everything was fine. She didn't have to listen to her thoughts. It was just the anxiety. Another layer to the shitty committee constantly yacking it up in her head. Besides, this was Danny's life. She'd done her best to play nice and hopefully hadn't bungled too much. She'd just wait until she could get Danny alone and let him know she wanted to catch a cab home.

See? An easy plan. In no time she'd be back at home, pajamas on, and curled up with Toothless and a good book. She opened the bathroom door, only half aware of where she was going, and ran smack into Zeke.

Chapter Seven

"You okay?" Zeke tried to keep the question light, but it was an ironic one considering he was anything but okay himself. The second Gabe had quite literally walked into his arms, he'd wrapped her up tight to keep her from falling, but now couldn't find the gumption to let her go. Everything about her next to him was perfect. Her scent, soft and subtle, yet with an exotic edge. Her breath whispering against his chest. Her soft breasts pressed against him. Of everything he wanted in that moment, moving her wasn't one of them.

She's Danny's sister, you moron.

The thought lashed hard and unforgiving. About the only thing that could fuck things up for Danny with the brotherhood would be his sister. If Zeke stepped across a line right now with Gabe, there'd be no telling how many ways things could go sideways.

"Hey." He forced his arms from around her and eased back, holding onto her shoulders and keeping her steady.

A little part of him died when her hands slid free of his hips and she tucked the tips of her fingers in her jeans pockets. Instead of meeting his gaze, she studied her boots. "I'm just tired. I think I'm going to grab my purse and catch a cab home."

A cab would be the safest bet. Yeah, he'd gained a

whopping foot letting her go, but the way his blood was revved right now, he'd need more like miles to cool things off. Heck, he could offer to take Danny home and suggest she take Danny's Chevelle. "Why don't I take you?"

Her head snapped up, surprise leaving her lips slightly parted and her pale blue eyes wide-open. The edges around them were puffy and red, though, and her eyelashes spiked in tight clumps as though she'd been crying. "I can't ask you to do that. You're with your friends."

"I don't mind. Sitting still's not my strong suit. I've already shocked half the guys making it as long as I did." He urged her back down the hallway to the game room. "Let's grab your stuff, and you can tell Danny good-night."

Oddly, extracting himself from the night's entertainment proved easier than he'd anticipated. Trevor and Danny were both reveling in their growing mounds of chips, and Axel, Beck and Knox were too focused on making a comeback to put up much protest. Only Jace lifted an inquiring eyebrow in his direction, silently stating he noted Zeke's possessive hand on Gabe's shoulder. After that, it was smooth sailing. Quiet, light and easy.

Zeke took the on-ramp to Highway 75 and goosed the engine up to the speed limit.

"What made you become a doctor?" Unlike the austere conversational tone a lot of people paired with that question, Gabe's was genuinely curious.

He checked the lane on his left and shifted to the HOV lane. "The short version? An inability to stay still for extended periods of time and a hair-trigger temper."

"You? Angry? I mean, you get really focused sometimes, but I've never seen you angry."

"Ah, but you've only seen me a few times. Could be

I'm a part-time whack job and you just haven't had the joy of experiencing my ugly side."

"I doubt that." She propped her elbow on the door and fiddled with the end of her hair.

He loved watching her do things like that. Those carefree, easygoing mannerisms that made him think of tropical beaches and hammocks. "Actually, my temper used to be pretty bad. My job keeps me even now, plus I do a lot of high-octane sports to burn off excess energy. Most things don't bother me anymore, but I've got my triggers."

"Such as?"

"Bullies. People with superiority complexes. Assholes in general."

She laughed at that, the sweet, airy sound unwinding his muscles and making him crave more of the same.

"So what made you decide you wanted to work on cars?" he said.

She shrugged and tucked her hair behind one ear. The soft blue light from the state-of-the-art navigation Danny had incorporated in the car's redesign cast Gabe's delicate profile in an angelic glow. "It's just what I know how to do. It was comfortable." She frowned and rubbed one hand along her thigh. "Danny would say it's safe."

"Is it?"

Her head cocked to one side, eyes soft on the road in front of them. "Maybe. I like it, though. The quiet. Being able to let my mind wander while I work. You like a thrill, but I like the calm."

"There's nothing wrong with that." Hell, he'd never had a calm moment in his life, but if it was anything like how relaxed she made him feel, he could see the appeal. For some reason, just being in her gravitational pull flipped his overdrive into neutral.

The drone of tires against the highway filled the silence. That was another thing he liked about being with her. She didn't need to fill every empty second with meaningless chatter. When she had something to say, she said it. When she didn't, she soaked in what was happening around her.

She turned from gazing out the passenger's window and caught him watching her. "I'm sorry I jumped all over your friend for checking Mrs. Wallaby's house."

"Beckett?" He scoffed and refocused on the road. "Don't sweat him. The guy's Teflon when it comes to emotions."

"And Jace?"

That was a damned good question. Her cautious nature wouldn't necessarily prevent Danny getting into the brotherhood, but it sure wouldn't help. Granted, nothing they did was immoral or caused innocents harm, but in the wrong hands, particularly in the hands of someone without the full story, it could sure cause them problems. Hoping Jace hadn't registered her suspicious mindset was like hoping Texas wouldn't see triple-digit temps in August. "Jace is the last person to jump to conclusions."

At least he hoped that proved to be the case.

He exited onto Interstate 30 and glanced in his rearview mirror. "You mind if I ask you a personal question?"

Her torso straightened, and she squirmed a little in her seat. "Okay."

"You know they have meds that help with the anxiety. You ever thought of trying one?"

She hung her head. "I guess Danny told you more than I thought."

"I'm a doctor, Gabe. Hearing someone has Social Anxiety Disorder doesn't faze me any more than hearing someone's got high cholesterol. Especially in today's day and age. We're twice as connected. Expected to do ten times what our parents or grandparents ever had to do. You'd be surprised at how many other people feel exactly what you feel."

"Do they take medicine?"

"Some of them. Depends on the severity and their lifestyle needs, but it's definitely not something to be ashamed or afraid of."

She lifted her chin and stared out at the highway.

"Think of it this way," he said. "A diabetic takes insulin. Do you think less of them?"

She faced him. "That's different. They have to have it to live."

"Actually, it's exactly the same thing. Except instead of dealing with insulin, it's dealing with serotonin. And if it allowed you to experience more of life without putting yourself through physical hell, it might be worth a shot."

She pursed her mouth as if she were fighting back an argument.

God, he was an idiot. He'd finally got her talking, and then he had to go and stomp into difficult terrain. "Sorry. It's the doctor in me. I didn't mean to push."

"It's okay." She shook her head and chuckled.

"What?"

"Just had a funny thought."

"And?"

A small smile played at the corners of her mouth and a wayward strand of blond hair brushed her cheek. "We may not live our lives the same, but we've got one thing in common."

"What's that?"

"Bullies."

The word catapulted him out of his peaceful state, his

grip on the steering wheel making the hard plastic groan in protest. "Bullies how?"

Her gaze locked on his hand clenched around the gearshift, and she placed her hand on top of it and gently squeezed. "Relax. I didn't mean now."

Bit by bit, her touch penetrated. He dragged in one slow breath after another, concentrating on the warmth of her hand and the hum of the highway. "Tell me about them."

She pulled her hand free and he almost reached across to reclaim it.

"I didn't always keep to myself," she said. "Not when I was little. Some stuff happened at home with my mom."

Stuff as in the arrest that had sparked their dad filing for divorce and full custody of the kids. With Knox's far reaching technical abilities, Zeke probably knew more about the technicalities of what happened when Gabe was young than she did, but he figured she'd share when the time was right. "And?"

"I didn't deal with it well at school. One thing led to another, and I had a few run-ins with some not so nice girls. After that, I kept myself as far away from everyone as I could. Over time, it was just easier to stay that way than try again. So, yeah. Bullies."

For the first time since he walked in her house this afternoon, he wanted to pace. Or run. Or beat the shit out of something. If he could reach across the console and thread his fingers through hers without looking like a flaming Nancy, he'd do it in a second. Especially if it gave him a little more of that calm goodness she radiated.

"Man, you weren't kidding about the quick trigger," she said.

The playfulness blasted through his tension-riddled muscles, as fresh as if someone had rolled the window down and let the cool night air smack him straight in the face. "Nope. It doesn't come out much anymore, but when it does, it's not pretty." He hesitated, not at all eager to share more, but compelled to do so after everything she'd offered. "It's embarrassing as hell after the fact, but when it's live, it's like I'm not even in my body."

She snickered none too delicately and covered her mouth with one hand. "Your anger and my silence. Aren't we a pair?"

They were, actually. She'd said more to him in the thirty-minute car ride than he'd heard her say in the past few days. And he'd managed to actually sit at a poker table with his brothers without getting up once to pace. At least until she'd left and hadn't come back.

He pulled into her neighborhood and navigated the slow curving street beneath the soft streetlights. Their almost pink tint gave the already cozy environment a dreamlike quality. No wonder she had Realtors knocking on her door day in and day out.

He killed the engine and opened his door.

Gabe's voice shot through the car's interior as he climbed out. "What are you doing?"

He propped one hand on the window and the other on the roof, and ducked so he could see her. "I'm walking you to your door." With that, he slammed the door shut and rounded the back of the Camaro. By the time he got to her side, Gabe had managed to get her own door open, but her ribs had slowed the process of prying herself from the deep bucket seats. He held out a hand and pulled her upright.

"Really, you don't have to do this," she said. "I can let myself in."

"I know you can. Doesn't mean you will." He waved

a hand at her purse then waggled his fingers. "Give me the keys."

"Why?"

"You had a guy knock you on your ass next door a week ago, it's late, and your brother's not here. At the rate he and Trevor were going at it, he might not make it home at all. Give me the keys. I'll check it out, you can lock up behind me, and we'll both sleep easy."

She rolled her eyes and tried to throw a long suffering sigh at him, but her ribs cut it short. Still, she handed the keys over.

He made quick work of the lock and flipped the main switch to the living room by the front door. "Wait here. I'll check the back rooms."

Toothless hopped down from his spot on the arm of the sofa, froze long enough to consider whether he needed to bolt, then walked a long path around Zeke toward Gabe. As names went, Gabe really couldn't have picked a better one for the fickle cat. All he needed was a set of wings and some fire breathing skills and he'd be a twin for the movie's dragon.

The sliding glass door was locked up tight, as was the door that led out of the utility room toward Danny's detached garage. Neither bedroom light was on, but he flipped the switches and scanned the rooms anyway, making sure everything appeared in place.

He strode down the dark hallway to the living room and found Gabe cradling Toothless in her arms like a baby. "Everything looks good."

"I knew it would be. The thing with Mrs. Wallaby's house was a fluke and bad timing." She stroked under Toothless's chin and he arched his neck higher, making room for more of her touch. Even from ten feet away, the cat's purrs rivaled a speed boat. The damned cat had it good. Very good.

"Well, I'll leave you to it," he said. "I'm sorry things didn't go better for you tonight, but maybe we can try again sometime if you're up for it." He smiled and ambled to the front door, his mind scrambling for an excuse to stay.

"Zeke?"

He paused at the threshold, cursed the rush that coursed through him at the sound of her voice, and faced her.

She glanced at the kitchen, then scanned the couch. "I was going to watch a movie for a little bit. It takes me a while to unwind enough to go to sleep after something like tonight." She trained her gaze on her fingers still slicking through Toothless's glossy black fur. "I was wondering…" Her chin lifted as though she'd processed an uncomfortable swallow. "Do you want to watch one with me?"

It was official. Gabe had lost her freaking mind. She'd already shown Zeke and all of Danny's other friends she was an awkward idiot, and now she wanted to drive the point home inviting him to stay and watch a movie?

Zeke shuttled his gaze between her and his Camaro parked outside, his mouth opening and closing at least twice while he ran his fingertips through his closely cropped beard.

"It's okay," she said, waving her hand as though it was no big deal. "It's late, and you want to get back to your friends. It was a stupid—"

"Yeah, I'll stay." He looked almost as shocked agreeing as she'd felt inviting him in the first place.

"Really?" She nearly groaned out loud the second her

unfiltered response took flight. If she could've snatched it out of the air and stuffed it back to whatever idiotic vault her mind had yanked it from, she'd have done it in a New York second. "I mean, your friends probably expect you back there, and sitting with me watching a movie has to rank high on your boring scale."

Something about his smile sent her insides winging like a flock of startled birds from a tree. "I've felt a lot of things around you since last week. Bored isn't one of them." He ambled to the tall bookcase next to her knock-off flat screen and stuffed his hands in his pockets. "Did you have something particular in mind?"

Normally after an event like tonight, she'd watch a guaranteed tearjerker, or a high-octane chick flick. Probably not the best selection for Zeke, though. She meandered next to him and scanned her DVDs. An action movie would be a good bet for a guy like him, but then she'd still be amped by the time it was over and in no shape to fall asleep.

Her gaze snagged on one of her favorites. Suspense, murders, with just enough lightness and romance to take the edge off, but not enough to make Zeke uncomfortable. "Have you ever seen *The Big Easy*?" She slid it out of its space on the shelf and handed it over to him. "It's older, but it's got a good cast. Plus, it's in New Orleans."

His gazed slid to her. "You like New Orleans?"

"Well, I've never been, but I've read a lot about it in books. I always thought it sounded really nice. The history and the food. Writers always make it sound like a magical place."

"It's a great place." He flipped the case over and studied the back. "Dennis Quaid and Ellen Barkin, huh?"

"Yeah. Dennis is really young in it and has a sexy Cajun accent."

"Got a thing for accents, huh?" He grinned big enough to hit her with the dimple. "How do you feel about Portuguese?"

Oh. My. God.

Even without a mirror shoved in front of her face, she could tell her cheeks were about twenty shades of raging red. If any more blood rushed to her face, she'd go up in flames.

He coiled his hand around the back of her neck and smoothed his thumb along her jawline. "Relax, *gatinha*. I didn't mean to make you uncomfortable." He stepped back, giving her space to catch her breath. "So is that what you normally wear when you watch your movies?"

She glanced down at her jeans and boots. "Oh, heck no. Usually I'm in my pajamas and have a huge bucket of popcorn, beer, my phone and the remote within grabbing distance."

"You plan for the long haul, huh?" He waved her toward her bedroom and moseyed to the kitchen. "You change then, and I'll drum up the popcorn and beer."

He'd already disappeared into the galley when the full force of what he'd just maneuvered her into registered. Or was it maneuvering? She traipsed down the hallway in a stupefied haze. That had to be it. Zeke wasn't anything like Jimmy Franklin. He was the kind of guy who unscrewed your water bottle for you and waited until you started eating before he appreciatively inhaled your food. And he wasn't interested in her. If anything, he probably viewed her as a little-sister type and felt bad she'd had a rough night.

She snatched her pajamas from the bottom dresser drawer, a soft pink cotton nightshirt that hung down to her knees, but was made of the softest cotton she'd ever felt. It would have been nice if she'd been able to find one that wasn't two sizes too big for her, but the outlet she'd found it at didn't always work to a bargain hunter's advantage.

She plunked down on the edge of her bed and pulled on her gray knitted socks. They were thick and probably looked more like leg warmers than socks, but they were the perfect, cozy addition when curled up on the couch watching movies. She snatched her phone and Googled *g-a-t-i-n-h-a* in the Portuguese translator.

No way. *Kitty*? Really?

She stomped down the hallway, double-checking the translator along the way. The scent of fresh popcorn hit her right before she made the kitchen and sure enough, there was Zeke, emptying a full bag of popcorn into the same bowl she always used. The guy was freakishly efficient with things like that. "I looked it up."

"Looked what up?"

"Gatinha."

The way he smiled, she was a little surprised her panties didn't melt. He shook the rest of the popcorn from the bag. "Yeah? What'd you find out?"

"You think I'm a kitten?"

He tossed the empty popcorn bag in the trash and took his time turning around, as if he were weighing how he wanted to answer carefully. "I think you're like a feral kitten. One who's hungry and has a bowl of cream right in front of her, but can't quite decide if she wants to lick it up, or hiss and hightail it back into the woods."

He did? And was that a good thing or a bad thing? To her mind, it seemed kind of nice, but then she had a wonky way of looking at the world compared to most people. "I'm not sure how to take that."

"Take it the way I meant it."

"How's that?"

He picked up the bowl and handed it to her. "That you're wild and sweet."

Even with the oversize white plastic tub between them, her heart hammered like he'd plant a kiss on her at any second. He wouldn't, obviously. But it was still a nice image, one unlike anything she'd have conjured for herself. "Thank you."

"You're welcome." He picked up the two beers he'd opened for them, and motioned with one toward the living room. "Now let's get our movie going. I've got a shift at seven in the morning and want to make sure I get a few hours in beforehand."

Oh, damn. He really was here out of pity. Somehow she'd known that deep down, but knowing she'd be responsible for him slogging through work tomorrow sat wrong in her conscience. "I didn't know you had to work tomorrow. You don't have to stay if you don't want to."

He nudged her shoulder and prodded her on toward the couch. "*Gatinha*, one thing you need to know about me is that, when I say I'm wired most of the time, it means I'm *really* wired. As in I get very little sleep. I can't tell you the last time I got eight hours straight. So if anything, you're helping me wind down enough to sleep a solid four hours at least."

He paused, studied something on the end table closest to him, then set his beer down and picked it up. The stack of Realtor cards she'd brought home from Mrs. Wallaby's house over the past few weeks were pinched between his fingers. "These are all the people who've stopped by your house?"

"No, those are the ones who've left cards for Mrs. Wallaby while she's been gone. I chuck the ones we get. The last thing I want is to move."

"How long has she been gone?"

Gabe propped a bunch of pillows next to her to support her ribs and tucked her feet beside her on the couch. "A few weeks."

"Gabe, there are at least ten here."

"Yeah, I told you they come by a lot." She punched the power button on the remote. "I'll man the remote if you'll pop the movie in."

For a second, he looked like he wanted to dig deeper, but he tossed them back to the end table, picked up the movie and slid the disk in the player. A few practiced clicks from Gabe on the remote and the movie came to life, aerial shots of swampland and the gulf mingling with an upbeat Cajun song.

Zeke killed the kitchen and dining room lights and settled on the end of the couch opposite her.

Accustomed to the routine, albeit without a hot doctor along for the ride, Toothless hopped onto the couch between them. It took him a few casual passes and a whole lot of feline nonchalance, but he finally crept close enough to Zeke to give a careful hello.

Zeke held out his hand and waited.

Toothless stared long and hard at the offering then rubbed his cheek on Zeke's fingers. The purring roared right behind the capitulation, welcoming Zeke's scratches behind the ear like a strung out addict.

"Fickle damned cat." Gabe focused on the murder investigation underway in the movie. God, she'd seen this movie so many times, she could quote it in her sleep. Zeke would probably think it was stupid, or at least seriously outdated, but there was something inherently sexy about it without being over the top.

Before she knew it, the world fell away. All her blunders. All her oddities. Even Zeke's steady, strong presence so close and yet so far away. The characters, the sites and the emotions sucked her in, so much so she bit her lip at a particularly sensual scene, imagining the heroine was her instead of the leading lady. To be kissed that way, a man's hand fisting her hair while his mouth devoured hers.

Zeke shifted at the far end of the sofa, ripping her from her steamy moment on the screen. Except he wasn't watching *The Big Easy*. He was watching her, and he looked hungry. Big-bad-wolf hungry.

"You're not watching the movie," she said.

"Watching you is better." No saucy gleam in his eye to indicate it was a joke. No follow-up snicker to suggest she should brush it off. Just his warm, husky voice and so much heat in his eyes she could barely breathe. "You liked what you saw."

"Um…yeah. It was hot."

"Which part?"

What did he mean, which part? You couldn't dissect any portion of a Cajun Dennis Quaid putting the moves on anyone. "All of it?"

He rubbed one finger below his lower lip, thoughtful.

She managed a deep, shaky breath and refocused on the TV. "It doesn't matter anyway. I love movies and romance, but I'm a realist. Passion like that doesn't exist. Doesn't mean I can't enjoy the fantasy."

She kept her gaze locked on the movie, but her senses couldn't quite unlock from Zeke. It was like her whole body was supercharged and tuned into his presence. So much so, when he reached out and wrapped his big hands around her ankles, she nearly leaped off the couch.

He carefully picked her feet up and urged them over his lap. "Stretch out. It'll be easier to breathe."

"I don't want to crowd you."

"It's your couch, Gabe. I'm the one who crashed your

movie, so relax." He gripped one foot and slowly massaged his thumb along the arch.

Holy. Freaking. Cow.

The man had amazing hands. Confident and strong without manhandling her. Perfect pressure mixed with a languid sensuality. Even better, he didn't seem to be in a hurry, giving slow, diligent attention to each foot. Staying still was hands down the hardest thing she'd ever done, second only to holding back her satisfied moans. When his hands shifted to her calves, she gave up trying to watch the movie and simply let her eyes drift closed, imagining them much, much higher.

He's just a friend.

Actually, he's Danny's friend.

He's just being nice.

Okay, all of that was true, but he had an exceptional talent for touch. If he weren't already making bank as a doctor, she'd recommend he look into work as a massage therapist.

Eventually, his strokes slowed, the twists and turns of the movie luring him in until he stopped altogether. It was still nice. Cozy and connected, his hands rested on top of her feet, sending his heat through her thick socks and warming her clear to her soul.

Perfect.

She closed her eyes. Colors from the screen flashed behind her eyelids, and the familiar dialogue droned well-worn through her mind. God, she hoped she never forgot this feeling. So peaceful and protected.

The actors' dialogue faded farther and farther away, and the sweet lull of sleep pulled her under.

Thirty minutes past midnight. In another six and a half hours, Zeke was due at work for a twelve-hour shift. Logic told him to get his ass in gear, get home, and at least try to get a few hours of sleep, but all he could do was sit at his end of the couch and watch Gabe sleep. Her breaths were shallower than he'd like to see, but it didn't surprise him with her only being a week out on healing. The way she'd adjusted to the injury, bracing and protecting her ribs when she moved, was impressive. Most people just planted themselves on their bed and avoided moving.

But not Gabe.

Toothless lay curled up next to her, his body tucked into the crook of her hips. The television's pale blue menu screen cast a soft glow on Gabe's face. He didn't have the first damned clue how the movie ended. As soon as that love scene had come on, the only thing he'd been able to concentrate on was Gabe. The way she licked her lip then bit it. How her eyes got big and glossed over. At one point, she'd snagged a handful of popcorn, held the fistful up to her mouth, and flicked a few pieces into her mouth with her tongue. He'd been rock hard and ready to go ever since.

For the first time in the past hour, he shifted, those insanely homely, but cute as fuck socks of hers tickling his fingers. He'd never rubbed a woman's feet before. Had never wanted to. With Gabe, it had been nothing short of erotic. And she'd liked it. A lot. He'd bet the brotherhood's accumulated wealth she didn't have a clue just how much her body had given her away. The soft little sighs and the tiny shifts from her hips. Talk about tilling fertile soil for his wicked thoughts. The fact that he'd kept his hands from coasting up and under her nightshirt to that pert ass of hers practically guaranteed him a fast track to sainthood.

Passion like that doesn't exist. Doesn't mean I can't enjoy the fantasy.

She'd said it without the least amount of levity, and he still didn't get it. How a woman could look like she did, be as sweet as she was, and not have a man frequently lighting her match, he still couldn't comprehend. She couldn't be a virgin. If that was the case, she'd think sex was all fairy tales and roses, not be a pessimist about it. Which meant either she'd had shit for lovers, or a few nightmare sexual experiences to go with the rest of her years in high school.

His temper twitched beneath his skin and pounded his temples. If it was the latter, someone had better pray like hell he never found out. That was one scenario he'd have no issue giving his anger full throttle to avenge her.

Damn it, what was he thinking? This was Danny's sister. Not a woman he had any kind of personal connection to. Not a woman he *should* have a personal connection to.

He eased up from the couch, carefully lifting her feet off his lap as he did and laying them softly on the couch.

She still didn't stir, her breath moving slow and steady between barely parted, but full, kissable lips.

All week long he'd ruminated about those lips, fraught as the temptation was. Even if she wasn't Danny's sister, she wasn't the type for a one-night tumble. Gabe was 100 percent long-term material. The type who deserved care and attention. Since when did he want that?

Since you found someone worth it.

Nope. That wasn't a notion he needed to entertain. Heck, he didn't even need to be in the same state as an idea like that. He snatched the empty popcorn bowl and drained beer bottles then tidied up the kitchen. DVD player and TV switched off, he stood beside the couch.

Gabe still hadn't moved. Not even an inch. The easier route would be to leave her there, but her ribs would be screaming mad when she woke up. She'd be better if she could stretch out and roll around if she needed to. Then again, waking her up seemed a rotten thing to do.

He spun and strode down the hallway. The light from the living room cut across her bedroom, spotlighting her small bedside lamp. He flipped it on and studied the room. Like Gabe, it was a whole lot different than most of the other women's bedrooms he'd been in. Unpretentious and welcoming. The comforter was a soft, denim color, and a slew of throw pillows in white, black, and a color that wasn't quite pink but wasn't red either, were casually stacked against the headboard. A simple, wide rug in the same colors stretched out in front of the bed, and two antique blue nightstands anchored each side.

He gauged which side of the bed she slept on by the alarm clock and pulled that side down. The sheets were nothing special, just plain white with tiny pink flowers scattered everywhere, but well-worn and sinfully soft. The kind of soft a man would appreciate most without a stitch on and curled up around a woman like Gabrielle.

Well, so long as she wasn't a prospective brother's sister. Looking after her as a doctor or for Danny was one thing. Anything more crossed a line that could well create a whole host of problems. He strolled back to the living room and gently rolled her to her back.

Toothless hopped down, pranced toward the bedroom, and looked back as if to say, *"You coming?"*

He had to admit, he totally dug the cat. Gabe couldn't have found a better fit for her if she'd tried. And to be honest, he'd envied the hell out of Toothless getting to feel Gabe's tender touch through the last half of the movie. He crouched next to her, slowly lifted her arm, and wrapped it around his neck. He'd just slid his arms under her thighs and shoulder blades, when she startled awake.

"What?" Her head jerked from side to side, trying to register what was going on. "What are you doing?"

"Shhhh. Go back to sleep." Straightening, he cradled her close and headed back down the hallway. He'd halfway expected her to try and wriggle herself free, but instead she accepted his quiet admonition, laid her head on his shoulder, and gave back into sleep.

The whole scenario was weird. Awkward and yet somehow quintessential. Holding her didn't just feel right, it felt necessary.

You're toeing a seriously dangerous line, buddy.

He shook the thought off and laid her in her bed.

Her eyes fluttered open, sleepy and unguarded, but so damned sexy his dick practically saluted on demand.

"Socks on or off?" he grumbled.

She didn't answer, just stared at him as though her conscious mind was having a hard time weaving reality and dreams together. Damn, he wanted a taste of those lips. To really wake her up and show her exactly how real passion could be.

"Socks on or off, *gatinha*?" If he didn't get the hell out of her room now, he'd do a whole lot less wanting and a shit-ton of doing.

Her husky sleep voice rasped past her lips. "Off."

Fuck. At the rate he was going, his cock would have bruises from his button fly. He slid her socks off and bit back a moan. He'd forgotten those dainty feet of hers. No polish, just soft and natural like the rest of her. He tucked them under the covers and pulled the blankets up to her shoulders. The smart thing would be to step away and hightail it out the door. He smoothed a strand of hair off her cheek instead. "Sleep good."

He turned before he could send her any more conflicting messages and flicked off the light. The door was nearly closed when her quiet voice hit him.

"Zeke?"

He paused, not daring to step back inside, but holding his spot in the doorway.

"Thank you," she said. "For helping me, I mean. And being a friend to Danny." The rustle of sheets nearly yanked him from his spot at the door. "For everything. Thank you."

"Don't thank me for doing something that's easy to do." He squeezed the door jamb a little harder. *"Boa noite, gatinha doce."* Good night, sweet kitten.

He pulled the door shut, strode down the hallway, and locked the house up good and tight. Her cozy porch with the outside light burning bright filled his rearview mirror as he drove away. Oh, yeah. There was a definitely a line, and damned if he wasn't ready to cross it.

Chapter Eight

Zeke strode out of the racetrack's main building to the parking lot, folded himself into his car's front seat and slammed the door behind him. Two hours he'd pushed his favorite race cars on the track and still no relief. If anything, he was jumpier than he'd been when he walked in. His skydive yesterday hadn't taken off his growing edge either. Neither had the rock climbing the day before that, or the half-day hike on Monday. In between it all, he'd had three twelve-hour shifts crammed full of all kinds of trauma. He ought to be as close to Zen as possible and sleeping like a rock.

The image of Gabe lying in bed last Friday night flashed bold and beautiful in his head. He wanted her. Not just sex, but *her*. To hear the sweet, easy cadence of her voice while she chattered about places she wanted to visit and movies she liked to watch. To watch her while she did simple things like cook for her neighbors, or maybe while she worked on her art. To have those big, vulnerable blue eyes of hers staring up at him while he buried himself deep inside her.

"Fuck." He fired up the engine and slammed the gearshift into first. A week now he'd put himself through this nonstop torture trying to stay away, but he was done with it. His body knew what was up. His conscience might be determined to dodge the idea, but the man in him had locked onto its target and wouldn't stop until it got its way.

And he was tired of fighting it.

He navigated the side streets then floored it up the westbound on-ramp for I-635. Traffic was already heavy, workers slipping out of their eight-to-five jobs a little early to start their weekend and clogging up everything but the HOV lane.

Forty-five minutes later, he pulled in front of the body shop where he'd first met Danny. Ironically, he'd just left the racetrack then, too, though he'd made one hell of a mess of his Stingray's back fender. The track's owner had recommended Danny's shop as a contact for fixing the damage.

He hoofed it across the blacktop parking lot to the farthest open bay. He'd barely rounded the door when Danny straightened from a crouch behind a fully primed Lexus ES. His hair was pulled back in a ponytail with a red bandana wrapped around his head. "Hey, Zeke."

"Hey." Zeke scanned the other bays but didn't see the shop's owner futzing around anywhere. "I'm not gonna cause any problems for you stopping by, am I?"

"Here? Hell no. Though I gotta say, you're a long way out from your normal stomping grounds for a Friday." Danny strolled to the open garage door and scanned the parking lot. "Please tell me you didn't ding the 'Vette again."

"It was a hell of a lot more than a ding, but no. She's fine." He jerked his head toward the Camaro. "You got a minute? Need to run something past you."

Danny pulled a rag out of his coverall's pocket, wiped his hands, and shouted to the heavyset man taping off the car in the next bay. "Hey, Steve. Gonna take a break. Be back in a few."

The man barely spared the two of them a glance, but chin-lifted an acknowledgment and kept on with his work.

Danny jammed his rag into his back pocket. "Gotta admit. Seein' you here's about the last thing I expected today. Can't imagine it's anything good if you drove all this way."

"Could be it's something good that made me drive out all this way, too." Zeke leaned against the back of his Camaro and crossed his arms. "It's not like you to jump straight into negative thinking."

"All right," Danny said. "I'll play. What's up?"

Across the street, cars darted in and out of the bustling 7-Eleven. The old-fashioned hamburger shop next to it was twice as busy with customers lined up out the front door and a drive-through line that stretched out into the street.

And yet, his mind was empty. The whole way here he'd molded and edited his words, only to have them vanish in an instant. "You know I introduced you to my brothers for a reason."

Danny frowned and scratched his bandana-clad head. "I guessed it was to help me out. Share a little of what you guys have learned."

"That's how it started, yeah. The thing is, I think you've got a shot at being one of us. A good shot."

"No shit?" Danny smiled huge, parked his hands on his hips, and looked around the parking lot as though he half expected someone to jump out and claim it was a prank. That's what he liked about Danny. Always so damned genuine and open it was scary. Just like Gabe when she wasn't preoccupied with keeping people at a distance.

"That's not something I'd joke about," Zeke said. "Problem is, it's not a done deal. Not yet. The brotherhood's slow to bring in new blood. Careful. I don't think I need to extrapolate on why that is."

"I may not be the sharpest blade in the shed, but I'm not the dullest. So, yeah. That makes sense."

"Then you get why I'm not keen on doing anything that would upset the situation while the guys are figuring out how they want to vote."

A genuine wariness moved behind Danny's eyes. "Upset the situation how?"

He didn't have to do this. He could shrug it off, come up with some bullshit excuse for his visit, and walk away. Hell, it was probably the right thing to do.

"Man," Danny said, "whatever you've gotta say, just lay it out there."

He was right. If Danny had any hope of being a brother, he'd have to take straight talk not just from Zeke, but all the other men, too. And walking away, no matter how valiant his conscience might make it seem, wasn't happening. "I could make shit go south really quick if I screw up with my next move."

"What move's that?"

"I'm making a play for Gabe."

Danny locked up tight and his smile died. With the two of them matched at six foot three, Danny's height wasn't exactly intimidating, but the way he jammed his hands in his pockets and rolled his shoulders back made Zeke think the rest of their convo might not go as smooth as he'd hoped. "Making a play how?"

"Not the kind you're thinking. Gabe's sweet. The kind of sweet a man protects. I get that and I respect it, but there's no predicting how things could turn out between us. We're complete opposites."

"Then why go there?"

"Because *not* going there isn't an option." It was the most honest thing he'd admitted since the day he laid eyes on her, and the truth behind his statement must have resonated with Danny too because a little of the tension in his shoulders eased. "I stayed with her a lot longer than I let on last weekend."

"When you took her home?"

"Yep. I didn't plan to do it. She asked me to stay, and I couldn't say no. Nothing happened. Nothing except sitting on the couch and watching some late-eighties movie." He paused long enough to meet Danny's stare head on. "Aside from the night I joined the brotherhood, it was the best night of my life."

Danny stared back at him, obviously a little shocked at the admission.

"I want you to know, I get the line I'm crossing," Zeke said. "I get what's at stake. That's why I wanted to come and give it to you straight before I move forward."

For the longest time, Danny just stood there, his eyes a little glazed over like someone had whacked him on the back of the head. He blinked a few times, studied the blacktop, then gazed out toward the interstate in the distance. Whatever he was thinking about, it was serious. Enough it appeared as though the whole damned world squatted on his shoulders. "There's more of a line there than you think."

Zeke forced himself not to move, but a thick, supercharged awareness prickled beneath his skin.

Danny faced him. "You think you're just putting my chances with the brotherhood at stake, but the damage you could do to her is worse."

"I get that."

"I don't think you do." Danny sighed, paced a few steps, and leaned next to Zeke on the Camaro's trunk. "You know my dad kicked my mom out when Gabe was little."

"You mentioned it, yeah."

"I'm guessing the brothers know the details, too."

Talk about your sticky wickets. "Brothers don't have secrets. So if you're asking if I know she got arrested and divorced about three months later, yeah, I know."

"Figured as much." Danny gripped the edge of the trunk and scanned the street in front of them. "What you don't know are the details. That Dad found my mom sleeping around with not one, but two men who were seriously bad news. What's worse, she'd take Gabe with her. He spent everything he had to get custody of the two of us."

"He sounds like a good man."

Danny smiled, his focus a little distant. "Oh, he was. Always cut to the point and never blew smoke up anyone's ass." He looked at Zeke. "Not even with Gabe. Gave her the truth about Mom the same way he did everything else. The problem is, Gabe thinks Mom seeking that lifestyle was because of her. That if she'd been better, prettier or smarter, Mom would've wanted to be home instead of somewhere else."

"That's whacked. She was just a kid."

"You know that. I know that. But that's the version Gabe got twisted up in her head. She might've gotten past the ideas if it hadn't been for a few other grab and tosses with guys from school. Somewhere along the way, she decided people don't stick around because there's something fucked up with her. So she keeps everyone at a distance to keep from getting hurt."

"She tell you that?"

"Nope. I might not be a doc like you, but I know my sister. I watched it happen. Saw her try to make friends and get the door slammed in her face one way or another. That's why she hangs with all the old folks in our neighborhood. They ain't going anywhere and she knows it. They're safe."

A need to be good enough. Man, could he identify with that. Growing up dirt poor around a bunch of snobby rich kids, he understood that desire all too well. Except where he'd come out swinging, Gabe had built a wall and kept her side of it very carefully structured.

"I'm not gonna lie to you," Danny said. "Of all the people I'd want for Gabe, I'd want someone like you. I liked watching you look out for her the other night. Liked the way she looked at you when you told everyone you were taking her home. But Gabe's not a good bet for anything casual."

"I'm not after casual. I wouldn't put your future or her happiness on the line for a quick hookup. And while I can't promise how things will turn out, I can promise I'll shoot her straight no matter what."

"And if I told you not to go there?"

Like hell that was going to happen. "I'm not sure I'd listen."

Danny hung his head and huffed out an ironic laugh. "Funny thing is, I take that as a comfort." He looked up. "She deserves someone who'd go to bat for her no matter what."

A car pulled into the shop's lot and parked in front of the main office, a potential new customer given the ugly dent in the front left fender.

Zeke held out his hand. "We good?"

Seconds ticked by.

Danny frowned and studied Zeke's outstretched palm, then straightened and shook it. "Yeah, man. We're good." He jerked his head toward the customer who'd just disappeared into the office. "I gotta go cover that. Appreciate you coming by."

"Appreciate you not ripping my head off." Zeke pushed away from his car and rounded for the driver's door. "Hey, is Gabe an early riser?"

"Depends. On a work week, yeah. But tomorrow's Saturday, so I'd guess she'll lay in a little. Never past eight-thirty or nine, though. Why?"

"I want to talk to her. Thought I'd pay her a visit in the morning."

That earned him an incredulous gape complete with raised eyebrows. "You could call her like every other man on the planet."

"You really think giving your sister fair warning of what I'm doing is a smart move?"

Danny's laugh rang out loud enough a few people from across the street turned and looked. He waved his hand and headed toward the office. "Point taken."

Chapter Nine

The low, throaty rumble of a souped-up engine dragged Gabe out of sleep. She pulled the covers up over her head and gingerly rolled away from the window. If she'd told Danny once, she'd told him a thousand times not to fire his Harley up this early. It always made Mr. Yates cranky, and cranky meant a long lecture about the safety of motorcycles. If she was smart, she'd stomp out there and tell him—

Wait a minute. That wasn't Danny's Harley. It rumbled, sure, but not like this engine. This was bigger. Definitely more horsepower.

She threw back the covers and carefully rolled out of bed, snatching her phone off the nightstand on the way. Who the heck would come to visit at eight o'clock in the morning on a Saturday? She peeked between the blinds.

Zeke's cherry-red Camaro idled in the driveway.

She gasped, and jumped back.

Holy crap.

More carefully than before, she pried the blinds apart just enough to check the rest of the driveway. No Danny.

Shit. Shit. Shit. And here she was in another freaking night shirt.

She rushed to the bathroom, flipped on the light, and groaned. Just once, she'd like to wake up and not look like she'd been on a ten-day bender. Movies made it look like other women woke up with sexy bedhead, but not her. She brushed through the ratty mess in long quick strokes.

The screen door's quick *whoosh* sounded followed by three firm raps on the door.

Tossing the brush to the counter, she stepped back and assessed her appearance. The tangles were gone, but one side was more smooshed than the other. The nightshirt was old, but it was pretty without being overly girly.

She hurried toward the front door. Worrying about what she looked like was silly anyway. He'd already seen her as dressed down as a girl could get. What difference did bad hair make?

Um, because you've obsessed about him for a whole freaking week and fantasized about kissing the bejesus out him on a nightly basis, that's why.

She froze two steps from the door. She hadn't brushed her teeth. What kind of idiot answered the door for a guy like Zeke with morning breath?

Maybe she should ignore it and pretend she wasn't here.

The knocks rapped again.

Yeah, ignoring him was stupid. Her truck was right outside so he knew she was home. "Hang on a minute." She dashed back to the bathroom and did a world record on brushing her teeth. Nothing her dentist would be satisfied with, but enough she wouldn't knock him over with a "Hhhhhello."

Pausing at the front door, she pulled in a slow, steady breath, smoothed her hand down the front of her nightshirt and wrapped her hand around the knob. He was probably just looking for Danny. No big deal. Act casual.

She swung the door wide, opened her mouth to say

good morning, and promptly lost the ability to speak. His hair was still damp from a shower, and he looked like he was headed out for some kind of sporting event. His black shorts paid homage to some seriously cut quads and his red shirt clung to equally defined shoulders and arms. In one hand he held a cardboard drink tray with two Styrofoam cups, and in the other a box of donuts from the bakery down the street. "Hi."

A simple *hi*. Like his ornery smile hadn't taken her day and completely turned it upside down. "Morning."

He lifted the box with the donuts and motioned toward the living room. "Are you going to invite me in, or did I hog too much popcorn last time?"

Gah, where was her head? She stood back and waved him in. "Sorry. I was asleep when you knocked. I'm slow to wake up."

"Then I guess it's a good thing I got coffee to go with the donuts so you don't have to make any." He sauntered toward the kitchen, set his sugary wakeup call on the table, and glanced over his shoulder. "You do cream or sugar?"

She shook her head and padded closer. "Danny's not here. He didn't come home last night."

"I didn't come to see Danny. I came to see you." He opened the box of donuts, pried the lid off one cup, and held it out for her. "I wasn't sure what kind of donuts you like so I grabbed one of everything."

Steam swirled off the coffee's black surface. He brought her coffee? And donuts?

"You do like donuts, don't you?" he said, still holding the coffee outstretched. "I'll have to reevaluate everything I've thought about you if you don't like donuts."

Logically her mind accepted what it was seeing and hearing, but her brain couldn't quite tie the pieces together. It just sat there, dumbfounded and worthless. "What's your current evaluation?"

He grinned, sidled closer, picked up one of her hands, and forced the coffee into it. "Right now, I think you're cute when you're sleepy." He stepped away and chin-lifted toward the donuts. "Drink your coffee and eat at least two of those. Doctor's orders."

She crept close to the box and peeked inside. The sweet, sugary scent of fresh pastries wafted to her nose. She loved donuts. Or any baked good for that matter. Granted, she didn't eat them as much anymore. Cheating seemed wrong when she was trying to help Danny eat better, but once upon a time she'd refused to end a single meal without dessert.

Zeke pulled out a kitchen chair, eased into it and sipped his drink.

One wouldn't hurt. Especially since Danny wasn't here to witness her dive into doughy depravity. She pinched one of the two chocolate-glaze donuts, closed her eyes and sunk her teeth in.

"Mmm." Soft and fluffy dough with just enough chocolate that melted on her tongue. Hands down the best wake-up treat ever. She licked her lower lip to catch a piece of chocolate before it could escape, opened her eyes and stilled.

Somewhere between her first bite of heaven and now, casual Zeke had exited the building. His stare was so intense, it felt like bits of supercharged air against her skin. Not a trace of his smile was left and his lips were slightly parted.

She swiped her lower lip where the chocolate had been. "Something wrong?"

His gaze locked onto the action, then snapped back to hers. Usually, his voice purred smooth and rich, but this time it came out thick and grated. "Not a thing wrong. Everything's perfect." He leaned back in his chair and blew across the top of his coffee.

Weird. For a guy who'd seemed pretty level-headed the few times she'd been around him, he seemed a little moody today. Then again, who was she to judge when it came to being temperamental?

She slid into her own chair and took another bite. "You know you don't have to keep checking on me. My ribs are still sore, but they're a lot better."

"I didn't come to check on your ribs. I came to see what your plans are for today."

Gabe popped the last bite in her mouth. "Not much. I went back to work this week. It's only office work right now, but it kept me busier than I thought it would, so I figured I'd relax. Maybe take some new pictures and read a book I bought this week." She sucked the last of the glaze off her thumb and finger.

Zeke stared at her, that frozen, fixated intensity aimed on her mouth.

"Sorry." She snatched a napkin and wiped her fingers. "Bad habit. I know it's gross, but it seems a shame to let good chocolate go to waste."

"I couldn't agree more." His words were playful, but the tone behind them was a little off. Distracted, yet aggressive. He sat up straighter and nudged the donut box closer to her. "Have another one."

"Do you know how many calories are in one of those things?"

"Absolutely. I also know I plan to keep you busy today, so an extra one won't hurt."

"Keep me busy how?"

"I'm taking you out."

"Out where?"

"On a date."

She hesitated with the donut halfway to her mouth. "A what?"

"A date. How long does it take you to get ready?"

Clearly, she'd stayed up too late reading last night. Or maybe it was the abrupt wake-up-and-scramble routine that had her brain on the skitz. "Get ready for what?"

A devilish, but oh-so delicious grin tipped the corners of his lips. "Just a little time out of the house. Some fun to go with the good weather. You might even get some pictures while you're at it."

Her shoulders relaxed and her lungs released the insufficient breath she'd been holding. So, it wasn't a date. More of a mercy thing to get her out of the house in exchange for the comfort food last week. Which was fine. Sort of. Yeah, for a second there, it had been nice to have the fantasy, but at least the extended friendship thing she could process a little better. "You're kind of bossy."

"You should see me when I work. Occupational hazard. So? How long?"

"To get ready? I don't know. Twenty minutes?"

"Twenty minutes." He shook his head and reached for his own donut. "Fucking amazing. Most women I know need an hour minimum." He bit into the plain glaze with the neon yellow, orange, and pink sprinkles, and crossed his arms on the table. "Eat up and get dressed, *gatinha*. I'm going to put your sugar rush to good use."

Chapter Ten

Zeke still couldn't believe it. He'd thought for sure Gabe was blowing smoke when she said she could get ready in twenty minutes, but at the eighteen-minute mark she'd strolled out of the bathroom dressed in a simple green T-shirt, jeans and sandals, ready to go. He paced beside her down the sidewalk and opened the passenger-side door. "You bring your camera?"

She paused mid-settling into her seat and glanced up at him. "For what?"

"Your art. Danny said everything starts with pictures."

"Oh." She dug into the side pocket of her purse, pulled out her phone, and wiggled it. "I just use my phone now. Why? Where are we going?"

"Wouldn't be any fun if I told you straight up, now would it?" He smiled and shut the door.

He'd barely circled the cul-de-sac and made it a few houses toward the front of the subdivision when Gabe tensed and leaned forward in her seat.

He eased off the gas and followed her gaze to the house with the moving van in front of it. "Something wrong?"

"Stop for a minute." She yanked the door latch before he'd even come to a full stop and wedged herself out of the bucket seats.

He killed the engine and popped his own door. "Gabe, what's going on?"

She stomped around the front of the car, all her sleepy morning lightness obliterated by her worrisome frown. "This is Mr. and Mrs. Malone's house. The last time I was here they didn't say anything about moving."

Two men in tan cargo pants and company T-shirts shuffled out of the open garage lugging an old, but comfy looking sofa. Beside them was a wiry man with thin, dark gray hair in black dress pants from the seventies and a powder blue cardigan. "Be sure and strap it down good. The wife won't like it if her sofa gets banged up."

Gabe lengthened her stride. "Hey, Mr. Malone. You get some new furniture or something?"

The old man's eyes lit up and he smiled huge, opening his arms wide for a hug. "Gabrielle! Always such a pleasure."

Without even a hint of hesitation, Gabe walked right up and banded her arms around the man. "You only say that because you like my meatloaf."

"Actually I love all your food, but I love your visits more." He pulled away and studied Zeke behind her. "And who is this fine young man?"

Zeke stepped up beside her and offered his hand. "Zeke Dugan."

"Well, that's a nice strong name." Mr. Malone shook his hand and smiled, but his eyes were stern and full of warning. Gabe's father might not be alive anymore, but she had a neighbor who had zero problem stepping in and looking out for her. "And what do you do, Zeke?"

"I'm a trauma doctor. I work locum tenens at some of the hospitals in Dallas."

"Locum tenens?" Gabe said.

Mr. Malone released Zeke's hand and focused on

Gabe. "It means he floats wherever he's needed. Gives a man variety and keeps things fresh." Then he aimed a subtle yet well-placed glare at Zeke that said he'd damned well better not be sporting any variety outside of Gabe.

Funny, he always thought he'd hate a parent-style inquisition, but the truth was he kind of appreciated it. Especially since it meant Gabe had more people looking out for her.

Mr. Malone wrapped an arm around Gabe's shoulders. "I have to say, it's nice to see you out and about with a nice man."

Gabe straightened quick and her eyes got huge. "Oh, he's not *out* with me. He's just keeping me company. I haven't been able to get out much and was getting a little bored."

Wait…what? He opened his mouth to ask what the hell she meant by *not out with her*, but Mr. Malone cut in too fast.

"Ah, yes. I'd heard you'd been hurt at Mrs. Wallaby's break-in. Nothing too serious, I hope."

"No, I'm fine."

Another mover trudged out of the garage, two boxes stacked high.

Gabe waved his direction. "What's going on? You donating stuff? I would have helped you. Or made Danny come for the heavy lifting."

"Oh, no, dear. Lucy and I sold the house to a nice couple a few days ago. We're moving into that new retirement community on the other side of the lake."

"But why? You love it here."

"Of course, we do. But the yard maintenance was getting to be such a chore, and a new Realtor brought us an offer we just couldn't ignore. Not to mention, Lucy's been jumpy ever since she heard about people breaking into Mrs. Wallaby's house. The Realtor mentioned there've been other break-ins in surrounding neighborhoods, too, so it seemed like a smart move. A young thing like you should be careful. Especially when your brother's not home."

"Excuse me." The mover who'd hefted out the boxes waited near the edge of the truck. "We're ready for someone to show us what you want loaded next."

Mr. Malone nodded and stepped away. "Gabrielle, I'm so sorry. Let me help them, and we'll go in and track down Lucy."

"No, it's okay," she said. "Go take care of your movers. When do you have to be out?"

"Not until the end of next week. This is just the first pass. Lucy and I will come by and visit tomorrow after church if you like."

"Should I make meatloaf?"

"My dear, you make whatever you like, so long as it's not too much trouble." He waved and shuffled into the garage.

Gabe's shoulders slumped and she huffed out a tired breath. "Weird."

No kidding. Though he doubted she was weirded out about the same thing he was. How the hell could she possibly think him waking her up with donuts and coffee on a Saturday morning was anything other than a bona fide date?

He got her back in the car and steered them out of the neighborhood and onto the highway. "Mr. Malone seemed nice. Are you close to them, too?"

She shook her head, eyes trained on the strip centers and restaurants whizzing outside her window. "No. Not really. I mean I talk to them, but not nearly as often as the folks in the houses closer to me. Maybe once a month."

"So why are you so upset they're moving? Seems like a retirement community would be pretty nice at their age."

She shrugged and looked at him, her scowl still etched deep. "Maybe. It just seems out of the blue. The last time I was there, Lucy asked me to help her dig a new garden. Then all of a sudden they change their mind? And what other break-ins? All the neighborhoods around us have gates and huge property walls. Who the heck could break in there?"

She had a point, though he figured he had zero odds of dragging her out of her worry. Some thoughts just needed time to percolate. Like how he was going to get it through her stubborn head that his time with her didn't qualify as charitable babysitting.

By the time he reached his exit, they'd burned through half the songs from John Mayer's *Born and Raised* album without a single word spoken. Not that he was complaining. He loved the fact that Gabe felt comfortable enough to keep her silence around him. Plus, it gave him time to formulate his plan of attack.

He pulled into the big intramural fields off Highway 75 and Gabe snapped back to reality. "Where are we?"

The parking lot was only halfway full this early on a Saturday and the fields were still slick with dew, which meant the next few hours were going to end up seriously muddy. "SMU's intramural fields. You're going to help me out while I work with some kids. But we'll cover that in a minute." He pulled into a parking space, punched the brake and faced her. "We need to talk about something else first."

The sudden change in topic and strange surroundings seemed to work to his advantage, because her scowl shifted to curiosity and confusion. "Talk about what?"

"I want to be clear on something. Clear enough that when I get out of this car, I do it knowing you're under no more illusions."

"Okaaay…"

"This is a date. A one hundred percent, man asks woman out, gets to know her, then kisses her stupid when it's over date. What this *isn't* is me being friendly with you in a purely platonic way."

She blinked. Then again. And again.

"Was that clear enough?" he said.

She swallowed, though it looked like the act took a ton of effort, and her cheeks turned a cute pink. "Why would you want to go out on a date with me?"

God. So fucking adorable. And sweet. He chuckled and cupped the back of her neck, not even remotely interested in forgoing touch with her innocent gaze locked onto him. Her hair slicked against his knuckles in a soft, silken touch. For a second, he was tempted to fist his hand around it and drag her across the console for a kiss in lieu of an answer.

"Because you cook for an army and take the leftovers to your neighbors," he said instead. "Because you'd take on a roomful of men you don't know with nothing more than those kitten claws of yours to protect your brother. Because you try to make that same brother eat healthy food even though you know he's cramming Big Macs down his throat when you're not looking. Because you could sashay around in a burlap sack without any makeup on and still make every damned man in her path rubberneck for a better look. You want me to keep going?"

She shook her head and tried to avert her face.

He tightened his grip and held her still. "You get this is a date now?"

"What if I don't want it to be a date?" she whispered.

Leaning in, he cupped the back of her head and ghosted his lips across hers in an almost kiss. "Then I'll find a way to change your mind."

Her sweet little gasp grated at what little control he had left. He couldn't go there. Not yet. Not if he wanted her to see he was willing to put in the effort. That she was worth going the extra step. He slid his hand down and fanned his thumb along her lower lip. "I don't mind fighting for your attention. After everything I've seen of you in the last few weeks, the fight will be worth it."

Knuckles rapped against his window behind him and Gabe jumped back, nearly knocking her head on the passenger-side window. Zeke glanced over one shoulder at the teenage boys waiting for him. Their none too subtle, yet thankfully muted laughter promised all kinds of razzing once he got on the field. He grabbed Gabe's hand and lifted it to his lips. "Bet that's the first and last time you'll ever be saved by three teenage boys." He motioned to her purse. "Get your stuff and let's go."

The boys were still laughing when he opened his door. "Yeah, yeah. Laugh it up. All three of you are running bleachers for touching my ride." He tried to make it sound stern, but the truth of it was he remembered being in their shoes. At fourteen and fifteen, everything and anything about, or leading to sex, was a male's primary source of amusement.

"Ah, come on, Doc." Tommy was just as lanky as Zeke had been at his age, all bone and no muscle. "We were just havin' a little fun."

"Mmm-hmm. So was I until you ruined it." Zeke popped his trunk, dug out two equipment duffels, and tossed the first one to Tommy. "Remember, karma's a bitch. Could be the girl's dad who knocks on your window when you're about to score a lip-lock." He tossed the second bag to Xander and sidled up to Gabe, waiting near the front of his car. "You guys get those on the field and get out of my hair. I wanna talk to my girl for a minute."

He hadn't thought her cheeks could get any redder, but the open male appreciation they aimed her way as they trudged past made her look like she'd spent a whole August afternoon in the sun. He wrapped one arm around her shoulder and guided her to the field. "You know anything about rugby?"

"Um." Her gait was a little awkward next to his, like her body wasn't quite used to ambulating so close to another one. Then again, it was probably kind of hard for her to put one foot in front of the other the way she kept glancing at his hand on her shoulder. "No."

"Well, you're about to learn. You remember Trevor, right? Cowboy? Thought he'd stake a claim before I did?"

"Stake a claim on what?"

His laugh rang out loud against the quiet morning. "Man, you really have no clue, do you?" When she just stared back at him with a blank look, he squeezed her shoulder and pulled her tighter against him. "You, *gatinha*. He wanted to stake his claim on you. Not that I'd have let him."

He steered them toward the bleachers. "So Trevor and I work with some boys who've gone sideways with the law. The best way to handle young guys prone to trouble is to give them an outlet. Something to look forward to. So, every Saturday, we give 'em a way to burn off energy with rugby. His team versus mine. It's nothing fancy or official. You're gonna be my timekeeper and snap me some killer pictures I can share with the parents the next time I email them our schedule."

"But I don't know anything about rugby."

"It's easy. Two forty-minute halves and a ten-minute

halftime. The only time you stop is if someone gets hurt. And I mean really hurt. Not just shaking their head and stumbling around and looking for who rung their bell."

They stepped onto the bleachers and Gabe dug in her heels.

The stands weren't packed to the gills, but they weren't empty either. Mostly it was a clump of twenty or so parents, mostly mothers, each of whom eyed them with curious stares.

"You made it sound like a private thing," Gabe muttered.

Zeke shifted in front of her and gave her shoulders a reassuring squeeze. He lowered his voice for only her. "I know you said you get locked up in the social stuff, but that's not going to happen this time. You've got a purpose in being here. I need a timekeeper and photos. If you start to freeze, remember what you're here for and focus on that. Plus, it's a rugby game. No one's going to expect you to be a conversational genius."

She cocked her head and frowned. "Why are you doing this?"

"Doing what?"

"Bringing me here. Introducing me to people you know."

So sweet. Untamed and beautifully innocent. He cupped the sides of her face. "Because I like you with me. Because I want people to know you're with me."

"You're trying to fix me." The words might have been accusatory, but the vulnerability behind them was so blatantly raw, his insides flinched.

"There's nothing to fix. You're perfect exactly like you are. I'm just giving you some tools for when you feel anxious. If they work for you, great. If they don't, that's cool, too. But I'd want you with me even if you sat in the corner by yourself and flipped everyone the bird. The only person's opinion I give a shit about when we're together is yours."

He leaned a fraction closer and inhaled her elusive, exotic scent. Her lower lip shone in the morning sunlight, slick and plump from the way she'd worked it with her teeth. "And, *gatinha*, you should know I'm really looking forward to the part of our date where I kiss you stupid."

Catcalls roared from the field, mixed with laughter and a few sharp whistles.

"Yo, Zeke." Trevor stood rooted in front of their avid teenage audience, hands planted on his hips and a goofy grin on his face. "Get our girl set up and let's get this going."

What a pain in the ass. As brothers went, Trev and he were probably the closest, but that didn't mean he didn't want to deck the guy with regular frequency. Like now. Maybe again later too for good measure. He chin-lifted to Trev instead and eased back.

Putting himself between Gabe and the boys on the field, he coiled his arm around her waist and led her to a prime watching spot. "Come on. We leave that pack unfocused much longer and they'll dream up some convoluted scam that gets us all thrown in jail."

Chapter Eleven

Seventy-eight minutes, twenty-seven pictures and only two minor social freeze-ups. Not too bad for a girl who'd rather suffer a root canal than volley random banter with a stranger. Especially when said freeze-ups came from curious mothers sniffing around for details on her relationship to Zeke. She'd bet all the money she'd saved for her new computer they were angling for a chance with either him or Trevor. Not exactly a long shot bet given the spectators were primarily estrogen based.

The digital timer on her phone flipped to seventy-nine minutes. One more and she'd be another step closer to the rest of their date.

A 100 percent, man asks woman out, gets to know her, then kisses her stupid when it's over date.

She still couldn't wrap her mind around all the things he'd said, let alone imagine what his lips would feel like against hers. Not the soft, teasing whisper of his lips he'd given her before the boys had knocked on the window, but a real one. Firm and heated.

Not for the first time, her heart kicked hard enough to hurt, and she eyeballed the parking lot. She still had time to run. To call a cab and disappear before things went too far, but that was the safe route. Danny was right. Not everyone had to be like her mother. And with the limited time she'd spent with Zeke, she wouldn't dare compare him to the other men she'd been with. He opened water bottles for her and actually had manners when he ate. No way did Zeke belong in any category remotely close to Jimmy Franklin.

The clock flipped to eighty minutes, and Gabe nudged the wide-eyed ten-year-old boy she'd finagled as an assistant about thirty minutes into the first half. The gangly redhead shot to his feet and blew on the ref's whistle with all he had, making half the people around them wince and cover their ears.

Gabe laughed, genuinely enjoying his delight. Recruiting the boy had been an intuitive stroke of genius. He'd paced, antsy and anxious, along the bleacher walkway, watching his brother on the field, obviously uncomfortable and without anything to do. Plus, he didn't seem to have a parent or guardian to look out for him. Gabe had wanted zero part in blowing the attention-garnering whistle, and keeping an eye on the boy gave her something to do like Zeke had suggested, so she'd recruited him. A perfect win/win for both of them.

Slowly, the mob of teens ambled toward the bleachers, Trevor and Zeke each surrounded on all sides. Both men gave time and attention to each kid, confirming they'd be around next weekend, then sending them on their way. When Zeke stopped and talked with the last boy on his team, her assistant leaned in and said, "That's my brother, Pete." Before she could comment, the boy hopped down the bleachers, waved back at her and jogged toward his brother. "Thanks for letting me help!"

Pete finished up with Zeke just as the boy reached them, and Zeke shot her a heart-stopping smile.

Oh, yeah. Definitely a stroke of genius on her part if it meant getting Zeke Dugan to look at her that way. She ducked her head and scrolled through the action shots she'd taken to hide her fluster.

Sharp, heavy footsteps sounded on the bleacher's metal walkway. "Anything good?" Zeke slid in beside her, his black shoes and socks smattered with mud. The heat coming off him was a welcome warm-up after her chilly morning.

She angled the phone so he could see and flipped through the pics, still not brave enough to look him in the face. "I think so. I can touch them up later and send them to you. The panoramas I took during halftime are nice, too."

Another set of cleats hammered against the bleacher's tinny surface. "Good game, brother. Your boys are gettin' too fast. I'm either going to have to steal someone, or recruit some ringers." He handed over a set of keys and hiked one of two equipment-laden duffels higher on his shoulder. "You two headed to the hangar now?"

Zeke leveled an *Oh, you did not just say that* look at Trevor.

"Oh. Right." Trevor raised his hands in surrender. "Sorry, man. Surprise. I forgot." He winked at Gabe and paired it with a smirk that said he wasn't sorry at all. "Y'all have fun this afternoon. And don't let Zeke hog the pictures. I want copies, too." He ambled toward the parking lot on the opposite end of the field, his easy cowboy stride not the least bit diminished by his rugby attire.

Gabe tucked her phone in her purse. "What was that about?"

"That's my brother giving me shit." He stood, held out his hand, and helped Gabe climb over the bottom row to the main walkway. "I think it's a universal standard for men to give each other a hard time when they see one of their comrades pull out all the stops for a woman."

"You're pulling out stops for me?"

"I don't know." He splayed his hand along the small of her back and focused on her mouth, his own lifting in a wicked grin. "You'll have to tell me what you think when the date's over."

The electric frisson she'd wrestled to a slow simmer during the match flared a notch higher, burning off the dregs of her anxiety and leaving her anxious for the day to come.

Ten minutes later, Zeke had them back on Highway 75 headed north. It probably made her the oddest duck in the country, but she loved watching him drive. The confident way he controlled the car and shifted gears, like he and the car were fused together instead of two separate pieces. Maybe it was the fact that she'd grown up with two confident drivers. Maybe it was the fact that she appreciated the way he manhandled the horsepower he had to work with. Whatever it was, it was sexy as hell.

"You hungry?" he said.

She tore her gaze away from his strong hand coiled around the gearshift and studied the nonstop businesses zooming past along the highway. She could've scarfed back three trips to an all-you-can-eat buffet two hours ago, but no way was she confessing that today. He probably already thought she had the appetite of a linebacker. "A little."

He chuckled, and the low sexy sound scampered along her skin in a phantom touch. "*Gatinha*, your stomach grumbled on the way to the car. If you need something, I want you to feel comfortable enough to tell me."

A breathtaking quiver whirled behind her sternum, the sensation twice as powerful as the one-liners from her favorite romance movies. It was like he was determined to break through every barrier she'd fought to build, literally dismantling it brick by brick. She tucked her hair behind her ear. "Okay, yeah. I'm hungry. Really hungry. Those donuts didn't last long."

"Good, because there's a ton of food where we're headed. If you can make it another five minutes, you can eat until you're too stuffed to move."

Five minutes was more like ten minutes. She barely noticed it though with his easy banter, asking questions about the match, what she thought of the parents, and how she'd talked Pete's brother into sitting with her. Through it all, he exited the highway and drove another three miles down a less-traveled country road. She was just about to razz him about how the predominantly female populated stands were there to watch Zeke and Trevor more than the boys when he pulled into a long and winding newly paved driveway. The black iron gate was open, and a rustic four-rung wood fence stretched out for what had to be a mile in either direction.

"Where are we?" she said.

"Trevor's ranch. The guy's got two loves; horses and planes." He navigated the long drive toward the dark wood home with the green tiled roof. If she'd fallen asleep on the highway and woken up at this second, she'd halfway think she'd been teleported to Montana, minus the hills.

Instead of pulling up to the main house, he drove around back. Two wide metal buildings sat off to one side with a miniature replica of the main house centered between them. Solid concrete lined the front of all three and led to a runway that stretched toward open acreage in the distance. "He's got his own airplane hangar?"

Zeke nodded and parked in front of the mini-house. "Honest to God, I'm surprised he only keeps one out here. If he didn't need a bigger runway for his jets, he'd probably keep the whole fleet out here. Of course, then he'd have too many people traipsing all over his property. He might get along good with people, but when Trevor wants to be alone, he doesn't want any reminders of civilization."

"Unless it's got wings."

"Exactly." He helped her out of the car, grabbed one of the duffels out of his trunk, and guided her into the house.

The inside was just as warm and cozy as the exterior. Exposed wood ceilings, honey-stained wood floors, and a rugged rock fireplace. None of the furniture matched, at least not in the classic sense. More like someone had picked loads of odds and ends and matched it together via magic. Unlike some leather sofas, the one lined up in front of the fireplace looked soft and comfortable, with loads of wear and tear giving it character.

Zeke strolled to the open kitchen and pulled a whole stack of plastic containers out of the fridge. "Momma McKee made us lunch. There's a little bit of everything here, so just take what you want and we'll leave the rest for Trevor."

"Who's Momma McKee?"

"Axel's mom, Sylvie." He set the containers out and started prying off lids. "She and Jace's mom, Ninette, live not too far from here at Jace and Axel's ranch, Haven. The way I see it, I've got three moms. Mine, Jace's and Axel's."

"That must be nice." More than nice, actually. She'd have killed just to have one. "Your friends seem like good people."

"You say that like you find it hard to believe."

It was a little hard to believe. Granted, she was slow to give people a chance, but she'd never met anyone like

Zeke and his friends. "I've just never known people who are so close-knit. You're kind of intense on your own. As a group, you're overwhelming."

"You'll get used to us."

Another long-term reference that plucked an old and out-of-tune chord in her heart. A part of her that only stirred in fantasies and imaginary happy-ever-afters. Across the table, all kinds of finger foods and sandwiches blurred into a misty haze, the prickling burn of unease and worry building up steam.

Footsteps clipped against the hardwood floors, and Zeke's hands rested on her hips a moment later. "*Gatinha*, turn that head of yours off for a minute. It's just you and me right now. An easy, fun date between two people getting to know each other."

His heat radiated across her back and his hands smoothed across her shoulders in a comforting touch. Relax. She could do that. Just focus on the moment. Not tomorrow or any day after it. Only right now. She pulled in a deep, calming breath and let it out slow.

"Eat," he said. "Take a tour or whatever else makes you comfortable. I'm going to take a shower, and then I'll show you your surprise." He kissed the top of her head and headed toward a hallway beyond the fireplace.

"Wait. What about you? Aren't you eating?"

"I'll cram something down when I'm done. You eat. Take it out on the patio if you want. Kick back and enjoy the view."

And then he was gone, leaving her alone with enough food to feed three starving men and enough time to give her thoughts too much room to wander. Her stomach let out a rumble of encouragement right about the time her gaze locked on a whole tray full of sweets. Tiny little tarts topped with glazed raspberries and blackberries, red-velvet cupcakes with fluffy cream cheese icing, and a whole mound of Mexican wedding cookies. Shoot, she could stick to that tray alone and be perfectly content for the rest of the day. Of course, then she'd have the sugar high from hell, and her nerves were already frayed.

She grabbed one of the ivory ceramic plates Zeke had laid out and piled on the goods. Three bite-size cucumber and cream cheese sandwiches on what looked like homemade bread, another with fluffy chicken salad and a few baby quiches she was pretty sure had bacon in them. For good measure she piled up a nice side helping of veggies and fruit, then snagged a fork and napkin and meandered to the back patio.

Unlike the front of the tiny home, the view from the backyard was all natural. No concrete, no metal hangars, no other homes in sight. She eased into one of two thickly padded loungers and curled her legs underneath her. Land unfolded for as far as she could see in soft, rolling planes. The grass had yet to hit full green, smatterings of winter's brown still giving the overall tint a rich sage color. A few trees dotted the acreage to the north, but to the south there was a thicker cluster. It was beautiful. Untouched and peaceful, just like her own backyard. Though, she'd still pick hers with the water over this one any day.

Ten minutes and a demolished plateful later, she pried herself from her comfy spot, ready for a reward in the form of a red-velvet cupcake. She shut the back door behind her, turned for the kitchen table and forgot all about dessert.

Zeke stood with the refrigerator door open, his torso leaned in while he shifted something inside the cooler. The rugby clothes he'd worn were gone, replaced by a pair of faded Levi's that molded his powerful thighs and butt, and absolutely not one other stitch of clothing.

He turned, a purple Gatorade in hand and flashed her with a big smile. "Hey. You like the view?"

Holy hell. What's not to like?

Logically, she knew he meant the backyard, but in that second she couldn't give a damn about anything except the man in front of her. She'd known he had a good build by the way his T-shirts fit him, but Mother of God, without a shirt he was lickably delicious. Not over-large where muscles were concerned but compact and defined. Perfect for tracing her fingers along each dip and curve. Or her tongue. She wasn't picky.

She licked her lip, her eyes drawn to the dog tags that rested between his sculpted pecs. Weird. He never said anything about being in the military. Then again, they didn't look like normal dog tags. They were nicer. Thicker with something masculine etched in black.

"Gabe?"

Her gaze darted to his, and she swallowed hard, her adrenaline-rushed fingers nearly fumbling her plate as she paced toward the table. "Sorry. I was…" *Ogling your body like an estrogen-rich teenage girl.*

"Yeah. Trevor's got a really nice place."

"Yeah, he does." He snatched the gray T-shirt draped over the back of the kitchen chair closest to him and pulled it over his head, but the devious grin on his face made it clear he knew exactly what had her so flustered. And he liked it.

Pulling the hem of his T down around his hips, he prowled closer.

She focused on the food, her pulse hammering loud in her head. *Think, Gabe. Say something. Anything.*

"Did you get something to eat?"

"I got enough." He stopped behind her, reached around and pulled the plate from her quivering hand. It clinked to the tabletop as he set it aside and turned her with hands on her hips. "The way you just looked at me, though, I think I'm juiced enough to go without food for days." His hands on her hips squeezed and he leaned in close, skating his nose alongside hers. His warm breath tickled her skin, tinged with a sugary scent, when he muttered, "Trying real hard to stay on plan."

Her lips parted on instinct, needing his mouth against hers more than she needed air. "There's a plan?"

"Oh, yeah. There's a plan. Otherwise, I'd have just kissed you this morning. But then we'd have never left the house." He lifted one hand and cupped her nape, resting his forehead against hers as he closed his eyes. He pulled in a deep steadying breath through his nose and tiny shivers wiggled down her spine. God, he even managed to make breathing sound sexy.

He straightened, kissed her forehead and took her hand in his. "Come on, *gatinha*. Time for you to fly."

Chapter Twelve

Zeke had done a lot in his life. Met amazing people, traveled to jaw-dropping locations and pushed his body with extreme sports, but not one of those experiences topped watching Gabe when Trev's little twin prop had lifted off the runway. Or when she'd all but plastered her nose against the window trying to catch all the aerial sites at once.

Or when she was aroused.

Her catching him sans shirt had been more luck than planning, but even a blind man would've caught her checking him out. Hell, the sexual tension burning off her in those few unguarded seconds was palpable enough it sparked against his skin. He wanted more of it. More of the way her full lips parted and her eyelids hung heavy over her pale blue eyes. More of the flush that stole across her cheeks and collarbone.

He shifted in the driver's seat and made room for his still semierection. The damned thing had all but popped the buttons on his Levi's all afternoon, which had made for a hell of an uncomfortable flight. Knowing they were only ten miles away from her house where he could make good on his promise of kissing her silly made it worse.

Gabe leaned across the Camaro's center console and held up her phone. "Look at this one."

The shot she'd taken as he'd flown her over her home was about as good as a person could manage with a three-year-old, knock-off smartphone. He'd have to get her introduced to Knox soon. Whether she had ideas of pursuing her art on a bigger scale, or just for the joy of it, she deserved the best. Something top of the line with loads of options instead of a no-name device that was out-of-date.

"I like it," he said. "Did you get the one flying back toward the house?"

She thumbed past a few more and angled the phone back where Zeke could see. "I didn't like that one as much. I like it where you can see the shoreline better."

He cocked his head and compared the two as she shuffled back and forth. The first one had more color. More life to it. "Yeah, I think you're right." Then again, almost everything Gabe had shown him on the way home seemed postcard ready in his book.

He downshifted and steered to the far right lane, angled for the exit that would take them across Lake Ray Hubbard's bridge and her house on the other side. "You going to work your magic on them? Or just keep them like they are for a souvenir?"

She pursed her mouth in a cute, considering mew and zoomed in on one in particular. "I don't know. I'll keep the original for sure, but I never know if the things I try on my computer will work or not. We'll see."

She shut the app and smiled up at him. No tension marked the edges of her eyes, and she'd reclined against the seats as if she rode with him every day. For the first time since he'd met her, she seemed unguarded. Like a glimpse of the girl Danny had mentioned she used to be was peeking out from behind the mask she held up against the world. Damned if that didn't make him feel about twenty feet tall.

"I still can't believe you can fly," she said. "Is there anything you haven't done?"

"Not learning to fly wasn't an option for me. The first thing Trevor does with anyone he deems family is get them behind the yoke. He uses safety as an excuse, saying it's good to have a backup, but the truth is he's always looking for a chance to get airborne."

She gazed out the windshield, her elbow propped up on the passenger door and fingers twirling a strand of hair around and around. Her mouth was soft with just a hint of a smile on the tips.

"You could learn to do it, too," he said. "Trevor never says no to a pretty woman, let alone a potential student."

One sentence and her demeanor went from bright and peaceful, to shuttered and cautious. She lowered her arm from the door and tucked both hands under each thigh. "Oh, no."

Fuck, he hated that. Hated how easy it was to upend the balance and knowing whatever gave her emotions such a hair trigger had to run deep. "'Oh, no,' you're not interested in learning to fly? Or, 'oh, no,' you don't think you can do it?"

Her head snapped toward him, a cute scowl pinching her mouth up tight. "I could do it if I wanted to."

"I couldn't agree more. Plus, you looked like you were having fun when I let you take the yoke. So, why not give it a try?"

She fiddled with her phone in her lap. "I couldn't ask Trevor to teach me. I don't even know him."

"You'll get to know him."

"No, I won't. I barely see him."

"You've barely seen him *so far*. If you're with me, you'll see plenty of him. Of all my brothers."

"Stop it." She paired the sharp command with a terse shake of her head and glared out the passenger window, her hands fisted tight in her lap.

Interesting. This hadn't been the first time she'd bared her claws around him, but the tension in this particular response was just short of explosive. A powder keg barely contained and nestled up tight to an open flame. Oddly enough, he liked it as much as her sweet side, which only made him want to nudge his *gatinha* a little more. "Stop what?"

"Talking about things like we're a long-term item. It's not nice."

"You don't like the idea of me being around long-term?"

Her mouth pressed to a harsh line and her chest rose and fell in sharp, shallow rasps. Damn, but he wanted her past this shit. How a woman could spend a day like the one they'd spent together and not realize how into her he was floored him. It also made him rethink finding the assholes who'd fucked with her in the past. At this rate he wouldn't stop at just pulverizing the bastards. He'd slaughter them and take his time doing it.

"Think about what you're saying, Gabe. Do you really think a man like me would introduce a woman to my family if I only planned to see them once? Or take the time to give you a day that made you smile if I weren't serious?"

She anchored her elbow back on the door and covered her mouth with her fist.

The clock on the custom navigation glowed a soft 2:07 p.m. Five more minutes until he got her home, then he'd have a few hours left to make his point. To reinforce she wasn't some inconsequential drop in the bucket. He let her have her silence until he pulled into the subdivision and parked in front of her house. Unfortunately, she popped her door before he could make it around to her side.

He snagged her arm before she could make the sidewalk and carefully turned her, mindful of her ribs. "Talk to me, *gatinha*. I can't fight what I don't know."

She tried to dig in her heels, to look anywhere but at his face.

He gripped her chin and steered it so she couldn't hide. "I'm bossy, remember? I can keep at this all afternoon."

"Why? Why keep pushing me?"

"Because I want you."

"You mean sex."

He tugged her against him so fast she gasped and clenched his arms for balance. He cupped the sides of her face. "I mean I want *you*. I want those smiles that make my day so bright it hurts. I want you to push healthy comfort food on me the way you do Danny and your neighbors. I want you curled up next to me on the couch while you watch movies and slip into make-believe. I want to do whatever it takes to make you look at me like you did this afternoon. And just so you can't accuse me of being a liar, I'll admit, I want the sex, too. Lots of it. I want to anchor my cock deep inside you and make you come so hard you forget about any other man who came before me."

As quick as he'd fired her temper, her pupils dilated and her body went live-wire hot next to his. Sweet Jesus, he wanted to hone that emotion. To stroke and nurture it until she shattered. But not until he could set this roadblock aside. "Talk to me, *gatinha*. What makes it so hard for you to believe I might be around long enough for you to get to know the people I love?"

"Because people leave." It was a whisper, nothing more,

but it clawed him from the inside out, the shear vulnerability in her eyes gutting him faster than any blade.

He pulled her tight against him, cradling her head against his heart with one hand while the other banded around her shoulders. Anger flooded his bloodstream, scalding through every vein in need of an outlet. A target for his release. He kissed the top of her head instead, breathing in her light, exotic scent until the blood-red haze clouding his mind ran clear.

Inside his arms, her breaths slowed and evened. Her arms were wrapped around his waist, hands fisted in his shirt.

He pulled away enough to meet her gaze, but kept a steady hand at her nape. "I can't promise you forever. Neither one of us knows what's going to happen in five minutes, let alone tomorrow, or the day after that. What I can promise is that I'll be upfront with you the whole way. If things aren't working for me, I'll share. No slinking away without warning, or dancing around anything. I'll ask you to do the same. We'll take one day at a time, but that means every day both of us putting ourselves out there. You'll get to know the people I love, and I'll get to know yours. If things work out, then you gain more family than you've got today. If they don't, then we'll both still have solid, good memories. Can you work with that?"

She nodded. It was small and hesitant, but her eyes sparked with hope.

He'd never forget that look. Not until the day he died. In a single second, she'd branded him. Marked and challenged him to conquer every damned one of her demons. "All right." He smoothed his thumb along her lower lip. God, he wanted to kiss her. To seal his promise in a way she couldn't ignore. That *she'd* never forget.

"We need to get inside, sweetheart. If we don't, the

first time I kiss you will be where all your neighbors can watch." Not to mention, he'd have a hell of a time stopping once he got started. He let her go and urged her toward the front door. "Besides, I've got to work a shift tonight, and I want to see the pictures you took on a bigger screen before I go."

Inside, the house was still and quiet except for Toothless, who leaped down from his perch on the front window ledge, leisurely assessed Zeke's presence, then demandingly greeted Gabe with a stern meow. He rubbed his side along Gabe's shins, spun and made another lap.

Gabe dug her phone out of her purse, tossed the bag to the floor, and swept Toothless up in her arms. She lowered her head close enough Toothless brushed his cheek against hers. "I know, I know. I missed you, too." She glanced back at Zeke and headed down the hallway. "Give me a second. I'll get my computer."

Oh, no. If she was headed to her room, then he was going with her. Just checking her ribs that first night had generated a whole library of fantasies in that same location. Never mind the places his head had gone when he'd tucked her into bed a week later. The prospect of actually breathing life into one of those fine ideas wasn't one he'd let pass. Plus, he'd have a chance to give her a few memories to chew on when she was lying in her bed at night.

She startled when he ambled through her bedroom door and fumbled her computer charger. It clattered to the top of her desk then slithered down to the floor.

He motioned to the laptop pinched between her fingers, sat down on her bed and leaned against the padded headboard. "That where you keep everything?"

For a heartbeat or two, she stared at him, her eyelids doing the blinky-blink thing as though her mind couldn't quiet register him visiting her room, let alone lounging on her bed.

Talk about the rooster in the henhouse. He hadn't had this much fun getting under a woman's skin in...well, ever. He grinned and crossed his feet at the ankle. "You okay?"

She snapped out of her stupor and studied the bed the way someone unfamiliar with silverware etiquette might gauge the settings for a sixteen-course meal. She opted for familiar, yet semisafe and sat on his side of the bed near his feet, opening the laptop and bringing the screen to life with a tap on the track pad. "I keep most of my pictures on the cloud because it's safer. Plus, this computer's old and not all that reliable. I saved up for a new one, but haven't gotten around to buying anything yet."

He eyed the distance she'd kept between them. "You should talk to Knox before you buy anything. He's got all kinds of contacts if you want lots of bells and whistles."

Her fingers froze over the keyboard and she opened her mouth as though to argue, but just as fast she frowned, closed her mouth and refocused on her work.

She'd fought it. Had wanted to push back about getting to know his family, but then knocked it back and rolled with it. It was beautiful. Such a small thing, but so utterly huge, too. Even if she'd handed him the moon, it wouldn't have meant as much as her fighting her fears.

She swiveled the screen so he could see it. "I think the rugby shots turned out good."

He cocked his head and pretended to study the screen. "I can't see. Come closer."

Biting her lip, she scooted a whopping five inches closer.

Zeke straightened away from the headboard, lowered

one foot to the floor, and patted the space between his legs. "Here."

She studied the spot he'd indicated then peeked up at him.

"Come on, *gatinha*. Show me the pictures."

Another scoot and her sweet ass was planted right where he wanted. He leaned in and splayed his hand between her shoulder blades, sliding it up and under her hair to the back of her neck. He nodded to the action shot of Pete on the screen. "I like that one. What would you do to it if you were going to work your magic?"

"Umm…" She moved her finger along the track pad, but it trembled so hard it took her a few times to click on the icon she'd aimed for. Still, she kept after her task, punching buttons, clicking here and there, and dragging the cursor in all kinds of directions. The whole time, one of her legs bounced in a nervous jitter.

The up-and-down glide of his thumb along her throat probably wasn't helping, but damned if he could stop it. Her skin was too soft and warm not to indulge. Too tempting. God help him once he managed to get his lips and tongue in the same spot. He'd bet everything he had she tasted as exotic as her scent.

"There," she whispered.

His mind semiscrambled out of his dirty thoughts. On the screen was the same photo, but sharper and bolder in color. The background had been altered to make the action look like something out of a sci-fi flick, but instead of drawing emphasis away from the player, it heightened the motion. "You made Pete look like a badass."

"It's not much." She coughed to clear the rasp in her throat and squeezed the edge of the computer. "I don't normally work with pictures like this."

"For a first time with sports, I'd say you knocked it

out of the park." He covered her hand with his. "You've really got a gift for this."

"Thank you." She still wouldn't look at him, just saved the picture and opened another one.

"Gatinha?"

She furrowed her brow and twisted her head only enough to peek at him from the corner of her eye. "Yeah?"

He swept her hair away from her neck and cupped the back of her head, urging her to face him. "Remember what I said about that kiss?"

Her pale blue gaze locked onto his mouth and her lips parted, her shaky breath whispering across his face.

"I want to give you that now. You okay with that?" God, he was an idiot for asking. How he would pull away if she'd said no wasn't even something he wanted to contemplate. Not with her sweet, innocent sensuality shining on him.

She dipped her chin in the tiniest nod and his cock jerked a celebratory high-five, pressing against his fly so hard circulation was a little sketchy.

Slowly, he eased the computer off her lap and slid it on the nightstand. He leaned closer, running his nose alongside hers. Much as he wanted the taste of her on his tongue, there was no way he was rushing this moment. The anticipation was too good. Too heady. More so than any adrenaline rush or high-octane sport.

He cupped the other side of her face, holding her firm as he murmured against her lips, "I've wanted to do this from the minute I saw you." He gave in and pressed his mouth to hers, swallowing her surprised gasp.

His hand fisted in her hair and he moaned. Christ, he was so screwed. One simple little kiss. One modest press of her lips and he was a goner. He licked the seam of her mouth, the barest trace of frosting from the last cupcake she'd snagged before they left exploding on his tongue.

She opened for him and sighed, angling for more. Every touch, every caress was perfect. Unhurried and natural. From the wet glide of their mouths against one another, to the slick tangle of their tongues, there wasn't a thing awkward about it.

Twisting, she splayed one hand on his chest—and winced.

Damn it, he'd forgotten about her ribs. He gripped her by her hips and pulled her astride him, easing their kiss enough to splay his hand along her injured side. "You okay?" God, he sounded like some dirty old man with a three-pack-a-day habit, and his lungs were working like he'd sprinted up about ten flights of stairs.

"I'm good." She ran her fingers along his jawline, nails playing in the scruff while her mouth brushed back and forth against his. "So good."

And then it was all her. Her hands, her mouth, her tongue devouring everything he gave her and demanding more. And God, was she hungry. More kittenish than ever before. Starved and eager for a warm bowl of cream and lapping it up before someone could take it away again.

She tugged the hem of his shirt, angling to slide her hands underneath.

He snagged her wrists, her pulse thrumming beneath his thumbs. He wanted her touch. Craved it. But he stood a snowball's chance in hell of keeping things in check if that happened, and he needed her long-term trust more than short-term pleasure.

She tugged her hands, trying to free them.

"Easy," he whispered against her mouth.

As soon as the words were out, she locked up. "Did I do something wrong?"

His mind hitched and tried to scramble back out of its kiss-induced haze. "Nothing's wrong. Not even close to wrong." Though the fact that she automatically jumped to that conclusion went a long way to answering a lot of unanswered questions, at least as far as her relationships with men were concerned. She might be shy on the up-take, but once the gate was open, she was a thorough-bred on a wide-open track. As aggressive as she'd been with that kiss, a lot of men might have been intimidated. Maybe put their shortcomings back on her.

Not him. He had zero problem letting her take her fill when the time was right. That time just wasn't today. Today she needed to know he'd not only keep up with her, but give her what she needed. "Lie down for me."

She eyed him from beneath lowered lids, suspicious and wary.

"I'm not through kissing you, *gatinha*. You already hurt your ribs once, and I want to give you what you need without that happening again, so do what I asked and let me take care of you."

"Take care of me how?"

"Lie down and find out."

For a second or two he thought she'd crawl off his lap and kick him out of the house. Given how revved his en-gine was, it was probably the smarter move, but instead she gingerly shifted and stretched out on the bed.

He rolled to his side, propped on one elbow beside her, and coiled his hand around the side of her neck. Chest to chest, their legs tangled together as though they'd lain together a thousand times before. The only thing un-natural about it was the tension in her neck and torso. He smoothed his hand to her shoulder, down her arm, then pulled her hand to his lips. Skimming soft, barely there kisses across each knuckle, he smiled down at her. "Relax." He pressed her hand to his chest then nudged a wayward strand of hair off her cheek. "There's nothing I expect. Nothing for you to do except what feels good for you."

She swallowed hard, a trace of disbelief sharpening her gaze.

He leaned in, inhaling her unique scent. "Stop thinking." He kissed her. Soft, more of a whisper than a touch. "Turn your mind off and let go." Another kiss, this one luring her pretty pink tongue out for a taste.

Fuck, yes. Just like that.

He took her mouth in one fierce claim, stroking her need with his own. Feeding her enthusiasm. Tongues, lips, teeth and touch, it all coalesced into one beautiful moment. Mindless and yet so profound it resonated through him like a living current.

Beneath him, her body arched. Her nails bit into his shoulders and she ground her sex against his thigh. So responsive and open. Eager and guileless. He might not be willing to push things too far where his pleasure was concerned, but that didn't mean hers had to go unattended.

He nipped and kissed along her jawline, easing her T-shirt up and teasing his fingers along the smooth expanse of skin at her waistline. "Let me take care of you, sweetheart." He scraped his teeth along the shell of her ear and smoothed his hand along her uninjured side. "Let me ease the ache."

A tiny mewl slipped free, and she bowed toward his touch, urging him for more.

"Say yes." He lifted his head and lightly skimmed fingertips along the underside of her breast through the soft cotton of her bra. "God, please say yes."

Her eyes opened, weighted and dazed with passion. Her answer came on a broken, shaky exhale that reverberated straight to his dick. "Yes."

Best. Answer. Ever.

He palmed her breast and gently squeezed, lifting the full mound and rasping his thumb across the taught peek.

Arching her neck, she let her eyes slip shut and speared her fingers in his hair, urging him closer. He shoved her T-shirt out of his way, tugged her bra down, and cupped her breast.

His cock punched hard and demanding against his jeans, anxious for its turn to play.

Not now. Not today. Today was about her. Fuck, the next several days needed to be about her if he wanted to build her trust. He ignored the building throb between his legs and rolled her berry-pink nipple between his thumb and finger.

She squeezed her eyes shut tighter and whimpered.

"I thought about this." He plucked the tight bud and skimmed his lips along the swell of her breast. "Imagined it a thousand times since that first night." He brushed the scruff on his chin against the tip. "Felt like a lech, but God I wanted to touch you like this. Tease you and take you in my mouth."

He did just that, drawing her nipple against his tongue and suckling deep as he plumped her other breast.

"Zeke." Christ, he could come just from the sound of his name on her lips alone. Raspy and grated, it was the sexiest sound he'd ever heard in his life. Both of her hands urged him for more, tugging his hair so hard it was all he could do not to roar.

He shifted to the other breast, licking a lazy path along the way. She needed more, but no way in hell was he stopping for strategic work. "Pop the buttons on your jeans for me."

The steady undulations of her hips hitched and froze.

Flicking his tongue along her untended nipple, he tweaked the one he'd left behind. "Don't think. Just do."

Slowly, she uncoiled one hand from his hair and gripped the opening of her jeans. The button fly *pop-pop-pop-popped* open.

"Perfect." He nibbled the underside of her breast. "Now get that hand back where it was and hold on." Before she could brace, he drew her nipple into his mouth and slid his hand down her belly, under her panties, and straight for the promised land.

Holy hell, if he made it through getting her off without coming in his jeans, it would be the single most amazing feat of his life. He flicked the nub in his mouth, wishing like hell it was the one under his fingers. She was drenched. Slick and soft and begging for attention. With every stroke, her hips lifted in greeting, eager for more.

He eased one finger inside her and her pussy fluttered and tightened. Lifting his head, he shifted upward, braced so he could watch her face. "Open your eyes."

She shook her head.

"Oh, yes. I want to see the look on your face when you come on my fingers." He set a rhythm, in and out, building in intensity. "Open them. Now."

He circled her clit with his thumb and her eyes snapped open.

"That's it." He added a second finger and groaned at the way her sex gripped him. "So sweet. Wet and tight."

Her nails dug into his neck. "Please."

"Soon, *gatinha*." He held her gaze and skimmed his lips against hers. "Soon, I'll claim you right here." He angled his wrist so his fingers grazed her sweet spot and pressed his thumb against her clit.

Her eyes widened and her thighs squeezed his hand so tight he couldn't have moved if he'd wanted to. Around his fingers, her pussy convulsed, sharp powerful contractions that made his cock jerk with need. God, she was beautiful. Vulnerable in the most unaffected way. Untainted by the trappings of so many women he knew. Oh, yeah. He'd claim her and tackle any demon she threw at him to keep her. To protect her.

Bit by bit, the tension in her thighs eased, and her hips rolled in the same lazy rhythm as his fingers. She smoothed her fingertips along his jawline, playing with his beard in a way that made him silently vow he'd never, ever shave the stuff. The look on her face was pure wonder, the pink on her cheeks utterly adorable.

He kissed her, slow and languid, further easing her from the peak. "Still think what you saw on TV the other night doesn't exist?"

She gasped and jerked deeper into the pillow. "You remembered that?"

"I remember every second of that night, especially the part where you got hot and bothered." He eased his hand from between her legs, held his hand between them so she couldn't miss the release coating his fingers, and licked.

Her jaw dropped, but her gaze didn't budge from his fingers until he'd finished off the last bit.

"That surprise you?" he said.

She nodded. She also looked like she was primed for round two. With her hair mussed and her clothes rumpled, it was all he could do not to give her exactly that.

"Then let me warn you up front. The next time you come, I won't be tasting it off my fingers." He kissed her again, righting her bra and tugging her T-shirt back down to her waist as he murmured against her lips. "From the taste I just got, I'd say you should be prepared to settle in for a long meal." He rolled away and stood beside the bed before he could change his mind and take advantage of her admitted shock. "Walk me to the door, *gatinha*."

She blinked, frowned, and glanced at the door. "You're leaving? But you didn't…" Her eyes went wide and she popped straight up in bed. "You said nothing was wrong."

Ah, hell. He should have seen that one coming a mile away. Probably one of many reasons he shouldn't have let things go as far as they did, even if it was one of the most bewitching moments of his life. "Easy, *querida*." He sat beside her and pulled her against him. "The last thing I want to do is leave you. Not with you all sex-kitten-cozy and primed for me. But, I start an all-nighter in two hours, and there's no way I'm rushing my first time with you."

With her cheek tucked tight above his heart, he couldn't see her relief, but felt her torso tremble on a shaky exhalation. "Sorry. It's a habit."

He eased her away and tilted her face to his. "Never apologize to me for being who you are. Ever."

Above his heart, her hand opened and closed in a loose fist. "Aren't you…well, you didn't…you know."

God, she was sweet. The first second he was confident she could trust him, he was going to sex her up and wallow for days in her sugary goodness. "Sex isn't tit for tat. And just because I didn't get off doesn't mean I'm walking away empty-handed. The look on your face when you came on my fingers? I'm gonna be wired all night with that image burned in my brain." He kissed the top of her head and stood. "Now, come on. Walk me to the door."

He ambled down the hallway and prayed she'd follow him. Yeah, he'd meant what he said, but that didn't mean his cock was good with his noble intentions. Another minute or two spying her creamy skin still exposed behind her open button fly and his resolve would be good and fucked.

Thankfully, her soft footfalls sounded behind him. He opened the front door, turned and hooked an arm around her waist. "You want me to call you when I get off work at seven? Or wait until after I get a few hours' sleep?"

For some reason, the question seemed to surprise her, her head cocking to one side as though it hit her out of the blue. "Before you go to sleep."

Perfect. That meant he'd have less time waiting to hear how things went after he left. It also probably meant her voice on the phone would have him stroking one off before he went to sleep. "All right. Before lights out it is." He ducked close for a slow, but soft kiss. "Thank you for a good day."

He was halfway out the door before her voice drew him to a halt.

"Wait!"

Before he could fully turn, she was in his arms, her hands around his neck and urging him down for a much longer, more thorough kiss. She pulled away slowly, uncertainty and regret pinching the corners of her eyes. "I've never had a day like today. A *date* like today. Thank you."

He chuckled and covered her hand at his chest, lifting it to his mouth. "I knew there'd be wild underneath all that sweet." He nipped her knuckles. *"Eu já sinto saudades."*

Reluctantly, he pulled away and opened the screen door.

"What's that mean?" she said, following behind him and propping the door open with her shoulder.

He winked before he turned for his car. "It means 'I miss you already.'"

Chapter Thirteen

Ding. Ding. Ding.

The annoying techno chimes pierced through Gabe's deep sleep and upset the otherwise quiet morning. Stretched out on her uninjured side, she hugged her pillow tighter and sucked in a deep, contented breath. Zeke's lingering scent filled her lungs, wisps of memories from the night before mingling with her warm cocoon and dreams she couldn't bear to let go of.

Ding. Ding. Ding.

Her mind inched a little closer toward consciousness, a soft sunrise glow peeking through her barely cracked blinds. It wasn't a workday, was it? No, it was Sunday. Who the heck called first thing in the morning on a weekend?

You want me to call you when I get off work at seven? Or wait until after I get a few hours' sleep?

Zeke.

She jerked upright up and her ribs kicked a brutal protest. Powering through the pain, she grappled for her phone and swiped the answer button. "Hello?"

A tiny pause filtered down the line before Zeke's whisky-warm voice followed. "Didn't realize it would be this hard."

Her heart might have been up and galloping at full

speed, but her brain was still apparently too sleep-muddled for conversation. "What's hard?"

"Hearing your voice first thing in the morning and not being there to enjoy it in person."

Whoa.

All the giddy flutters she'd painstakingly corralled one memory at a time the night before escaped her make-shift emotional cage and winged toward the stratosphere.

"We'll fix that soon enough," he added.

Another flutter kicked in, this one centered between her legs and eliciting a soft groan.

Zeke chuckled at that, but had the decency not to call her on it. "You sleep good?"

Still swimming in the deeply visceral response pulsing through her body, she eased against the headboard and fisted the blanket pooled across her lap. "Very good." Granted, it'd taken her two movies and half of a new book to get there before her mind stopped replaying their date in vivid detail, but eventually exhaustion had taken over and led her straight into phenomenal dreams. "How was your shift?"

"Long. Boring." He paused for a beat. When he spoke again his words were laced with pure mischief. "Plenty of time for me to remember my kitten stretched out on her bed."

Her cheeks burned as though witnesses crowded around her bed, but damned if she cared at this point. She could die tomorrow and not regret a single thing in her life after the day he'd given her. "Yesterday was nice."

God, what was she saying? He'd gone all out and she called it *nice*? Surely she could do better than that.

She cleared her throat and whispered, "More than nice. It was perfect."

Rustling sounded through the phone line, a soft fabric-on-fabric slide. "Perfect would have been me finishing out the day next to you instead of crawling into my bed alone and exhausted fifteen hours later, but I agree. We teed up a spectacular start."

"A start?"

His voice softened. "Yeah, *gatinha*. A start. For us. Now, tell me what your plans are for tonight."

An us.

As in not just a one-time thing.

She barely stifled the school-girl squee ripping up the back of her throat, drew her knees up toward her chest and tried for a casual tone. "Not much." Okay, not exactly the casual she'd hoped for. Closer to breathless and needy, but considering the adrenaline main-lining through her veins, still pretty impressive. "I usually cook and watch TV or read at night."

"Good, then I won't knock you too far off your normal game if I invite myself over?"

Another date.

With Zeke.

She smiled so big her cheeks ached and whispered, "I'd like that."

"Good. What time's dinner?"

"Umm…" What time did guys like Zeke usually eat? Everyone she shared dinner with in the neighborhood ate between five and six, but they were also usually in bed by eight. "Maybe seven?"

"Then I'll be there at six thirty to help."

He would? With Danny, she was lucky if plates ended up in the dishwasher. Her dad hadn't been much better when he'd been alive.

"Want me to bring anything?" he asked.

Like she'd be able to come up with anything on the spur of the moment with her thoughts whirring in all different directions. And holy crap! What the heck was she going to cook? "Maybe whatever you want to drink? I've only got tea for me and Danny's beer."

"Got it. I'll load you up on Bohemia Weiss. Anything else?"

At this rate oxygen would be good. And maybe something to take her pulse down a notch or two. "I don't think so."

"Well, you've got my number on your phone now. If you think of something call me. Otherwise, I'll see you at six thirty."

"Okay."

He chuckled. "Good night, Gabrielle."

God, she loved it when he said her name like that. Like she was a beautiful woman instead of just another one of the guys. She bit her lip, her heart thumping strong and steady enough to count for a week's worth of exercise. "Sweet dreams."

The rustle of his bedcovers came first, followed by his husky response. "Sweetheart, knowing my day's gonna end with me curled up next to you and my stomach full of whatever you cook, sweet dreams are a foregone conclusion."

It was official. Zeke had snagged one kick-ass cook in Gabrielle Parker. And by *kick-ass* he didn't mean some frilly Martha Stewart wannabe, but a down-home, this-man's-gonna-pack-on-some-pounds miracle in the kitchen. Never in his life had he knocked back three bowls of chili, but for the batch Gabe had whipped up tonight, he'd happily rallied for a third helping.

Sated and stretched out on the couch with Gabe spooned in front of him, the tail end of the vampire series they'd watched for the past hour was more background noise than actual entertainment. Hell, his favorite teams could be in the damned Super Bowl, tied with only two minutes left in the game, and he still wouldn't pay attention to the screen. Having Gabe this close, this loose and relaxed against him, was a much better draw for his attention. If his dick had its way, they'd have forgone TV about an hour ago and be sweaty and catatonic from some serious skin-on-skin action.

But he wasn't listening to his dick. Not with Gabe.

All through his shift, he'd puzzled over her fearful response the night before. Wondered what kind of experiences she'd been through to make her assume she'd done something wrong just because she'd been the only one to get off.

He shouldn't have gone as far as he did. That much was 100 percent clear. Now he'd have to find a way to slow things down without making her draw the same negative assumption, because when he took her for the first time it damn sure wasn't going to be with her worrying he wouldn't stick around to see daylight.

The oversize and faded red sweatshirt she'd worn tonight had slipped over one shoulder, leaving a delectable stretch of skin exposed. Even knowing the tricky terrain he'd have to navigate, he gave into temptation, swept her silky blond hair out of his way, and kissed the spot where her neck and shoulder met.

A shiver worked through her and her hand tightened on his where it rested against her belly.

Breathing in her soft scent, he skimmed his lips toward her shoulder, interspersing subtle scrapes of his teeth, soothing licks and gentle rasps from his beard.

She tilted her head and pressed her ass against his rapidly hardening cock. "Zeke."

Christ. All she'd done was give him better access and said his name, and he was ready and raring to go.

He threaded his fingers with hers and squeezed. It was either that or slide his hands under her sweatshirt and fill his palms with her tits, and that play wasn't in the cards. Not yet. Much as it scared him to broach it, he'd be a lot smarter to play her straight as to why before things got too much further down the road.

Propping himself higher on one elbow, he pressed one last kiss to her creamy skin then savored the unguarded bliss on her face. "Want to talk to you about last night."

Her eyes snapped open and her body went rigid.

"Easy." He hugged her closer to him and kissed the crown of her shoulder. "Just because I want to talk doesn't mean the topic's a bad one." Though her immediate reaction sure as shit emphasized taking things slow was the right approach.

She twisted her head enough to peer up at him. "Okay."

He urged her to roll the rest of the way over so she lay stretched out on her back beside him, then cocked one leg over her hip and reclaimed her hand in his. Whether he was trying to reassure her or keep her from bolting he wasn't sure. Maybe a little of both. But his instincts insisted on closeness, so he went with it. "I liked last night. A lot."

Some of the wariness on her face faded, and the television's soft glow highlighted the blush that lit her cheeks. "I did, too." As confessions went, it was tentative, but utterly adorable.

"Good." He smoothed his thumb across her knuckles, not feeling a tenth of the same surety he tried to convey. "What I didn't like was seeing you afraid after the fact."

She averted her face and, sure enough, tried to wiggle off the couch.

He held her fast. "Don't shut down on me."

She ceased trying to keep away, but still wouldn't look at him.

"This is important." He cradled the side of her face and urged her attention back toward him. "I want to be with you, Gabrielle. In every way. Not just sex. But I want to do it at a pace where I know you're not worrying on the inside. I want you to understand I'm here because of *you*. All of you."

Her gaze dropped to his chest and she relaxed her hands where she'd fisted them against his shoulders and tried to push him away. "So what are you saying?"

"I'm saying I want us to take our time. I want to get you to a place where you can be intimate with me and know we're there because I want to give and share pleasure. *Not* because I want to get laid."

That got her attention. "You mean that?"

Jesus, God Almighty, he wanted just thirty minutes alone with the motherfucker who'd put that doubt in her mind. Thirty unchecked, merciless minutes. "I absolutely mean that. I told you yesterday, I can't predict what'll happen between us for the long haul, but I can assure you it's more than just getting you in bed."

Tears welled in her eyes, but she wrapped him up in a fierce hug and buried her face in his neck before they could fall.

He rolled to his back and took her with him, protecting her ribs as he went and sheltering her inside his arms while she let the tears free. Up and down, he smoothed one hand along her spine while he cupped the back of her head with the other. Damn it, but he hated seeing her cry. Hated even more that he'd been the one to cause it, but sharing the way he had still felt right.

When her shudders died down and her breaths had slowed to a normal rate, he smoothed her hair away from her face and tucked it behind her ear. "Better?"

She sniffled and nodded, but kept her face where he couldn't see her.

"*Gatinha*. Look at me."

It took another few heart beats and a long enough pause to dash the back of her hand against her cheeks, but she finally did.

And the sight seized his heart, tear-stained cheeks, puffy eyes, and all. "God, you're beautiful."

She ducked her head in that endearingly shy way of hers and shrugged. "I'm just Gabe."

He chuckled at that, which earned him a mini-glare beneath her wet eyelashes.

"Just Gabe, huh?" He gently traced the line of her cheek with his thumb. Her jaw. Her lips.

She closed her eyes and let out a soft sigh.

With every inch he covered, her shyness fell away, replaced with the same open, sensual abandon he'd discovered last night. "Sweetheart, I don't think you've got a full appreciation for all that you are. All that the people close to you see." He palmed her nape and gently squeezed. "Look at me, Gabrielle."

Slowly, she opened her eyes. Where the room's shadows had left her pupils slightly dilated before, now the black was prominent against her pale blue irises, and her eyelids hung heavy with need. Even her breathing was faster and a little ragged.

So responsive. Gloriously perfect. One way or another he was going to fan that part of her and help it grow. More than that, he'd protect it. "You are absolutely, drop-dead gorgeous. Inside and out."

She frowned and opened her mouth.

"Beautiful," he repeated before she could speak. "Giving. Sweet. Smart. You may not see or accept that yet, but I'm going to repeat it until it sinks in and you believe it." He tugged her closer, guided her lips against his and murmured, "Until you *feel* it."

Her mouth parted on a gentle moan and her tongue tangled with his, the fluidness of how they meshed both urgent and natural. With the same abandonment she'd shown the day before, she straddled his hips and deepened the kiss, his curious kitten fired up and hell-bent to consume everything he could give her.

Her scent, her taste and her touch surrounded him. In that moment, everything good that was Gabe was his. A gift and a benediction that resonated so much deeper than sinew and bone it rocked him to the core.

As quick as the kiss had flared, she pulled away, her chest pumping to match his own. She bit her lip and dragged her gaze down his torso. "Does taking our time mean I can't touch you?"

Oh, he was so fucked. Well and truly fucked. His voice came out about an octave lower and a whole lot more ragged. "Not gonna lie, *gatinha*. When I said I want you, I meant *I want you*. Want to bury myself so damned deep inside you never forget the feel of me. So you, sitting where you are and looking down at me with those sexy eyes, touching's probably a terrible idea." He gripped her hips and fought the urge to grind his rock-hard cock against her sex. "That said, I'd also jump out of a plane without a parachute if it meant getting your hands on me, so if you want to explore, I'll hang on as long as I can without throwing slow out the window."

Her smile was instant and blinding, as if his honest words had supercharged her confidence in a flash fire. With tentative fingers, she touched his abdomen.

His cock jerked against the choke hold of his jeans and he hissed.

She yanked her hands back and fisted them as though she'd been burned. "What's wrong?"

Squeezing his eyes shut, he tried to find his center. Some tiny scrap of calm so he could give her what she wanted. "Not a damned thing." He pulled in a slow breath, opened his eyes, and guided her hands back where they'd been. "Your hands on me are a fucking miracle. I'm just doing my best not to cry uncle too soon."

Her lips crooked in a hesitant, but saucy smile, and her attention dipped lower to the obvious ridge beneath his fly.

"Don't even think about it," he warned. "I'm willing to a point, but I'm no saint. One of these days, I'll let you have your fill of me however you want it, but today those hands stay above my hips."

An emotion flared behind her eyes. Hunger for sure, but something else, as well. Something that made him wish the word *slow* had never factored in his plans. She tugged his T-shirt free of his waistband and slipped her fingers beneath the hem.

His muscles flexed at the contact, the soft press of her hands sweet torture.

She took her time, slowly ghosting the pads of her fingers against his skin and tracing each rise and dip of his muscles as though fascinated. Working from his abs to his obliques, she pushed his shirt up above his pecs. Her attention snagged on his dog tags resting against his sternum. "What are those?"

Wrangling his thoughts up out of the dangerous terrain she'd created, he forced his mouth to move. "They're from my brothers. We all have them."

She cocked her head and traced the tribal tree etched on the black background. "What's the *H* stand for?"

"Haven."

She frowned and lifted her gaze to his. "Jace and Axel's ranch?"

Something about the moment gripped him, holding him tight and forcing him to full alert. It wasn't danger. That he'd have recognized easily. This was something else. Something important. "They named their land Haven when they bought it, yeah, but for me and my brothers it's about what the word means. We built our family by choice. Doesn't matter where we come from, how ugly we've had it, or what we've been through, we've got each other's backs."

An odd expression moves across her face. A little surprise, but more than that, longing. "That's really nice."

I want to give her that.

One single second. One clear, concise thought and his whole world rearranged. Yeah, he'd known he wanted more than a quick tussle with Gabe, but the reality was he wanted *a lot* more. As in the home run to beat all others.

"It's everything." As the words slipped out, he wasn't sure if he was commenting on the importance of his brothers in his life, or making Gabe part of it. Hell, he wasn't even sure the two were separate anymore.

He tugged her forward and held her against his chest, needing the contact and the time to recalibrate.

"You okay?" Gabe muttered.

He swallowed hard and speared his fingers in her hair. Hard to call on that one. Part of him wanted to claim and mark her right then and there. The other half wanted to sprint twenty miles while his head figured out which way was up. "I had a stellar meal. I had an easy, quiet night watching TV and I've got a beautiful woman tucked against me. Outside of me not feeling you skin to skin right now, I don't think I could top tonight."

She giggled and snuggled closer, her weight the most natural thing in the world.

He'd known in short order Danny was meant to be a brother. Why wouldn't he recognize something similar between him and Gabe just as quickly?

Still, to bring her into his family he'd have to tread carefully—both for her and for him. The guys needed a chance to get to know her, and her social anxiety wouldn't make that an easy task. Plus, she'd already demonstrated a rigid perspective where the law was concerned. While he and his brothers never embarked on anything that went against their own code, that didn't mean their decisions always played within the rules. "I want to ask you a question and I want you to tell me the truth, all right?"

She nodded against his chest.

"That night you went with Danny to the compound, aside from that first panic attack, how comfortable were you?"

She pushed up enough to stare down at him. "What do you mean?"

Hell, he wasn't sure where he was headed with this. It was just an idea at this point. One that would require him finagling family night somewhere away from Haven to keep from breaking the brotherhood's rules, but would give her time to get to know his brothers a little better. It would also reinforce he wasn't looking to crawl in bed with her and then leave. "I mean, my brothers and I get together on a regular basis. Viv and the moms, too. I want to take you with me."

She blinked over and over, her face blank as though her brain couldn't quite decipher his words.

Well, fine. He'd try a different tactic. "I told you yesterday I mean to put myself out there where we're concerned. I'm not screwing around—not about what I want from you, or about you getting to know the people I love. To my mind, the best way to demonstrate that is to show you straight out of the chute I mean what I say. So, if I can arrange it, are you up for it?"

"We—we've only been out once. You want me to meet your moms?"

He grinned at that. "Well, technically, we've been on two dates now. And unless my shifts get in the way, or you bar me from your kitchen between now and then, I figure we'll have at least a few more under our belts by the time I can arrange something that works." He skimmed his knuckles along her jaw. "But once I do, are you up for it?"

She sat up, putting way too much distance between them even as her gaze went distant.

He braced, schooling his expression to the unaffected mask reserved for the worst of traumas at work. "You don't have to do anything you don't want to do, Gabe. It's just an idea. One we can work up to when you're ready."

Her attention drifted to his torso, lingered on his Haven tags long enough it registered like a physical touch, then lifted to meet his steady stare. "I don't need to work up to it. If you want me with you, I'm willing to try."

Chapter Fourteen

Things were changing. For the life of her, Gabe couldn't define when or how it'd started, but even putzing through her normal routines the past few days, her world was different. Riddled with a little less worry and structure, and sprinkled with a whole lot more hope and courage.

Like he had on Sunday, Zeke had joined her after his shifts at the hospital for dinner the past few nights and unwound with her in front of the television.

They'd kissed.

A lot.

Petted and teased each other until both of them were breathless and edgy, but nothing else. Now it was Wednesday, and things between them were stepping into a whole new realm.

She rubbed her sweaty palms on her hips and assessed her appearance in her dresser mirror. Of all the times for Danny to disappear, this had to be the worst. Granted, he was a guy and seldom gave more than one—or two— word responses when it came to her outfits, but having *some* kind of input before she came face-to-face with Zeke's family—or more to the point, his moms—sure would have been nice.

And this is why most girls have friends they can call.
She shook the nasty self-criticism off and refocused

on her image. Zeke had said to be herself, so she'd paired a simple navy blue tank with her favorite green and blue flannel and Levi's. She'd ditched her boots, though. They might be comfortable and add an extra kick to her confidence when facing down strangers, but the one pair of sandals she'd splurged on last year seemed to help soften her otherwise tomboy appearance.

Three quick raps sounded on the front door, and her heart kicked an answering echo.

On her nightstand, the alarm clock showed 7:25 p.m.

Five minutes early, which she'd learned was the norm for Zeke. The one time he'd been late he'd actually *called* five minutes early to give her an updated time, then had beat his modified arrival estimate by ten minutes.

Not letting herself overthink the big surprise he'd promised any further, she hurried to the front door and opened it.

Three nights in a row she'd greeted him this same way and every single time the punch of seeing him on her front stoop knocked her dumbfounded. Like her, he'd donned jeans and paired them with a simple black T-shirt, but while her overall look said blue collar, his said cover model.

"Hey," she managed.

His kissable lips curved in a slow, promising smile, and he prowled across the threshold, crowding close and wrapping her up at the waist. "Hey, *gatinha*." He pressed a soft, lingering kiss to her mouth and murmured, "You ready for your surprise?"

Not really. If she had her way, they'd skip wherever they were going and jump right to the kissing and groping. "Yeah," she said instead. "Though you're not helping the anxiety much keeping our destination a secret.

Stressing about making a good impression on your moms is bad enough."

He chuckled at that. "Makin' a good impression on Sylvie and Ninette is the last thing you need to worry about. They're gonna love you. And where we're goin' is right up your alley." He stepped away and playfully swatted her butt. "Get your purse so we can lock up. Movie night waits for no one."

"We're going to a movie?" As options went, it meant minimized socializing for her, but seemed kind of awkward for a family thing.

"Oh, yeah. Movies done brotherhood style. Double feature and everything. Now get a move on."

Ten minutes later he had her out the door and climbing into a black Escalade with windows tinted so dark any number of felonies could take place inside and no one would be the wiser. "I didn't really take you for an SUV guy."

In the driver's seat, he buckled up while she eyeballed the spacious tan interior. "It's not mine, it's Beck's. Or one of them anyway. He's got five he keeps on hand for security details. Says he'd rather use his own rigs than trust someone else's gear. Plus, Knox keeps tracking devices on all the vehicles in case anything goes south."

The same fear that had bubbled up the night she'd visited the compound and learned of Danny's involvement with Beckett's business whispered up through her happy buzz, but she forced it down. Tonight wasn't about Danny. Or fear. Or any other catastrophic idea her mind could come up with. It was about enjoying herself and savoring every second with Zeke—however long those seconds lasted.

On the horizon the sun made its final decent, and the crisp mid-April evening scent slipped through the open sunroof overhead. As usual for a Sunday evening, the weathered country road that led to the interstate was mostly void of traffic. "So where's the theater?"

"Ft. Worth."

At first she nodded an absent agreement—until the reality of their destination fully clicked. "We're driving nearly an hour away for a movie?"

"It's only an hour drive with traffic. This late, it'll be forty-five tops."

"But why? Dallas has plenty of places to go. Shoot, *Rockwall* has plenty of places to go."

"Not like where we're going. Though I heard a new place is going up in Lewisville."

She stilled, a whole host of suspicions welling up in seconds.

Zeke glanced at her and grinned. "Relax, *gatinha*. You'll love it. I promise."

The rest of the trip went fairly easy, Zeke's adeptness at casual conversation steering her thoughts further away from their destination even as the SUV ate up I-30. It wasn't until he'd navigated them just north of Ft. Worth's downtown and beside the river that his big secret clicked. The sight of the three huge screens, each angled different directions and reaching toward the darkening night sky, drew an immediate smile. "We're going to a drive-in?"

"Is there a better way to watch a movie?"

She barely managed not to press her nose against the passenger window as they neared the entrance. "I have no idea. I've never been to one before."

"Never?"

She shook her head, fascinated by how the big screens looked close up. Unlike the ones in movie theaters, these were a lot less smooth and made up of huge white sections bolted together. When they reached the little hut where people paid for admission, a slightly overweight but jolly-looking man took one look at Zeke and smiled huge. "And the last of the Haven clan comes straggling in!" He shook Zeke's hand like the two of them met up for beers on a regular basis and waved him through the gate without taking so much as a single dollar. "Your crew's already set up. Screen three. Previews start in about twenty minutes, so you've got time to get you and your girl settled in."

"Appreciate it, man."

"You bet." The clerk ducked down enough to catch Gabe's gaze through the window. "Have a good time, little lady."

Gabe had barely given the man a hesitant wave before Zeke was through the gate and headed toward the parking area on the far left.

"I take it this isn't an uncommon event for your family?" she asked.

Zeke scanned the arced rows fanning out from the huge wall that served as the screen, locked his sights on a cluster of cars congregated dead center, and chuckled. "*Gatinha*, anything considered uncommon by most is practically a given in our family." He turned down one row and cast her a quick wink. "You ask me, that's the best part."

Ahead on their same row, two other black Escalades to match their own, a black Silverado with a whole lot of chrome and a silver Chevy dually were backed into their spots. Centered in the row in front of them was a swank new white Mercedes sedan and a pretty Shelby Cobra painted an indigo blue to rival her truck. Several people meandered between the vehicles and lawn chairs set up for optimum viewing, and situated in the middle of it all were two long folding tables laden with food.

"I should have brought something," she muttered.

Zeke pulled just past the cluster of cars, moved the gearshift to Reverse, and twisted so he could back the SUV into the slot on the far end. "Brought something for what?"

"For the food. It's bad manners to show up for something like this without food."

Frowning, Zeke put the car in Park and gave her his full attention. "You remember the spread we had at Trevor's house on our first date?"

Boy, did she. And she'd done her best to put the hurt on a good chunk of it. Especially the sweets. "Yeah."

"So, you get from the quantity of food Sylvie made for just two people, she loves to cook. As in she could give you and your triple lasagna sessions a run for your money. In fact, odds are good she'll have us loaded up with a care package before the first movie is over." He punched the auto-tailgate opener overhead, opened his car door, then paused and grinned at her over his shoulder. "And about those manners. Anything based on respect you'll find we appreciate. But doing anything because someone with a stick up their ass said *it shall be so*, doesn't hold much sway in this group."

With that, he hopped to the ground and shut his door behind him, the warning *beep-beep-beep* of the back hitch as it lifted filling the otherwise quiet. Her own door popped open all of ten seconds later, and Zeke held out his hand to help her down. "Come on, *gatinha*. Gotta get you fed and settled before the previews start."

She could do this. It was just a movie, after all, and she'd already met the brothers once. Granted, she'd been a little snippy the last go-round, but she could do better this time. Easy peasy, right?

She wiped her sweaty palm on her jeans, took Zeke's

steady hand, and stepped out on the running board. As spring nights went, this one was perfect, a barely there breeze dancing across her fear-dampened skin in a calm, cooling touch. They were still at least thirty more minutes from full sunset, but the sky had deepened to a dark enough blue the stars winked with promise.

Knox, Beckett, Trevor and Jace all turned from where they surrounded one of the two tables and paused in filling their plates long enough to give her a once-over and easy smiles.

"'Bout time you got here," Jace said. "Though from the company you're keeping I'd say the wait was worth it."

"Hey, you're not the only one who gets to show off a pretty girl." Instead of heading over to join the rest of them, Zeke routed to the back end of their SUV, slid out two folding sport chairs, and started setting one up. She'd barely had a chance to gawk at the thick camping bedroll, blankets and huge mound of pillows setup inside when Zeke glanced back at the guys and said, "Speaking of pretty girls, where's Viv?"

Viv poked her head up from the far side of the black Silverado's truck bed, waved and offered a warm smile. "I'm on drink duty." She ducked down out of sight for all of two seconds, popped back up, then strolled into full view carting four longnecks. "We've got beer, sweet tea, wine and water. What's your poison?"

"Beer for me," Zeke said reaching for the second chair to set it up. "Gabe, what do you want?"

She opened her mouth to speak, but what came out was more of a strangled whisper than actual words. She cleared her throat and tried again. "Water's fine."

You have no business being here.
You don't fit in.

They'll look at you, judge you and laugh.

Zeke's touch registered at the small of her back, and Trevor's voice cut through her thoughts. "You okay, darlin'?"

She blinked the world back into focus. "Sorry. What did you say?"

"I said I hope you're hungry. Sylvie and Ninette took finger foods to the extreme tonight."

Well, she had been. Now she wasn't sure if food was a good idea. At least not until she figured out how close the bathrooms were in case her stomach revolted.

The same nasty sentiments circled around for another lap, but this time she shook them off. Maybe it was Zeke behind her, or the burgeoning hope she'd nursed the past few days, but she focused on relaxing her shoulders and forced a smile. "If she's got dessert, I'm starting there. I got too full before I could enjoy those last time around."

Zeke wrapped his arm around her waist, tucking her close to his side, and gave an encouraging squeeze. A silent *atta girl* and *I've got your back* all rolled into one. He guided her toward the table. "Rule of thumb—Sylvie always has dessert."

"God, that's the truth." Vivienne handed Gabe a bottle of water fresh out of the cooler and a Bohemia Weiss to Zeke. "It's like a bakery at Haven ninety percent of the time. I'm surprised I haven't had to buy a whole new wardrobe since moving out there."

Walking behind her as she spoke, Jace chuckled, palmed Vivienne's ass without the least bit of concern for anyone watching, and squeezed. "Sugar, as long as I'm breathing, you workin' off Sylvie's desserts is the last problem you gotta worry about."

The guys barked a chorus of hoots and hollers.

Vivienne swatted his hand playfully, but the look she paired it with said she planned to hold him to his word.

So simple. Easy. The same comfortable camaraderie Gabe had with Danny when no one else was around. She grabbed a plate and let the guys' idle chatter settle against her frayed nerves. The spread really was impressive. Far more than anything she'd ever try carting to a drive-in. Meatballs coated with what looked like the cranberry sauce she used for New Year's Day snacks, three different cheeses and twice as many crackers, sliders and potato skins that made TGI Fridays' offerings look wimpy. Over on the other table were cheesecake cups topped with caramel, chocolate cake balls, bite-size peanut butter and chocolate squares, and simple chocolate chip cookies.

A chipper, feminine, albeit thickly accented voice, sounded over her shoulder. "Now, there's a lass with a mind like my own."

Gabe hugged her empty plate against her chest and spun.

Not even a full arm span away stood an older woman with vivid auburn hair to her shoulders and a smile bright enough to light up the whole parking lot. In each hand, she held huge tubs of popcorn glistening with enough butter on top to guarantee a clogged artery. "I'm Sylvie McKee. Axel's mother. You must be Gabrielle."

Even without the introduction or the accent to guide her, Gabrielle would have figured out which son was hers with one look at Sylvie's eyes. Like Axel's, they were a deep forest green, except hers twinkled as though she knew an exciting secret.

At the far end of the table, Zeke filled his plate. Enough distance to let her stand on her own, but close enough she knew he'd be there if she needed him.

She let out a slow breath and refocused on Sylvie. "It's nice to meet you."

"The pleasure's all mine, lass." She leaned in and dropped her voice in a conspiratorial manner. "It's not very often we have family night away from Haven, but if it means we get ta meet our boys' ladies sooner rather than later, I may have ta vote we change up the venue more often."

The odd statement threw Gabe for loop, but before she could puzzle over what it meant, Sylvie placed her popcorn tubs strategically with all the other hearty food, then guided her over to the dessert table. "Now, if ye'd rather start with dessert, ye'll get no beef from me, but save the cookies for after the first show. We've got ice cream in the cooler and I plan ta make sandwiches out of them."

Oh, yeah. This was definitely a lady she needed to get to know. And even better, being with Sylvie didn't send her anxiety through the roof. It was more like chatting with Mrs. Wallaby over morning coffee than coercing her tongue to form polite conversation.

With the same focus as a mom prepping dinner for a five-year-old, Sylvie started loading up Gabe's plate with one of everything. "Zeke tells me you're quite a cook yourself."

"He did?"

Leaning against the dropped tailgate of the silver dually, Zeke popped a meatball in his mouth and nodded his head at something one of his brothers said, but his eyes were on her. Watchful and considerate even as a soft smile played across his face.

"Och, lass. The boy's over the moon w' ye. Kept me on the phone for a full twenty minutes extolling your lasagna and askin' me ta bring more cupcakes for tonight. I told him ye deserved somethin' new for our movie night, but if ye get a hankerin' for them, I'll whip them up next time around." She pointed at two strawberries she'd plunked to one side of Gabe's plate. "Try those. Cream cheese frosting on the inside. It's like ye've died and gone ta heaven."

It wouldn't take strawberries to make that happen. Not plain or stuffed with cream cheese frosting. The first movie hadn't even come on yet and she was already floating in a way she'd never felt before. Danny was right. These really were good people. Friendly and unpretentious.

And Zeke had shared them with her.

Footsteps crunched against the fine gravel that made up the parking lot, and Axel's rich and gravelly voice broke through her thoughts. "Should've known Zeke had shown with Gabe when Ma hightailed it out of the concession stand without flirting with old man Dodger first."

Spinning, Gabe found not only Axel, but a woman about Sylvie's age with platinum hair to her shoulders. Both hauled two handfuls of the same monstrous-sized popcorn tubs as Sylvie had, but it was the woman she assumed was Ninette that held her focus. Where Sylvie was all things vibrant and homey, Ninette oozed intelligence and a strength gained only by experience.

Not the least bit flustered by Axel's obvious taunt, Sylvie cocked an eyebrow at him and started filling up her own plate with desserts. "Oh, haud yer wheesht! Someone has to look out for the lass and teach her how ta keep ye bloody boys in line." She waved Ninette closer. "Ninnie, come meet Zeke's Gabrielle."

Before Ninette could make it halfway to the table, Knox and Beckett intercepted and relieved her of her popcorn. Knox glanced at Gabe, grinned and said plain as day, "Told you she was a looker."

"She is, indeed," Ninette said with a genuine smile.

Hardly. Not compared to Ninette. She might be old enough to have a son in his early thirties, but her skin was still soft and radiant enough to give some women half her age a run for their money, and her eyes were a stunning blue. Not at all the woman she'd pictured as Jace's mother.

Ninette glided toward them, a soft sway to her hips that spoke of confidence and open sensuality. "Have to admit, it's nice to see another one of our boys fired up to bring a new woman around." She glanced at Gabe's near-to-overflowing plate and chuckled. "An even bigger bonus for Sylvie if you're a sugar lover."

Strong arms slid around Gabe's waist a second before she found herself firmly pulled against Zeke's front. "Don't steer her away from the sweets, *mamãe*. Our first kiss came after Sylvie's cupcakes, so I'm a fan."

"Zeke!" Her cheeks flamed hot in an instant.

Ninette and Sylvie both let out guffaws loud enough to draw looks from others outside their group. Before their laughter had fully died out, Ninette snagged one of the frosting stuffed strawberries and motioned to the cluster of men behind them. "Sugar, we've raised two boys and all but adopted those other four. Nothing they say or do is gonna shock us or sway what we think of you, so let that shit go."

Sylvie shrugged and popped a bite size cheesecake in her mouth. "Well," she muttered around the morsel, not the least bit concerned about talking with her mouth full, "unless Zeke here tells us ye've a stash of sexy man-candy photos tucked away yer not willin' ta share. Then we'd have to ban ye from our merry group on the basis of bein' stingy."

More laughter filled the deepening night, Viv's beautiful voice mingling with the deep rumble of the other men and wrapping Gabe up as surely as Zeke's arms around her.

"See?" Zeke murmured low in her ear. "I told you, they'd love you."

Nearly an hour later, cozied up beside Zeke in the back of their SUV and so full on delicious food she could barely breathe, she had to concede his point. Danny hadn't been wrong. Zeke's family wasn't like anything she'd ever imaged. Every one of them were unique, and yet they came together in a colorful tapestry that allowed the people within their circle to let down their guard and just *be*. A safe place.

A haven.

Her eyes drifted closed, the soft back-and-forth glide of Zeke's thumb along her belly lulling her farther and farther from the cybercrime plot unfolding on the screen.

Zeke's low voice near her ear sent a pleasant shiver down her spine. "You want me to take you home?"

She shook her head, too replete and content to even think of disrupting their cocoon. "I like it here."

He chuckled and shifted so he could better see her face. "Made you a fan of drive-ins, huh?"

Peace, that precious, but all-too elusive gift she seldom felt except when alone or with Danny, whispered through her. "I'm a fan of you. And your family."

Something moved across his face. An emotion she couldn't quite tag, but that energized the space between them with a pleasant hum. "You mean that?"

"I do."

He smiled, his gaze moving over her face as though cataloguing every detail. "You were comfortable? No panic?"

"No." At least not anything she'd been unable or unwilling to navigate. Though she chalked most of that up to his very even-keel clan.

"You think you might be up for something more? Maybe a dinner out?"

"With your family?"

He shook his head. "Just with me. I've got a dinner thing I'm supposed to go to Saturday night. They're a bore, but I need to go for my job. Normally I duck in and out, but it'd be nice to have someone with me." He dragged his thumb along her jawline. "To have you with me."

You've pushed the envelope enough already, don't you think?

You'll do something stupid and then he'll find out who you really are.

Then he'll be gone.

No. She wasn't listening to that trash anymore. Wasn't going to let the negative thoughts weigh her down. Not this time. She'd done just fine today. Heck, with Zeke beside her, she could probably do anything.

She snuggled closer to him and nodded. "What do I need to wear?"

Chapter Fifteen

Talk about a stranger in a foreign land. Gabe meandered through the department store's never-ending racks of clothes and stared at the headless white mannequin near the main aisle. Going by the frilly outfit pinned and tucked to the sterile plastic form, she'd assumed this was the formal section, but everything around her looked like it belonged on some frail and elderly librarian.

God, she was screwed. Seriously, big-time, in-over-her-head screwed.

A spunky, feminine voice sounded behind her. "You need some help?"

Gabe spun and found a smiling, curvy girl about Gabe's age with a hand cocked on one hip and the other loaded with clothes on hangers. For this particular department store, she was dressed pretty edgy. Technically conservative if you went by just the black pants and shirt, but thrown way out on the edge with the bold silver earrings and vibrant turquoise headband wrapped around her unnaturally tinted maroon hair.

The woman smiled and smacked her gum. "You looked a little lost. They just moved everything around, so I thought you might need some help."

Help. Yes, help would be good.

Are you insane?

She'll see how clueless you are.

How pathetic you are.

Instead of grabbing the lifeline the lady had offered, Gabe shook her head and averted her face, wishing she could crawl underneath one of the racks and hide until the coast was clear.

God, this was so stupid. She needed help and it was right there in front of her. She could totally do this. She'd met Zeke's family not once, but twice—mothers included. All she had to do was dredge up a little solo courage. She sucked in a fortifying breath and turned.

Goth girl was gone.

Gabe hurried out to the main aisle and spied the top of her wild, yet artfully coifed hair bebopping around the corner. "Wait!"

Goth girl backed up, but the smile she'd offered before was gone, replaced with a wary, or maybe hurt, expression.

"I'm sorry. Shopping's not exactly my thing." Gabe gripped the hem of her flannel shirt and shrugged. "Normally I just wear stuff like this, but I need something nice for a dinner."

The girl sidled closer, draping the clothes over one arm and giving Gabe the once-over. "What kind of dinner?"

A dinner she was bound and determined to make it through, no matter what it took. "My…" Crap, what did she call him? Did you still call a guy a boyfriend after high school? "The guy I'm seeing. He said it was a work thing and he's wearing a suit, so I'm guessing there will be some bigwigs. Maybe his boss."

"What's he do?"

"He's a doctor. An emergency room doctor."

The girl gaped back at her. "Whoa. Nice." She sauntered a little closer and held out her hand, her multi-jewel-toned bracelets clinking with the sudden motion. "I'm April, by the way."

Gabe shook her hand and shared her own name. "So what do you think? Any ideas?"

April frowned and scanned the far end of the building. "Well, you could go the LBD route."

"LBD?"

"Little Black Dress." April shrugged and went back to smacking her gum. "It's not really my thing, but lots of women say that's the go-to outfit when you're not sure what to wear. If it's formal, you'd still come off classy. If it's casual, you'd look slick. Hence the *can't-go-wrong* part."

Well, that made sense. Not that she'd have the first freaking clue where to find one. "Do you have any of those?"

"Girl, that's a staple in these kinds of stores. Not that there's anything wrong with black. I mean, *helllooo*." She motioned to her outfit. "I just don't go for dresses. God did not intend for my Lily Munster complexion to be shown from the waist down."

Gabe rolled one foot back on its heel and waggled the toe of one boot. "My complexion doesn't bother me, but it's hard to match steel-toed boots with dresses."

April snorted and slapped her thigh. "Oh, I don't know. My friend Theresa matches steel-toed boots with tights all the time." She waved Gabe down the aisle to a different section. "Come on, we'll see what we can find."

Forty-five minutes and a dressing room littered with clothes later, Gabe tried on her favorite for the fifth time. Surely trying on clothes counted as exercise. God knew, she'd given her belly a workout sucking it in on a few of the numbers she'd wiggled into.

Damn, but this one looked good. And that was saying something considering she knew nothing about fashion. It was simple, which made her feel a whole lot more comfortable, the top half something April had called a halter while the bottom half clung to her hips. Unlike some of the others that had barely covered her ass, this one hit just a little above her knees. She felt classy. Elegant.

A knock sounded on her dressing room door. "You still alive in there?"

Man, April had been a godsend. And to think she'd nearly let her walk away. "Yeah, I think I picked the right one." The price was going to set her back on her new computer and phone for a little while, but if it meant she wouldn't embarrass Zeke, it would be worth it. She opened the door. "What do you think?"

"Niiice." April juggled the armful of stuff in her arms and swirled her finger in a circle. "Lemme see the back."

Gabe turned and glanced over her shoulder. "Does it fit right? I mean, it's supposed to be snug, isn't it?"

"Girl, it's perfect. You couldn't have picked better. Now…" She bulldozed her way past Gabe into the dressing room and plunked her armload of stuff on the chair tucked into the corner. "I figured if you're a work-boots kind of gal, you didn't have much in the way of cute shoes, so I grabbed you these. You said you were a seven, right?"

Holy. Crap. She hadn't even thought about shoes. Or underwear. Or a purse. From the looks of the pile spilling onto the floor, April was totally on the case. "Um, yeah."

"Good." April held up a pair of shiny black heels. "These should be perfect. And they're on sale. So's the purse. Couldn't do much on the bras and panties, though. That's the store's bread and butter."

Gabe carefully took the shoes and studied them from every angle. "I'm going to kill myself."

"No, you won't. Those have platforms on 'em. They look crazy tall, but they're really not. See how all that works for you. I gotta run before my boss jumps my ass again. I'll swing back in ten and see if you're good." She hustled out of the tiny room and waved. "And if I don't catch you, have a killer time!"

Waving April off with an enthusiasm she didn't feel, Gabe slunk back into the dressing room. She re-checked the price tag on the dress. Then the shoes and all the other goodies. She knocked the merchandise to the floor and plopped on the chair. Okay, so this was going to take a wallop out of her savings instead of a dent. It would still be worth it. The only other option at this point was to call Zeke with some kind of lame excuse and, deep down, she really wanted to go. To try and be pretty, or maybe even sexy, just once.

Satisfied everything fit the way it should, she gathered up the things she wanted and trudged with full arms to the register. So what if she'd have to wait longer for her computer. This would be a good thing. A step in the right direction. And how freaking awesome was it she'd met a person like April to help her get ready for it all? It kind of made her wish she'd asked the girl more about herself. Where she hung out and what she liked to do.

She paid for her purchases and scanned the racks behind her for any sign of April. She'd just tucked her receipt in her bag and hefted her purse on her shoulder when the top of April's head went traipsing above a rack of casual tops.

Gabe hustled that direction, hoping she wasn't about to make a complete idiot out of herself.

So what if you do? No one else is watching. Logically, she knew that was the truth, but it didn't lessen the spotlight sensation she always felt in situations like this. "Hey, April."

April stopped, searched for the source of the voice, locked onto Gabe and grinned. "You got 'em! Yay!" Bustling closer, she poked a pen in her messy up-do. "Did you get the undies, too? They're crazy expensive, but I'll bet they'll be worth it."

"Yeah, I got them." She glanced down at the bag. "Actually, I got a cute red pair just like them, too. Well, not red, really. More like scarlet."

"Mmm-hmm. Smart girl." April cocked her head. "Need something else?"

"Well…" *Just say it.*

Say thank you at least.

"I just wanted to tell you thank you for helping me. And…" She wiped her hand on her jeans. "I wanted to give you my number. I thought maybe we could grab coffee sometime if you live somewhere close?"

April's head jerked backward, a confused expression on her face.

Oh, God. She probably thought Gabe was asking her out for a date or something. "I mean, I just thought you were fun to hang with, and I don't have a lot of friends where I work."

Much better. Less desperate and more reasonable.

It seemed to work, too. April smiled that big, wholehearted smile of hers, jerked her pen out of her hair, and pilfered an unused price tag from the stack in her hand. "You bet. I'll jot my number down and you can text me yours later. They don't let me keep my cell phone on the floor." She held it out as soon as she was done. "First phone call better be as soon as the date is over, though. I wanna hear how the undies score."

Chapter Sixteen

Makeup, three different kinds of hairbrushes and more styling products than Gabe had owned her entire life littered her bathroom's one-sink vanity. Two hours since she'd stepped into the shower and embarked on her first girly crusade, and she still wasn't sure if she'd hit the mark. She'd kept the eye shadow light for fear of straying into overdone hooker territory, but the smoky grays and soft black liner seemed to make her eyes a little bolder. The rich red lipstick had made it all of five minutes before she'd washed it off and gone with a softer, barely there pink.

She smoothed her hand down the front of her dress and twisted enough to check the back. No tags and no strings hanging off anywhere, so that was good. Surprisingly, April had been right about the pumps. They really didn't feel too uncomfortable and she'd practiced wearing them practically since she got home. Shower not included.

The *swoosh* and *ka-chunk* of the front door opening and closing rattled through the otherwise quiet house. She'd locked it before she'd jumped in the shower, so it had to be Danny.

Sure enough, his voice bellowed from the living room.

"Jesus, Gabe. What'd you do? Buy every issue *Cosmo* ever made?"

Shit. She'd forgotten about the magazines. And technically it wasn't every issue ever made. More like the past twelve months since that was all the secondhand bookstore had available. "Give me a minute and I'll clean them up."

Swiping the makeup into her top drawer and tossing the brushes into the one below it, she double-checked her hair one last time in the mirror. It wasn't anything fancy, just her usual loose arrangement, but it looked poofier than normal. Shiny, too.

She hustled to the living room and gathered up the magazines. "Can you hand me that one on the end table?" she said to Danny, straightening the pillows on the sofa as she worked. She turned and found Danny frozen in the middle of the room, his gaze locked on her dress. "What?"

Danny just stood there, dumbfounded.

Dropping the magazines on the coffee table, she straightened and smoothed her hands down the low cut V neckline, making sure everything was where it was supposed to be. "Does it look bad? I was going for casual dressy. The girl at the store said this could go either way."

He blinked a few times like she'd suddenly slapped him out of a trance. "Where are you going that's casual dressy? And with who?"

"With Zeke. He's got some doctor dinner thing. Does it look bad?"

"It's…" He pushed his skully back and forth on his head. "Wow. I've never seen you like that." His bewilderment vanished in a single beat, replaced with a heavy frown. "He being good to you? You being careful?"

"Danny!"

"What? You're my sister."

"And he's your friend. He's a good guy."

"He is. But he's also a *guy*. Meaning he has a dick. He sees you like that, that's the only fucking thing he's going to think with."

A huge flutter rippled low in her belly, so powerful she pressed her hand to her abdomen before she could catch it. God, she hoped that was the case. Zeke's intentions might have been noble with the whole *slow* thing, but she'd reached a point where she was ready to play dirty if he didn't change his tune. "Stop worrying. He's being good to me. Really good." She shrugged, a little uncomfortable admitting anything further, but if it kept Danny from acting like an ass around Zeke, it would be worth it. "I like him."

He fisted his hands at his sides and stared at her in that scary way her dad used to when she was in trouble.

Three solid raps sounded at the door.

Danny still didn't move, just studied her with his lungs cranking heavier than normal.

Well, shit, she wasn't letting Zeke stand out there all day just because Danny had his briefs in a twist. She broke the starefest and started forward.

"I'll get it," Danny grumbled and turned for the door. He jerked it open hard enough the blinds covering the front window clattered.

"Hey, Danny." From her angle, she couldn't see Zeke, but the confusion in his voice didn't really make a visual necessary. "Something wrong?"

Danny grunted, stomped out from between them, and into the kitchen.

Zeke shut the door behind him, strolled a few steps deeper into the living room, and took his sweet damned time eyeballing her head to toe, the heat behind his gaze so potent she nearly melted. "Well, I guess that explains a lot."

Holy. Freaking. Cow. Zeke in a suit was a thing of beauty. Black on black, the outfit put off a seriously intense vibe, but the lack of a tie and his tanned skin peeking out from just below his collar took some of the edge off. She started to move toward him, eager to smooth her hands along his shoulders, then stopped. "What explains a lot?"

Zeke grinned and ambled closer. "Why Danny's so angry." He rested his hands on her hips and skimmed his lips along her cheekbone. *"Você é linda."*

"What's that mean?" Whatever it meant sounded really, really nice. But then, Zeke could order a hamburger and fries in Portuguese and make it sound sexy.

"It means he's gonna try to get that dress off you the minute he gets home. Don't need to speak Portuguese to know that." Danny upended his beer for a huge gulp and stalked down the hallway toward his bedroom. "No fucking way I'm coming home tonight. Some noises I don't need to hear coming out of my sister's room."

"Danny!"

"It's okay, *gatinha.*" Zeke chuckled and rested his forehead against hers. He pulled in a long, slow inhalation, opened his eyes and kissed the tip of her nose. "It means you're beautiful."

"So, I picked okay? I didn't have a clue what to buy so the girl at the store helped me find something. I mean, it probably wasn't the swankiest place in town, but she was helpful, and some help is better than no help, right?" She clamped her mouth shut and fingered the starched edge of his shirt where it opened near the top. Her whole life she'd kept her mouth clamped up, but she had to go and pick tonight to get chatty.

"You were nervous about what to wear?"

She nodded.

"You could have just asked me. I could have saved you a lot of worry. Hell, I could have taken you shopping. I'd like spoiling you a little."

"I didn't want to look stupid."

He straightened to his full height and frowned. "Right." He stepped back, scanned the room, and settled his gaze on the kitchen table. With a hand on her upper arm, he guided her to it, sat in one of the chairs and pulled her between his knees. He glanced down the hall toward Danny's room, then focused on her. "We need to talk."

Oh, shit. The last talk they'd had they'd downshifted to *slow*. The only other gear slower meant *nada*. She edged backward, heart clamoring with a whole lot more speed than her feet.

He tightened his hands on her hips and tugged her back in place. "Not that kind of talk. I mean talk about being honest with each other."

As fast as her panic had set in, the tension in her shoulders ebbed and her lungs started working again.

Smoothing his thumbs back and forth in a calming stroke, he inhaled deep. "You get after this week that I'm after more than a quick tumble?"

Boy, did she get it. Hard to miss a guy's intentions when he put her in a one-on-one situation with the women he'd honored with the title of mother. "Yeah, I get it."

He paused a minute, studying her. "That mean you're ready for more?"

All of a sudden, the space around her went from light and easy, to thick and supercharged. Part of her wanted to dodge a verbal answer and drag him back to her room for something more tactile, but her new and blossoming courage punched forward and answered first. "Yes."

"Good. Then let's cover something else." His hands slid around and cupped her ass, pulling her even closer. "Even more than you understanding I want you for you, I want you to feel confident enough with me to ask for what you need. Communication with sex is a must for me. Absolute straight talk."

She traced the seam where his sleeve connected to the shoulder. Silence stretched between them and her brain kicked and sputtered trying to come up with words to fill it.

"On our first date, I went with my gut," he said. "Everything I read in your body language and actions told me you needed that release, so I went with it. But if I'd been wrong, if that had been too much for you, I'd want to know you'd feel safe enough to tell me to stop." He cupped the side of her face and steered it so she couldn't avoid his gaze. "That also means if you want something, you'll ask for it."

"Are you…" Ugh, just once she wished she could come off as smooth and sophisticated as him. In her head, the words came out just fine, but getting them all the way to her tongue was a whole different game. "You're not wanting a list or something right this second, are you?"

He smiled so big her anxiety scattered. "I'm not after a list, no. Just to know you'll ask me if something comes to you."

"Okay, good. Not exactly an impromptu subject."

"No, it's not. But since we're talking straight, there is something I need to ask you." He laced his fingers with hers. "Are you on any kind of birth control?"

Heat seared her cheeks, and she was mighty tempted

to study the tips of her new black pumps. She held his gaze instead. "No."

"Do you want to be?"

She probably should be. She might not have talked much in school, but she sure as shit listened. Almost all the other girls had talked about getting on the pill at one time or another, but she hadn't dared to broach that subject with her dad. Of all the times she could have used a mother to talk with, that and starting her period had been the hardest. "When I've…you know. We just used condoms."

Zeke fanned his thumb along the pulse point at her wrist. "We can do that if you want, but there are other options, unless you've got a medical reason you can't take them."

She shook her head. "None that I know of. I just never needed to."

"So you're not against it."

"No."

He pulled one hand to his mouth and kissed her palm. "When's the last time you were with a man?"

God, this was embarrassing. Probably smart to talk about, though, considering he'd figure out her lack of experience sooner or later. "It's been a while. A couple of years." More like three, but no need to toss gas on the already fuming blaze.

"And you always used condoms?"

She nodded.

"I'm not gonna lie. The idea of being with you skin to skin makes me hard enough I could come just thinking about it." He squeezed her hand. "How do you feel about me getting tested? I'll show you I'm clean, and we'll get you a form of birth control you're comfortable with."

No condom. Nothing at all between them. She swallowed and tried to ignore the very vivid image her mind conjured up to go with the thought. As conversational topics went, this had to be the weirdest and most awkward ever, but it was also comforting. More evidence that Zeke was nothing like the men she'd slept with before. "I think I'd like that."

His eyelids lowered and a low rumble percolated up his throat. His hands cupped the space just above her bared knees and skimmed upward, fingers teasing just under the hem of her dress.

"Zeke?"

"Mmm-hmm."

"That day when we...when you..."

He opened his eyes and locked his gaze on hers. "When I got you off with my fingers?" His wicked grin made her squeeze her legs together tight. "Oh, yeah. I'll die remembering that day." His fingers inched a little higher. "What about it?"

"I liked the things you said. How you talked to me." She smoothed her fingers along the opening of his shirt, focusing on the warmth beneath. "It helped me not think of anything else. I couldn't worry. All I could do was listen to you and feel."

He pulled his hands from beneath her skirt, stood and palmed the back of her neck. "I like that. I like that a lot." He lowered his mouth to hers, not quite touching but skimming close enough her lips tingled with the need for contact. "You think you could give that to me, too? Let me hear what you're thinking when I touch you? When I kiss you?"

She gasped and his mouth closed over hers. God, she loved the way he kissed, powerful and yet languid as though he had all the time in the world to savor what sparked between them.

He pulled away and rested his forehead on hers. "Can you do that for me?"

Her hands fisted in the hair near his nape and the space around her heart grew weighted and tight. "I doubt it will come out as sexy as when you do it, but I'll try."

"That's all I need, *gatinha*." He pressed another, far more chaste kiss to her lips and backed away, lacing his fingers with hers. "Now, let's get this dinner over with so I can whisper dirty commentary in your ear and peel you out of that dress later."

Chapter Seventeen

Gabe braced both hands against the bathroom stall walls, closed her eyes, and tried to slow her breath. Lined up in front of the multi-sink vanity of the hotel's ballroom bathroom, a gaggle of women chattered about their dates, the food and what they had planned after they escaped the charity's boring event. Couldn't they just shut up and leave?

She rested her forehead against the door's cool metal. They had to finish soon. For crying out loud, she didn't know what she was doing with lipstick and even *she* could have touched hers up by now.

Five more agonizing minutes later, the clique shuffled out the door, their high heels clacking on the smooth, luxury-tile floor. The door whooshed shut, leaving blissful silence. Now all she had to do was make sure the anxiety attack and subsequent cold sweat that had driven her to the bathroom in the first place hadn't sent her mascara running down her face. Talk about your nightmare dressy debut. Everyone had been politely conversational and sweet on the surface, but they were nowhere near as comfortable to be around as Zeke's family. More like tiptoeing through a masquerade ball riddled with landmines. As soon as the acid churning in her stomach had collided with the not-so-enticing dinner, she'd bolted for the restrooms. While she hadn't actually puked, it had been a close call.

Hair fixed, face checked and a fresh stick of gum later, she teetered toward the door on newborn-deer-shaky legs.

Zeke leaned against the wall opposite the women's restroom door, his hands anchored in his slacks pockets and one ankle crossed over the other in a classic *GQ* model pose. He straightened the second she crossed the threshold. "Hey, *gatinha*." He skimmed his knuckles along her cheek. "You okay?"

"Better now." Embarrassed as hell at the near sprint she'd made through the big room with its round tables and crisp white linens. "You didn't have to come check on me."

His soft, concerned expression sharpened in an instant. "You're kidding me, right? You think I'd chill at the table and not be here if you needed me?"

Well, when he put it that way… "Yeah, sorry. I didn't mean to imply…" Shit, she just really needed to unplug for about thirty years and give her head a break. "I'm not thinking too good."

He pulled her tight against him, wrapped her up and kissed her forehead. "You seemed to do okay at the drive-in. Any idea what triggered you?"

For a few seconds, she simply let his warm and summery scent settle against her senses. Once her heart settled into a decent rhythm, she lifted her head and met his steady gaze. "Not sure this will make sense, but there's a big difference between your family and the people here."

Tucking her hair behind her ear, he grinned in a way that said he absolutely understood. "Yeah, *gatinha*. That makes perfect sense." He pulled in a slow breath and stepped away, keeping one hand pressed at the small of her back. "Let's go home."

She dug in her heels. "No. I'm good." She motioned to the main room. "This is your thing. It's important. I can do this. I promise, I'm—"

"Gabrielle." Low, but definitely stern and brooking no argument. "First, I don't give a damn about this event. I've given my face time and that's enough. Second, that chicken was closer to a dog's squeaky toy than a suitable meal. Third, and most important—" he gripped her chin and held it firm "—I would never force my woman to sit through an event if I knew it hurt her."

Oh. My. God.

My woman.

The overall sentiment of him not wanting to cause her discomfort probably should have been the main driver in the major loopty-loop going on in her stomach, but her head couldn't quite make it past his possessive claim. In that second, she'd have committed murder for him if he asked it, so snagging a free hall pass out of social hell was a no brainer. "Okay."

He smiled and tapped the tip of her nose. "Okay."

The wait at the valet line was nonexistent. By the time her nerves had settled and her brain had come around to the idea it could stand down from its full-scale panic, Zeke had the Camaro blazing down Highway 75 toward Rockwall.

"I don't get it." Her wayward thought slipped out unchecked, which just proved how whacked her internal processing was.

"Don't get what?"

She smoothed her dress's soft fabric along one thigh. He'd asked her to be open. To share her thoughts. If she couldn't touch on this one, she'd never do well with anything as intimate as sex. "Why me? I mean, you couldn't put two more different people together. You're used to loads of money, and I live paycheck to paycheck. You don't sit still, and I have a hard time getting out of second gear for anything."

"Oh, I'll get you out of second gear." Zeke grinned and checked his rearview mirror. "And you can't base compatibility on money. I might have money now, but my family was dirt poor growing up. The only reason I have what I do today is because of the profession I chose and my investments with the brotherhood."

"But that doesn't cover how different we are in our lives. I just don't get it. Why would a guy who lives life on the edge want to be with a woman who's happy sitting for hours on the back porch?"

"I've been able to sit still with you."

"But why? For how long?"

He stared out over the road in front of them and tapped his thumb atop the gearshift. "Let me ask you a question. When you're with me, are you uncomfortable?"

"No."

"You enjoy the time we spend together?"

"Um…" Surely this was a trick question. "Yes."

"Then maybe it's not a question of how different we are. Maybe I've been in a hurry my whole life to experience all the things I've done and seen for a reason."

"What reason?"

His head turned toward hers. "To share them with you."

She couldn't move. Couldn't breathe. Hell, lightning could've struck dead center of the car and it wouldn't have generated so much as a blink. Everything she'd been through, every tear and every fear, she'd walk through again to be in this moment. "Zeke?"

"Yeah."

The bridge of her nose stung and tears threatened behind her eyes. "I'm not stupid. I know there's no guarantee what will happen with us, and I know if it doesn't work out, it will hurt. Bad." She swallowed, just barely biting back a quaver in her throat. "But you make the risk worth it."

He clenched the gearshift hard and his eyes widened. Any trace of the casual man who'd strolled beside her at dinner and introduced her as though she were the finest treasure was gone, replaced with primal, possessive predator. In that moment, if the road hadn't demanded his attention, she had no doubt he'd have forgone any pretense of foreplay and physically claimed her in any and every way he could. Instead, he pulled in a long, sexy inhalation, reached across the console, and coiled his fingers around her wrist. His thumb stroked along her pulse point. Back and forth. Light, but sparking with intent. Only when they reached the entrance to her subdivision did he release the contact, navigating the short drive to her house far faster than any of her neighbors would care for. He'd barely killed the engine before he was out of the car and rounding the tail end of it for her.

This was it. The moment she'd craved and fantasized about ever since that first kiss and yet, now that it was here, she wasn't altogether sure she could handle it. The way he'd touched her, the way he'd kissed her, showed not just confidence, but loads of experience. All she could claim on her résumé was her quick, fumbling loss of virginity with Jimmy and a lackluster tumble with a guy from junior college.

Her door swung open and the cool night air swept across her bared shoulders and legs. Zeke held out his hand.

For the longest time, all she could do was stare at

it, paralyzed by the shift placing her hand in his would create.

"Take my hand, *gatinha*." So confident. Demanding and yet thick with understanding and support, as if he knew how hard her fears rioted inside her and refused to let them win.

She could do this. If he could fight for her, be patient and sensitive with her anxiety, then she could fight, too. She twisted in her seat and placed her hand in his, pushing upright on wobbly legs.

Their footsteps clipped against the sidewalk, swallowed almost instantly by the night's weighted, damp air. He slipped the keys from between her fingers, unlocked the door and drew her across the threshold. The dead bolt snicked shut behind her and sent chills scampering down her spine.

Striding past her toward the kitchen, he shrugged his suit jacket off his muscled shoulders and hung it on the back of one of the dinette's chairs. He crooked his fingers and opened his hand, palm up. "Give me your purse."

Easy for him to say. Or maybe he knew exactly how taxing such a request would be, given the white-knuckled grip she had on the tiny black clutch. She crept closer, goose bumps rippling along her skin as she held it out. "You're not mad, are you?"

"No, not mad." With one hand, he pried the purse free and set it on the tabletop. The other manacled her wrist as he had for most of the drive home and lifted her palm to his mouth. Pressing a kiss to the center, he closed his eyes and inhaled deep.

God, she loved it when he did that. It was such a simple thing, a deep, almost preparatory breath, but every time he did it her body sung with anticipation. "Then why aren't you talking?"

"Because what you said meant something to me. I'd rather show you my gratitude than speak it." Lowering her hand, he turned and led her down the dark hallway to her room, the light from her small bedside lamp casting a soft glow through the open doorway. He closed the door behind them and steered her to the foot of the bed. "Sit."

The command should have rankled. Heck, from anyone else it probably would have, but the power behind it was a thrill in and of itself, the intensity of his emotions vibrating against her skin.

He toed off his shoes, yanked off his socks, then started unbuttoning his cuffs. What other men might have made look awkward, Zeke transformed to seduction. Every second his eyes stayed on hers, purposeful and potent.

And you're just sitting here like a bump on a log.

Surely she could do the same for him. The least she could do was try. She slid one hand down her thigh, the soft fabric of her dress tickling her palm as she aimed for one of her pumps.

"No."

She froze at Zeke's low, but seriously firm order. "But you're—"

"I'll tend to you." He shrugged off his shirt, and her breath caught in her throat. At least once a night over the past week she'd savored his powerful shoulders and muscled torso, exploring every hard ridge and plane with avid, searching fingers, but usually over his shirts or scrubs. She'd definitely not garnered the same full-on view she'd had the day at Trevor's bunkhouse. Heck, she'd halfway talked herself into believing she'd imagined how good he looked, but nope—it was real.

He prowled to the nightstand, the same dog tags he'd worn on their first date dangling between his pecs. Turning away from her, he pulled something out of his pocket and laid it beside the lamp.

No, not something. *Somethings.* As in at least three condoms. Maybe more. Her heart kicked into a jog, and she licked her suddenly very dry lips.

Zeke stalked back to the end of the bed and crouched in front of her, his knees splayed on either side of her legs. He smoothed his hands just above her knees and gently squeezed. "Straight talk, Gabrielle. No pressure. No expectations. Do you want this?"

Just the image of his long, tapered fingers against her flesh catapulted her thoughts to the way they'd felt stroking between her legs. How strong and firm they were when they'd pushed inside her. A shudder rattled through her, and she barely bit back a moan. She squeezed her knees together instead and whispered, "Yes."

His thumbs drew lazy, taunting circles on the inside of her thighs and her legs trembled. "You going to tell me why you're so nervous?"

Why was he talking? She couldn't think when he touched her like that. Couldn't breathe.

"Tell me. Help me make this good for you."

She covered one of his hands with hers, instinctively seeking the connection, the support she knew she'd find. "I'm afraid."

"Of?"

"Doing it wrong," she blurted. "The last few times…" God, he had to think she was an idiot. Yet his expression was steady. No smiles, just his patient, intense gaze locked on hers while his fingertips painted wicked designs along her inner and outer thighs. "The last few times things didn't go so well. At least not after."

The soft, gliding touches against her skin morphed to something stronger, a hint of anger to match the fire burning behind his gaze bound behind an iron will. He traced her jawline. "Then I think we need to turn that mind of yours off long enough to re-write that ending."

God, yes. She'd give anything to erase those horrid memories with this one. Even if nothing happened beyond a kiss, it would be enough.

Ghosting his palms down the backs of her calves, he pulled off her pumps, keeping his gaze on hers like he had since they walked through the front door. As if, in doing so, he left himself open and vulnerable. Giving her not just his touch, but everything he felt inside, as well.

His thumbs worked in soft circles along her arches, up to her ankles, then up the inside of her legs. He'd barely skimmed beneath the hem of her dress when he slowly stood and pulled her to her feet. He turned her to face the bed, moved her hair to one side, and tugged her zipper down. Instead of sliding the dress off her shoulders, he trailed his fingers down her spine. "Trade me places, sweetheart."

Before her mind could translate the directive, he'd pivoted them both so he sat on the bed, her standing between his thighs with her back to the dresser and mirror behind her. He slid his hands up her arms and goose bumps lifted in their wake. His eyes locked with hers. "I've wanted to peel this dress off you since I walked in tonight."

He released her straps and let them fall over her shoulders. Bit by bit, the fabric rasped against her heightened skin, cool air dancing across each exposed inch until the fabric pooled at her feet. Only then did he lower his gaze, leisurely mapping the flesh he'd uncovered while his palms scorched a claiming brand at her hips. His lips parted on a slow, sexy sigh. *"Perfeição."* He smoothed his rough fingertips toward her abdomen and lifted his gaze to hers. "Pure, sweet perfection."

She wanted to believe him. Wanted it more than anything. Had even felt girly in her dress and heels, but underneath it all she was just Gabe. A mechanic with a closet full of jeans and T-shirts. "I'll never be like those other women tonight. Not really."

"I don't want those women." His gaze flicked to something behind her and he stood, turning her and holding her in place with hands at both shoulders. "I want this one."

Her heart jolted at the reflection in the mirror. Her pale torso on the backdrop of his muscled and tanned one. The strength behind his hand splayed across her soft belly. Her wide and unknowing eyes contrasted with the burning predator's gaze behind her. An artist's dream, the lighting in the room making the image that much more intense by the nearly black-and-white coloring.

"Look. See what I see." He skimmed the thin black lace along the bottom line of her bra. "You buy these while you were out today?"

She nodded. Or at least she thought she did. Every shred of her attention, thoughts and sensory, were lasered on his touch. Every nerve ending perfectly poised and waiting for where he led her next.

"Very sexy." He swept her hair off her neck, skimmed his lips up the exposed column to the back of her ear, and growled, "But you make me hard with just the simple white ones."

A delicious quiver fired at her core even as she bit back a moan. "I was kind of hoping you hadn't noticed those."

"I haven't missed anything where you're concerned. Especially when my hands were on you and your back was arched and begging for more." He fingered the latch between her breasts. "I like this. Easy access. Convenient for me. And you." He eased his hands away and rested them on her shoulders, holding her stare. "Take it off for me."

Holy shit, she was in trouble. So far over her head, she couldn't swim to the surface in time to survive even if she wanted to. The slow, smoldering embers he'd nursed whipped to a flash fire and her lungs gasped for air. Her shoulders pressed backward, breasts aching for release and more of his touch.

"Come on, *gatinha*. Peel the bra away and show me."

Her heart kicked an unrelenting beat and her blood practically hummed from its high-speed chase through her veins. Pink fanned across her cheeks and collarbone, and her palms grew damp. He'd already seen her once. Technically, it wasn't a big thing. Shouldn't be anyway. Just a repeat performance. Totally normal.

She fingered the front latch, her breasts tightening to the point they ached. The snick of its release ricocheted loud as a bullet in her head and she flinched.

"That's it," he whispered, his wolfish gaze trained on their reflection while he nipped and kissed a devious path around the shell of her ear.

She peeled the lace free, the delicate fabric slicking across her taut nipples and drawing a broken moan up her throat.

Zeke growled and caught one strap at her elbow. He flicked the garment to the ground and cupped each of her breasts as though he couldn't contain himself any longer. "Sweet, pretty nipples." He toyed with the tips, and her whole body reverberated in response. "Did you like my mouth on them?"

Oh, yes. And now she had a rock-solid visual to go

with the sensation. Her own personal erotic image seared into her brain.

He pinched and rolled the tight peaks between his fingers and thumbs. "Did you replay the way I sucked on them after I was gone? At night when you were alone?"

A tiny whimper slipped out and her eyelids grew so heavy she could barely keep them open. She covered his hands, urging him for more and grinding her ass against his hard shaft.

"I thought about it," he said. "The way your nipples felt in my mouth. The way you fisted my hair and rode my fingers." He trailed one hand straight down her belly and slipped his fingers beneath the waistband of her panties. "Gonna get my mouth somewhere else tonight, Gabrielle."

Oh. My. God.

Her brain offered up a graphic to go with his dirty promise and her sex clenched, her eyes relenting to the sexual weight as her hips flexed on instinct. Lace rasped past her hips and thighs then whispered to her ankles. His hands skimmed butterfly soft along the curve of her hips then slid inward, gently pressing the insides of her thighs. "Feet apart. Give your man room to work."

Her eyes snapped open, her feet eagerly obeying without even the slightest input from her conscience.

He trailed his fingertips through the neatly trimmed curls atop her mound and licked his lower lip. "You see?"

Oh, she saw all right, and could barely breathe around all the sensory input. *Cosmo* must really know their stuff when it came to feminine landscaping because she'd never seen a man so focused. So fixated and hungry. As lost in the moment as her.

His fingers dipped lower, slicking through her folds. He rolled his hips against hers and groaned, pressing the heel of his hand against her clit. "Fuck, so wet and ready for me."

Unlike the first time, he built a fast and furious pace, demanding her response with each back-and-forth glide, yet never pressing inside. His lips, teeth and tongue laid siege to her shoulders, neck and the sweet spot behind her ear. His breath fanned hot against her skin while his wicked fingers took her higher and higher.

God, she wanted more. Needed it. The fullness of him inside her. The weight of his body and the flex of his muscles. She gripped his forearms, digging her nails into the powerful sinew even as her hips followed the rhythm he demanded. "Zeke."

"Yeah, baby?"

Holy smokes, his voice. Gritty and so powerful it ricochet through every nerve ending. "I need more."

"Oh, yeah." His eyes opened and a low grumble vibrated against her back. "You definitely need more."

A second later, his lips were on hers, the mix of his heated torso and cold metal dog tags pressed against her. It was wild. Furious and unscripted. A duel of impatient, demanding caresses and ravenous kisses. He cupped her ass and lifted, urging her legs around his waist as he laid them both on the bed.

His lips blazed a path between her breasts, hands plumping her aching breasts and fingers relentlessly working her tight nipples. When he didn't sidetrack and take one of the aching tips in his mouth, her mind clued into his intended destination and squeezed his shoulder. "Zeke."

He kept going, licking and sucking her sensitized skin and sliding his hands under her ass. "Yeah?"

Shit. Shit. Shit. She wasn't ready for this. Yes, she

wanted it, but God what if she did something wrong? Or didn't do something she should?

Just say something.

"I'm scared."

He stopped and lifted his head. His lips were as kiss-swollen as hers felt and his breath fanned fast and warm against her stomach. "Scared of what?"

Honesty. He said that was what he wanted. To know what she needed. She swallowed and squeezed his shoulders. "I've never... What you were going to do... I haven't done that."

His lips curved in a wicked, stomach-flipping grin, and he pressed a sweet kiss just below her belly button. "Well, that's a delightful development." He licked his lower lip and scooted farther down on the bed. "There's really nothing to it." Wedging his shoulders between her thighs, he pressed upward so her legs draped over his shoulders and pressed a soft, lingering kiss atop her mound. "You just lay back, turn that busy mind of yours off and let me work your pussy 'til you come."

His tongue connected with her clit and her hips flexed on reflex.

Zeke splayed his hand over her womb and held her steady. "See?" He did it again and a high-octane jolt fired out in all directions. "Just like that. Only better and for a whole lot longer."

Better. Definitely better. And it wasn't just his tongue, it was his mouth, too. God, the slick heat of his lips and the way he devoured her. Why the hell had she never expected this from a man? Demanded it? For crying out loud, she was twenty-four years old and had missed *this*? It was pure sin. Decadent and delicious.

She found his rhythm, holding him to her with fists in his hair and surrendering to the dark sensation. A slow stretch filled her entrance, two fingers pressing deep. Her thighs tensed, release so close she wanted to scream, but didn't dare for fear of ruining the moment. His lips wrapped around her clit, he sucked and—

Boom.

Her core clenched his fingers, the pure intensity of the orgasm reverberating all the way to her toes. Over and over again, her sex pulsed around his fingers while he feasted. Talk about intimate. It was like they didn't have any walls left between them. Like he'd torn them down and left her bare in the most delectable way possible.

He nipped and teased the inside of each thigh, the scruff on his jawline tickling as he did so. The Portuguese he murmured against her skin she couldn't ever hope to understand, but the tenderness behind the words rocked her to the core. So sexy, and yet sweet.

She combed her fingers through his hair, watching him leisurely work his way up her body. "You wanted me to tell you what I like?"

He gently scraped his teeth along the underside of one breast. "Always."

"I liked that a lot."

Propping himself up on one forearm, he grinned down at her and slicked his fingers through her swollen folds. "That's good, *gatinha.* 'Cause I liked it too and you're gonna get it a lot." He deepened his stroke and circled her clit with his thumb.

She gasped and her hips jerked on reflex. "What are you doing?"

Leaning down, he ghosted a kiss across her mouth. The remnants of her release lingered on his lips and daaamn if that didn't feel naughty. "Takin' you back up."

"You're what?" She gripped the back of his head, trying to pull him closer for more of his addictive kiss.

He fought the tug, smiled against her lips, and deepened his strokes. "Next time you come, I'm going to be inside you."

"But I already—"

"Yeah, and you're gonna do it again." He eased back enough to study his fingers working between her legs, groaned and released her, scrambling off the bed. He undid the fastenings on his pants in quick, jerking motions and shoved them and his briefs straight to the floor.

Whoa.

Zeke Dugan was not limited to just an upper-body awesomeness. He was a full-body work of wonder. Muscles everywhere, not bulky and not lean, but somewhere in between and so perfectly defined she couldn't wait to explore.

"Damn, Gabrielle. You keep looking at me like that, I won't make it five strokes." He snatched a condom off the nightstand and crawled toward her, kneeling between her thighs and draping her legs over his thighs. He tore the package open.

She skated her finger along his bunched quads, gaze locked on his thick erection and the prominent veins running root to tip. "But I haven't gotten to touch you yet."

He leaned over her, forearms anchored on either side of her head and his dog tags resting between her breasts. He studied them a moment, a thought or emotion moving behind his eyes she couldn't quite identify. Closing his eyes, he skimmed his knuckles along her sternum and down between her legs. "Put your hands on me. Feel all you want. Just please, God, say you can do it with my cock inside you."

She could work with that. Totally a win-win if it meant feeling his body next to hers. "Yes." She wrapped her legs around his waist and undulated up along the side of his shaft. "Definitely a yes."

A low, broken grumble crawled up his throat, and he hung his head. "Jesus, I'm not even inside you yet and I want to come." Grasping himself by the root, he slicked his cockhead through her wetness and lined himself up. His gaze locked onto hers, a lightning-bolt potency behind it that shook her to her core. "Feel me, Gabrielle."

Oh, God. How could she *not*? He was every dirty fantasy and ideal hero wrapped into one. A feral protector, poised above her and ready to stake his claim. She gripped the back of his neck with one hand and splayed the other across his chiseled abs.

He pressed deeper, stretching and filling her with such slow purpose it rippled to the top of her head. Pleasure and pain. The purest intimacy and darkest sin.

She wrapped her arms around him, luxuriating in the way his muscles bunched beneath her palms and the fine sheen of sweat that coated his skin. Only when he was seated fully inside her did he draw his hips back, the flared head of his cock rasping perfectly within her sex.

"Zeke." She smoothed her hands across his flanks and scraped her nails across his taut skin, rolling her hips in encouragement. "More."

"Hell yes, more." He drove himself forward, still nowhere near unleashing the power burning off him, but filling her completely. Then again. And again. Slow out and fast in, he worked himself inside her, his gaze roving as reverently as his touch across her breasts, her hips, and where they joined.

Tension built low in her belly, slower to grow than her first release but packed with the promise of so much more and hovering just out of reach. And oh, how she wanted it. The clench of her sex around his cock. The toe-tingling push and pull of his shaft against her sensitized walls. She dug her heels into his ass and fisted her hands in his hair. "More. Harder."

A low, satisfied chuckle rattled from his chest. "Fuck, knew you'd be wild." He shifted back to his knees, gripping her hips as he moved and taking her with him so he towered above her. A conqueror taking what he wanted without the least hesitation. He thrust against her, the deepened angle driving the tip of his cock against the perfect spot inside her and slapping his tight sac against her ass.

"Look at that pretty clit. Swollen and ready to send you off." His voice dropped to a low grumble, the foreign words he used none she'd ever heard before but dirty enough they'd likely singe her cheeks if she went on tone alone. He dipped one thumb between her legs before she could ask, sliding beside where his iron length pistoned in and out of her and slicked her wetness up to the tight nub. "Give it to me, *gatinha*."

Yes. God, yes. Just like that. Her thighs jerked and squeezed his hips.

He circled her once, twice, punctuating each touch with his pounding thrusts. "Come on my cock and take me with you."

He pinched her aching clit between his slick fingers and her world exploded.

Perfect. His hard to her soft. His strength to her give. His claim to her surrender.

His shout rang out above her and his hips slammed against hers, his unyielding length jerking inside her. *This* was what all the fuss was about. The connection. The sensations and the gut-clenching emotions. With each languid glide in and out he bound her, wrapped her heart and thoughts in a gossamer cocoon. Sheltered her from the raw vulnerability raging between them.

His lips skimmed her cheeks, her eyes, her lips, more of his lilting Portuguese falling over her like early-morning mist.

She wrapped her arms around him, combing her fingers through his well-mussed hair with one hand while the other explored the sweat-slick skin along his back. If she could lock herself in one moment of time, this would be it. The serenity of it. Untouched by reality or the fears she'd battled throughout her life.

"I like you like this." He lifted his head enough to make eye contact. The tension and focus he usually carried was gone, replaced with the same leisurely peace slipping through her muscles. He smoothed his knuckles along one cheek. "Soft and purring after you've sunk your nails in deep."

Her eyes popped wide. "I didn't."

"You did." He grinned and nipped her lower lip. "And don't even think about keeping them from me next time because I liked it."

Before she could argue, he shifted slightly and slipped his hand between them. "I need to deal with this condom. You stay put, yeah?"

She nodded and he slipped free, drawing a disappointing whimper past her lips.

"I know, baby," he whispered against her mouth, and then rolled from the bed and padded to the bathroom, giving her another sigh-inducing view.

God, what a night. What a life-altering, heart-searing night. After what he'd given her, she might as well claim tonight as her first time with a man, because the other two experiences weren't even close. A paint-by-numbers attempt with all the wrong brushes and colors compared to a master artist's crowning work.

Definitely worth the risk. No matter what happened tomorrow, even in the next second, she wouldn't change a thing.

He ambled back to the bedside, a lazy panther grace behind each step. He smoothed her hair off her cheek. "You need anything? Water?"

You.

She shook her head instead, the feelings dammed up at the base of her throat too overwhelming to speak without unleashing a torrent of tears.

For the longest time, he just stood there, studying her face. He flicked off the lamp and darkness blanketed the room. The bed dipped beside her, his summer-warm scent engulfing her a second before he spooned against her and banded his arm around her waist. "You okay, *gatinha*?"

Okay didn't cover it. Didn't even begin to scratch the surface of everything swirling in her heart. She covered the possessive hand he'd splayed above her belly and nestled in deeper against his heat. "I'm perfect."

Chapter Eighteen

Zeke shifted beneath the covers, the scent of something sharp and unpleasant dragging him from sleep. Damn, but he didn't want to move. Didn't want to think. Gabe felt too good next to him. All warm, soft and sweet.

But the scent was off.

His eyes popped wide and his muscles tensed. That was smoke. A lot of it. He rolled to his back and glanced toward the windows facing the front yard. A soft, golden glow flickered behind the blinds, wavering and at the wrong angle to be a street light.

He tossed aside the covers and rolled to his feet. Prying open the blinds, he peeked outside. "Shit." He clicked the lamp on and snatched his pants off the floor. "Gabe, get up and dial 911."

She pushed herself up on her elbows, her gaze unfocused and heavy-lidded. "What?"

"I need you to dial 911, sweetheart. Your neighbor's house is on fire."

That got her attention. She scrambled to the window, not the least bit concerned, or not yet aware, she didn't have a scrap on. "Mrs. Wallaby's?"

"No, the other one."

She gasped as soon as she looked outside. "Oh, my

God. That's Mr. Yates's house." She shot across the room and grabbed her robe off the back of her closet door.

Zeke wrestled into his shirt and jammed his feet into his loafers, not bothering with socks. "When's the last time you saw him?"

"Yesterday afternoon when I got home from shopping."

"Which side of the house are the bedrooms?"

"The end closest to our house." She hurried out to her purse on the kitchen table and dug out her phone.

Zeke strode toward the front door. "As soon as you get the fire trucks on the way, call Danny and let him know what's up. Tell him to call Beckett."

"Wait! Where are you going?"

"I'm going to see if he's in there. You call 911."

"But you'll—"

"Gabe, make the call. I'll be fine." He ducked out the front door before she could argue and jogged across the dew-slick yard. If the bedrooms were closest to Gabe's house then the fire had clearly started in the kitchen, because the whole far end and a good chunk of the center was engulfed in roaring flames. Another five or ten minutes and he wouldn't be getting anyone out of there.

Farther down the street, a few slow moving shadows worked their way down the lamp-lit sidewalks, but no one quick or nimble enough to help him scout the home's interior. The front door was locked. Fire or not, it was solid enough it wouldn't budge with nothing but his shoulder for leverage. He ran around the back of the house, the patio with its sliding glass door thankfully a good distance from the fast-moving flames. Not expecting much in the way of luck, he tugged on the handle.

Low and behold, the damn thing slid open easy as pie, thick, choking smoke rolling out into the already tainted night. He covered his mouth with his arm. "Mr. Yates?" He ducked low and crept along the edges of the murky living room to the hallway on his left. "Hello?"

Nothing. Not a single sound save the roiling flames licking their way closer and closer. Both bedrooms were empty, though one was unmade, the covers angled back as though someone had left in a hurry.

Shit, that meant another trip back toward the front. His eyes burned and his lungs ached with the weight of so much smoke. Another few minutes and he wouldn't have any choice but to bail, but damned if he wanted to let Gabe down. Not in this. Her neighbors were everything to her. As much of a family as his brothers were to him.

He inched toward the middle of the living room. "Mr. Yates?"

There. A faint groan followed by a weak cough.

Zeke plowed ahead, heat blasting on all sides and sharp sparks snapping as the fire consumed everything in its path. The smoke shifted, exposing pajama-clad legs and bare feet. Sucking in the deepest breath he could, he crouched, hefted Gabe's neighbors in his arms and hauled ass for the back door.

The fresh air slapped his sweat-coated cheeks and long, racking coughs seized his chest. He kept moving, distancing himself from the inferno and rounding toward the cul-de-sac and the rapidly growing crowd. Sirens sounded in the distance, but all Zeke could focus on was drawing a steady, clean breath and finding a decent place to lay Gabe's neighbor out.

"Zeke!" Gabe hurried into his blurry vision. She'd replaced the robe with loose gray sweats, and her eyes were wide with panic. "Is he okay? Are you?"

"Fine." His voice sounded like hell, not exactly the confident tone he'd hoped for, but at least he was breathing. If he was lucky, Mr. Yates would be, too. He laid the man down near the sidewalk. His respirations were faint and his pulse weak, but there nonetheless. So long as he could get some oxygen in the man soon, he'd be over the biggest hurdle. "He have any medical conditions?"

Gabe kneeled next to her neighbor, holding tight to his hand and smoothing the hair off his head. "Not that I know of. He's retired, but he's really healthy. Does his own yard work and walks all the time."

A definite bonus considering the overtime his lungs were doing.

"Did you see what caused it?" she said.

"Had to be the kitchen. That's where it was centered when I first woke up and saw the flames."

"That can't be it. He doesn't cook. Hasn't since his wife died. He either heats what I give him in the microwave, or has food delivered."

The firetrucks squealed to a stop not twenty feet away, the ambulance right behind it.

Zeke stood and waved the paramedics over. "He needs oxygen."

The men complied, hurrying their direction laden with a portable tank and duffels full of first aid gear.

Zeke sank to his ass, knees bent and elbows resting on top.

"You sure you're okay?" Gabe dropped beside him, her neighbor forgotten in favor of wiping the sweat and grime off his face.

"Yeah." He covered her hand with his and sucked in another breath. "Better once I get this shit cleared out of my lungs."

On cue, one of the medics knelt beside him and held out a mask. "How long were you in for?"

"A few minutes. Maybe five. Nothing long enough

for serious damage." Zeke took the mask, pride taking a backseat to making sure he was strong enough to look out for Gabe. One inhalation after another, he focused on the unruly blaze. The building was a complete loss, a fact evidenced by how the firemen focused more on containment than actually dousing the fire.

That can't be it. He doesn't cook.

That weird, sixth-sense vibe resonated out in all directions. If Mr. Yates didn't cook, then what else would have started the fire? And why the hell hadn't his back door been locked?

"Man, what the hell happened?" Danny strode up beside him, his gaze locked on the blaze.

Beckett ambled their direction, his attention far less invested on the fire and more focused on the thickening crowd.

Zeke laid the mask aside and stood as Beckett ambled up beside him.

"For a tiny neighborhood, this place gets a lot of nasty action," Beck said low beside him.

"No shit," Zeke answered back in kind. He glanced at Gabe beside him. Her fingers were laced tight with his, but her worried gaze was locked on Mr. Yates. He pried his hand free and nudged her toward the slowly rousing man. "Go talk to him."

"But you're—"

"I'm fine. Sweaty and dirty, but fine. Go talk to him. You might want to chat with the neighbors lined up over there too and let them know everything's okay."

Danny tore his stymied stare away from the blaze and the firemen scrambling around it. "I'll cover the neighbors. Gabe, you stay with Mr. Yates."

The two had barely cleared hearing distance before

Beckett jumped in. "You don't think this was an ordinary fire, do you?"

"Too coincidental," Zeke said. "Gabe says the owner never cooks, but it had to have started in the kitchen."

"Could've been a one-time thing. Hungry people do desperate shit. Could have been wiring, too."

"Maybe. But you wouldn't believe how often Gabe gets hit up by Realtors claiming they've got high-scale buyers looking for lake property. Remember those two houses down the street that already sold? If the people were so hot to use the land, then why are they still empty? Plus, a couple down the street who had no intention of selling are headed to a retirement community after they got an offer they couldn't pass up. You already know about the break-in with her other neighbor. Now a fire?"

Beck crossed his arms and scanned the elderly crowd. "What are you thinking?"

"Beats the shit out of me, but something's not right, and my woman lives here."

Beckett arched an eyebrow. "Must be getting serious if you're using that kind of language. You want me and Knox to dive in?"

Damn. He hadn't even been cognizant of his phrasing, not that he had a problem with it. If anything, it felt right. Scary as hell, but definitely on target. "Yeah, I think that's smart."

Beck hesitated a beat, rubbing his hand across his mouth as though he couldn't quite bear to utter what came next. "You know if we start spending brotherhood resources on this, the rest of the guys are gonna want to know what you're up to. You ready for that?"

Gabe's sweet, soft voice as she talked to her neighbor lilted behind him. He twisted in time to catch her squeezing Mr. Yates's frail hand and laying a tender kiss to the top of it.

Three weeks. Three weeks of her growing and facing her worst fears, some of them just to be with him.

You make the risk worth it.

The sweetest words anyone had ever shared with him. And man, did he understand the sentiment. For her, he'd do just about anything. "Yeah, I'm ready."

Chapter Nineteen

Gabe had pulled some long nights, but never like this one. Even with her eyelids sagging like concrete curtains, she wasn't altogether sure she could sleep. In her whole life, she'd probably only slept away from home five times, let alone at some place as swank as Zeke's town house, but Zeke had refused to let her stay home. *Too much smoke*, he'd said.

Located on the edge of Dallas's trendy Uptown area, Zeke could easily make it from his house to Baylor's Level One trauma center in under ten minutes. Everything in this part of town reeked of new. All shiny and perfect.

The shower in the attached, oversize bathroom shut off and Gabe snuggled deeper under the soft gray sheets. Probably something like seven-thousand thread count, knowing how high-class everything else was in his place. How he'd made himself so comfortable in her house was nothing short of a miracle. Where her place was all earth and softer jewel tones, his had a definite black, gray and red theme throughout. A manly, contemporary feel.

Zeke padded out of the bathroom, one towel slung low over his sexy hips and another draped around his neck while he dried his hair with the ends. He headed for the ebony dresser across the room with its circular mirror hung above it. "I thought you'd be asleep already."

She shook her head. "A little too wound up." Not a thing marked the top of the dresser. No pictures. No knickknacks. Not even a speck of dust. "How long have you lived here?"

Zeke paused, glanced over one shoulder at her, then went back to rummaging through the middle drawer. "A couple of years, I guess. Maybe three." He pulled a folded pair of black pajama bottoms free, shook them loose and stepped into them. "Hey, I was thinking maybe after we catch some sleep, I'd take you out so you can pick up that new computer you've been wanting. Heck, Knox might be available if you want the extra input."

"Nah, I'm not in a hurry." And she wouldn't be for at least three or four more paychecks.

"You were a few weeks ago. You said you'd planned to do it the weekend you got hurt."

Gabe fiddled with the sheets, avoiding eye contact.

"Gabe?"

She let out a sigh, hating the truth, especially with so much wealth prominently displayed around her. The last thing she needed was another demonstration on how ill-suited she was for him. Still, he'd asked for honesty, and last night had been the most spectacular of her life. Largely due to both of them being 100 percent candid. "I can't go yet. I need to save up again. I used some of it for other stuff."

Zeke ambled to his side of the bed, picked up his phone and started punching buttons. "You having to work the desk at the garage is docking your pay that much?"

"That's some of it." Honesty, she'd give him, but that didn't include an itemized list. "I'll make it back. Then I'll go shopping with Knox."

He set his phone aside and narrowed his eyes. "You spent it on the clothes, didn't you?"

Ugh. Skirting topics was so much easier with Danny. Leave it to Mr. Trauma Doc to zero in on the details at Mach ten. She shrugged. "It was worth it. I liked the way you looked at me."

Dragging back the covers, he crawled across the bed and stretched out next to her. "Next time you don't have something you need, you tell me."

"I don't need you to take care of me. I can handle stuff on my own."

"I know that," he said. "But it would make me feel a whole lot better if you'd let me share the load." He rolled so he gave her just a hint of his weight and rubbed his nose alongside hers, his perfect lips just inches from hers and his voice shiver-inducing deep. "Besides, I've got more than enough cash to spoil you a little. What's the point in a man making bank if he can't play sugar daddy now and again?"

His kiss unwound all her anxious, negative thoughts like none of her pep talks could. Sweet and yet still sexy. Unhurried and indulgent as though they'd been lovers for years instead of hours.

The crisp, shrill ring of his phone on the nightstand jolted her from the relaxed cocoon he'd created.

He groaned and rested his forehead against hers. "You gotta be kidding me." Rolling to his back, he snatched the device off the nightstand and swiped the answer button. "Yeah?"

Whoever was on the other end of the line didn't talk loud enough to reach Gabe's ears, but whatever they said zapped Zeke's focus to a laser point. "Where was he shot?"

No wonder he'd gone superalert. Gabe propped herself up on one elbow.

"How long ago?" he said, sitting up on the side of the bed. He stood and zeroed in on Gabe, tilting the phone away from his mouth. "Give me a minute. I gotta get some answers on this." He strode from the room, barking more questions in a clipped, authoritative tone he'd never used around her before, not even the night she'd been injured. While she was glad it wasn't aimed at her, it was crazy sexy in a supersmart, hot-doc kind of way. McDreamy didn't have shit on her man.

Her man.

God, she loved that phrase. Just the idea of it put her in a twirly, dance-around-the-room, Cinderella kind of mood.

A ping sounded from her canvas hobo bag on the floor.

Weird. The only person who ever called or texted her was Danny. Or nowadays, Zeke, and she'd never received any calls or texts at five o'clock in the morning. She dug to the bottom of her bag and grinned at the screen.

April: Hey, girl! You didn't call! How'd the date go? You rock the dress?

How cool was that? She had a man *and* a friend. Best day/night *ever*. She typed out a quick response, her heart humming about as fast as her thumbs worked the keyboard.

You're up early. LBD was perfect! Made for a long night, though. Maybe grab a coffee later today and I'll share the details?

The answer came a whopping fifteen seconds later.

April: Up for the gym. Gotta work my fat ass into bathing suit shape. Work until five tonight. Can meet after or tomorrow. Let me know when. PS: Late nights are the best kind. ☺

Actually, with the night they'd had, after five was probably a good idea. Then again, Zeke had mentioned going shopping for a computer. Was that off the table now? Yeah, she'd told him she wanted to take care of it herself, but he also had a way of getting what he wanted once he'd made up his mind. After last night, passing up any available time with Zeke seemed criminal, even if it was only window shopping.

She crawled out of bed and strolled toward his voice in the living room.

Zeke's back was to her, one hand holding the phone to his ear and the other propped on his hip. "You sure you're willing to put us out there for a guy like that? Moreno's about as trustworthy as a hungry snake. Need for a truce or not, this is my license we're talking about."

Moreno. She'd heard that name before, though she couldn't quite place it.

"Yeah," he said, "people who peddle drugs tend to end up in the wrong place at the wrong time." He ran a hand through his hair, turned and spied Gabe in the doorway. As fast as her presence registered, his expression blanked.

That's where she'd heard the name Moreno. He was a local drug dealer whose name was mentioned almost every other day on television.

Zeke held her gaze. "No, I get it. All right. Keep his feet elevated and pressure on the wound. I'll meet you there." He started to pull the phone away from his ear then put it back just as fast. "One more thing." He paused as though waiting for someone to answer on the other end, his gaze burning with an intensity that sent shivers down her spine. "You need to call a rally. There's something we need to talk about."

With that he punched the home screen to end the call and tossed the phone on the couch, striding her direction. "Thought you were going to get some sleep."

Sleep? No, she'd been too hyped up from her fan-freaking-tastic night that had nearly ended in a horrid tragedy. Apparently, she'd gotten her cart in front of the horse on the fan-freaking-tastic part. "I got a text." She waggled her phone as if that might somehow explain things. "I made a friend yesterday. The girl from the store. She texted me to see how things went. We were thinking of meeting for coffee after she gets off work."

He smiled and pulled her into a hug. "That's great, *gatinha*. That's a big step for you."

She wanted to hug him back, tried to lift her arms, but couldn't quite muster the enthusiasm. Could only stand there, dumbfounded and weighted with dread.

Pulling away, Zeke anchored one hand on her shoulder and steered her face to his with firm fingers at her chin. "What's going on in that head of yours?"

Just a World War III panic attack. One side featured all the reasons why she should've kept Zeke at a distance, and the other, hopeless-romantic side cast puppy dog eyes and urged her to hug him and forget what she'd heard. "Where are you going?"

His lips pressed into a hard line and the hand on her shoulder tightened.

"I heard you talking about drugs," she pressed. "About losing your license. What's going on?"

He kept his shrewd eyes on hers, thoughts shifting behind his gaze so fast she couldn't even begin to fathom what they might be about.

Well, to hell with that. She'd done the things he'd asked. Put herself out there in a way she'd never done before. "You asked me to be honest. That should go both ways, right? I don't have a mom because of drugs. I almost lost my brother to them. I'm not giving them a third chance to screw up my life."

Exhaling hard, he cupped the back of her neck and gave her a semismile, though it had a bittersweet edge to it. "Yeah. Honesty's a two-way street." He spun her around and wrapped an arm around her shoulders, guiding her back to the bedroom. "Let's get you curled up in bed and I'll tell you what I can."

On a scale of one to ten, opening the huge-ass can of worms in front of Zeke with a man bleeding out like a stuck pig fifteen minutes away had to rank a thirty, even if he did hate the slimy bastard doing the bleeding. He pulled the covers back on Gabe's side of the bed.

Gabe eyed the empty space, then her purse beside the bed.

Oh, hell no. No way was he letting her walk out of his house without a fight. Though how he was going to be honest and not give her extra fuel to hightail it home was a mountain he wasn't sure how to climb. Hell, he wasn't even sure how much of his conversation with Jace she'd heard. If he knew some of the finer nuances of what had happened to her family when she was young, it might help, though. "Tell me about your mom."

"I thought you were going to tell me about where you're going and how you've got a hand in drugs."

"I don't have a hand in drugs. I wouldn't. But, before

I go there, I'd like to understand where you're coming from."

Her eyes slid to the side, her cute little mouth puckered up as though she couldn't decide whether she wanted to fight or share. "She got caught up with some bad people. Men who had a side business peddling small-time drugs."

"And?"

"And they weren't very nice." She plopped down on the side of the bed, her head bowed as she laced her fingers between her knees. "She'd take me with her when she went to see them because she didn't have anyone else to leave me with. I was too little to understand what she was doing when she'd disappear into the bedroom with them, but I figured it out later. They used her to front a lot on deals with customers they didn't know. I was there the day she did a deal with an undercover cop and got hauled in. That's when Dad found out what she'd been up to. He kicked her out and spent all his savings to get sole custody of me and Danny."

"How old were you?"

She finally lifted her gaze. "Eight."

Fuck. Talk about a head trip for a kid. No wonder she had a thing for rules and keeping to herself. "And Danny? You said drugs almost took him, too."

She nodded and went back to studying her hands. "In high school. He started running around with a bad crowd and they liked to experiment with drugs. Their part-time jobs didn't do much on funding their needs, so they broke into houses. Danny got busted. The only reason he didn't end up in juvie is because Dad got him a decent lawyer and beat some sense into him." She looked up at him. "But I'm guessing you already knew that."

"Most of it." Though Danny hadn't shared the part about his dad beating sense into him. Kind of made Zeke

wish he'd had a chance to meet the guy. He sat next to
Gabe and tugged her hands apart, taking the one closest
to him and wrapping it up in both of his. She'd nailed it
when she called him on the honesty thing. She deserved
the truth. Or at least as much as he could give her. "Look
at me, *gatinha*."

She twisted her head so a strand of her honey-blond
hair hung over one cheek, those beautiful blue eyes of
hers filled with raw, open fear.

Damn, but he couldn't take it. They might be side by
side, but it was too much distance. Too much disconnect. He twisted on the bed and pulled her around to
face him, guiding her legs so they wrapped around him.
He cupped the side of her face. "I do not condone heavy
drugs. Why anyone would willingly put some of the shit
they do in their body is beyond me. I see too many of
the side effects in my job. I'd be lying if I said I hadn't
shared a smoke or two with friends when I was growing
up, and I've got no problem with people who kick back
with weed on occasion, but the hard stuff? No. Personally, beer's about all you'll catch me with. Sometimes a
Scotch when Jace and Axel pull out the good stuff. Most
of the time, I want a clear head, but I won't judge other
people for their choices. So I can absolutely tell you, I
do not involve myself with drugs."

"But you know people who do. Like Moreno. He's
on the news all the time as being suspected for dealing drugs."

Well, that cleared up how much she'd heard. "I don't
know him. Not outside of the same pictures you've seen
on the news. What I do know is he's an ass who's caused
Jace a ton of problems in the last few months peddling
really nasty stuff in his and Axel's clubs. The problem
tonight is Moreno's brother is hurt. And while I might

not like Moreno or what he's done to Jace, there are very few people in this world I could walk away from without helping if it was in my power to make them better."

"He could go anywhere for help. Walk in any emergency room."

"It's not that easy. Not for everyone." He tucked her hair behind one ear, savoring the soft brush of her skin against his fingertips. "Let me ask you a question. If you were me and you could help a hurting person who didn't feel like they could walk into a normal doctor's office, could you walk away from them? Even if you didn't agree with how they lived their life?"

"No."

"That's all this is. Me helping someone else." And simultaneously earning a marker from Moreno. Bartering done old school. But that information put his brothers out there and that he wouldn't share until he'd claimed her.

She wrapped her hand around his wrist, the slightest tremor marring the touch. "That's all? No drugs?"

"No drugs. I promise."

The grip on his wrist tightened and her shoulders eased on a heavy exhalation. "Okay."

Thank. You. God. He kissed her forehead, then her nose, then her lips, the last making him hate Moreno even more now than he had five minutes ago, which was a helluva lot already. "I gotta go. You okay to sleep while I'm gone?"

She nodded and eased away from him, slipping her feet under the covers.

"I'll call you when the guy is stable. If you decide to go anywhere, be sure to call me and let me know, okay?"

"Yeah, I can do that." She curled up on her side facing him and tucked one hand under her head. Seeing her there, so sweet and tucked up tight in his bed, re-shifted every priority in his life.

Man, he was a goner. He just hoped like hell his brothers wouldn't balk when they heard what he had to say. Maybe three weeks ago he'd have chosen his brothers over her, but now he wasn't so sure.

He started to stand then stopped. He'd given her the truth about Moreno, but not the truth he'd realized when he'd fallen asleep with her in his arms. As much as she'd put herself out there the past few weeks, she deserved everything. "I told you the things I did because I trust you. What we've got going between us…" Hell, he wasn't sure what it was. He wasn't even sure there were words for what he felt. "I've never been in anything like this. It's huge and so deep I can't see the bottom of it."

"Me, too," she whispered. "It's scary."

He leaned in and pressed a soft kiss to her lips. "I'm not sharing what I did because I'm afraid, *gatinha*. I'm telling you because, for you, wading into the deep end's worth it."

Chapter Twenty

Fatigue wasn't something Zeke fought often, but between the overnight fire and stabilizing Moreno's brother on three hours of sleep, he was ready for some serious shut-eye. He pulled into Haven's long drive behind Jace's pimped out black Silverado and followed his brother toward the main house. Tired or not, every time Zeke passed those front gates, a little part of him let out a relieved sigh. No one but the brothers, the women they claimed or the moms came here. While it was Jace and Axel's main home, it was also the brotherhood's safe place. Their solace away from the daily grind. And man did he need the relief. Now more than ever. What he had to say to his brothers could go ten different kinds of bad for him, Danny or both.

At least he knew Gabe was okay. Getting her text after she'd napped, saying her friend was coming by to get her for coffee had shaken a little of the tension out of his shoulders. If she'd wanted to bail on him, she wouldn't have bothered with a text, but would've just slipped out of his house unannounced and hid at home.

Or maybe called the cops on him.

He killed the engine, wrenched his aching body out of the car and trudged toward the spacious wraparound porch with its plentiful Adirondack chairs and mountain-lodge design.

Jace waited for him, one hand stuffed in the pocket of his faded jeans and the other fiddling with the ever-present toothpick nestled on one side of his mouth. "Appreciate you taking care of Moreno. I know he's not high on your list."

"You know I wouldn't tell you no."

"No, but you don't like what he does. Hell, I don't either, but it earned me a marker my clubs needed." He grinned. "Probably peeled you away from that sweet thing you've been spending so much time with lately, too."

"Yeah, about that." Zeke rubbed the back of his neck, the kink that'd been building the past twelve hours sending a sharp jolt up the back of his head. "Gabe heard us talking on the phone."

Jace's grin died. "How much?"

"Enough to make her ask questions." Questions he wasn't altogether sure his brothers would appreciate the way he'd handled. "I like her, Jace. A lot. Enough I couldn't lie to her. She doesn't know who I was on the phone with and she doesn't know the extent of it, but I told her what I was doing."

Jace scratched his cheek, his beard bristling with the sharp movement. "That why you asked for a rally?"

"Yeah." In the driveway, all the other brothers' cars were already there, which meant little to no waiting before he fessed up on what he'd done. Or where his head was at. If anyone would understand, Jace would. He'd been in a similar position just a few months before, and he'd come out okay. "It's time. I'm just not sure how the rest of the guys are going to feel about it."

Jace clamped one hand on his shoulder and squeezed.

"The only reason they wouldn't back your play is if they thought Gabe wouldn't do the same." With that, he slapped Zeke's back and ambled through the front door without so much as a backward glance.

Well, shit. Didn't that just yank the rug out from under all his idealistic plans. Truth be told, he wasn't altogether sure Gabe would have his back. Not at first anyway. Yeah, she'd come around when he'd taken time to explain, but he had a pretty good idea there would be a whole lot more in the way of explanations in his future before there was any blind acceptance.

Inside, the soft strains of a television show drifted down from the huge entertainment room. Bigger, masculine rumbles and the steady thump of old-school rock billowed up from the basement. He hit the bottom step just as Knox let loose with his cue and broke the racked pool balls with a wicked *thwack*.

"Damn, Zeke. Don't you sleep?" This from Beckett, who stood with the butt end of his own pool cue anchored on the floor and the shooting end gripped loosely with two hands near his chest.

"Bloody patients aren't too fond of doctors napping while they dig bullets out of their shoulders." He pulled his chair out from under the twelve-foot conference table Jace had bought shortly after they moved into Haven. Every brother had brought their own chair, one that represented a piece of their past, or a place in their life they needed to remember. His had to be one of the ugliest. A battered ivory kitchen chair on casters with obscene orange, black and yellow paisley, but it never let him forget where he'd grown up. It also reminded him his mom and dad didn't want for a damned thing these days, even if he only saw them once every year or two.

Jace settled in his own chair at the head of the table.

"Knox, table the game for now so we can get our business done. Zeke's earned a quick one after the day he's had."

"And night." Axel sat opposite Jace and reclined in his chair, feet up on the edge and hands laced over his belly. "You get Moreno's word he'll keep his shit out of our clubs?" he said to Jace.

"As much of a guarantee as I think he's capable of."

Trevor settled beside Zeke. "All the same, I'd keep Otto and his crew in place. Moreno might honor what he said, but an open playground only offers up fresh opportunities for new players."

"Agreed." Jace rapped his knuckles on the table and focused on Zeke. "All right, brother. You wanted a rally. You got it. What's the topic?"

Man, talk about ripping the Band-Aid off and diving into deep territory. "Not sure how much everyone's heard by now, but last night there was a fire out by Gabe and Danny's house. The next-door neighbor."

"The same one with the break-in?" Trevor asked.

"Other side," Beck said. "Danny and I were out working a job when Gabe called. I hung around and did some checking with the fire crew. Nothing official slated when I left, but it's looking like a well-placed arson job."

"And you're nosin' around why?" Axel said.

Zeke swiveled and met Axel's curious stare. "Because I asked him to." He let the news sink in for all of two heartbeats. "Something's going on out there. Break-ins, people who've lived there forever bailing with little to no notice, fires where there shouldn't be fires, Realtors knocking on Gabe's door every five minutes. It's a forty-year-old neighborhood. It ought to be the dullest place in a fifty-mile radius. Not drawing in first-responder traffic every week. I've got a bad feeling on this one."

"Whatever's tweaking you, I think you're right." Knox

leaned forward and folded his arms on the table, a Pilsner bottle clenched in one hand. "I only looked a little before I headed out here, but the three houses that have sold in Danny's neighborhood all have ties to one investment company. All sold to different buyers initially, but all of them turned around and sold to a company called Lakeside Investments."

"What about the increase in crime?" Zeke said. "One of the Realtors told the seller down the street all the surrounding neighborhoods were seeing higher break-ins."

"Nope," Beck said. "The only reports of violence that tie with this kind of activity in the last six months are in Danny's neighborhood. Considering that neighborhood is one long street with only twenty houses on it, that makes for a high tally."

Trevor pushed back in his chair enough to cross one booted foot over his knee. "You got anything we can leverage against Lakeside? Something we can turn over easy to the cops?"

"None." Knox tapped one finger near the base of his beer, slanted one of his devious I'm-in-the-know-and-you're-not smiles up and down the table and delivered his next little tidbit with a teaser ending. "All the records I've found are tied up tight. Nothing sketchy that ties them to the break-in or the fire."

"But?" Axel prodded.

"I did some digging on Lakeside's executive team. More than one of their top guys have a history of getting caught with their fingers in the financial cookie jar. I'd bet they've got some serious pay dirt in their office."

Quiet filled the room, each man looking from one to the other.

"You suggesting we go in?" Jace said.

Knox shook his head and reclined back in his seat.

"I'm not promoting anything. I'm just saying if this is something we want to shut down, then we need to get inside and see what they've got."

Beckett locked gazes with Zeke. "Sorry, brother, but we've got no skin in this game. Might be cleanest for me to give it to some buddies of mine at DPD. Maybe see if they'll dig into it."

Like hell they didn't have skin in this game. They had a lot of it. Him in particular. "Danny's damned near one of us. If we'd already voted on him and learned shit like this was going on in his neighborhood, it wouldn't even be a question."

"You say that like Danny's the only one you're concerned about," Axel said, "but I'm not so sure the pretty lass isn't an equal part."

"Don't go there, Axel," Zeke said. "Don't cloud Danny's part in the brotherhood with who I'm with. He deserves more than that." And yet here he'd gone and muddied it up for Danny, tangling with Gabe.

"Hold up." Jace sat forward and held up a hand. "Yeah, Zeke's gettin' deep with Gabe, but that's a separate issue. One we'll cover. But Zeke's got a point. I think we cover the issue of Danny first. It's time. He's paid his dues and shown his colors. Making the call on him answers our next steps on covering his turf."

Thank God.

Zeke jerked a nod at Jace and let out a slow breath. "I brought Danny in. He's a good man. Honorable, smart and willing to throw himself out there for any of us. The only thing he needs is the same direction and support we give each other. There's no doubt in my mind he'll pull his weight."

Jace zeroed in on Beck. "You work with him the most. What's your spin?"

"I'm with Zeke. He's solid. Smart. Maybe not all that bookish, but deadly on the street. Got balls bigger than Texas. Shit you not, I've seen him stare some crazy motherfuckers down and not flinch."

"That a yes?" Jace said.

"Yeah, I'm in."

Jace shifted to Knox. "You got any input?"

"I'm leaning on the rest of you. What I know of him, I get no bad vibes. Everything I've found on him checks out, and I've dug deep. Mom's a lost cause. She hits Danny up for money now and then but steers clear of Gabe. Nominal cash really. At worst, she's someone we might have to jump in and bail out a time or two, but so long as she stays at a distance, she's not a risk."

"What about the sister?" Axel said.

Zeke clenched the armrest and the knot at the base of his neck wrenched tight enough to make his eye twitch. The question was a fair one to ask, one he'd ask himself if he were in Axel's shoes, but damned if he didn't want to slug the Scottish bastard. He answered before Knox could. "Gabe could be a problem if she finds out too much. She's all about rules and neat, tidy boundaries. Especially the law. With everything that went down with her mom and Danny when he was young, it's how she's coped. Black-and-white is good. Gray isn't."

"Black-and-white's not bad," Jace said. "It just means you gotta bite your tongue around her."

And there was his problem. He'd already proven just how inadequate he was on that score this morning. He hung his head and studied his blood-smattered tennis shoes.

"You think you can do that?" Axel said.

Zeke met Axel's stare. "Am I eager or interested in

telling her everything we're into? No. The more innocent she stays, the better. But I can't lie to her. I won't."

On his left, the worn black leather lining Jace's chair
groaned as he shifted in it. Otherwise the room rang silent.

"All right," Jace said. "Let's table Gabe and keep focused on Danny. Trevor, what's your vote?"

"I'm in."

"Axel?"

Axel dragged his fingers through his beard and studied Zeke.

Damn it, this was exactly what he'd wanted to avoid.
If he hadn't started things up with Gabe, Axel wouldn't
have even hesitated.

"Never seen anything in Danny that gives me pause."
Axel shifted his gaze to Jace. "I'm in."

"Yep. Me, too." Jace rapped his knuckles on the table.
"That's a solid vote. If Danny's on board, then he's in.
Which means digging into Lakeside is a no-brainer."

Beckett chuckled and took a swig of his beer. "It also
makes the person getting inside their office a no-brainer.
No one better on our crew for this scale of a job than
Danny. With Knox's help, it should be straightforward."

Trevor focused on Knox. "You got any idea what he'd
be up against?"

"Not yet, but me and Beck can scope it out. Probably
take two or three days to get a good idea on what we're
talking about."

"What do we do in the meantime?" Zeke said. "Danny
can handle himself if there's trouble in the neighborhood, but I don't like Gabe being home by herself. Her
ribs are better, but she wouldn't hold up defending herself if things went bad."

Beckett pushed back on the rear legs of his chair and

crossed his arms over his chest. "Then we arm the house. I'll put a man on watch until we get it wired."

"Yeah, wiring her place is going to raise more questions." More than he'd be able to juggle without raising more suspicions.

"One thing at a time," Jace said. "We need intel for the company first. Zeke, you brought Danny in. You going to be the one to make the offer?"

Hell yes, he was. From the first day he'd met Danny, he'd known this day would come. No way was he passing it off to someone else. "Yeah. I'll cover it."

"Good." Jace pulled the toothpick from his mouth, leaned into the table and crossed his arms, gaze pinned on Zeke. "Gotta deal with the other piece, brother."

Yeah, he did. Though how he was going to deal with the outcome if he didn't have their support, he couldn't fathom. For ten years, these men had been his lifeline. The last thing he wanted to do was live a life without them, but letting go of Gabe wasn't an option either.

He sucked in a deep breath. "The thing with Moreno. Gabe walked into the room when I was talking with Jace on the phone. She's got no clue who I was talking to, but she heard Moreno's name and called me on it. I told her as much truth as I could. Told her I couldn't refuse helping someone even if I didn't condone the kind of dope he pushes."

Not one man said a word, but every one of their expressions got tight.

Axel lowered his crossed feet from the table and sat up straight. "You think she'll do anything with that info?"

"She knows where Sanctuary is. She could've called the cops and sent 'em straight to me while Moreno and his brother were there, but she didn't. I think she's trying to be reasonable and let some of her rigidity go, but

I can't guarantee what will happen if she figures out it wasn't a one-time deal."

"That's a high risk," Jace said. "You gain us more points prying bullets out of rough crews than any amount of cash ever could."

Trevor shifted in his chair beside Zeke. "What is she to you?"

Wasn't that just the million-dollar question of the day. One he'd been wrestling with since the first day he met her. "The truth? I've never met a woman worth taking this kind of risk before. Not until her."

"Ach, Christ." Axel reclined in his chair, all the tension that had held him moments before replaced with his usual easygoing, playful demeanor. "Another lad headed down the bloody tubes."

"I'm not going to lie to you guys," Zeke said. "What I've got with her, it's good. Real good. I don't know if we'll make it. Not with how cautious she is, but if we do? Man, the gamble would be worth it."

The room got quiet, every man waiting for him to leap.

Except Jace, who was more than happy to push. "You claiming her?"

And there it was. The time for him to man up, or go home. Oddly enough, the words came easy. Like they'd been there all along. "Yeah, she's mine. No telling if she'll be willing to stick it out for me long-term, but there is no question I'm on board. The problem is, I don't want her putting my family in danger."

"Fuck that." Axel sat upright, elbows perched on his wide knees and hands clasped between them. His eyes burned with an intensity he seldom let show, but when he did, it was all consuming. "You want her, you find a way to make that happen. I may be the last man ready to settle down, but if you're willing to throw down for a woman, then we back your play and we take the risk together. You're my brother. I trust you."

Jace chimed in right behind him. "Agreed. If she's yours, she's ours, too. We'll manage the risk." He looked to Trev, Beck and Knox. "Any issues from the three of you?"

"Nope."

"None."

"Hell no." Trevor grinned and slapped Zeke on the back. "Gonna be fun having a front seat, though."

Of course, it was Trev who'd find humor behind the risk. The two of them had come into the brotherhood at the same time, and in all the years Zeke had known him, the laid-back cowboy had only lost his cool three times. Three explosive, wrath-of-God, lethal-ending times. "Careful, brother. You get too close to front and center, you might find yourself courting your own problems with a female."

"Not likely." He plucked his beer off the table and raised it in a mock salute. "I'll take a full stable to a single filly any day."

"Amen." Beck lifted his own beer and knocked back a huge slug.

"You boys don't know what you're missing," Jace said, "but you'll pull your heads out of your asses eventually." He rapped his knuckles on the table. "All right. Business is done. Gabe's protected and Danny's in. We'll meet back here on Friday, add one more chair to the table and figure out how to bring Lakeside down."

Chapter Twenty-One

Storm clouds lined the western sky, moving fast toward the lake. Between the time Zeke had left his Uptown town house and the time he'd turned into Gabe's neighborhood, the early-evening sun had disappeared behind a thin veil of gray and now cast an eerie, green pall for miles.

He pulled in behind Danny's Chevelle, killed the engine and jogged up the front stoop, strengthening wind gusts whipping all around him. Another thirty minutes and every weatherman in the Dallas/Ft. Worth area would be nursing an adrenaline high in front of their cameras, pissing off television viewers with their interruptions and juggling storm spotters better than a circus entertainer. He knocked on the front door.

Gabe's voice rang out behind the solid wood. "It's open."

Sure enough, the knob twisted smooth as butter, a fact that had him scanning the neighborhood for confirmation Beck had followed through on his promise to put a man on watch.

Four houses down, just out front of one of the empty homes sat a baseline black Ford F-150. No bling at all. Just a nondescript truck with heavily tinted windows, its nose pointed so it had a straight-on view of Gabe's house.

He pushed the door open and nearly whacked Gabe's outstretched hand in the process.

She jumped back. "Oh, I thought maybe I'd locked it. Didn't you hear me?"

"Yeah, I heard you." He shut the door and locked it. "The question is why the front door isn't locked."

"The door's never locked when Danny's home."

"Well, it should be." And would be whether it made her ask more questions or not. "You've got too many damned Realtors knocking on your door for my comfort. Not to mention the break-in next door."

She frowned up at him, deep furrows scrunching up the space between her eyebrows. "What's got you in such a sour mood? And I thought you had to work tonight."

Fuck, but he hated keeping her in the dark. Hated that he couldn't just lay shit out for her and trust she'd take him and his actions as they came. He pulled her against him and kissed the top of her head, her scent wrapping him up just as tight as her arms at his waist. "I just want you to be safe. I know you're not used to it, but I want you to promise me you'll keep the doors locked."

"But, I—"

He squeezed tighter. "Promise me, *gatinha.*"

She leaned back enough to study his face.

"Call me an overprotective Brazilian man if you want. Just tell me you'll do it."

The frown twisted to a quirky purse of her lips, and one eyebrow arched at an angle that said she thought he was nuts. "Fine." She pulled free and sashayed into the kitchen. "Now, what are you doing here instead of work?"

"I switched. I'm going in tomorrow morning instead." He followed her and found shredded lettuce, grated cheese and tomatoes prepped and laid out in separate bowls. In the large skillet, enough chicken strips to feed eight starving men sizzled over a low flame, and a huge stack of flour tortillas waited beside it. Damn, but he loved taco night. He moved in behind her at the stove and nuzzled her neck. "It's too hard to work overnights now when I know what I could be sleeping next to at home."

"Jesus." Danny strolled into the kitchen. His once black Aerosmith T-shirt was so faded it ran closer to gray, and his hair was damp from a recent shower. He popped the fridge open and pulled out a beer. "Not sure I'm ever gonna get used to seeing you making a play for my baby sister."

"Already made my play." Zeke squeezed Gabe's hips, kissed her temple and lowered his voice just for Gabe. "Now I'm just making sure I keep what I've got."

She giggled and stirred the chicken, but her sweet ass pressed harder against his hips, as if on instinct.

He smacked her on the butt and ambled over to the table. "How much longer before dinner? I've got a problem with the Camaro I need to show Danny and thought I'd do it before the rain hits."

Danny groaned and thunked his beer on the table. "Ah, man. Not another ding from the parking lot."

"I admit, the hospital garage is an affront to all automotive works of art, but no." Outside the sky had grown even darker and the trees lined up and down the neighborhood whipped in the wind. "You got room in the garage? Looks like it's gonna pour any minute, and it might be better if I pull it around so you can get the right light on it."

"Yep." Danny stood, taking his beer with him. "Just finished up my last job and delivered it yesterday. Got nothing else in there right now."

"Fine, but hurry up," Gabe said. "I'll have food ready in fifteen minutes, tops."

Not as much time as he'd like, but enough to say what needed saying. In less than five, he pulled the Camaro into the single-bay garage just as the first raindrop splattered against the back window.

Danny flipped the bold fluorescents on and stood off to one side, hands on his hips while he studied the driver's side. He rounded to the other side as Zeke popped the door, gained his feet and headed for the garage door.

"Man, if there's something wrong with your ride, I'm not seeing it," Danny said.

The high steel door rattled until it slammed against the cracked concrete, trapping what was left of the unvented exhaust.

"That's because there's nothing to see." Zeke strolled to the window on the opposite end of the garage with a direct line of sight to the house. "Got a few things I need to run past you that didn't need your sister's ears."

Outside the sky opened up, rain pounding the metal building for all it was worth. A second later, a nasty crack of thunder filled the night.

Danny leaned against his workbench and crossed his arms, not the least bit concerned with Zeke's cloak-and-dagger. Hell, if anything, he looked comfortable. "All right, shoot."

Zeke mimicked the pose, but did it leaning against the hood of his car and wrapping his fingers around the lip of the hood. "We'll start with a softball. I wanna know where your head is about me and Gabe."

"Told you before. I couldn't pick a better man for my sister. I'm shocked as shit you've gotten as far as you have, but she seems happy. If she's smilin', then I'm smilin', too."

"You weren't smiling when I picked her up for dinner a few nights ago. From the scowl on your face, I half expected you to throw a punch. Tonight was better, but you still seem on edge."

"Yeah. Not my most comfortable moment." Danny hung his head and huffed out a laugh. He reached for the skull cap he usually wore, realized it wasn't there, then tucked his hand in one pocket. "I want Gabe to have someone. I want to know she's with someone good like you. But for twenty-four years, that hasn't been much of a reality. Takes a little getting used to. Especially that night you picked her up. I knew damned well what kind of thoughts were in your head. No matter how much I like you, a mental picture of my sister in a starring role didn't sit well."

"So, no change on where your head's at as far as me being with her?"

"Nope. Like I said, she's happy. Putting herself out there. Hell, there was even a chick here when I got home this afternoon. Some girl she met at the mall."

"You mean April. Gabe met her while she was out buying the dress." Two girlfriend outings in under a week. Definitely a plus in the way of Gabe taking chances.

"So what else is on your mind?" Danny said.

For the past few months, he'd spent a lot of time thinking about how Axel and Jace had brought Zeke and Trevor into the brotherhood. How his life had turned on a dime in only a handful of sentences. Now that he had the chance to do the same for Danny, he wasn't so sure how to go about it. "Had some stuff come to a head with the brotherhood today."

"Come to a head bad, or good?"

Zeke laughed, the power behind it ricocheting off the garage walls. Leave it to Danny to cut through the shit. "Bad that led to good." Across the yard, he caught a few glimpses of Gabe moving around in the kitchen. Setting the table, if he had to guess. If anyone would want her to keep on having her peaceful life, it would be Danny. "Don't you find it odd how many Realtors are out here knocking on doors?"

Danny shook his head. "Not really. It's prime land. One of the sales guys claimed Dad could make a small killing if he'd sell his acre. Dad just wasn't interested. He was a lot like Gabe. Liked the quiet. Liked the people and the lake."

"Yeah, well, I thought it was odd. Especially with the break-in at Wallaby's and the fire next door."

Danny frowned, but other than that held his stance.

Zeke plowed ahead. "I asked Beck and Knox to do some digging. Knox thinks I'm on to something. The houses that have sold all ended up in the hands of a company called Lakeside Investments. Apparently, some of the execs on their board have a thing for creative financing deals. And by *creative*, I mean the kind the feds and financial industry frown on."

"You think they're pushing people out?"

"Looks that way, but we've got nothing to prove it. To dig further, we're going to have to get in their offices. Knox has a hunch they're smart enough to keep whatever info they've got offline."

"And you need me."

"I didn't say that."

Danny's gaze slid to the side, narrowed, then zipped back to Zeke. "Then what are you saying?"

"Don't you want to know why we'd be digging into this?"

Danny's stare shifted to the window and the house beyond. "Given you're into Gabe, I'd guess she's the main reason."

"She's part of it. I want her safe and I imagine you do, too, but there's more to it than that. Brothers watch each other's backs. That means we're watching yours."

Danny froze, but a wild and supersized tension gripped his body. "I'm not a brother."

"You weren't. You are now. Assuming that's something you want to be a part of."

Pulling his hand out of his pocket, Danny gripped the side of his workbench and sucked in a deep breath. His gaze darted around the room, momentarily landing on random items like he was trying to factor whether the room around him was real or some mental hoax.

God, he remembered that feeling. That surreal moment when things you didn't even know you'd hoped for clicked into place. The instant, unequivocal acceptance given without a price tag of any kind. Belonging by choice and knowing good people had your back. "You need me to run that by you again or did it register?"

Danny blinked a few times and zeroed in on Zeke. "It registered. Fuck, yeah, it registered."

"I take it that's a yes?"

"Oh, yeah. It's a yes." Danny smiled huge and pushed off the workbench, his hand outstretched. "That's the best damned news ever."

A handshake. Christ, he had a long way to go in getting this guy to learn things were different. Zeke took the hand offered and pulled him in for a hug, slapping him on the back. "You're a good man, Danny. You deserve a big family. Now you've got one."

Danny's arms tightened sure as someone had jolted him with serious voltage before he stepped back and studied the floor long enough to get his wits around him. After a beat or two, he looked up. "I don't have words."

"You don't need any. We've all been there. That said,

we're throwing you in fast. You weren't wrong on the job that needs to get done. Before our vote, Beck would've been the one to run the job, but he said you're the best man for it now. If we want to get to the bottom of this deal, we need inside."

Danny nodded, his energy pinging around the room like a six-year-old boy hopped up on a case of chocolate. "Yeah. No, I'm good. And I'm in. Whatever they need."

Zeke grinned. Definitely a long way to go. "It's not *them* anymore, brother. It's *us*. And we're looking out for your home." He pushed away from the car and padded to the window for a better angle on the house. The rain had eased a little, and they were already pushing Gabe's dinner timeline. Knowing her, she'd stomp over and drag them both in by their ears. "Timing-wise, we're moving fast. We're rallying at Haven Friday night after Crossroads and The Den close. I figured we'd drive out together and get you hooked up with keys to the house."

Danny's jaw dropped, his adrenaline rush held hostage by the latest information. "Shit. I forgot about that. Beck said Haven's nice."

"Haven's great. Jace's and Axel's moms, Ninette and Sylvie, live out there. They're awesome. But have a mind on what you tell them. You may not have grown up with much of a mother, but you've got two now and they'll be in your business nonstop."

Danny smiled for all of two seconds before a frown swept in. "What about Gabe?"

Yeah, that was the hard part. The rest of the guys had seen the reason in moving slow with Gabe, but then they weren't Gabe's big brother. "The brotherhood's got few rules, but one of the biggest is that Haven is family only. That means no women unless they're claimed. And by claimed I mean you may as well put a ring on her finger."

"And you're not there yet." Danny nodded. "That's cool. Better not to rush—"

"I claimed her." Every time he said it, his body buzzed as sure as a lightning bolt had worked him from the ground up. "She's mine, protected by me and my brothers. Whether or not she'll ever get to the same place as me, I don't know, but I'm all in and will bust my ass to get her there, too."

Danny's eyes narrowed at the unspoken ending in Zeke's voice. "But?"

"A claimed woman doesn't just mean she's family and protected against whatever happens to her in this world. It means she's worthy of no secrets. Not from me and not from the brotherhood. I'm willing to do my part to earn her trust, but I don't know yet if she wants me enough to trust me. To take me as I am. Until I do, I can't put my family at risk."

With a heavy sigh, Danny stared at his boots. "Yeah. I get that." He looked up, more emotion bared in his dark eyes than Zeke had ever seen. "Don't give up on her."

"I'm not even close to the edge, brother. Got a whole lot of patience where she's concerned. Wouldn't have put myself out there with the rest of the guys if I didn't." He jerked his head toward the garage door. "Now get that thing open. Gabe's cooking waits for no one."

Danny barked a sharp laugh and stomped over to the cord, yanking it upward in one practiced move. "Don't give me that shit. It ain't dinner you're looking forward to."

Chapter Twenty-Two

A sharp, incessant vibration yanked Gabe from sleep, the clatter coming from Zeke's side of the bed. She propped up on her elbows and blinked her eyes into focus.

On the opposite nightstand, Zeke's phone flashed against the darkness.

"Zeke." She shook his shoulder. "Zeke, your phone's ringing."

He knifed upward, going from the deepest sleep she'd ever seen him in to wide-awake and scanning the room. "What's wrong?"

"Nothing, but your phone is ringing." She flopped back down to her pillow, her old digital alarm clock glowing 2:00 a.m. in soft neon blue.

The bed shifted and sheets rustled in the darkness.

Her eyes slipped closed, sleep pulling her back into its comforting depths as Zeke shuffled around the room, the brush of denim against skin overloud in the darkness.

Wait.

Her eyes flew wide and her heart lurched. He hadn't talked to anyone, had he? Or maybe she'd fallen asleep and missed it. Whatever had happened, Zeke was up and moving swiftly. She pushed up to one elbow. "Who was it?"

"It wasn't a call. It was my alarm. I have to be some-where."

"What?" She double-checked the clock. "It's two in the morning. I thought your shift didn't start until seven."

Already in his jeans, he pulled the T-shirt he'd worn the night before over his head. "It doesn't, but I have to be somewhere. So does Danny."

"Now? Who does anything this late?"

Zeke's sigh slid through the shadowed room, the faint moonlight through her window accenting how his shoul-ders sagged with the sound. He grabbed his shoes off the floor and padded to her side of the bed, sitting near her hip to put them on. "My brothers are meeting tonight. It starts late because it's Friday." He nodded toward the clock. "Or it *was* Friday. Weekends are rough for some of the guys because of the clubs, so we get together after closing time."

Your mom slipped out late, too.

Look what that got you.

"You don't think that's… I don't know…weird?"

"Babe, just because I keep odd hours doesn't mean I'm up to nefarious deeds."

He had a point. Not that she had any history with friends to gauge normal behavior on, but after the fun she'd had visiting with April the past few days, she'd at least try to pry her sleepy ass out of bed if it was the only time she could see her friend.

For you, wading into the deep end's worth it.

He was trying. Putting in the effort in a way no one else ever had for her. Giving her the truth when she asked for it. Even now. He easily could have said it was a trauma case, but instead he'd given her the facts straight up.

She shrugged and curled up on her side. "Okay."

Finished putting on his shoes, he twisted and smoothed

her hair off her face. With the window behind him, his face was all angles and shadows, but the glow from her alarm was enough to highlight the intensity behind his eyes. The same lasered focus he wore when working with a patient. "What kind of man do you think I am, *gatinha*?"

He'd posed it simply. Lightly spoken. But the depth behind what he asked loomed bottomless and deep. She hesitated, giving her thoughts time to surface. "I think you're the first person outside family I've trusted in a very long time."

He cupped the side of her face, his eyes roving her features as though seeking reassurance. "Do you?"

She jolted against the pillow, the soft, carefully spoken words ricocheting through her. Not once in the time she'd known him had he sounded so vulnerable. So raw and uncertain. "I'm trying."

His lips softened on a wistful smile, and he traced her lower lip with his thumb.

She parted her mouth on instinct, her body igniting with the simple touch, craving the caress only he could give her.

Leaning in, he pressed a gentle, lingering kiss to her mouth and whispered, "I know you are. Just give me what you can." He stood, but pressed another far more innocent kiss to her forehead. "Go back to sleep. I'll head straight to work this morning, but I'll be back tonight. Be sure you keep your doors locked, all right?"

She nodded, too dumbfounded by the odd tone of their conversation and the emotions they'd stirred. The dim overhead light from the stove painted his outline the second he opened the bedroom door. More than anything, she wanted to scramble across the bed and ask him not to go. To keep him here with her.

To make sure he doesn't run away.

She sat up, the sheet clenched tight in one fist. "Zeke."

He paused, one hand on the door jam and the other on the knob. "Yeah, sweetheart?"

Her insides twisted, panic spiraling her thoughts in all directions. Everything was fine. She'd said she trusted him, now she needed to show it. She pulled in a steadying breath and settled back against the mattress. "Be careful."

In shadow, she couldn't see his face, but a smile lit his voice. "Always, *gatinha*."

It took a thirty-minute drive and a whole lot of handshakes and backslapping from the brothers before everyone gathered round the table for Danny's first rally, but the delays had been worth it. The slack jaw and wide-eyed wonder on Danny's face when he'd caught his first glimpse of Haven had yanked Zeke ten years back in time. To the buzzed, angry and unbalanced man he'd once been with nothing but intellect and street smarts to navigate life. The brotherhood had grounded him. Taught him and backed him while he found his way. And now it was Danny's turn.

Danny trailed behind Zeke down the basement stairs and gaped at the room's rough interior. "Wow, your decorator did not get the memo down here."

Trevor handed Danny a bottled beer. "The moms got full say upstairs. Down here, it's just us. Nothing except what reminds us of our past and where we're going."

Axel motioned toward the simple ladder-back chair at the table. "We brought that one down from the kitchen for tonight. You'll need to pick one of your own and bring it over another time."

The men gathered around the table, Zeke taking his place in the chair next to Danny's.

Jace settled in his black leather banker's chair at the

head of the table. "Zeke bring you up to speed on what's going down in your neighborhood?"

Danny fidgeted, obviously a little uncomfortable with his place at the table, but still buzzing with so much hyped-up energy it practically bounced off the walls and ceiling. "Yeah. Said we need to go in if we want to find anything but that it should be straightforward."

"Yeah, well, it's a little more complex than we thought." Beckett tossed an architectural plan on the center of the table and unrolled one end toward Axel. "Security's tight. Nothing the seven of us can't get around, but they've got a lot of fail-safes. One fuckup and the moms will be bailing our asses out of jail."

Beck leaned in and pointed out key concerns while Knox rattled out a bunch of jargon Zeke couldn't follow. Danny ate it up, nodding his head about every other sentence. The rest of the guys hung back and waited for the *Reader's Digest* version.

"It's doable." Danny zeroed in on Beckett. "If you take the CFO's office, I can handle the big guy's."

"What are we thinking time-wise?" Jace asked.

"I need more intel," Beckett said, "but I'm thinking next weekend. Security's always lax then."

"What about Danny's house?" Trevor said. "We ever going to get it wired up?"

Danny glanced at Zeke beside him. "Zeke's right to be worried about Gabe asking questions. She's loyal to a fault, but until she knows people, she's leery. If Beck and his crew started wiring the place up out of nowhere, she'd want answers. But I've got an idea."

Beckett lifted an eyebrow.

"That night at the compound," Danny said, "you mentioned me wiring up Mrs. Wallaby's house. She may have said no to our upgrade, but what if we play it up that I took a notion to trying my hand on our own house?"

Beckett shrugged and crossed his arms. "If it was Wallaby's house, that might work, but I wouldn't have put much more than a basic system in her house. What I'd put in yours you couldn't install alone." He grinned, not the least bit repentant about his upcoming jab. "Not and have it actually work."

Danny harrumphed and reclined in his chair, the discomfort he'd shown before displaced by the easy camaraderie.

"So get her out of the house." Trevor looked to Beckett. "How long do you need?"

"With a decent crew and no interruptions? A twelve-hour day. We'll have to wire the whole thing since they don't have anything pre-existing."

"Gabe's back on regular duty at the garage, so if you do it on a weekday, you'll burn an easy eight while she's there," Danny said.

Trevor swiveled toward Zeke. "Then all you need to do is pick your girl up, take her out for a long dinner."

"Or, better yet," Jace added, "take her to your place for the night."

They were right. Outside of coming up with an excuse on why she should spend the night at his place, the plan was simple and straightforward. It still didn't sit right. "I don't like lying to her."

"You're not lying to her. You're just not waving a bloody red flag in her face." Axel swirled his Scotch in his thick crystal tumbler. "Besides, how a woman could fault a man for keeping her safe, I'll never know."

Jace scoffed and kicked back in his seat, feet outstretched to one side and ankles crossed. "Goes to show you've never been with a woman longer than one week."

"That's by choice," Axel shot back. "You might like strapping yourself down to one lass. Me? I like strapping down as many as I can get my hands on."

Guess that answered how much Axel trusted Danny. His proclivities when it came to sex weren't exactly a secret, but the casual share was a whole lot more personal info than he'd expected Axel to reveal at Danny's first rally.

Undaunted by the info bomb, Knox snatched the diagrams off the table and started rolling them up. "No one said you had to keep Gabe in the dark. Danny can tell her as soon as he's done. Hell, he'll have to if we expect her to use it."

"He's right," Danny said. "She's my blood so I'll take the brunt. If I say it's best to keep things quiet, then it's on me. Not on you."

The idea still rubbed him wrong. "She's your blood, but she's my woman."

"And you'll be the one who levels her out after the fact," Danny said.

True. Outside of her new friend, April, Zeke wasn't altogether sure Gabe had anyone to talk to about anything. "What about after? When she learns more of the details. More about what's behind the security?"

Beckett thunked his beer down on the table. "You're overthinking it, man. Let's jump one hurdle at a time. We'll get the house secured, see what evidence we find, and then figure out how to break the news, if there even is any. Like Axel said, gonna be kind of hard for her to rip you a new one if all you're doing is making sure she keeps breathing."

Danny scanned the men lined around the table. "So when do we do this?"

Jace chin-lifted to Zeke. "It's his call. He's the one making sure our girl's well and truly occupied."

The tongue-in-cheek comment earned a whole lot of dirty grins and rumbling chuckles. While he sure as hell didn't mind muddling Gabe's mind, he still wasn't thrilled with the underhanded agenda. "I've got a seven-o'clock shift this morning and a Sunday-night overnight. If you want to run the system on Monday, I can pick her up at work and take her to my place."

Beck jerked a tight nod. "Done. I'll get the installers ready to go. Danny, Knox and I will work out the details for the Lakeside gig next Saturday and give everyone a rundown midweek."

"Then it sounds like Danny's first rally is done." Jace stood up, rapped his knuckles on the tabletop, and ambled over to Danny with his hand outstretched. "Welcome to Haven, brother."

Chapter Twenty-Three

Six o'clock on a Monday near Dallas's Mix Master was no place for the weak of spirit. Not unless you could appreciate the frenetic energy with a beautiful woman on a third-story rooftop while the sun crept toward the western horizon. For the past hour, Zeke had lavished Gabe with the comfort foods he'd grown up with via the roof of his town house and their private urban picnic while the rest of the world scrambled to make their way home. With two bites of *pavé* left on his plate, Zeke set his fork aside and slid the decadent dessert across the table to Gabe. "You gotta try this one."

"Mmm." Gabe motioned to the varied plates of food with the tip of her fork and shook her head. She still had one bite of *brigadeiro* left, but if the rapturous expression on her face was any indicator, the chocolate truffle wouldn't last long. "No way. I'm finishing off whatever sinful thing this is and calling it quits. I can barely breathe as it is."

"Just a bite." He nudged the plate closer. "It's chocolate, cookies and coconut. How can you say no?"

"It's the *only* thing I've said no to. I'm almost in a food coma."

She did have a languid presence about her now, far different than the protesting woman he'd dragged out of work a few hours ago. Since then he'd plied her with cheese and beef filled *pastéis*, which weren't too far off from the more popular empanadas, *moqueca de camarão*, a creamy shrimp stew made with coconut milk and palm oil she'd compared to clam chowder, and fried *coxinhas*, which was basically fried mac 'n' cheese minus the noodles with chicken thrown in for good measure.

She lowered her fork for the last of her truffle, but shifted paths at the last minute, digging into the *pavé*. "Oh, damn," she said around her mouthful. "That's good, too."

"Of course it's good. It's Brazilian." He winked and stood, ambling to her side of the table. "You ready for the best part?"

She dropped her fork on her plate and raised both hands in surrender. "No way. I'm done. No more food."

"Ah, the food was just a ploy." He pulled her to her feet and guided her with one hand at the small of her back toward the chaise loungers situated near the terrace railing. "There's something I want to give you and figured overwhelming you with culinary goodness would make you too relaxed to put up a fuss."

"Give me what?"

He motioned her toward one of the loungers and sat on the one beside it. "Just something I thought you'd like." On the small table beside him sat the white box he'd left out before he'd intercepted Gabe at work. He set it on her lap and anchored his elbows on his knees, hands clasped between them to hide his fidgets. "Open it up."

For two excruciating heartbeats, he thought she'd refuse, her hands positioned on either side as though she might hand it back to him. Instead, she cautiously lifted the lid and set it on the concrete at her feet. The tissue paper inside the box rustled in the gentle evening breeze. Pinching the delicate white paper between her tiny fingers, she peeled it back and sucked in a sharp gasp. "You didn't."

"I did." And he'd given Knox carte blanche to go as overboard as his nerdy inclinations dictated.

With the kind of reverence usually reserved for sacred artifacts, Gabe lifted the new state-of-the-art laptop from inside. Beside it sat a brand-new phone with enough power and memory behind it to power a small data center.

"I told Knox how you work," he said. "The programs you use and how you import. He said those were the best for graphic work and that they run on parallel operating systems so they'd make interfacing easier." He paused, retracing his conversation with Knox. "At least, I think that's what he said. When Knox gets wrapped up in gadgets, I only catch about a tenth of what he actually says."

She smoothed her hand over the laptop's soft aluminum surface, her fingertips trembling.

He fisted his hands tighter, forcing himself to stay put, but damn, this gift-giving thing made him antsy. "If they're not what you wanted, we can exchange them. I just thought "

Her head snapped up, the awe on her face staggering in its beauty. "They're perfect." She studied the gifts on her lap, swallowed, then met his gaze again. "They're way more than I can accept, but they're exactly what I would have bought myself."

"If they're what you want, then keep them."

"I can't do that. It's too much."

"Gabe, you dropped a good chunk of your savings for a dress to wear on a date with me. Would you have bought it and all the fancy stuff that went with it if I hadn't asked you to the dinner?"

She ducked her head and tucked the laptop back in the box, though her face was painted with regret. "That's not fair. It's not the same."

"It is the same." He grabbed her hand before she could cover the gifts back up. "You did it to be with me, and it damned near made me swallow my tongue. Which, by the way, means I enjoyed it a hell of a lot. So, why can't I do this for you?"

"Because it's about four times as much."

"Since when does the price tag matter? You didn't skimp for me."

Her eyes widened, the tiniest bit of hope zinging behind them.

"Take the gifts." He laced his fingers with hers and leaned closer. "Let me do this for you."

"But you're already giving me more than I can ever give you."

And he was deceiving her even as they watched the sun set, even if it was for her protection. "You're wrong on that. You have no idea how much you give me. For the first time in my life, I don't have to chase some kind of thrill just to take the edge off. I can actually sit still and enjoy what's going on around me. I'm even sleeping for a change. Being next to you settles me. Or, maybe what I've been chasing my whole life was you, and now that you're here, I don't have to run anymore. Whatever it is, I like it. A lot. Don't discount what a gift you being in my life is."

Untwining her fingers from his, she stroked his jawline, fingertips playing in the scruff. "You think I'm a gift?"

"I think you're everything. Worth everything. Worth any risk."

She frowned. "What risk?"

His heart stuttered and his lungs seized. Granted, keeping her in the dark with the Lakeside break-in was a risk in itself, but there was a bigger insecurity where she was concerned. One he could absolutely share if he had the balls to do it. He covered her hand with his, reveling in the soft sensation beneath his palm and the open curiosity on her face. "I always thought love was a risk. One I wasn't willing to take. You're worth it."

Her mouth parted on a soft gasp and she tried to pull her hand free.

Zeke tightened his hold and kissed the center of her palm. "Relax."

"I can't relax. I don't… I mean, how am I supposed to interpret that?"

"It means I love you, *gatinha*. All of you. Just like you are." He clasped her hand between both of his, needing the simple contact more than he needed air. An anchor to hold him steady while his senses rocketed on an adrenaline high. Nothing he'd ever done, no high-octane sport or thrill ride, beat the euphoria of that moment. "I know it probably seems fast, but I think I knew it the second I laid eyes on you. Never once have I felt that for another woman. Never said it to anyone else, but it's true."

"You love me?"

He traced her lower lip, her fluttering breath warm against his thumb. Funny how she quieted everything inside him. The same shocking peace that came the second his parachute unfurled from a free fall and offered him absolute silence. *"Eu te amo e cada dia que passa eu me apaixono mais por você."*

"What's that mean?" she whispered.

He slid the box off her lap, set it on the small side table and pulled her to him, guiding her knees so she straddled his hips. Cupping the back of her neck, he pulled her close. "It means I love you, and every day I fall a little more."

Her hands fisted in his T-shirt and her breath ghosted across his face. "I don't know what to say."

"You don't have to say anything. Just listen and know it's not only Danny anymore who'd do anything to keep you safe." He lowered his voice. "There are no rules where you're concerned, Gabrielle. No risk, no chance that wouldn't fall under an entirely different criteria where you're concerned. I need you to understand that."

She combed her fingers through his hair, her eyes searching his face with a mix of curiosity and suspicion. "That sounds a little ominous."

More like a Hail Mary he hoped she'd remember when the time came to lay his cards on the table. "Your man just admitted he loved you. My gender requires I macho that shit up or they'll yank my man card." He squeezed his arms, hugging her closer to him. "Proper form is for you to lay those plump lips of yours on mine and kiss my ego into the stratosphere."

She smiled so bright that the sun seemed a little dimmer in comparison. "I can do that."

Chapter Twenty-Four

Zeke Dugan loved her. Not just liked, but *loved* her. Gabrielle Parker. A nobody mechanic with enough social dysfunction to make people point and laugh. Even after an hour of long, indolent kisses and sunset watching, his words still hadn't sunk in. Now she sat nestled between his legs on his oversize couch, perusing the new toys he'd given her.

He pointed over her shoulder at the email icon. "Knox said everything's set up and ready to go. Fully integrated."

She clicked the image and, sure enough, the program opened, new emails flying into her inbox. "How'd he do that? I mean, doesn't he need passwords?"

Zeke stilled behind her, so silent and motionless she wasn't even sure he was breathing. When he spoke, his voice seemed thin. Uncertain and vulnerable, just like the night he'd left to meet his brothers in the middle of the night. "Most people would."

She twisted and barely bit back a gasp.

Wariness painted his features, but his eyes were sharp. As though he were waiting for something. "I promise you, not just anyone can get to that information. Cybersecurity is one of Knox's specialties. He works for a lot of corporations and helps them safeguard their secrets.

I didn't know he'd take me asking him to set you up so literally until it was already done."

"But if he can get into my accounts, then what's to stop anyone else from doing it?"

"That's why he added his contact information in your app. He wants to sit with you when you have time so he can walk you through how to better protect yourself." He tucked a strand of hair behind her ear, but the move lacked his normal confidence. "Don't think of it as an invasion of privacy. Think of it as your own personal cyber consultation."

Well, there was that aspect to it. And better someone she knew, or in this case someone close to someone she knew, than someone out to steal what little savings she had. Still…

She faced forward and reclined against his chest. "A little notice would have been nice before he did it. At least I could've taken embarrassing stuff offline before I'd hired him."

"Embarrassing?" This time it was Zeke who adjusted for a better view of her face. "Like porn?" He knocked her hand away from the track pad and popped open the internet browser. "Now I'm compelled to find what secrets you've got stashed away."

She snatched the laptop, swung her legs off the couch, and set the computer on the coffee table. "No porn." She slid him a sideways glance as she shut the cover. "But I might have a few…um…graphic pictures saved here and there."

He snatched her by the wrist and tugged her toward him. His voice rumbled low in that drop-dead sexy way he always used when he was about a second from sliding his cock inside her. "Yeah?"

Oh, yeah. Definitely drop-dead sexy.

He nuzzled the sensitive space behind her ear, his warm breath sending delicious ripples down her spine. "Now I feel compelled to finagle a private viewing."

She giggled, but it came out huskier than her usual laugh, her body ramping fast for more of his decadent touch. "Ask Knox. I bet he's seen."

"Maybe." He pulled away, much to her dismay, and gripped her chin between his fingers. "But if you knew Knox a little better, you'd know he's seen so much crap online that nothing fazes him. And I mean nothing. A few dirty pics or porn history wouldn't even tweak his radar. Hell, if anything, a lack of dirty stuff would throw a flag more than anything kinky."

Part of her wanted to push the issue, but the sweet, puppy dog look on his face obliterated her forced frown. She pursed her lips to fight back the smile. "You and your brothers are weird."

"Weird, but devoted. Once you're in, you're ours whether you like it or not."

She sat back, more than a little stunned by the statement. "I'm not *in*. I barely know the man."

"*Gatinha*, I've told you I love you three times in the last hour. Knox is my brother. You don't get more in than that."

"Maybe you should define—"

Her new phone rang and vibrated against the glass-topped coffee table. For a second, she considered punching the decline button, but changed her mind when she spied Danny's number on the front. Her brother might get chatty at home, but she could count on one hand the number of times he'd phoned her without an agenda. She scooped it up and scowled at Zeke. "I'm not done with you."

He grinned, as unrepentant as always.

She swiped the button on the home screen. "Hey, Danny. What's up?"

"Oh, good, you've got your phone on," Danny said. Before his voice had even died off, what sounded like a high-powered drill shrilled in the background. A muffled sound distorted the audio, but she could still make out Danny yelling at someone. "Hey, you guys wanna give that a rest a minute?" The smothered sound disappeared and Danny came back online. "Sorry 'bout that. Been a busy day. I just wanted to give you a heads up you'll be getting some test calls in the next thirty minutes or so."

"Test calls?" She pulled her phone away from her ear long enough to check the time. "And what the heck are you still doing at work after seven o'clock? You never work this late."

"I'm not working. At least not at the shop. And the calls are from the monitoring center."

"Monitoring center?" Beside her, Zeke swiped his fingers against her laptop's track pad, navigating some colorful website, not the least bit clued into her confused conversation. "Are you drunk?"

"No, I'm not drunk," Danny said. "The monitoring center is the place that dispatches emergency services if an alarm goes down at the house."

"We don't have a security system."

"We do now. I put one in today. Beck and some of his boys helped me do it. It's part of his sign-on bonus. Said no self-respecting security guy is worth his salt if he doesn't practice what he preaches."

She blinked. Then blinked again, rewinding what he'd said and still not coming up with anything that made sense. "Hold up. What signing bonus? And how could you install a security system when you were supposed to be at work?"

Movement sounded through the line, a shuffling sound as though Danny were moving somewhere quickly, followed by the *thunk* of a closing door. His voice dropped to that I'm-your-big-brother-and-you're-gonna-listen-to-me voice. "I got a signing bonus because I quit the shop and went to work for Beck."

"You what!"

Zeke's head snapped up at her outburst. He set the laptop aside and gave her his full attention, which kind of sucked considering he could only hear half of the shit coming through the line.

Danny kept going. "I'm going to work for Beckett."

"Doing what?"

"Everything. Home installs, consults, private security."

"You mean guarding rich people."

"That's a piece of it, but yeah, that, too."

He was out of his mind. No one just up and quit their job on a whim. Especially Danny. "But what about cars? You love working on them."

"I love doing my own thing. Doing the hot rods. Not patching up someone's fender bender and picking stock colors. Plus, Steve's an asshole. Beck's cool. He gets me. And he's willing to teach me something new. Plus, he's letting me set my own schedule so I can take on more custom work. Even said he'd back me financially so I can grow into that full time if that's what I want."

He quit his job.

Moving away from you.

Leaving you.

A bone-chilling cold pierced her stomach and a low, grating buzz droned inside her head. Quitting meant change. He'd probably be gone more. Might even decide he needed a place of his own. Someplace where his sister didn't cramp his style. Or worse, what if he got hurt looking out for some stranger? She'd already lost her dad. Her mother couldn't even remember to send cards on her birthday, let alone be a presence in her life. If she lost Danny, then—

"Gabe?" Zeke covered her hand and pulled it away from her neck, yanking her back from her manic thoughts and the murky darkness that went with them at the same time. "Sweetheart, take a breath and give me the phone."

She nodded and handed over the sleek device, nearly fumbling it in the process.

Zeke reclined on the couch, pulling her against his chest as he went and wrapping her up tight. "Hey, Danny. What's going on?"

God, he was warm. Warm and solid against the negative chatter battering her from the inside out. She inhaled deep, grounding herself in his summery scent and the steady beat of his heart beneath her cheek. The words he shared with Danny didn't matter. Only the rumbling comfort of his voice did.

He tossed the phone to the couch long minutes later and kissed the top of her head. "You okay?"

She was now. Embarrassed as hell she'd panicked like a two-year-old, but steadier now that she'd had time to center herself. "What did he say?"

"Mostly, he was worried about you." He shifted enough to gauge her expression. "You want to tell me why your brother trying out a new job sent you in a tailspin?"

Not really. Heck, she wasn't even sure it would make sense even if she tried. "He just caught me off guard. Walking away from something you've done your whole adult life is kind of a big thing."

"*Gatinha*, doing a job and loving it are two entirely

different things. Can you honestly say he was happy working at the shop?"

Was he? Now that she thought about it, she couldn't remember the last time he came home in a decent mood. If he ever talked about the shop, it was to bitch about his boss. "No, but he likes his custom work."

"And Beck is willing to work with him on that. Danny likes the security work. A man exploring…trying things on for size…that's healthy. The only way a person finds what they love in life is trying. Before I met Jace and Axel, I didn't know that. Now I do. We want to share that with Danny. Why is that bad?"

She pushed against his chest and sat upright, studying his expression. "What if it doesn't work?"

"Are you asking about him working security? Or are you asking if we'll stick around for him?"

I hope they're around a lot more. I hope they let me in their circle so I can learn from them and make my life better like they have.

Serious topics weren't something Danny dove into often, but when he'd shared those words with her after she'd first met them, he'd never been more solemn. "You guys mean something to him. I don't want to see him get hurt."

He traced the line of her cheek, his smile soft and patient. "We're not going anywhere. Not for you, or him. Danny's as much family to my brothers as you are to me. The only difference between the two of you is he's ready to jump."

If he'd somehow linked directly to her mind and conjured a picture from her thoughts and emotions, he couldn't have summed it up any better. Ever since she'd met him, it seemed he'd drawn her closer and closer to the edge of a giant bluff. Her hopes and dreams whispered of paradise and urged her to trust and leap, but her fears could only focus on the distance. On the danger and the risk.

"It's a long way down," she whispered, hating the anxiousness that laced her admission, but proud she'd voiced it all the same.

He palmed her nape, pressed a gentle kiss to her lips, and murmured against them, "I'll catch you."

She closed her eyes, his velvet promise sweeping clean and bright as a spring breeze through her guarded heart.

Resting his forehead against hers, he squeezed her neck. "Don't overthink this. You might be content in your work, but Danny's not. He's bored. Frustrated. You know where that's led him in the past. We're just opening some new doors."

She pulled away enough to meet his gaze. "That's the part I don't get. Why?"

"Because he's a good man and he deserves it."

So simple. Almost too simple and too good to be true, but if Zeke and his brothers could make Danny happy, she'd bite her tongue and pray for the best. For both of them. "I think he deserves it, too." She smoothed her fingertips along his sternum, the dove-gray cotton T-shirt soft beneath her touch. "And you're right about my work. I like what I do. I like the peace behind it. Puzzling things out and letting my mind wander." She lifted her gaze to his. "But I'm not content with everything in my life."

He arched his eyebrow, silently prodding her for more.

Part of her wanted to retreat. To wave the topic off or find some shallow excuse for what she'd started to unveil and keep her secrets safe. Another, more daring part, demanded she take that first step toward the cliff. "People. I'd like to have more friends. Trust people more." She hung her head, a smile tugging on her lips as she thought of all the times her brother had lectured her on her reclusive ways. "Danny says I hold people off on purpose so I can't get hurt."

"Is he right?"

She shrugged. "Probably."

Zeke snagged her wrist and tugged her forward until she toppled against his chest. "You know, I used to be a lot like that."

"You did?" She tried to push upright, but he held her firm. "There's not a shy bone in your body."

His voice took on an easy tone. Almost distant as though he strolled easily through long forgotten memories. "Shy wasn't my problem. Bullies were."

She relaxed against him, splaying her hand over his heart and resting her head on his shoulder while the setting sun cast his living room in deeper shadow. Outside the picture window, Dallas's downtown lights twinkled against a deepening blue skyline.

"I told you my family was poor," he said, "but I was crazy good with books and learning. My grades earned me scholarships to one of the nearby private schools for junior high and high school. Great for my education, but hard as hell on my social life."

"How?"

From her place against him, she couldn't watch the emotions play across his face, but she felt them all the same, a prickling unease that lifted goose bumps along her arms and shoulders.

As if sensing her response, he wrapped her up tighter, warding off the chill from his emotions. "Kids are mean. Especially when someone's different. It's hard to blend in with rich kids when you've got a thick Brazilian-Philly accent and no money to dress like them."

"They were mean to you?"

"People buck what they don't know." He huffed out an ironic laugh. "And to be fair, I wasn't exactly nice back to them. I told you I had anger issues. Still do if I don't keep a tight leash on them and keep myself evened out. Back then, though, it was bad. I got to the point where it was either isolate myself from everyone, or get kicked out of school. Watching how hard my parents worked to make ends meet, I knew how important school was, so I sucked it up and went with option A."

A helicopter glided above the two tallest buildings in the distance, its rotors filling the room with a low, muted pulse. Even its landing lights took on a mystical glow in the twilight. "What changed things?"

"I met Jace and Axel in college." His thumb moved in a slow, back-and-forth slide against her shoulder. "I was tending bar at a college hangout near campus. Some snotty jock tried to force a fellow bartender into a yes when she'd clearly said no, and I snapped. It took both Jace and Axel to pull me off the bastard. I lost the job, but I found my brothers."

She shifted enough to gaze up at his face. "So they helped you, and now you're helping Danny."

"Something like that." He hesitated a minute, his eyes narrowing as though he struggled to string his words together the way he wanted them. "The thing is, once a person's got their base, people they know they can trust in their corner, it makes dealing with everything else easier. It doesn't matter if you've got one or ten you can rely on. If they're there, you can face the rest of the crowd a lot easier. You don't have to be defensive with the world at large because you know at the end of the day, your real friends aren't far away."

And she'd spent the vast majority of her life keeping most people at a distance. Except Danny and her father.

God, no wonder she was a basket case. Though, in the past month things had been different. She'd not only begun to let a man into her life, both emotionally and physically, but she'd willingly walked into at least two social situations. Scary ones that necessitated at least a modicum of small talk. In the past, she'd have chewed off her own arm to avoid that kind of torture.

And she'd made a friend. A real life honest to God girlfriend.

All in the past month.

Since she'd met Zeke.

Because he was in her corner. Grounding her even when she was freaking out over demons he couldn't see.

She swallowed, barely managing the act with the knot of emotion clogging her throat. "I have you."

He smiled and tugged her back against him, the patience and understanding in his easy embrace further tempting her to jump. "Yeah, *gatinha*. You've definitely got me."

Chapter Twenty-Five

Thirty more minutes until Operation Swan Dive commenced. Careful to keep her new ivory shirt out of the mess she'd created, Gabe wiped up what was left of the splattered chocolate cake batter on the kitchen counter and gathered up the last of her pots and pans for washing.

Nearly a whole week since Zeke had told her he loved her and they were still solid. Five and a half days of easygoing, uncomplicated happiness so bright and blinding it rivaled the May sunshine glinting off the lake outside her kitchen window.

And nothing had ripped the rug out from underneath her.

Well, not with Zeke at least. Something was wrong with Danny. Not that he was overly angry or anything. More like distracted and refusing to talk about whatever was bugging him. Hence, the chocolate Bundt cake cooking in the oven. Where poking and prodding to uncover what was on her brother's mind wouldn't work, sweets would.

Always.

Too bad her plans with Zeke wouldn't be as simple. Cooking she could do in her sleep. Handing over her heart was a whole different recipe she didn't have a clue how to prepare for. April, on the other hand, had offered all kinds of sexy tips to build into her special night. Most of which entailed blowing what was left of her savings on purchases she'd guaranteed would make Zeke remember every last detail.

The timer on her phone let out an impatient trill at the same time a knock sounded at her door. She poked her head around the corner of her galley kitchen.

Zeke's cherry-red Camaro sat beside her truck in the driveway, the early afternoon sun sparking off the spotless exterior.

So much for having the mess cleaned and her makeup re-touched before he got here. "It's open!" Ducking back to the oven, she snatched her oven mitts. The heat hit her in a waft powerful enough to stir the hair around her face, and the rich, sweet scent of fresh cake flooded the kitchen.

"Gabe?"

"In here." She flipped the oven door closed and eased the cake on the counter to cool. "I thought you weren't going to be here for another thirty minutes?"

Zeke meandered around the corner. "I thought you were going to start locking the front door." He glanced back over his shoulder. "The alarm system wasn't even on."

Okay, so maybe they hadn't had a completely uneventful five and a half days. Zeke might not get upset about many things, but the three times he'd busted her not locking the door and using the alarm—which was now four times—had set him off good. She still couldn't figure out what all the fuss was about. "I've lived in this house my whole life, Zeke. I told you I'd try, but that's not going to change overnight."

Satisfied she had the bulk of her cleanup done and eager to get his mind on something else, she tossed her dish towel to the countertop, spun toward him and smoothed her hand over her blouse. It probably wasn't anywhere near as fancy or trendy as the stuff the women where he worked wore, especially paired with jeans, but the peasant look and the delicate lace made her feel sexy, and April said that was what counted most. Plus, she'd splurged on some delicate, sparkling sandals. "What do you think?"

Sure enough, her ploy worked. His gaze travelled the length of her, slowly taking in the subtle way she'd pulled her hair back and pinned it, then on to appreciate her clothes and new shoes. "I like it." His anger seemingly forgotten, he sashayed closer and curled his hand around the side of her neck. "What brought this on?"

"I wanted to be pretty." Ugh, maybe she should have practiced her verbiage as much as she practiced her makeup. "I mean, I wanted to do something special. For you."

His mouth softened, and any distance he'd left between them was gobbled up in a second. He lowered his voice and slid his nose alongside hers. "Told you at least a hundred times now. I love you. Not what you wear."

His rich scent wound around her, the soothing timbre of his voice scrambling all her well-laid plans.

Shake it off, Parker. Get your head in the game. Focus.

"I, uh…" She licked her lips and tried not to focus too long on his mouth just a kiss away. "I didn't do it for approval." Slow and steady. All she had to do was put herself out there and share the truth. "I like the stuff I usually wear. I mean, everything I own is comfortable, but I also wear it because it doesn't draw attention. If you don't draw attention, then you don't ever have to get your hopes up and you never have to risk." She let her voice trail off, hoping what she'd said didn't register like the nonsense it sounded like coming out of her mouth.

He backed away and studied her face, a hint of surprise and a whole lot of pride sparking behind his eyes. "You're putting yourself out there for me?"

"I'm trying." It should have been terrifying—utterly devastating based on past experiences—admitting such a thing, but with the way he looked at her, as though he reached for her soul instead of seeing only on the outside, kept her solid as a rock.

"It looks good on you. The clothes *and* the attitude." He skimmed his knuckles along her jawline and grinned. "Of course, you realize there's a side effect to this little exercise, right?"

"Side effect?"

Fingering the low cut neckline, he teased her skin. "The more you dress up, the more time I'll spend taking those clothes off you."

She scoffed and batted his hand away, wrapping her arms around his waist. "The only chance I've had to wear clothes the last week is when we're in public or you're at work."

"Which proves I'm good at what I do." His playfulness ebbed and he cupped the side of her face. "And considering you've made such effort, I think it's only wise I practice my skills and get you out of that top."

"Oh, no." She stepped out of arm's reach before he could make good on his promise. "You can't undress me yet. Not until I finish Danny's bribe." She tested the side of the Bundt pan.

"Holy shit, is that a cake? I thought you were sworn to all things healthy?"

She placed her cake plate over the top of the pan and carefully flipped the cake. "There's a time to be healthy, and there's a time to take off the gloves and sweet-talk your brother in the most literal way."

Eyes glued to her work, he crept closer. "What's up with Danny?"

"No idea. He's been acting weird the last few days.

Distant. Every time I try to talk to him, he gets pissed off. You don't think he's in trouble with Beckett, do you? I mean, his job is okay, right?"

For a flickering moment, a look she couldn't quite categorize shot across his face. Whatever was behind it, he masked it quickly with a shrug. "He's got no issues with Beck. At least none that I know of. And even if he did, it wouldn't last long." He grabbed her wrist as she pulled the Bundt pan free and looked her square in the eye. "I told you, *gatinha*. He's family. We might fight, but we don't leave each other hanging."

Family. That had to be the second or third time he'd referred to Danny that way. For that matter, he'd included her a time to two. Did that mean they considered Danny a brother now? Was that something she could even ask? She knocked the topic out of her thoughts, grabbed the chocolate icing, and poured it over the top.

Zeke swiped his finger through a pool of syrupy goodness at the bottom of the cake and popped it in his mouth. "The way that looks, I'm kind of hoping you'll hurry up and piss me off. Hell, I'm even thinking I'll fake being mad."

"What makes you think I'd make you a cake? Maybe I'd bribe you other ways." A light, happy giggle bubbled up behind her playful retort. She was flirting! And doing a decent job of it, too. She set the icing aside and grabbed the powdered sugar, sprinkling it lightly over the top.

Her gaze snagged on a smudge of oil beneath her fingernails and she nearly tumbled the small bowl of sugar to the countertop. White puffs billowed up all around her as she scrambled to the sink.

"Gabe?" Zeke was beside her in an instant, snatching her hand out from under the water and smoothing his fingers across her hands as he scanned for whatever had hurt her. "What'd you do?"

She tried to tug free of his hold, but he only clamped down harder. "It's nothing. I just saw some grease I missed from last night at the garage."

Zeke froze for all of two seconds, then released her hand and shut off the water. "*Gatinha*, you jumped like you'd been burned. What's that about?"

Her cheeks burned as hot as when she stayed out in the sun too long and the space along her hairline dampened. Talk about a mood killer. Only *she* could go from flirting and seducing her man to a fumbling catastrophe in a second. "I was embarrassed."

"Why?"

She rung the dish towel and squared her shoulders. Klutzy mechanic or not, she was done with ducking her head every time she got embarrassed. "Because I was trying to make an effort, and I missed the grease. I didn't want you to see a mechanic today. I wanted you to see a woman."

He chuckled, slow and broken at first, then building to a full-on laugh.

"You're not helping." She crossed her arms and tried to keep a stern face, but it was really hard with him laughing so hard.

"Babe." He pulled her against him, his shoulders jerking beneath each guffaw, especially now that he was trying to hold his laughter back. "There hasn't been a time in the weeks I've known you that I've *ever* thought of you as anything but one hundred percent, make-my-dick-stand-up-and-take-notice woman. And the next time you worry about grease under your nails, factor in the fact that I think it's hot as hell my woman can not only tell the difference between a carburetor and a crankshaft, but can replace either one if she needs to."

She snickered and let her forehead drop against his chest. "You're right. I shouldn't have freaked out. It was just knee-jerk."

"You're learning something new. Freaking out's part of the process." He threaded his fingers through her hair at the back of her head and tilted her face up to his. "Now, do I have to wait for Danny to get his peace offering first? Or can I have a slice of cake in advance?"

How in the name of all that was holy had she gotten this lucky? Most men would have run screaming at all her social crap within an hour of meeting her, if not sooner. But here he was, moving right past her childish freak-out without so much as a backward glance. "I'll make you a deal."

"Ah, negotiating. I like it. What's your offer?"

"You let me show you the rest of what I bought today, and if Danny's not home by the time I'm done, I'll cut you a slice."

"Done." He grabbed her hand and tugged her toward her bedroom.

"Hey, wait!" She tried to dig in her heels, but as traction went, her sandals really sucked. Not to mention he had at least eighty pounds on her. "You can't just agree that fast. You didn't even bargain."

He slapped on his best Marlon Brando interpretation and did that movie-mafia yada yada hand gesture. "You made me a deal I couldn't refuse." She'd barely passed her bedroom door, when he shut it behind her and ambled to the bed. Apparently, he planned on settling in for a while, because he shucked his boots and socks and stretched out on what he'd claimed as his side of the bed. "All right. Bring on the fashion show. But do me a favor. Stretch the clothes changing to a maximum."

She cocked her head and anchored her fists on her

hips, trying to keep a straight face. "Maybe you should have negotiated better."

"Keep talkin' and I'll renegotiate by paddling your ass."

A spanking.

In the space of a nanosecond, her sex grew damp and a slow, demanding pulse set up shop between her legs. Leave it to Zeke to send a miniorgasm ripping through her when he was all the way on the other side of the room. She couldn't have moved or come up with a decent thought if someone had come through the bedroom door with guns blazing.

His goofy grin slipped and his eyes heated. "What just happened?"

Oh, no. No way was she going there. Not yet. Putting words around what felt good and sharing where her head was at with sex was one thing. Diving into fantasies she could barely admit to herself was something else entirely. "Nothing."

"Nothing my ass. You totally shut down. Surely you know I'd never hurt you. Ever. I'd cut off my own hand first."

She knew. She also knew that, while her exterior might have shown a shuttered expression, her insides were still revved up and ready to go. While she might be chicken when it came to dirty confessions, there was no way in hell she'd leave him thinking she'd even considered he'd cause her pain. "I wasn't upset." She licked her lip, for all the good it did her with her desert-dry mouth. "I was actually thinking you promising a spanking wasn't the best incentive to get me to behave."

This time it was Zeke who went crazy still, his sharp gaze shifting from concern to blazing devilment in a single heartbeat. "Now, there's a promising development."

His mouth curled into a wicked grin that fanned the flames licking through her core. He crossed his feet at the ankles, jerked his head toward her walk-in closet and readjusted the rapidly growing bulge behind his Levi's. "Show me what you bought, and we'll see how bad of a girl you've been today."

Oh.

My.

God.

Surely he didn't mean what she thought he meant. Yeah, it was a fantasy. Lots of women probably had the same one, but to actually act it out?

"You keep standing there and I can pretty much assure you'll end up over my lap sooner rather than later."

She bit back a squeak and her toes curled in her sandals. "Um…" No big deal. All she had to do was carry on with her original plan. Where things went from there would just happen.

She swallowed and tried to look casual on her way to the closet. It wasn't like she could drag things on too long. Yeah, she'd bought a few other new tops and some fun flats and flip-flops, but the bulk of what she'd spent her money on was folded in the top drawer of her dresser. Once she showed him the bra and panty set she'd donned this afternoon, she couldn't imagine she'd get around to modeling those.

Stopping at the farthest edge of the closet, she toed off her shoes and pulled her shirt over her head.

Movement sounded on the bed behind her.

She didn't dare turn around, was too afraid to confirm he'd shifted for a straight-on view of where she stood. If he had, he wouldn't suspect much yet. From the back, her bra would look just like all her other boring white ones, but the front? Big difference.

With trembling fingers, she popped the buttons on her waistband and shimmied her jeans over her hips.

They'd barely cleared mid-thigh when Zeke's low, hungry growl rumbled behind her.

She smiled despite the adrenaline racing through her veins. So, Zeke was a fan of thongs. *Good to know.* When she'd first pulled her jeans on over them, she wasn't so sure she could adjust to the feel of her butt cheeks rubbing against the rough denim, but if that was his response, she'd grow accustomed to the sensation.

Taking her time, she neatly arranged her jeans on the hanger, then plucked her blouse off the floor and repeated the process.

"You're taking too long."

She peeked over one shoulder, though not enough to actually make eye contact. "I thought you said to draw the changing part out as long as possible."

"I changed my mind."

Her eyes slid shut and a near silent whimper whispered past her lips, a wild and unruly swirl of flutters sweeping through her belly. Her voice, when she managed to speak, came out husky and breathless. "I thought trauma docs were decisive, think-on-their-feet types."

"I'm about to do a lot more than that on my feet if you don't get over here."

Smoothing her hand down the front of the blouse she'd hung on the highest rod, she dragged in a slow steadying breath and turned, only to have it escape on a shaky exhalation.

Gone was the patient man who'd lectured her about locked doors and alarm systems, replaced with 100 percent pure predator. He sat at the edge of the bed, his feet firmly planted on the ground and legs far enough apart she could easily walk between them. His carnal gaze lei-

surely assessed her head to toe, a starving wolf antici-
pating its main course.

Sheer need propelled her feet forward, instinct lending
what she hoped was a sultry sway to her hips. "I didn't
buy much. Just a few underthings." She trailed her fingertips between her cleavage, drawing his gaze to the
delicate see-through lace. "You said you liked the white,
so I stuck with the same color."

He held his silence and fisted his hands on his knees.

"The lace feels really good. Like silk." Emboldened,
she gently cupped her breasts and halted just between
his knees. His mouth was close enough his warm breath
fluttered against her chest. "So? On a scale of one to ten,
what do you think?"

He'd created a monster. A remorseless, sex-kitten
monster. Zeke stroked the creamy expanse of Gabe's
torso, displacing her hands with his own so her breasts
filled his palms. "On a scale of one to ten, I'd say your
shopping trip scored a perfect ten." He plumped the full
globes and dragged his thumbs across her pretty pink
nipples showing through the delicate fabric. "Your tits,
though, are off the fucking chart."

Her breath left on a shaky exhale and her whole body
trembled beneath his touch. Whether she realized it or
not, she angled herself closer, nearly brushing one puckered bud against his lips. "Does that mean I shouldn't return the other colors tucked away in my dresser?"

God help him, his nuts were already drawn tight and
ready to explode and he'd barely even touched her. He
forced his hands to her hips and eased back enough he
wouldn't be tempted to suck one of those tempting peaks
in his mouth. Eventually, he'd get a taste, but not yet. Not
until he was sure where her head was at. "What it means
is if you didn't get at least two sets in every color, we're

going back to the store. Tomorrow. Today, I think my kitten wants to play."

Another shudder, this one paired with tiny goose bumps flaring out along her arms and the tops of her breasts.

"You want that, *gatinha*?" He traced the line of her thong around her waist and to the small of her back where it dipped between her cheeks. "Want to see what it feels like taking my hand on your ass?"

Her fingers bit into his shoulders and she shifted her weight from one foot to the other, her breaths coming short and shallow. She opened her mouth as if to say something, then bit her lip instead.

"There's not a wrong answer there, Gabrielle. Nothing to be embarrassed about. This is you and me. Safe. Honest. If you want to explore, I am one hundred percent on board."

"You don't think it's…a little weird?"

It was a step. A good one. And one he had a very solid answer for. He pried one of her hands from his shoulders, stood, and guided her palm so it covered his aching cock. The contact ripped a groan up his throat. "That give you a clue how I feel about the idea?"

She gently squeezed his length and rubbed the heel of her palm up and down. "You don't think I'm a freak?"

"Who gives a fuck?" He flexed into her touch, halfway tempted to jerk his fly open for skin-to-skin contact. "If you're a freak, then I'm one, too. If we both want it and it feels good, then nothing else matters. Now, are we playing, or are we saving that for another time?"

Releasing her grip on his cock, she slipped her hands beneath his shirt and guided it up around his pecs. She leaned in close. Pressing her parted lips to his sternum, she lifted her innocent, yet hungry gaze to his and flicked her tongue against his skin. "I think I'd like to play."

His cock jerked in agreement, his pulse throbbing through his shaft. He yanked his T-shirt over his head and tossed it aside, eyes riveted to the way she plied her lips, teeth and tongue against his skin. Utterly devoted with no pretense of putting on a show. Innocence packaged as a wet dream.

And she'd just given him the green light on some seriously decadent fun. Fuck, he was a lucky bastard.

She fumbled with the waistband of his jeans.

Zeke clamped onto her wrists. "Easy." No way was he freeing his dick. Not yet. The damned thing had a mind of its own when she was fully dressed, let alone when all she had on were a few scraps of lace. "You in a hurry?"

She tried to pull her hands free with zero success. "Yes."

He grinned and earned himself a frustrated little pout from those naughty lips of hers. "That's too bad, 'cause there's no way in hell I'm rushing this." He sat back on the bed behind him and tugged her in between his knees, his hands still manacled around her wrists. Beneath his thumbs, her pulse beat a wild rhythm.

"I don't know what to do," she whispered.

God, she was sweet. Yet the energy coming off her was wild and untamed. He guided her hands to his chest. "There's nothing for you to do. Nothing except go with the flow." He teased her nipples through the sheer fabric with soft, barely-there circles from his fingertips that made her arch for more. "If you get scared, get uncomfortable for any reason, you say 'red.' Okay?"

Her gaze shot to his, her pupils dilated to the point the black nearly consumed the blue. "A safe word."

A low chuckle slipped from his chest, the fact that

his little angel caught on to what he meant so quickly knocking her halo off-kilter. "I'm thinking maybe I need to have Knox show me a little of your browser history after all." He tweaked her nipples, rolling them between his fingers.

Her eyes slid shut on a grated moan and her hips undulated as though she felt the touch between her legs.

"On second thought, how about you take me on a tour instead?" He peeled her bra straps over her shoulders. "Show me all the dirty sites that get you off." He reached around her and flicked the clasp.

She gasped, the sound closer to relief than surprise.

Slowly, he eased the fabric away, her breasts full and tipped by nipples so hard they had to hurt. "Would you do that? Show me all your dirty secrets?"

"Zeke." A plea. Simple and ragged. She coiled one hand around his neck and threaded the fingers of the other through the hair at the back of his head, urging his mouth toward her tits. "Can we hurry now?"

"Oh, no." He licked one distended tip and blew across the slick path he'd left behind. "I want to explore just how naughty my girl really is." He pulled away and grinned up at her, ghosting his fingertips up and down the sensitive stretch just below her belly button.

No way in hell was there a woman sexier than Gabrielle Parker in that moment. Eyelids heavy and languid, full, kissable lips slightly parted, and sexy blond hair falling soft around her face. She was totally in the moment, drifting on every touch and word. Damned if it didn't make him feel like a fucking god.

He palmed her ass. "Something tells me you're a very bad girl." He smoothed his hands down the backs of her thighs then back up, gently warming her flesh. "You know what happens to bad girls, right?"

Her hips twitched and a tiny squeal passed her lips.

Oh, yeah. She knew. Knew and was eager for it. Ready and practically purring. He splayed one hand at the small of her back. "Bend over, sweetheart. Show me what you want."

Her body trembled, but she folded herself over his lap without even a breath of hesitation.

"Hands straight out in front of you so I can see them." He stroked one hand down her spine. "What's the word I asked you to use, *gatinha*? What stops everything?"

"Red." Quiet, but quick on her tongue.

"Good girl." He dipped his fingers between her legs, smoothing his fingers over the delicate lace. It clung to her labia, the fabric soaked. "My girl's wet."

God, he could play with her for hours, just like this. Hell, even with his dick hard enough to bust out of his jeans, he wouldn't forgo this moment. He hooked his fingers in the waistband of her thong and inched it down her ass. "Spread your legs, sweetheart."

The sheer lace pooled on the floor, and damned if she didn't lift her ass when she opened for him, baring a decadent, beautiful view of her sex.

"Oh, baby." His mouth watered and his tongue practically danced for a taste of her slick folds. He rubbed her taut cheeks, prepping the creamy surface for the slap of his hand. "You should see what I see. Your ass turned up for me, your pink pussy swollen and ready for me." He gave into temptation and slicked two fingers between the apex of her thighs. "You're drenched." Back and forth, he worked her, building her need higher and higher. "You want this bad, don't you?"

"Yes." Instant. Greedy.

He smacked one cheek before he could second guess himself.

She bucked beneath him and let out a startled cry. Her thighs clenched tight. "Zeke!"

"Uh, uh, uh." He tapped the inner seam of her leg. "You're not hiding that sweet pussy from me. Not now. Unless you want to use your word?"

"No." Her body quivered, but she opened herself on a ragged exhale, even wider than before. "More."

His cock jerked so hard his hips damn near lifted off the bed and his eyes rolled back far enough he could have given his own neuro exam. Jesus, God Almighty, she was perfect. A fucking dream. He swiped his fingers through the middle of her sex and over her clit. "Good girl." He circled again and landed another swat. Then another. And another. Each strike targeted for a fresh patch of skin and interspersed with rewarding, yet demanding strokes through her slick folds.

With every smack, her hips rose in anticipation. She fisted the comforter in each hand, her head thrown back so her hair trailed in a wanton mess down her back. The ragged sounds coming out of her throat—Christ, he could come from those alone.

He plunged a finger inside her and she cried out.

"So good." Pumping deep, he worked her core, adding a second finger before he pulled them free and swatted closer to her sex. "Love how pink your ass is." Pump, pump, smack. "Lift for me more. Show me how bad you want it."

She groaned and tossed her head, but did as he asked. Her pussy quivered around his fingers.

Smack. "Don't you dare come. Not until my mouth is on you." He could already taste it, her sweet cream coating his tongue and the back of his throat. Hell, her scent alone was enough to make a man want to live between her thighs. "You ready for that? Want to come in my mouth?"

"Yes!" She pushed back against his fingers, her whole body strung taut with the need for release.

Fuck it.

"Slide with me, *gatinha*." He grabbed her hips and dropped back on the bed, lifting her so she straddled his mouth with her hands braced on either side of his hips. "I'm so eating this pussy."

Oh, yeah. Sweet and thick, her hips eagerly grinding against his mouth. He palmed her inner thighs and spread them further, swiping his tongue against her swollen flesh. "Get my cock out."

She fumbled with the buttons once, twice, then finally got a decent grip. A yank of the denim and a shove on his briefs and his cock was free, filling those quick, enthusiastic hands of hers. No one had ever worked his dick the way Gabe did. Not like it was a means to an end, but like she couldn't wait to jack him off. Couldn't wait to get her lips wrapped around his shaft.

Wet heat surrounded his cockhead, and he flexed into her mouth.

She hummed and tightened her fist at the base, taking him deeper as she stroked his length.

He'd never last. Not like this. And damned if he was finishing this without watching the look on her face when he shot inside her.

Holding her firm against his mouth, he speared his tongue inside her.

She lost her rhythm, her thighs bearing down on either side of his head.

He dipped one hand to her clit, circled it once, twice, then squeezed the swollen little nub.

Her cry rang out above him, her hips writhing against

his mouth and sex pulsing her sweet release to his waiting tongue. Christ, he loved the taste of her. Loved the wild, unpretentious way she gave herself to him. No hesitation. No worry. Not in the bedroom. Outside of it, maybe. But here, it was raw, sensual goodness.

Her grip around his shaft tightened, the earnest strokes she started before, ramping back up again.

"Oh, no." He swiped his tongue between her folds one last time. "I'm not done with you. Turn around."

"But—"

He smacked her perfectly pink ass. "Get that ass turned. Gonna die if I don't get my cock inside you."

Either the swat, or the promise of riding him, got her moving, but her muscles shook from the mix of her release and adrenaline. She straddled his hips and braced one hand on his chest, the other gripping his shaft.

"That's it." He urged her knees wider, craving her slick, wet heat. "Guide me in."

So beautiful. Her hair loose on either side of her face and her eyes still glazed and languid from her release. She notched the tip inside her entrance and her eyes slid closed on a whimper.

"God, yes." He flexed upward, filling her in one solid thrust. This is where he needed to be. Right here. Connected just like this. Her scalding sex clutching his cock in a perfect vise. Hands down, the best thing he ever did in his life was prove he was clean so he could feel her skin to skin. So he could spill inside her. Mark her.

He powered deeper, holding her hips and rocking fast and hard into her sex. Her tits jiggled with each impact, the hard tips begging for attention. "Lean down here. Want those nipples in my mouth."

"Zeke." Her nails bit into his chest, the plea in her voice drawing his nuts up tight, ready to release.

"Now, baby. Wanna give it to you again before I come."

She angled closer, dangling those tight pink points right in front of his mouth and lifting her hips for all he could give her.

He flicked his tongue against the peak. "Finger yourself. Do it hard so I can feel you on my cock."

Her hand slid between them, her fingers dipping down to rub against his shaft.

He drew her nipple deep and sucked, pistoning against her willing sex.

"Zeke!"

"Fuck!"

Her pussy fisted around him, slow, merciless pulses milking his shaft. His cock jerked inside her, jetting his release deep inside her. Powerful. A God-damned miracle of sensation he felt all the way to the arches of his feet. Every time he thought things might even out between them, maybe find a leveling out place, she upped the ante. Drew him deeper and deeper until he couldn't care less about surfacing.

He wrapped her up tight, her sweat-misted body trembling next to his and her cheek pressed directly above his hammering heart. "Love you, *gatinha*." He threaded his fingers in her hair. "Love you so much."

She froze inside his arms, even her breath halting.

"What?" He urged her head up so he could see her face. "What's wrong?"

She lifted her head, an uncertainty stamped across her features that should absolutely *not* be there after what they'd just shared. "I just…" She swallowed hard, licked her lower lip, then smiled. It was shy and a little crooked, but it shot straight through his heart and anchored in his soul. "I love you, too."

Chapter Twenty-Six

Gabrielle loved him.

Ever since he'd put himself out there, Zeke had craved hearing those words. Puzzled over whether or not she'd ever feel safe enough to give them to him and how it might feel if she did.

Nothing compared to reality. Especially with her body naked against his, his come filling her and his dick still semihard inside her. Hell, the damned thing was already stirring for another round, ready to show its appreciation.

He cupped the side of her face and rolled his hips against her. "Say it again."

She giggled, the sound as cute as the deeper flush spreading across her cheeks. "I love you, but you're not taking me for another ride. Not yet. I've gotta ply Danny with cake and get answers before he disappears to wherever he said he had to go." She leaned in close, pressed her perfect breasts against his chest, and rasped, "But if you want me to show you the alternate colors I bought on my shopping trip, I could model the rest tonight."

Tonight.

Fuck.

Maybe not the perfect declaration of love after all. Perfect setting? Yeah. But the timing? Completely jacked. He rolled them to their sides and his cock slipped free of her wet heat. Damned if the lost connection didn't feel ominous considering the circumstances. "I can't. I gotta head out in a few hours. There's something I need to do." Something that could land him and the rest of his brothers in jail if they didn't do things right.

She traced one finger down his sternum. "Let me guess. You guys are having one of your brotherhood powwow things."

"Yeah." Though not in the traditional sense. Not unless she considered breaking and entering traditional. He huffed out a frustrated breath and rolled to his back, keeping one arm hooked around her shoulders and her body tucked close to his side. Keeping their plans from her had never set right in his gut. Now it only felt worse.

She propped herself up next to him and splayed her tiny hand on his chest. "Hey, you okay?"

Man, wasn't that a loaded question. Part of him was tickled shitless. Over the moon she'd finally taken a chance on him and tempted to ignore tonight altogether. The other part was getting its ass kicked by his conscience for not saying something to her sooner.

Her hair spilled over one shoulder, the afternoon sun slanting through the windows sparking off the honey color. He speared his fingers through it, savoring the slick, heavy strands. "I know what's wrong with Danny."

As soon as he said it, his brain scrambled for bullshit excuses to cover and backtrack. Pronouncements of love and steaming-hot sex aside, if she took things even a tiny bit the wrong way and went to the cops, she could really cause them problems tonight.

But this was who he was. His brothers and the way they lived were part of his life. If he didn't show her all of who he was, could she really love all of him? "You ever think it's strange how many Realtors you've got knocking on your front door?"

Her gaze slid sideways long enough to show she considered it then shrugged. "Not really. It's been going on for a while now. At least three years."

"Well, I did. Especially after the fire. So, I had Knox do some checking."

She lifted her eyebrows in silent question.

"Turns out all the houses that have sold in this neighborhood have ended up in the hands of one real estate investment company. One that's got top management with seriously shady backgrounds."

"So?"

He sat up, leaning back against the headboard and pulling her in closer. "You heard Beck say he'd checked Mrs. Wallaby's house after the break-in. If it had been some random hack wanting electronics or quick items to fence, they wouldn't have bothered making a clean entry. Your neighbor's house was absolutely clean. No theft. Not one thing out of place. No one was ever supposed to know her property had been breached. The only time that happens is when people are looking for something. Usually information."

She sat back, a tiny pout pursing her kiss-swollen mouth. "You're overexaggerating. Who'd want information from Mrs. Wallaby?"

"Someone who wanted to force her to sell."

The pout morphed into a frown, but what he was saying still didn't seem to click.

"Think about the fire," he said. "You said yourself, Mr. Yates doesn't cook. But when Beck scoped things out with the fire chief later that night, they said it looked like a kitchen fire. Didn't you say he'd gotten up in the Realtors' faces and told them he'd never sell?"

"So, what? You think this company is behind everything?"

"*Gatinha*, I don't think you get how valuable the land your house is sitting on actually is. If a company cornered this neighborhood, they could make serious bank selling out to a big investor."

She swallowed, a spark of comprehension finally registering behind her gaze. "Okay, so what's that got to do with Danny?"

And here we go.

For a minute, he toyed with dodging the rest of it. Or at least stalling until after tonight. "After Knox dug into the investment company, I talked it over with Danny and the rest of my brothers. Every one of us thinks the people who run this company are willing to do some risky shit to get their hands on your land. And by risky I mean willing to force you and everyone else that lives here out if you don't play along. The problem is, Knox can't nail down enough proof through data online."

"Then tell the police. That's what they're there for."

God, she was sweet. Pure and good and everything right with the world. He cupped the side of her face. "It's not that simple. People in law enforcement have rules they have to follow. Processes they have to work within. They can't just move on suspicion. My brothers and I can. We *will*. If we find out the company's on the up-and-up, then we'll step back and leave it be. Or at least take precautions to get them out of your hair every five minutes. If they're not, we'll package everything up with a shiny bow and hand it over to the cops. We're not out to go vigilante on their ass. We're just out to make sure the investment company doesn't catch on to what we know until it's too late."

"Wait, what are you saying? Get information how?"

"We're going in. Tonight. That's what Danny's focused on."

"What!" She glared at him for all of a heartbeat then scrambled off the bed. "No. You can't do this. He can't do this. If you get caught, you'll lose your license. Or worse." She snatched her bra and panties off the floor. "And Danny…" She shook her head, her temper building steam as she yanked on her panties. "Jesus, you said you cared about him. Said you'd help him build his life, not fuck it up by breaking the law." She jerked a T-shirt out of her dresser drawer and yanked it over her head. "Do you know what happens to people when they break the law? They go to jail. They lose their lives. *They leave people behind.*"

"Gabe!" He snatched her wrist and pulled her between his legs. "*Gatinha*, listen to me. Danny is my brother. Even if you weren't in the picture, I'd do this for him because family has each other's backs, but it isn't just him. It's *you* we're talking about. *My* woman."

"It's. Against. The. Law."

"Which would be a huge fucking deal if I thought we'd get caught, but we won't. I know my brothers. I know what they're capable of and so do they. If we didn't think we could handle it, we'd deal a different way."

"Then find a different way. You're making a huge deal out of nothing."

"You getting hurt isn't nothing. Or have you forgotten your run-in with their henchman? A little bit deeper of a wound and your ribs could've punctured your lungs. What if you hadn't had your phone with you?"

"You're blowing it out of proportion."

"Really? What about your neighbors? What if I hadn't woken up when I did the night of the fire? Or hadn't been able to get in Mr. Yates's house? He wouldn't be kicked back in a retirement community waiting for his house to be rebuilt, he'd be in a casket. How much more unsafe does this situation need to be?"

Her lips clamped up tight, but her chest huffed up and down as if she'd sprinted a mile. "I believed in you. I told myself the fact that you had your own private emergency room was just me not being in touch with the real world. That you were being a good guy taking care of not-so-good people despite how they got hurt. I rationalized my boyfriend getting out of bed at two o'clock in the morning to meet his friends was completely understandable. That I just didn't know how friendships worked because I'd never had any. I even went so far as to twist up a man being able to hack into my personal accounts on a whim as a benefit instead of something terrifying. But that was complete shit, right? This is your world. You guys do this kind of crap all the time. It's not a one-time deal, it's a way of life."

"You're right." He stood and seized her with one hand behind her neck, his face nearly nose to nose with hers. "My brothers and I grew up in a different world. A rough one. But we grew up *right*. We know right from wrong. We have honor. Our code might not live up to your letter of the law, but it is always honorable. More than that, we protect the people we love. And you are most definitely loved. So much sometimes it hurts. I've said it before, but apparently it didn't register, so I'll say it more clearly. Like it or not, there is nothing, absolutely nothing, I won't do for you. Especially if it means keeping you safe."

Her voice dropped to a scary pitch and her body shook. "Get out and stay away from my brother."

His fingers clenched, muscles straining beneath a flood of adrenaline so powerful his veins burned. He should have kept quiet. Should have sucked it up and waited. Earned her trust over the long haul instead of throwing her in the deep end. "Your brother's a grown man. What he chooses to do is on him. As for me, I told you I loved you. That comes without conditions. Exactly as you are. You said you love me. I trusted that. Hoped you'd take me the same way. Either you don't have a fucking clue what love is, or you're just too scared to face it and you're using the first excuse to hightail it to safe ground."

He let her go, her startled gasp ringing in his ears. Fastening his jeans, he snatched his shoes and T-shirt off the floor. Christ, what a clusterfuck. He'd never be able to focus tonight. Not with this shit hanging over his head.

"This isn't an excuse. I trusted you."

"To what? Stay inside the lines so I didn't rock your tidy world?" He tugged his shirt down and sat on the side of the bed, jamming on his boots. "Life is messy, Gabe. People are imperfect. But you know what you can count on one hundred percent? *Me*. I'm not your mother. I'm not the narcissistic assholes you went to school with. I'm the man who loves you. Who's doing his damnedest to keep you safe." He stood and ambled so he towered over her. For the first time since he'd met her, the angry twitch he'd wrestled his whole life was back and flailing him with a razor-edged whip. "You may not agree with me, but I'm asking you to support me."

"You want me to pat you on the back and say this is a great idea?"

"No, I want you to tell me what you think, take the fucking time to see it from my angle and back my play no matter what. It's what I'd do for you." He gave into temptation and gripped both sides of her face. "You get tonight. Then I'm back here in the morning and we're talking this shit out."

"No, we're not."

"Oh, yeah we are." He grinned, a perverse and twisted part of him loving the throw down even if it did mean tomorrow could end up screwing his world thirty different ways. "You might be willing to run at the first sign of trouble, but I'm not." He kissed her hard and fast before he turned for the door. "That's a fact you can bank on."

Chapter Twenty-Seven

For the fifth time in under ten minutes, Gabe made another pass through the pictures she'd taken the past week and wiggled in her rickety pub chair. Comfort-wise it was probably the worst seating choice at the Gypsy Coffee House, but its dim lighting and corner location made the inconvenience worth it.

She swiped her phone's home screen with her thumb and a lakeside landscape slid into place.

Too bland. Swipe.

An urban bridge.

Too dull. Swipe.

The new family Lake Center.

Too much color. Swipe.

The nighttime skyline outside Zeke's town house filled the screen.

Perfect.

But too painful.

Yeah? But who gave you the phone to take that picture with? And the computer that went with it?

She dropped the phone to the tabletop and pinched the bridge of her nose. God, it was like a free-for-all in her head. Ever since Zeke had stomped out, she'd had enough back-and-forth, nonstop arguing to make her wonder if she should add multiple personality disorder to her social anxiety hang-up.

The muted strains of acoustic guitar from the main room died away and a round of semienthusiastic applause billowed up in its place. Surely, April would be here soon.

She flipped the phone back over and punched the button on the front. The fingerprint sensor unlocked the screen so fast she barely registered 8:12 p.m. on the lock screen before it redirected her to her photo app. Her favorite picture of her and Zeke together stared back at her.

God, she loved that shot. He'd taken her to a hole-in-the-wall diner for breakfast the morning after he'd told her he loved her and asked the waitress to take the picture. The accommodating older woman had taken a ton of them, eager to get the shot just right.

There wasn't a bad one in the bunch. Yeah, the lighting was off in a few and she could have framed them better, but with Zeke in them, they were perfect. His arm looked natural around her, his smile wide and easy and his gaze focused on her instead of the camera.

But he was a criminal. Maybe not a convicted one. Not yet. But he would be if he got caught. And if he was willing to break into a major corporation, no matter what his reasoning was for doing it, what else would he be capable of? For all she knew, the things she'd pieced together were just the tip of the iceberg.

April's perky, no-holds-barred voice cut the dark corner's quiet. "Hey, what's up?"

Gabe punched the off button on her phone and stood for that still-awkward hey-how-are-ya moment she'd yet to master. The first time they'd met for coffee she hadn't known whether to fake one of those BFF hugs she'd seen other girls give each other, or shake hands. Thankfully,

April had stepped right in and offered one of those casual half-hugs. "I didn't get you in trouble at work, did I?"

"With the phone call?" April waved the concern off and hung her purse on the back of her chair. Like always, she was dressed mostly in black, her wide magenta belt the only color accenting her simple cotton tunic, leggings and combat boots. "Nah, I had it on silent and was working the floor. No one noticed. Sorry I couldn't get out sooner, though. You sounded pretty worked up."

Worked up was putting it mildly. The first hour after Zeke had left she'd been so wound up with her internal debate, it was a wonder she hadn't hyperventilated. Calling Danny hadn't been an option. Between the way he'd acted the past few days and the things Zeke had told her, he was clearly on Zeke's side of the fence. The guys in the shop gave her funny looks if she talked about anything but sports or cars, so they were out. That had left April. And while they'd gotten to know each other a little the past few weeks, dialing her number had been one of the single hardest things she'd done in a while.

"Yeah, I..." She fiddled with her phone. "Something happened."

"At work?"

"No, with Zeke."

April slumped and rerouted the coffee she'd been about to take a sip of back to the table. "Ugh. Please say he's not a cheater. Cheaters are the worst."

Despite her foul mood, Gabe managed a weak chuckle. Leave it to April to lay things right out in the open and give it an extra kick at the same time. "No. He's not a cheater. I'm just not sure it's smart to keep things going with him."

"Why? Last I heard he was twenty kinds of awesome."

"He is. He was. I mean..." Shit. How the heck was she supposed to sum all this up and not sound like a loon?

She worried her fingers along the weathered groves on the dark stained table. She might not agree with what Zeke and her brother were doing, but she didn't want to get them in trouble either. "There's this thing going on. A situation in my neighborhood."

April leaned in and crossed her arms on the table, clearly warming up to the story.

"My brother and Zeke think a group of people are up to something bad. Something that needs to be stopped. But instead of telling the police about it, they want to take care of it themselves."

"Okay?" She lifted her eyebrows as if to say, *"And what's the rest of it?"*

"What they want to do is illegal."

April frowned. "Illegal as in they plan to hurt someone?"

"I don't think so. I mean, he said they planned to turn things over to the cops after they figured out what was going on, so no."

"So, they're gathering evidence or something?"

"Something like that. But it's dangerous. I mean, if these people are capable of doing what Zeke and Danny think they're doing, they could get hurt."

April sat back in her chair, shoulders slumping. "I still don't get it."

"What's not to get? They're doing something wrong, and it could get one or both of them hurt."

"Did they say *why* they were doing things the way they want to do them?"

"Zeke says turning things over to the cops right now would give the bad guys time to hide evidence and disappear. That the police have to follow certain procedures."

"So, it's not necessarily that they have anything against the cops, it's just they don't want the bad guys to get away with anything, or hightail it before they can get caught." Taking a slow sip of her usual to-go cafe mocha, April studied her over the plastic top, then carefully set her drink on the table and crossed her legs. "So, the nuts and bolts are you've got a protective brother and boyfriend who're trying to do the right thing big picture—wise, but aren't going about it in a way you're too excited about."

Thank God, someone actually understood. She nodded, so freaking relieved to know she wasn't a complete nutcase that she let out a heavy exhale with it.

April cocked her head. "And you told him how you felt about it?"

"Yes."

"And he's still doing it anyway?"

"Yes."

"And that's why you're upset? Because he's not changing his mind?"

Gabe opened her mouth to throw out another *yes*, but snapped it shut instead. Was that why she was mad? Surely not. "No, I'm upset with him because what he's doing is wrong."

"Looking out for you is wrong? I mean, I get it's not on the up-and-up, but it's not like he's out to hurt anyone, right? He's just getting what's needed to protect you. And the only ones at risk are him and his friends. Not you."

So much for finding someone who related. Gabe grabbed the straw out of her untouched water and poked the ice floating on the surface. "Breaking the law isn't a gray area. If everyone tried to use that kind of justification and did what they wanted, the world would be a nightmare."

"The world already is a nightmare." April studied her for long seconds, slowly pivoting her coffee between her fingers and thumb. "Are you really considering walking away from a guy that had you on cloud nine twenty-four hours ago?"

"Wouldn't you?"

"Um, no." She snatched the straw out from between Gabe's fingers, tossed it to the table and grabbed Gabe's hand, giving it an encouraging squeeze. "You're absolutely right. Breaking the law is usually a black-and-white situation, but people are all different shades of gray. You can't fit anyone into a perfect tidy box because we're human. Fallible. Every man, no matter how hot, smart or attentive, is going to fall short somewhere. If I had a guy who fell short tiptoeing into gray matter trying to take care of me, I'd tally that up under the I-can-deal-with-it column."

Gabe tugged her hand free, tempted to make some lame excuse and leave. She'd thought for sure April could help her. Yeah, the woman had a rebel image, but in the few weeks Gabe had known her, she'd been super strait-laced and just as OCD as Gabe. She actually put towels on her floor mats in her car to keep them from getting dirty. You didn't get more uptight than that.

"I don't get it," April said.

"Don't get what?"

April shook her head. "You've got your neat-and-tidy quirk and are as shy as they come, but you accepted me right off the bat even with all my weird bullshit."

"So?"

"So, what makes a mostly easygoing woman who thumbs her nose at all things girly get so rigid with law and order? It's completely out of character with the rest of you. What gives?"

People were everywhere. Cops and tenants from other apartments standing around gawking while they hauled her mother away in handcuffs. Police cars lined the front of the building, the blue-and-red lights swirling so fast they made her nauseous. For ten minutes, one of the cops had held her hand and stood beside her until her dad and Danny had shown up.

"I could have stopped her." Her own, distracted voice startled her out of her memories.

Across the table, April watched her with the same kind of shrewdness she'd come to expect from Zeke. "Could have stopped who?"

For years she'd kept her past buried, yet here they were fighting their way out from the darkness. "My mom."

"Stopped her from what?"

Gabe hung her head, tears blurring her clenched hands in her lap and acid filling her gut. Years she'd kept the story to herself. Beyond the police, her dad and a visit to a shrink five years later, she'd never rehashed it. Never wanted to. But all of a sudden the memories were right there in front of her, tangled with all the fear and confusion she'd wrestled since her fight with Zeke. "When I was eight, my mom was arrested. Possession with intent to distribute."

That night still registered as clear as if it happened yesterday. The apartment reeked like the bottom of Toothless's litter box, and the place was so cluttered and dirty there hadn't been a single place she'd felt comfortable sitting down. "She used to take me with her. She said we were going out to have fun with her friends, but she always put little baggies in her purse before we left. I thought about saying something to Danny or Dad, but I didn't want to make her mad. She and Dad fought all the time back then, and the only time she was really nice to me was when we went out."

"She took you with her?"

Gabe nodded, her shoulders sagging. "I guess she figured taking me was better than leaving me at home."

"That's whacked."

Gabe shrugged. "It only happened a few times. The last time she sold to an undercover cop. Turned out her friends were really guys she was sleeping with behind Dad's back. They needed a flunky willing to front for sales, and she needed men who made her feel young again. The trade didn't work out so well for her in the end."

"How in the world do you think you could've stopped that? You were eight."

"I told you. I saw the baggies in her purse. I saw her walking up to people outside in the parking lot while I waited in the apartment. I was little, but I wasn't stupid. All I had to do was tell my dad. Or even Danny. They'd have done something, and I wouldn't have lost my mom."

"Lost her how? She got jail time?"

Gabe shook her head. "No. Although, I bet she wishes it would have been that simple. She copped a plea and turned over her friends to the cops in exchange for probation. By the time she got home, Dad had hauled her stuff off and had filed for divorce. He spent every dime in savings on attorney fees, but got full custody of me and Danny."

"And you think if you'd have done the right thing your life would have ended up with some fairy-tale ending?"

"Well, at least I would've had a mom. I mean, don't get me wrong. Danny and Dad gave me a really good life. A solid one. But it's not easy growing up in a house with only men. It's…awkward."

"And smelly."

Gabe smiled at that. She couldn't help it. April always managed to lift her up. And surprisingly, she felt a lot lighter having shared. Clearer than she'd felt in a long time.

"Gabe, I don't know how to tell you this, but there's no guarantee you blowing the whistle on your mom would have changed anything."

"There's no guarantee, no. But I'd have at least had a chance."

"Tell me something." April folded her hands on top of each other on the table. "When's the last time you saw your mom?"

Forever and a day, and not one of them went by without her wondering why she didn't see her more. "Just after my twelfth birthday. She came over unexpectedly with a late birthday card."

"And? How'd it go?"

Gabe glared at the table, the pain and disappointment of the past piling onto all the other emotions from the day. "Not so great. She'd been there about five minutes when she asked me if I'd feel Dad out for a loan. Danny overheard it, yanked her out of my bedroom and kicked her out of the house. I heard Dad on the phone with her later that night. Hell, the whole neighborhood probably heard him. He made it *really* clear she wasn't welcome at the house anymore."

"That's too bad."

"I know. It sucked not having a mom."

"No, I mean it's too bad you haven't seen her. Then maybe you'd drop this crazy idea that you could have changed things."

"But I could have."

"No, you couldn't. Nothing you do can change someone else. People change themselves." She tilted her head to one side. "You saw her four years after she was arrested. Was she any different?"

Well, now that she thought about it… "No."

"Right. So she'd been busted by the cops, divorced, kicked out of her home and lost her kids. Don't you think that would be the mother of all wake-up calls?"

Um…maybe. She didn't give voice to the thought, but it didn't matter because April answered for her.

"Yeah, it would be. For any *sane*, reasonable person. But there are some people who just don't get it. No matter what we do, or what we try, they just can't get there. Maybe if you'd seen her more, you could've realized that's who she is. And Zeke isn't her. Not based on the stories you've told me the last few weeks."

I'm not your mother. I'm not the narcissistic assholes you went to school with. I'm the man who loves you. Who's doing his damnedest to keep you safe.

It was the truth. Not once in the time she'd known him had he been anything but steady. Considerate. Caring. Not just with her, but with everyone. The rugby kids, his brothers, even strangers. And he'd taken Danny into his extended family. Taken an interest in his future and set out to really make good things happen.

Danny. He was another example of goodness. Yeah, he'd started down a criminal path, but unlike her mother, he'd woken up and changed his ways.

Well, mostly. She still wondered how he'd ponied up for the back payments and the mortgage for the house, but there was no comparing Danny or Zeke to her mom. Both were good, solid, reliable men. So were the other brothers.

Danny's as much family to my brothers as you are to me. The only difference between the two of us is he's ready to jump.

Was she being shortsighted? Danny had claimed a million times she used every trick in the book to keep people at bay. Maybe this was another one. No different than her introverted social life or her boyish clothes.

April sat up straighter, drawing Gabe out of her thoughts as she reached across the table and nudged Gabe's hand. "Hey, you okay?"

No, not even close. "Not yet," Gabe said instead. "But I will be."

Chapter Twenty-Eight

Backed into a shadowed parking space across from Lake-side Investment's corporate office, Zeke thumbed the volume down on his stereo and re-checked his voice mails and text messages.

Again.

Still nothing.

He checked the discreet headset tucked inside his ear, the muted background conversations from Axel, Danny, Beck and Jace mingled with Knox's nonstop keyboard clicks.

The passenger-side door *kachunked* open and Trevor folded himself into the low-slung bucket seats, three large pizza boxes stacked in his lap. Unlike all the other guys who'd worn the expected all-black cargos and long-sleeved T's to their pre-meet, Trev had kept his attire to the usual jeans, button-down and a seriously badass pair of Lucchese boots. Then again, their role in tonight's event was distraction.

Zeke motioned to the pizzas. "You planning an after-party, or does sneaky shit make you hungry?"

Trev grinned, dropped a beat-up ball cap on top of the boxes and shoved the whole mess toward Zeke. "More like your diversion."

"You want me to be a delivery man? Really?"

"Hey. Not my fault you were working when we laid out the details."

Beck's voice sounded through the headpiece. "Don't knock pizza as a distraction, brother. We got lucky tonight. Two guys, both in their early twenties, working on a Saturday. You walk in there this late with those pies and the only thing they'll be interested in is who gets the last slice."

Zeke popped the lid on the top box. "Deep-dish cheese? You could have at least copped for some decent toppings."

"Yeah, well, don't expect a tip either." Trev fiddled with his own headpiece. "By the time they dig into them, they'll be cold."

Jace's chuckle rumbled through the line. "You forget the kind of crap you were willing to eat at twenty-one?"

"Hell, I don't remember what I ate yesterday," Trevor said.

"You guys are talkin' food and I've got a sweet lass waitin' with somethin' else for me to eat at the compound," Axel said. "What say we get this shite on the road?"

Knox barked a sharp laugh from his office at the security firm he shared with Beckett. "It's always about sex with you."

"Kind of the pot calling the kettle black, aren't you?" Axel said.

"All right," Beckett interrupted, though the humor was evident in his own voice, "let's review the drill. Zeke, you get the security crew away from their desk. How's not important. Just get 'em far enough away, Trev's got time to plug the flash drive in the main computer, and the rest of us past the desk and into the stairwell."

"What about the cameras?" Trevor said. "You said they're mounted on both corners up front. That's got a prime shot of the desk."

"Once I'm in it, won't matter," Knox said. "I'll copy footage of the guys and lay it over whatever's recorded."

Beckett picked back up. "As soon as Knox overrides their security, he'll disable the alarms and will have a direct line to their monitors. Unless they've got unexpected surprises on the inside, it'll be smooth sailing until we're ready to get out."

"What's the likelihood we'll find surprises?" Zeke said.

Unlike the rest of the guys with their easygoing banter, Danny's voice was rock solid. Focused. "My guess is low. The hack Knox had to come up with to get through their system makes me think they'll be overconfident with their frontline defense."

Well, that was something, at least. Considering he'd boasted about him and his brothers knowing what they were doing, he was kind of banking on being able to argue with Gabe first thing in the morning instead of waiting on someone to post bail. "Do me a favor and avoid surprises."

"I'm with ya on that one," Danny said.

"One more thing," Beckett said. "Trev staged something a little bigger to get the guys out of our path when it's time to exit."

Trevor's answering chuckle came out a little on the sinister side. "I never did like that car."

"What car?" Zeke said.

"Remember that piece of shit Volkswagen I had to tow out of The Den's parking lot a few months ago?" He waggled his eyebrows. "Boom."

Damn. Clearly Trev didn't fuck around when it came to distractions. "You didn't."

"I did." He jerked his head toward the street lining the

front of the building and grinned. "Mr. Johnson would be proud."

"Who's Mr. Johnson?" Jace said.

"That son of a bitch chemistry teacher my senior year. And here he thought I wasn't listening."

"You boys wanna focus and get on with this?" Knox said. "My fingers are twitchy."

"Well…" The way Jace drew it out, Zeke could practically picture the toothpick rolling from one side of his mouth to the other. "We can't have the man at mission control with twitchy fingers. All set?"

"Yep."

"Yeah."

"Go."

"I'm in."

Zeke grumbled and popped open his door, hefting the stack of boxes out in front of him. "I make it all the way through college without delivering one fucking pizza, and I ruin my stretch after I'm an M.D." He waited until Trevor was out of the passenger side and hit the locks on the Camaro. "And no blowing that piece of shit Volkswagen before my ride's in the clear."

"Deal." Trevor hustled toward a hidden alcove just off the main entrance. "Give me five, then go."

Zeke pulled the grungy cap on, tugged the bill low, and checked his watch. Just after ten. More times than he could count, he'd considered texting Gabe, but had tucked his phone away before he could give in. He'd promised her space and she sure as hell deserved a little time to process the bomb he'd dropped on her, but fuck if it wasn't gutting him from the inside out. Maybe he shouldn't give her until tomorrow. He'd seen firsthand the whacked ideas her mind could conjure. More time tonight only meant more arguments to wade through tomorrow.

Trevor's hushed voice sounded in Zeke's earpiece. "Ready."

Right. Cue Pizza Man. He ambled toward the building, careful to keep his head down when he entered, just in case. Instead of stopping at the front desk, he angled toward the farthest bank of elevators.

"Hey!" A lanky guy with dirty-blond hair and a lingering fight with acne popped out of his seat and hurried around the wide black desk.

Zeke kept going, pretending he hadn't heard.

Keys jingled behind him, interspersed between heavy feet moving at a near jog. "Hey, mister. You have to check in."

The elevator bank was only a few more steps away. If he pushed it, maybe the second guy would get up off his ass and follow suit.

Clipped words he couldn't quite make out sounded behind him, followed by more footsteps. Sure enough, both men rounded the corner just as Zeke pushed the elevator's up button, though the way the second dude was breathing sounded like he could have gone without the sudden sprint.

Blondie was the first to shout. "Hold up!"

Zeke feigned surprised. "What?" He pried his headset out of his ear and held it up. "Sorry. Guess I had the music up too loud. Something wrong?"

The heavy-set dark-haired guy sauntered forward like that tin shield on his rent-a-cop uniform actually stood for something. "All visitors have to check in first. And no one called us about a pizza order."

"What do you mean? They said it was on the eighth floor."

"Ah, man." Blondie shook his head and stuffed his hands in his pockets. "Sorry to break it to you, but whoever called in your order either gave you the wrong address, or is pranking you. The eighth floor here is empty. Couldn't be anyone there."

Talk about not having all the right intel before he made his moves. He'd kind of hoped he'd keep the guys away by talking them into riding along for delivery. "Are you fucking kidding me?" He glanced down the rest of the elevator banks with the shiny silver exteriors then back at the men, making a show like he was considering tossing the boxes. "I hate this job. Fourth damned time this week it's happened, too." He scowled another second, milking every moment he could by staring out the big plate glass windows and pretending he couldn't decide what to do. "You guys hungry?"

Not surprisingly, it was hefty dude that answered first. "Are you kidding? I'm starved."

Go figure. Zeke shrugged and strolled toward them. "Better you two get 'em than me have to lug 'em back to the shop again. Think my car's gonna smell like pepperoni for the rest of its life." He handed over the boxes and tucked his earpiece back in. "Don't suppose you're willing to chip in a little to cover the cost?"

Both shook their head, but at least Blondie had the good grace to look apologetic. "Wasn't planning on ordering anything until after shift change."

"That's cool."

Trevor's voice cut through the headpiece. "Clear."

"Yup, we're in, too," Danny said.

Thank God.

Zeke slapped hefty dude on the shoulder and headed back the way he'd come in. "You two enjoy. Sorry if I jacked up your night." He waited until he was a few steps away and threw in a "Hate this job," for good measure.

Trevor's laughter vibrated through the earpiece. "You sure you never delivered a pizza, brother?"

"Fuck you, Trev," Zeke said low enough the men trailing him couldn't hear it. He pushed open one of the glass entryway doors and stomped out toward the parking lot.

"Hell, he probably didn't even catch a buzz from that little routine," Jace said. His voice was low and a little winded, the echo of footsteps from the stairwell ringing in the background. "Kind of tame compared to jumping out of airplanes."

"Gotta say," Trevor said, "the bit with the headset was creative."

Knox cut through the banter. "I'm in. Sensors are going down."

And that was it. Before Zeke and Trevor had even met back at his Camaro and moved it farther away from the building, the rest of the guys had split and breached both offices. While he was damned glad they'd made it safe inside, he'd have given a lot to have something to occupy his time while he waited. "You sure the car thing's the best kind of distraction?" he said to Trevor beside him.

"Well, another bogus pizza delivery's not going to cut it, and I'm too old and proud to streak, so yeah, I'm going with fire."

"You sure you know what you're doing?"

Trev scoffed and slumped lower in the passenger seat. "Piece of cake. Nothing huge, just a mini light show for our hungry friends."

Danny's nearly whispered, but very tense voice cut through their banter. "I think I found something." Papers rustled before silence filled the line. "There's shit here on Wallaby and Yates. All the sales down the street are lined up in here, too. Lots of shit about their finances and some reverse mortgage papers."

"Let me see," Beckett said.

Another pause.

"Not a good time for suspense," Jace said. "We need to bail?"

"Hell no." Beck was all business, clearly on to something. "Zeke, what's Succinylcholine?"

"It's a muscle paralytic. Why?"

"What would you use it for?"

"Relaxes the muscles for surgery. Or with a ventilator."

"If you give someone too much, what happens?"

"Exactly what it sounds like. It paralyzes the muscles. Cardiac arrest most likely." He shifted in his seat. "You wanna tell me what the fuck this is about?"

"They killed my dad." Danny's voice. Flat and loaded with disbelief. "They've got his cholesterol meds listed here. They knew what he was taking."

"How old was he?" Zeke said.

"Sixty-three. Two years from retiring."

He had to hand it to someone. As moves went, it was pretty slick. "Not likely for an autopsy then. Not unless the family requested one."

"We didn't even think about it." Though, from the devastation in Danny's voice, it sounded like it was a decision he'd second-guess for a very long time.

"Son of a bitch." The sharp clunk of a drawer closing followed Beckett's sharp words. "They've got copies of the security system we installed on Danny's house, records of who comes and goes, and all kinds of other details for the last two weeks."

"What the fuck?" This from Knox, clearly pissed anyone had violated his security.

"What the fuck is right," Beckett said. "If we're reading this right, they're casing Gabe."

* * *

Two hours Gabe had driven around the lake, her thoughts whipping like the wind through her truck's open windows. No destination. No purpose behind the trip beyond the hypnotic drone of her engine and the time to think.

They were right. Zeke. Danny. April. Her father. Even the therapist all those years ago. Every one of them saw and tried to tell her what she'd refused to see. She really didn't let people close. Or if she did, she pushed them away the first chance she got. Heck, now that she'd dared to let the idea settle, she even wondered if the social anxiety was just another ruse from her psyche.

She pulled into her driveway and shut off the lights. Silence filled the cab, only the random pings of her heated motor as it began to cool and cicadas in the distance breaking the night's quiet. The empty concrete where Danny and Zeke usually parked was shrouded in shadows. That's the life she had to look forward to if things didn't change. No friends. No family.

No Zeke.

A pang twisted behind her sternum and her stomach lurched. God, the things she'd said to him. After everything he'd done for her, all the kindness he'd shown, she'd gone and acted like a shrew. She still thought the way he and his brothers were going about things was wrong, but he was right in calling her out on the way she'd approached it. Loving someone didn't mean controlling them. It meant accepting them. The good and the bad.

Didn't it?

Frustrated at the prospect of more internal debate, she yanked the door's latch and slid down to the concrete, her purse whacking her in the hip as she landed. She dug for her keys, cursing the fact that she'd gone and left the porch light off again.

She hesitated at the thought, memories of Mrs. Wallaby's break-in stomping mercilessly through her. Shaking the eerie sensation off, she glommed on to her keys and let out a frustrated breath. She'd just been in a hurry, that's all. Too keyed up and eager for a friendly ear to pay attention to what she was doing.

She slid the key home, twisted the dead bolt and leaned her hip into the door to open it. A slow vibration registered through her purse, her ringtone muted by the overflowing contents inside. The next time she went shopping she was definitely downsizing. Hobo bags were just too convenient for carting around way too much unnecessary stuff.

Digging toward the bottom, she rummaged through the latest shop magazines she'd tucked inside and her billfold, her keys jingling between her fingers—and froze.

The alarm wasn't beeping. Wasn't it supposed to beep when she came in? She flipped the little cover for the keypad and groaned. "Yeah, it's supposed to beep, but only if you arm the damned system, Gabe."

The phone stopped ringing and her shoulders sagged. Great. Not only was she clumsy and forgetful, but she was talking to herself in the dark.

"I'm not going to complain."

A man's voice. Deep and one she didn't recognize. She jolted toward the door, instincts pushing her for escape.

A hand clamped around her wrist and yanked her back against a hard, muscular chest. Another hand wrapped around her throat. "A nice system like that's a shame to waste. Appreciate you making my job easy, though." The man squeezed her neck enough to make it clear how vulnerable she was. "Don't even think about screaming. You do and this will go worse than it needs to. Got it?"

She nodded, her frantic agreement as jerky as her heart. Over and over, she blinked, trying to focus on the soft green light glowing from the alarm's keypad. She palmed her keys, careful to silence their jingle against her sweaty palms. "What job?" Though after what Zeke had shared this afternoon, she had a feeling she knew.

"Just cleaning up some loose ends." He maneuvered her to the couch and shoved her forward, yanking her purse away in the process and tossing it well out of reach. A second later the lamp came on, painting her living room and her captor in a soft white glow. He yanked the curtains closed, his dark jeans and black hoodie only accenting how big he was.

He turned and her lungs seized. No way could she mistake those eyes, the vibrant green unusually bold and impossible to forget. "You're the guy from Mrs. Wallaby's."

"Like I said, loose ends." He unzipped the hoody and pulled a gun from a harness inside.

Shit.

Her ringtone sounded again, the vibration that went with it rattling against the table leg her purse had come to rest on.

He lifted the gun and ambled closer. "You so much as twitch toward that phone and you'll be dead a lot sooner than I'd planned."

She swallowed. Or tried, for all the good it did with her parched mouth and throat. Was it Zeke? Danny? God, why hadn't she listened to him? She should have called him as soon as she left April instead of driving around the lake. "I'd rather not be dead at all."

"Then you should have playcd nice."

The phone stopped ringing and a little piece of her dicd along with the silence. There had to be something she could do. Some way to buy her time. Maybe if she played dumb he'd trip up and give her a chance to run. "I don't know what you mean."

"You should've sold like your neighbors did. Would've saved the people who want your land the need to get creative. Though you being the victim of the break-in next door makes it a little easier for me to stage your downfall." He grinned and a shiver rippled down her back. Pure evil burned behind his eyes, a complete disregard for anything decent. "Gotta say, casing your place the last few weeks gave me a lot to look forward to. That man of yours is gonna hate losing you on a regular basis."

A whimper ripped up her throat and she pulled her knees in toward her chest, her hands fisting close to her chest. Sweat trickled between her breasts and her breath came in short, choppy huffs. The metal of her keys bit into her palms so hard it was a wonder she didn't bleed.

Her keys.

God, how could she have been so stupid? One of the bells and whistles Danny had added to the system was the panic fob on her key chain. If she could push it without the guy catching her, all she'd need to do was buy more time.

The man stepped forward, motioning his gun toward the hallway. "Get up."

She shook her head and tucked the hand with the keys behind her back, holding the other hand palm up as if to ward him off. "Please don't."

Behind her back, she shifted the keys, clumsily trying to find the plastic sensor with her sweat-slick fingers. "Just call the people you work for. I'll sell. I won't repeat anything you've told me." The hard plastic slicked against her fingertips. She gripped it tight and punched the button hard, holding it in place and silently counting the three seconds she needed for the alert to reach dispatch.

"Lady, you do not want to push me. The money I'm making on this deal is enough to tide me over for the rest of this year. Me enjoying that sweet body of yours is just a bonus. One I can easily walk away from. Now get up, or die there."

Chapter Twenty-Nine

One ring. Then another.

"Hi, this is Gabe. You know what to do at the beep."

"Damn it." Zeke punched the end button. "She's not answering."

"If she ain't answering, something's wrong," Danny said. Like the rest of the team, his words came sharp between heavy pants while the men stepped up their efforts to sweep the rest of the offices. "Swear to God, she carries that thing everywhere."

"Yeah, well, she was kind of pissed when I left." As in off the charts, cut his nuts off while he was sleeping angry. "Not thinking I'm high on her answer list. I came clean on what we were doing tonight, and she kicked me out of the house."

Axel grumbled through the headset. "The lass has a funny way of showing appreciation for someone having her back."

"She was freaked. Cut her some slack," Zeke volleyed back. Though why he felt compelled to stand up for her he couldn't fathom. He'd thought pretty much the same thing more than once since he'd stormed out the front door.

"I don't like this," Danny said.

That made two of them. The longer Zeke contemplated all the possible scenarios, the harder it was for him to keep his car in park. "Beck, you still have a man there?"

"Pulled 'em off after we installed the system. She'll be fine as long as she's inside and it's active."

"Yeah, well, she's not using it."

A whole string of surprised responses sounded through the line, but Danny's was the strongest. "What?"

"She's trying," Zeke said, "but I busted her this afternoon and a few times before that. She forgets."

"Hold up, let me check the system." Knox's lightning fast keyboard strikes clattered through the audio. "Negative. Nothing activated. Sensors show movement, though."

"I know the locks are thrown 'cause she threw the bolt hard behind me. Beck, how long to get a guy out there?"

Jace cut in before Beckett could answer. "You two are closer. Go."

Trevor twisted in the seat beside Zeke. "Uh, in case you missed it, you're still inside."

"Then Knox'll have to up his game and get creative," Axel drawled. "Trevor, stay with Zeke. Go."

It was all the incentive Zeke needed. In one smooth move he ripped his headpiece out of his ear, jammed the stick shift into first, and pealed out of his dark parking space.

"Roger that," Trevor said. "We're out." It wasn't until Zeke hit the highway and shot straight to the HOV lane that he broached next steps. "You got a certain way you want to play this?"

Yeah, he did. He'd like to show up, find out Gabe was just nursing a serious grudge, and then spank her sweet ass for real. That dark, sixth sense that had bailed him out of one too many scrapes and saved a whole lot of lives insisted he wasn't going to get that lucky. "This is not my forte, brother. I'm thinking you get that or I wouldn't have been the one on pizza detail. Unless it's a brawl, then I'm a contender."

"You bring the heat Beck gave you?"

"I take bullets out of people. Not in a hurry to make more business for my peers than there already is. Besides, my aim is for shit."

Trevor shook his head and huffed out an ironic laugh. "Only fucking guy I know who goes into a sketchy situation with possible thugs involved and doesn't carry a firearm."

Zeke glanced at his brother. Despite his cool exterior, Zeke was pretty sure Trev could strike as fast as a snake if he needed to. "You bring yours?"

"Is the pope catholic? Of course, I'm armed." He anchored his elbow on the door and rubbed the back of his hand against his chin. "What's the layout of the place?"

"Simple. Master on one end, living and kitchen in the middle, and two bedrooms on the other end."

"Alternate entrances?" Trev said.

"Two. A sliding glass door that heads out to the patio and separate steel door that heads out of the utility room."

"Right, so if something looks fishy, one of us goes to the front door and the other tries the back."

"And if it's locked?"

The color display in the center console lit up before Trevor could answer, Knox's name splashed across the top. Zeke hit the accept button. "What's the status on the guys?"

"Guys are great," Knox said, albeit a little distracted sounding. "Wet but great."

Trevor cast Zeke a confused look. "Wet?"

"Kicked off the fire alarms to get 'em out of the stair-

well and that kicked off the sprinklers. What's your ETA
to Gabe?"

Zeke gripped the steering wheel a little harder, the
telltale prickle he'd learned to avoid at all costs ghosting
down his spine. "Ten minutes. Maybe seven."

Silence echoed through the line for all of a heartbeat
before Knox spoke. "Gabe punched the panic button on
her key fob. I've got her system hard-wired so the alarm
comes straight to me and Beck first. You want me to hit
the cops on this, or hold off until you're there?"

Heat fired through him, merciless, unrelenting rage
flooding his system with the need to seek and destroy.
At that moment he wouldn't need a gun to do murder.
Whoever dared to set their hands on Gabe, he'd happily
serve justice with his bare hands. "Bring 'em in quiet.
I don't give a shit who gets there first so long as someone gets there."

"I'm on it," Knox said. "Anything else?"

"Yeah." Zeke floored the accelerator. "Patch Danny
in. I need an alternate way into the house."

Like hell she was dying tonight. Not here on the couch
and sure not at the hands of this deranged bastard. Whatever happened, Gabe was not going down without a fight.
"Why were you at Mrs. Wallaby's? She wasn't even in
town." It was a long shot as delay tactics went, but better than nothing.

"And you weren't supposed to be there either. All I
needed was information the execs could use to squeeze
her out, but then you showed and jacked the plan."

"And the fire?"

The empty smile on his face sent cold railing through
her already shivering body. "Yeah, I set it. Another reason my bosses want you out of play. If it weren't for you

and your family, we'd have a lot deeper inroads in this neighborhood already. Now, get your ass up."

Her mind scrambled, desperate for some other topic to stall him with. She huddled deeper into the couch, somehow sensing that the second she was on her feet, the faster time would tick past.

"I said move it." He clamped a hand around her upper arm and yanked her upright, semipropelling her across the living room.

Gabe went with the motion, tucking her arms tight to her body as though she expected a blow and hiding her keys from view. Against his gun they wouldn't help much, but it beat going at him with her bare fists.

Headlights flashed behind the closed curtains and the roar of what she was sure was Zeke's Camaro rumbled outside her house. A car door slammed and heavy footsteps jogged up the steps.

"You gotta be shittin' me." Her captor grabbed her, the gun's muzzle pressed uncomfortably hard against her back.

Knock, knock, knock. "Hey, Gabe! You in there?" *Knock, knock, knock.*

"Trevor." Of all the people she'd expected to show up at her front door, he had to be on the tail end of the list. All she knew was she was damned glad someone was there. She glanced up at her captor. "He's one of Zeke's friends."

Before the man could say anything, the doorknob rattled and Trevor's voice rang out again. "Jesus, Gabe, I hope you're decent. Danny and Zeke sent me out to pick something up for them. I'll just be in and out, okay?"

In one harsh push, Gabe found herself smack dab in front of the door.

The bad guy shifted behind the door, his gun trained

through the door toward Trevor. "Get rid of him," he growled. "You fuck this up, he's dead."

The door opened before she could get her hand on the knob. "Hey." She stared up at Trevor, her thoughts too jumbled to come up with anything. All she knew is if she moved so much as an inch backward, one of Zeke's best friends wouldn't be alive long.

"Hey, Gabe. Sorry to barge in on you, but Zeke and Danny are working on a new hot rod and needed me to pick up some plans he said he left here." He stepped forward. "Just give me a minute—"

"No." She splayed one hand on Trevor's sternum and pushed back as much as her shaking arms would support. "I mean…" Shit, what did she mean? And how the hell had he opened the door? "Danny keeps all his designs out in the garage." She opened her eyes as wide as they could go and tried to motion behind the door with a shift of her gaze.

He held her gaze, the sharp intensity behind his blue eyes not at all a match to his light-hearted tone. "Cool." He held out the keys he'd used to open the door. But that couldn't be right. Those keys weren't Danny's. "Which one of his keys gets me in there?"

She fumbled with the set, the jangling metal grating her frazzled nerves. There had to be something else she could do. Something else she could say.

Trevor's hand closed firmly over hers. "This one?"

Something in his eyes gave her comfort, warning and bolstering her in one calming glance. "Yeah." She cleared her throat. "That one. He keeps his plans over on his workbench."

"Okay, got it." He squeezed her hand, a cold calculating message behind his stern face. "I'll head over and get them. You lock up tight, all right?"

Lock up. As in *don't* lock up. And she was supposed to do that with a guy pointing a gun at her how?

Trevor stepped back enough she could close the door, his gaze lasered onto hers. She closed the door with him still standing there, her heart thrashing as if she'd just closed herself in her own coffin. She leaned against the old wood, covering the lock with her torso as a sob ripped up her throat.

"Smart girl." Her tormentor gripped her arm and jerked her away, his hand reaching for the bolt.

"You jerk!" She kicked out, her boot connecting with his forearm.

Before she could catch her balance, he backhanded her across the cheek and wrapped her up in a choke hold. She fought with all she had, writhing inside his unforgiving grip.

"Now I see why the doc dug in," he grumbled as he wrestled her down the hallway to her room. "Got fire underneath all that innocent bullshit you throw out. Looking forward to gettin' some of that myself."

"Fuck. You." She kicked his shin, the heel of her boot making solid contact before she let herself go slack. The ploy worked. He lost his grip enough for her to slip free, turn and swipe her keys across his face. With nowhere to go but the dead end of her bedrooms, she plowed past him toward the main room, throwing her shoulder into the move as she went.

"Bitch." His footsteps sounded behind her and his hand clamped onto her shoulder, spinning her around so fast her stomach lurched. Just as fast, another hand wrapped around her wrist and yanked her out of the hallway into the utility room.

Zeke.

It was a second at best. A shadowed, freeze-frame

instant of time for her senses to process his scent and his touch, but it was enough. She spun into the motion, huddling into the cocoon of his body, immediately surrendering to his lead.

A blast filled the small space, a violent white exploding against the darkness alongside it. Then another from somewhere farther away followed by a heavy crash.

"Zeke?"

He slumped against her, his weight more than she could hold and pulling her down to the ground.

"Zeke!"

The laundry room light flashed to full bright, blinding her for precious, disorientating seconds. Before she could blink her eyes into focus, a blurry figure tugged Zeke off of her and rolled him to his back.

Sirens sounded in the distance, lots of them coming in fast.

She scrambled to her knees and froze at the blood coating the linoleum floor.

Trevor pressed his big hands to the wound blossoming at Zeke's shoulder, his phone tucked between his ear and his shoulder. "Knox, get us an ambulance. Intruder's neutralized, but Zeke's down."

Chapter Thirty

This was why Gabe hated hospitals. The fake lemony scent masquerading unpleasant odors. The sterile colors and uncomfortable chairs. The unnatural tension slithering up and down the hallways. The mere idea of a grim reaper had to have come from such a place, the ugly black cowl and scythe a visual representation of the terrorizing emotion wafting out of each room.

She squeezed Zeke's hand in hers and smoothed her other along his forearm, careful to avoid his IV. Milling around her, most of his brothers had gathered, Beckett and Knox the only two who hadn't shown since they'd brought Zeke back from surgery. The rest had meandered in and out, some offering her coffee, others giving her space.

The machine monitoring Zeke's heartbeat bleeped out a steady rhythm, her own pulse wearily thrumming in sync. Thirteen hours she'd waited, not the least bit interested in sleep. At least she wasn't relegated to the waiting room anymore. Shortly after Zeke's release from Recovery, the men had informed the nurses she was more than a visitor and had a right to be beside Zeke while they waited for him to wake up.

Not a visitor, but not welcome. At least not if the

guarded looks Jace and Axel cast her way every now and then were a guide to go by.

"Hey." Danny leaned up from the long bench beneath the room's window and motioned longwise along the cushion. "Pretty sure this thing folds out. How about you lay down and get some sleep?"

"No." It came out sharper than she'd intended, but the tension and the lack of sleep were making her jumpy. No way was she closing her eyes until she could see Zeke was awake. Until she could hear his voice and know with absolute certainty he was okay. She swallowed, cursing herself for the hundredth time for not listening to Zeke the day before. For not trusting him. "They really killed Dad?"

"Yeah, Sugar Bear. The only thing we need to do now is prove it."

She still couldn't wrap her head around it. From what they'd gleaned in Lakeside's files, the execs had presumed Dad's past due mortgage payments would send the house right back to the bank upon his death. They sure hadn't counted on Danny coming up with enough money to bring the account current *and* pay off the note.

Two quick knocks rapped against the door before it eased open.

Trevor and Jace shot to their feet only to nod and drop back into their seats when Beckett and Knox walked through.

Beckett chin-lifted toward Zeke and stuffed the tips of his fingers in his pockets. For a heavily muscled guy who looked like he could take out any threat bare-handed, he seemed surprisingly uneasy. "Any change?"

"The doc was in about an hour ago," Trevor said. "Between the anesthesia and pain meds, he said Zeke would be out of it most of today."

Axel pushed off the wall where he'd kept to his feet for the better part of the past hour, his voice as grated and rough as the scowl on his face. "What's the news on our shooter?"

Knox scanned the room, his gaze landing on hers long enough to make her want to curl up in an invisible ball. She averted her gaze instead, focusing on Zeke, willing him to wake up.

Jace's menacing voice sounded from behind her. "It was almost her instead of Zeke. He'd want her to have the facts."

Funny, because she wasn't sure she wanted them. Wasn't sure she could juggle any more ugly realities beyond what she'd already learned in the past twenty-four hours.

Knox shrugged and slid one of the industrial chairs around so he could straddle the back. He crossed his arms on top, his supersized Starbucks dangling between his fingertips. "Shooter was a midlevel thug. The wound Trev gave him was superficial enough they treated and released him to short-term holding. With the info Beck handed off to Rockwall's homicide guy and the kind of sentence they had to hang over him, the guy rolled on a plea deal quick."

"The search warrant was a no-brainer at that point," Beckett said. "They're moving on the offices now."

"What about the records?" Axel said.

"Contained," Knox said. "With one suspected and one attempted murder, the cops moved fast. The building was on lockdown before the execs even got up this morning."

Trevor shifted and held out his hand to Danny. "Congrats, brother. Looks like you and your neighbors are safe."

"Brother." Danny shook his head, bewilderment and

relief mingling with his obvious fatigue. "Still weird hearin' that." He clapped his hand against Trevor's and shook it hard. "Appreciate you guys havin' my back. And Gabe's."

Laughter filled the room, low and respectful of the place they were in and Zeke still asleep, but easy and relaxed all the same.

Brother.

The room fell away, her thoughts tumbling over each other and crashing into a new reality. Danny had finally gotten what he wanted. Not just friendship, but family. Support in a way she could never give him. Not really. And where did that leave her? Especially after the way she'd reacted to Zeke's honesty the day before.

Alone.

Unless she dared to changed things.

If she wanted to be a part of Zeke's family she'd have to offer them the same open acceptance and care they'd shown her. To trust and support them the way Danny and her father had supported her, even if her mother was AWOL. They'd always been there, even when they didn't agree with how she'd approached life.

They'd also taught her to own her mistakes. To suck it up and do the right thing even when it terrified the ever-loving crap out of her. She lifted her chin, a little of the fledging determination she'd nursed during her drive around the lake the night before pushing up on wobbly legs. "Zeke and I fought yesterday."

The room fell silent, the weight of every man's stare slicing straight to her.

"He told me what you were going to do and I freaked out. It terrified me." She licked her lips. "I was wrong."

"You get what we did was for you, right?" Jace said. "For your brother. For your neighbors."

She jerked an awkward nod, but didn't dare meet Jace's penetrating stare. "Now I do, but then all I could see was the bad. Every worst-case scenario. And rightly so. Look what happened."

"Sugar." Jace's command was soft and low, but it was a command all the same, demanding her attention.

Gripping Zeke's hand tighter, she lifted her gaze.

"I get you not understanding or even agreeing with how he planned to go about it, but it was his choice to make. His love to give."

Another chunk of the wall she'd begun to build that day she'd watch her mom hauled away in handcuffs crumbled, powerful fractures creeping to the very base of the archaic structure. Zeke loved her. Had said it as plainly as possible, but until Jace's words it hadn't registered this heavy. This powerful. He didn't love her only on the surface. He loved her enough *to risk*.

Jace stayed rock still, his eyes steady and calm. "I know all about your past. Every one of us do. As to Zeke and the danger, it was his call." He cocked his head, considering. "Were you hurt?"

"No."

"Right. Because he kept you from it. That's our way. The way we do things might not always line up with your or society's idea of what's right, but they won't touch our family. The seven of us? Maybe. But the ones we claim as our own? Never."

Claimed.
Part of a family.
Loved.

"Can I ask you something?" she whispered.

"You can ask," Jace said. "If it's ours to give, we'll share."

She didn't have to ask. Could simply try to pick up the

pieces and mend things with Zeke and ignore the suspicion slithering through her thoughts. But if she could face the truth—all of it, no matter what it looked like—wouldn't that make a better foundation to build on? "This wasn't a one-time deal, was it?" she said before she could change her mind. "Taking matters into your own hands… the people you deal with…that's the norm for you, right?"

For the first time since she'd waded into the conversation, Jace broke his stare and traded looks with his brothers. Not a single word was spoken, and yet the room crackled with tension.

Jace refocused on her. "If you're asking if we get up every morning looking for ways to juke the system, no. Doesn't mean we live confined to it either. If there's an action that's in the best interest of family or our livelihood and it doesn't fuck with an innocent, then we won't shy away from it. But I'll tell you this. There's not one thing, not one decision or action we take, we can't honorably get behind or have a damned good reason for doing it. We follow what actions *we* deem are right. Not the path society tells us we have to walk."

Truth. The unvarnished underbelly laid bare.

Only the steady beep from the monitors beside Zeke broke the deafening white noise, and every man watched her, waiting.

Uncurling his arms from across his chest, Axel leaned a hip on the arm of the long bench. "Need you to understand somethin', lass. The only reason Zeke didn't lay this out for you was fear of outing us. You askin' direct gives us the chance to do it for him. We're doing it here, in front of him, to the woman he was willing to die for. It might scare the shite out of you, but hope to God it doesn't, because we want you right where you are. Beside him. That's what would make him happy."

It absolutely did scare the shit out of her. Not so much from the usual fear of abandonment so much as the danger it implied. But what was the alternative? Life without Zeke? Going back to the empty existence she'd essentially plodded through her whole life?

No. She didn't want that for herself. She wanted more. Wanted the promise of all that was her and Zeke together. Wanted not just the safety of her blood relationship with Danny, but the security and warmth that came with a family built by choice. *Her* choice. All she had to do was find the courage to claim it.

Chapter Thirty-One

A slow steady beep and the chatter of a television program wiggled through Zeke's consciousness. Neither of them were loud, more background noise than anything, but enough to drag him up from the bowels of some seriously deep sleep.

He shifted beneath the covers, the plastic-coated groan of the unforgiving mattress beneath him and a whole lot of *stay-the-fuck-still* from his body halting him in seconds. Jesus, what kind of bender had he gone on last night? Even the prospect of opening his eyes made him want to sink back down into sleep.

The all too familiar scent of disinfectant coalesced with the sounds all at once.

The hospital.

His muscles unwound on a heavy exhale. Just a shift. A long one, judging from the way he felt. Must have been a helluva trauma to knock him out this hard.

Except monitors weren't in the doc's lounge.

And he damned sure never slept this hard on shift.

Shit. The shooting.

His eyes snapped open. Trevor, Jace and Axel were parked on one side of the room, their focus locked onto the latest CNN report, while Knox tap-tap-tapped away at his keyboard on the other.

"What…" He coughed to loosen the thick congealed gunk at the back of his throat. Man, but he could go for about ten Big Gulps of H2O right now. "What time is it? And where's Gabe?"

The question jerked his brothers out of their boredom induced comas. Trevor tossed the remote to the bench beside him and stood, stretching as he went. "About damned time you woke up. You were out all day yesterday. You got any idea how shitty hospital TV is?"

"I told you I'd stream you some good stuff." Knox shut his laptop and set it on the rolling table he'd commandeered as part of his mobile command center.

"Not sure the nurses would appreciate your Jenna Jameson compilation as much as we would." Jace uncrossed his booted feet from the chair he'd propped them in, swiveled for a full upright, and zeroed in on Zeke. "How you feeling?"

"Better if I knew where the hell my woman is."

"Relax, brother." Unlike the rest of them, Axel kept his semireclined pose and laced his fingers behind his head. "Gabe said she had somethin' to do this morning, but she'd be back soon."

She had something to do? Like her nails or hitting the mall? Christ, she must be really pissed off. If she were the one in a hospital bed, they'd have had to pry him away from her. Talk about a kick in the nuts.

Trevor swiveled his chair and positioned it a little closer to Zeke's bedside. "Thought I told you to get out of the line of fire, not into it."

"Yeah, well, the laundry room was smaller than I remembered it." He tentatively shifted his shoulder only to have it bark a demanding *STOP!* And wasn't that just the perfect way to get his mind off a disenchanted woman. "We get what we needed out of the shooter?"

"And then some," Trevor said. "Beck hasn't copped to it, but rumor has it he sweet-talked one of Rockwall's finest into a brief, but unguarded chat with the guy before the cops took over with interrogation. Spilled everything he knew as soon as he figured out his canoe was up Shit River. The cops got a warrant, swarmed the offices and have Lakeside's top dogs in custody already."

Damn. Talk about sleeping through the good part. "An unguarded chat, huh?"

Knox snickered. "Everyone needs a little time to reflect. Beck's good for muscling people toward the light."

On Knox's side of the bed, the room's computer hovered on an oscillating arm mounted to the wall. Funny, he'd never considered working for a hospital might score him access to his own records on demand. He motioned to it with his uninjured arm. "Swing that thing around here, would ya?"

"Yup." Unsurprisingly, Knox manned the keyboard and started typing on the login screen.

"My user name is—"

"I know what it is." Knox hit the enter key and stepped back, moving the computer into Zeke's line of sight. "I also know what your password is. You use the same one on all the networks."

Axel snorted and shook his head. "Nosey bastard."

"That's fucked up," Trevor said.

"Nah, that's just Knox," Jace added.

Zeke scrolled through the patient history. Two transfusions. Clean entrance and exit of the bullet. Limited bone fragmentation, but the drive-by the bullet did through his lung had done a number. "Damn, no wonder I was out. At least I got Moen as a surgeon."

"Christ, he's a cocky one," Axel said. "Only understood about every third word he said."

"Some people say the same about you," Knox said, leaning in toward the screen for a look over Zeke's shoulder.

"Only the ladies, brother. And that's because I use ma brogue ta get 'em thinkin' of all the naughty things I'll say when ma mouth is between their thighs."

Fucking Axel. Always thinking about sex and his next conquest. Normally he'd appreciate the levity, especially considering he was stuck in this hospital bed for at least one more night, but right now all he wanted to do was get up and pace. Too bad the pain meds and the level-ten ache in his upper back meant that was a shaky idea at best. "Gabe say where she was headed?"

Trevor and Jace glanced up at the television screen.

Knox kept his gaze rooted to the computer.

Axel shrugged, but something in his expression looked a little off. "Wasn't all that talkative. Went outside just after eight this morning, made a call, then came back saying she'd be back as soon as she could."

Eight o'clock. On a Monday. But she couldn't have gone to work. Not if she'd said she'd be back soon. "Who's got my phone? I want to call her."

Jace looked to Trevor, who shrugged and kept avoiding eye contact. "I left it at Danny's house."

"Fine." Zeke held out his hand to Knox. "Give me yours."

"Why mine?"

"Because you're an information whore, which means you've got her number and every other detail you might need in a pinch on the damned thing."

Knox rolled his eyes, but unlocked it and handed it over.

Sure enough, Gabe's number was there. He punched

the call button and waited, every ring sounding louder and longer.

"Hi, this is Gabe. You know what to do at the beep."

The long tone sounded. Zeke opened his mouth to speak, but hit the end button instead. Something was off. Really off. He scanned his brothers, every one of them suspiciously pre-occupied with everything from the television to some vague happening outside his window. "Someone want to tell me why you're all acting like you just got caught robbing a blind old woman?"

A whole lot of back-and-forth eyeballing between the four of them commenced.

"Not going to ask this again," Zeke said. "Where's Gabe?"

Jace cleared his throat. "Not exactly sure, but Beckett and Danny are tailing her."

"Why would they need to tail her?"

Knox spun the computer out of reach and settled back in his seat. Trevor glared at Jace, and Axel nodded.

Jace dragged a toothpick out of his pocket, a dead giveaway without a single word spoken Zeke wouldn't like what came next. "Because we're worried she might be sharing information she shouldn't and want to be prepared if she does."

He looked to Trevor. Then Knox. Then back to Axel and Jace. "I want details. Now."

"Well, for starters," Trevor said, "she knows about her dad."

"That wouldn't make her run to the cops. That would prove what we did was right. What else?"

Jace lifted his chin, the hard lines on his face making it look like he was braced for a right hook. "We laid everything out. Who we are. How we operate. If she thought this was a one-time deal before, she doesn't now."

Fuck. Of all the shit ideas he'd heard in his lifetime, going full confession with Gabe in the frame of mind he'd left her in had to be a bullet to the top of the list. No wonder why they were antsy. With her mind and enough time sitting in one place to stew, let alone a hospital with a bullet hole in his shoulder, there was no telling what her mind had conjured up. He tried to force himself upright and out of bed, but the pain slammed him back against the mattress, echoes of the foolhardy action reverberating out in all directions. He gritted through it and shot a mean glare at Jace, now standing by his bed. "She wasn't ready."

"First off, she asked," Jace said. "You said you wanted to give her honesty and we honored that. Second, I think you're selling her short. Up until she left this morning, we couldn't peel her away from you. Even went so far as to say she'd been wrong to send you in without letting you know she'd have your back."

"But you still sent Danny and Beck after her."

Jace chuffed a short laugh and twirled his toothpick with his tongue. "I might be optimistic, but I'm not stupid."

Zeke snatched the phone up off the bed. Knox intervened enough to let the fingerprint reader do its security magic then handed it back off to Zeke. Despite his fingers feeling like over-plump Vienna sausages from all the fluids, he fumbled through the contacts to Danny's number.

It barely finished the first ring before Danny's clipped voice barreled through the line. "Hey, Knox."

"Not Knox. Zeke. Where's Gabe?"

A rock station droned low in the background, buffered by heavy traffic.

"Danny, where the fuck is she?"

"She's okay." In the awkward silence, he could almost

picture Danny fumbling for his skull cap. "She's..." A car door slammed shut and a cluster of feminine laugher rose then faded off to nothing. "Just sit tight, will ya? Honest to God, I'm a little shocked. Surprised as hell actually, but Gabe's fine. I just don't think she'd want me knowing where she is right now, let alone you. Not yet."

The steady throb around his wound sharpened as if they'd replaced the bullet's path with razors and a vision-wrecking stab pierced his temples. Zeke checked his IV. Antibiotics, fluids and a morphine self-dispense. Sucked that it was in his right arm, but he could handle taking it out left-handed. Scrubs would be easy enough to drum up, but he'd have to get past his brothers first. Tricky.

Danny's voice dropped, low but about as sincere as a man could get. "Zeke, listen to me. She's fine. I think this is a good thing. Me and Beck are keeping an eye on her. My guess is we'll be back in one, maybe two hours. Just hang tight and let her tell you what she's doing."

A good thing. As in not betraying his brothers or doing anything that could get her hurt. He gripped Knox's phone tighter and the high-tech miracle creaked in response. Every heavy breath lashed with more pressure on his wound. "You sure?"

"Very. I swear to you, man, if she's doing what I think she is, it'll be worth the wait."

Debatable. Danny was the one with eyes on Gabe, while he was on his ass and immobile. "Right." He thumbed the phone off and tossed it on the bed. "Fuck."

Chapter Thirty-Two

For a place where people spent a whole lot of time sitting on their ass waiting, one would think hospitals would at least offer up decent pay channels. Zeke eyed the morphine dispenser next to his right hand. He wasn't a pussy. Not by a long shot. But in the last hour waiting for Gabe to show, the throb in his back had morphed from bad to branding-iron hot with no hope of relief from the heat. If anyone knew better than to let the pain get out of control, it was him, but damned if he'd be jacked in the head when Gabe showed.

He closed his eyes and focused on Axel and Jace working through some new promo idea for Crossroads. Knox hadn't budged so much as an inch for the past thirty minutes, his lightning-fast fingers on the computer excluded. Just watching the guy settle into his zone made Zeke itch to move around.

And Trevor. You'd have thought he was kicked back in his living room the way he navigated the remote control. The only thing missing was a beer dangling from his fingers.

A soft knock rapped against the door a second before it whooshed open.

Zeke snapped his head up, his heart jolting hard enough to leave tracks on the monitor's screen. "Gabe."

Her cheeks were red and her eyes puffy, but a tentative smile curled her lips. "You're awake." She scanned the room and hesitated, her smile dimming. "Okay if I come in?"

"No one here gonna stop you from seein' your man, lass." Axel stood and jerked his head toward the door.

Jace followed his lead. "We'll wait outside."

She started to step out of everyone's way, then shook her head. "Actually, could you stay?" She bit her lip and rested her gaze on each man. "And could you find Danny and Beckett?"

"Find Danny and Beckett for what?" Danny's voice filtered through the room before he came into view, Beckett prowling right behind him. With a chin-lift to Zeke, Danny wrapped Gabe up in a casual half hug. "Hey, Sugar Bear. What's going on?"

"I need to talk to Zeke, but I'd like for you to stay." Her gaze slid to Beck, the uncertainty behind them enough to jolt Zeke into action.

"No one's talking about anything until you're about ten feet closer." He motioned her toward him, the lack of pain meds making the simple gesture on par with the breast stroke, even on his good side.

Careful to skirt Beckett in his crossed-arms, badass pose, she faltered to his bedside, her white-knuckled grip on her purse strap holding steady even once she'd reached him. She laid her other hand inside his outstretched one, the touch tremulous. Her lashes were clumped together, more confirmation that however she'd spent her morning, she'd done it crying. "Hey."

"Hey, *gatinha*." Leveraging her hand in his, he tugged her closer and smoothed her hair away from her face. "You okay?"

She smiled. A shaky one at best, but the promise of

it chiseled at least a layer or two of the worry he'd built up in the past few hours. "I think I'm supposed to ask you that question."

Cupping the back of her neck, he urged her toward him. "I'd be better if I got a kiss."

Her gaze skittered to the men watching on the other side of the bed and braced one hand beside his head. "I don't know if that's a good idea," she muttered. "I mean, you're hurt and—"

"I'm a doctor. First thing they teach us is kisses make everything all better."

She studied his face, gaze roving over every detail as though searching for some assurance he was really awake and alert. "You scared me."

So much in one simple statement. Whether the comment related to what he'd done with his brothers, or the fact that he'd bled all over her utility room floor, he wasn't sure. Maybe both. But there was no missing the depth and sincerity behind it.

"Then I'll kiss you and make it better." He kissed her, using what little energy he had to draw her mouth to his. So simple. A perfect mesh of his lips against hers, lingering and soft. Mindless of their silent audience.

"I'm sorry," she whispered against his mouth.

He tangled his fingers in her hair, the thick silk spilling against his forearm and her sun-and-sin scent eradicating the room's grating sterile stench. Grazing his nose alongside hers, he drew in a deeper breath, reveling in it. In her warmth and sweet innocence. "Nothing for you to be sorry for. You didn't do anything wrong."

"But I did." She backed away, covering his hand with hers and twining their fingers together. "I should have listened to what you were telling me. At least tried to understand why you were doing the things you were instead of making everything cut-and-dried."

She swept her wary gaze around the room and swallowed big. Squaring her shoulders, she lifted her chin. "I talked to April."

"This morning?"

"No, after you left Saturday night. She reminded me that the law might be black-and-white, but people are all kinds of shades of gray." She squeezed his hand, her palm clammy against his. "I want to be able to see more gray. To not feel so trapped by old ideas."

His breath hitched, and for a second it felt like his body might float right out of the bed, even with the pain weighting him down. As first steps went, what she was saying was huge. Especially with her history. "Okay. We can work on that."

"No." She focused on their joined hands and her mouth hardened for a second before she looked back up. "*I* need to work on that." She glanced at Jace. "I can't freak out every time something happens. If we're going to have a healthy relationship, then I need to be willing to deal with the stuff that happened with my mom. I can't hold every situation for the rest of my life up against one finite time in my life and use it as an excuse to keep people away." She cast a quick, but soft smile at Danny. "And I need to make friends. To learn how to be comfortable in social situations without anyone there as a buffer."

Danny smiled big enough to show teeth, his whole face lighting up like he'd won the lottery. "Atta girl."

"Proud of you, *gatinha*," Zeke said. And he was. Damned proud. But even after what she'd shared, her body was still strung up tight and her movements jerky. Definitely not the body language of someone who'd finished unloading whatever was on their mind. "You understand that no one expects you to tackle all this shit overnight, right? Least of all me. There's not a person in this room who hasn't faced a demon or two."

"I know. But there's something I could do to help." For the first time since she'd walked into the room, she pried her hand off her purse strap and wiped it on her hip. "I remembered what you said. How you compared the anxiety stuff to diabetes or cholesterol. So I called the doctor's office when they opened this morning. The psychiatrist who saw me in high school. The receptionist probably thinks I'm a basket case since I broke down and bawled on the phone, but she took pity on me and gave me a cancellation slot."

"That's where you were this morning?"

She nodded, rooted around inside her purse and pulled out a small orange bottle. The pills rattled against the hard plastic as she handed it over. "I had it filled on the way here. The doc said it's a small dose to start with. That I'd work my way up."

Paroxetine. Twenty milligrams.

A perfect choice for her with minimal side effects.

"I'm going in every two weeks," she said. "At least for a while until he's sure I'm good with the medicine. He said we'd work on some coping techniques, too. New ways for me to think about social situations."

Okay, not just a huge step. More like a monumental leap. But even with the big olive branch thrown out there in front of him and his brothers, it was the underlying heart in her, the gentle guilelessness that wound through everything she did and how she approached life, that left him dumbfounded and head over heels. "Love you, *gatinha*." Not giving two shits how bad his body protested the move, he snagged her around the waist and pulled her to him, hugging her tight against his side and kissing the top of her head. "For the record, though, you didn't need to lay all this out in front of the guys."

"Yeah, I did." She gently eased back and tucked her hair behind her ear. Unlike the mottled red that had stained her cheeks before, now they were an endearing pink. One by one, she met his brothers' stares head on. "I need you to know I trust you. I may not always like the way you do things, but I know you're good people." She saved Danny for last. "And you're good to my brother."

"Hell yeah, they are." Danny came up behind her.

He'd barely gotten a hug in before Jace had rounded the bed and pulled her into one of his own, kissing the top of her head the same way Zeke had. "Gonna be good to you, too, sugar." He chin-lifted toward Zeke then winked at Gabe. "Think you've had enough social practice for today, though. We'll clear out and give you time with Zeke. Figure you're the only shot we've got at keeping him in that bed until he's discharged."

"Welcome to the family, lass." Unlike Danny and Jace's tame, brotherly hugs, Axel grunted and did a mountain man bear grab. He dropped his voice to a mock grumble at her ear. "We'll guard the door while you give your man a proper good morning."

The rest of the guys followed suit, offering their praise and support in their own unique ways, but the hug from Beckett had to be the most entertaining. Given how big he was compared to the rest of the guys, Zeke was a little afraid Gabe was going to leap across the bed to keep her distance, but then she squared her shoulders and wrapped him up around the neck. Honest to God, even the bullet was worth it to see that awkward hesitation while Beck recalibrated and returned the embrace.

With everyone else but Gabe out in the hall, Danny

paused at the door, his hand braced on the latch and his eyes on Zeke. "The day you came into my shop? Best day ever. For me and her."

"Thinking it was my lucky day, too." He waved Danny out the door. "Now beat it. My woman's had a rough morning and needs some one-on-one."

Danny's sharp bark of laugher echoed down the hall even after the door clicked shut.

Zeke patted the bed beside him. "Crawl up here."

Her eyes popped wide, gaze darting to the tubes and wires forking out to all the high tech around him. "No way. I'll hurt you. And besides, the nurses would kill me."

"They tussle with me, I'll tussle back when I'm healed up. Payback's a bitch." He shifted to the far side of the bed, his back protesting the commotion with a good old-fashioned stab that made his eyes roll back in his head. He waved her toward the sliver of space, moving the tubes out of her way while his breath sawed in and out of his chest. At this point, even breathing hurt. "Come on. Had a rough few days. Need you up here to make it better."

She crawled in, careful not to jar him or put any pressure on his torso. Only when she'd snuggled up beside him did he take a decent breath. She rested her hand over his heart. "This okay?"

"Almost perfect." He motioned to the morphine pump tethered to the lowered handrail on her side of the bed and closed his eyes, forcing his thoughts to center on Gabe's soft body beside him instead of the hammering throb at his back. "Wouldn't mind if you push that red button, though."

The bed wiggled for a second, the waterproof covering on the mattress an unfortunate reminder of his surroundings. A tiny beep sounded, assuring him a fresh dose of pain relief was on the way.

Slowly, Gabe eased back against him and he guided her head to his shoulder. Now he could relax. Could concentrate on healing and getting the hell out of this place where he could hold her like she deserved to be held. Tucked up close with her legs tangled with his.

"I'm sorry I wasn't here when you woke up," she whispered.

Bit by bit, the morphine unwound his muscles, a soothing numbness rolling through his body in an unhurried glide. Even though logic insisted it wasn't real, the world around him shifted into slow-mo, Gabe's presence a protective cocoon against both the pain and reality.

He rubbed his cheek against the top of her head and gave into the drug's pull. "You were where you needed to be. Not going to complain when you're taking care of yourself. You're here now. That's all I need."

Epilogue

If you had to be outside in mid-July in Texas, the best way to do it was poolside on a lazy Sunday afternoon. Adding your boyfriend, six brothers (those by blood *and* those by choice), one of their wives and two mothers (also by choice) made it a little slice of heat wave heaven.

Gabe smashed out the last of enough half-pound hamburger patties to feed all the men two times over and let Sylvie and Ninette's easy chatter settle over her. Beyond the kitchen window, Haven's property stretched as far as she could see, a mini paradise of thick, plush grass so green it probably cost Jace a fortune to maintain it. In the center of it all sat a lagoon-style pool surrounded by wispy, tropical plants you'd expect at a high-end beach getaway. A mountain-resort gazebo perched off to one side, the bridge to reach it spanning crosswise across the pool while a bubbling brook meandered along the opposite side.

Zeke's laugher rang out, muffled by the thick, double-paned glass between them, but still rich and warm despite the distance, his wide smile stretching ear to ear. Reclined on an outdoor lounger big enough to hold a three-hundred-pound man, he had one leg cocked with his forearm resting on top of his knee and the other stretched out easy in front of him. Most of his brothers surrounded him, Jace, Axel, Knox and Trevor all in similar loungers lined up in a haphazard half circle. Every one of them was shirtless, their Haven tags and board shorts the only attire they'd bothered with after rolling out of bed.

Zeke took a pull of his beer, his Adam's apple bobbing with the simple act and sending her stomach on a pleasant dipdy-doo. Unlike the rest of the men's boring navy blue or black trunks, his were a pale turquoise. On anyone else, they might've come off girly, but on him they were a *GQ* Summer Special Edition centerfold equivalent. Especially with his dark tan skin accenting the exotic hue.

Jace's mom, Ninette, sidled up next to her at the counter, perusing the stack of hamburger patties while she wiped her hands on a dish towel. "How many more do we need?"

"You said two for each of the guys and one for each of us, so this should give us at least three left over."

Ninette patted her arm and smiled. "You're learning." She turned to Viv stationed at the monster kitchen island on hamburger-garnish duty. "Jace say what time Beckett and Danny are due out here?"

Viv checked her watch and tore another lettuce leaf in half. "They were headed out thirty minutes ago, so unless they got a wild hair on the way here, I'd say they'll be here anytime."

"All right, then." Ninette folded her towel and tossed it on the counter. "Let's get the food outside and put the men to work at the grill."

"Ach, don't let Axel man the meat this time." Axel's mom, Sylvie, was just as boisterous as her son and a good enough cook Gabe had put on five pounds within a month of knowing her. "My boy might tend ta the lasses' needs, but he's got no attention span when it comes ta cooking."

A mix of chuckles and snickers filled the kitchen, each woman loading up with armfuls of food and condiments, and lumbering toward the open sliding glass door. It was such a simple act. Four women working together to prepare a celebration, sometimes jabbering over sales and television series surprises, and other times coasting in companionable silence. But it was never weird. Not like she'd been afraid it would be. If anything, the past few months had surpassed all her hopes, Haven's women banding around her in an unshakeable foundation of support.

She'd grown closer to April, too. While their relationship was special in its own right given it marked her first foray into her new and growing reality, she still wasn't family. Haven was exactly what they'd named it. A safe place only for family.

And today was special, just for Danny.

The women filed outside, the summer heat hitting Gabe in a none-too-subtle slap. In the background, the Dallas rock station she'd grown to expect at any Haven gathering pumped vintage Bob Seger through the air.

Ninette slid two casserole dishes onto the long glass patio table. "Jace, pry your ass out of that chair and fire up the grill. Axel, you've had enough time sitting pretty, too. Get up and get all the ladies a cold one while we set up the fixings. Trevor, get Beckett on the phone and find out how much longer until he's here with Danny."

One by one, the men unfolded themselves from their cushy poolside spots, grumbling good naturedly as they set about their assigned tasks.

Trevor tagged his phone off a side table. "I'm starting to notice Zeke hasn't drawn a short straw in a long time."

"Son, you get a bullet in your back, I'll give you a month or two to be lazy." Ninette winked at Gabe and lowered her voice. "That doesn't mean you should follow suit. Our boys are spoiled enough as it is. You keep yours in line." With that, she hustled off to get another armload of food.

Our boys.

Hers.

Nearly eight weeks since Zeke had been shot, and the idea that this thing between them was real still sent goose bumps skittering out in all directions.

Stepping clear of the gazebo's stainless steel fridge, Axel kicked the door shut with one foot. In typical man style, he'd loaded his arms up trying to avoid more than one trip.

Gabe slid the burger patties onto the grill's side work space and hurried to help him. "Here, give me a few."

"Ah, lass. You're a sweet angel."

Behind her, Sylvie scoffed. "Don't be thinking I don't know yer game, Axel McKee. Yer kissy-kiss might fool Gabrielle this time, but I'll be takin' her aside and explaining yer tricks before the night's through."

"Me?" Axel splayed his big hand over his heart, feigned indignation and rolled out the brogue. "Ye think I'd ply our fair Gabe with dirty tricks?"

"Ye'd ply anyone w' a skirt and we both know it."

He winked at Gabe and strutted toward his mom. "Can't blame a lad for learnin' from his mother's sweet-talkin' ways." He leaned over her shoulder and planted a big smooch on her cheek.

Gabe ducked her head and meandered toward Zeke. Yeah, she'd had the same kind of light relationship with her dad when he'd been alive, but it was always brief and never with spectators looking on. The funny thing was, her new clan had locked on to her bashful side to public displays of affection and seemed hell-bent on showing her a new way of life via limitless hugs.

She held out one of the two ice-cold Bohemia Weiss to Zeke. "You know the spoiling won't last forever."

He could have kept his seat and soaked it up, but stood instead, prying both bottles free and setting them aside on the table next to his chaise. He pulled her flush against him and wrapped her up tight. "It absolutely will last forever. I plan to do a lot of spoiling where you're concerned."

And…cue more goose bumps. Definitely not a response that should be possible with the temperature at ninety-five degrees and the humidity dancing around ninety, as well, but the word *forever* in connection with Zeke could make a woman's body do all kinds of wonky things. A part of her said to be pragmatic. To edit out the word *forever* when it popped up and keep her focus on right now.

Not that anything in the right now was rough. If anything, the past two months had been perfect. Between finding balance with her medicine and fighting through the fears from her past, her whole world was opening up. Broadening in a way she hadn't thought possible.

She smoothed her hands across Zeke's pecs, the puckered scar where the bullet had exited his chest dowsing her light thoughts.

"Hey." Zeke covered her hand with his and tugged it up for a kiss. "Let it go. It's over."

Yes, it was. Along with a dump truck full of other burdens she was determined to let go of. Tilting her head back, she smiled up at him. "I love you."

"I love you, too, *gatinha*." He pressed his lips against her forehead, the touch reverent despite the whirling activity around them.

The side gate swung open and Beckett lumbered through, the huge ice chest he lugged in front of him clunking with every step. "I've got the birthday boy and two extra cases of beer. Who's ready to party?"

Never a question that went without cheers in this crowd. What was laid-back and easy before, ratcheted up to a full-on party complete with music, food and general male insanity. Watching them never got old. Outside of Haven, they worked their assess off, each of them focused on their responsibilities to a degree that was almost scary. But here, tucked away in this private, safe place, they let down their guard.

And Danny was part of it.

By the time the guys had blown through all of the food and at least a six-pack of beer each, the sun had passed the five-o'clock mark, inching its way toward the horizon. Zeke reclined on the oversize chaise, his legs on either side of Gabe so she could lay against his chest.

Not surprisingly, Ninette was kicked back at the family-sized patio table trying to talk Viv into hitting the mall for some big sale the next day, an endeavor she'd finally given up ever getting Gabe to agree to. Shopping for a purpose? Sure. Get in, get out, go home. Shopping all day just for giggles and grins? Um…no.

Next to her and Zeke, Trevor was outlining some new expansion project for his private charter service, the accelerated hand gestures that went with the details a good indicator of how many beers he'd knocked back so far.

Zeke's thumb shuttled a slow back-and-forth path against the back of her arm. Her eyes slipped closed, every muscle relaxing into the moment and soaking up the cool shade around them.

One of the loungers groaned, and wet, heavy footsteps sounded across the poolside's decorative concrete.

A second later, a Five Finger Death Punch remake of a Bad Company song cut off mid chorus.

She snapped her eyes open in time to catch Axel slipping something out from under a few of the still folded beach towels on the table next to Zeke. "Now that everyone's got a belly full, it's time Danny gets his party favor."

"Don't buy it, Danny," Beckett said. "Axel's just in a hurry for cake."

"And you've had Ma's cake, so you know damned well that makes me a wise man." He held out a simple, unwrapped mahogany box. It was long and slender like what she'd expect a bracelet or watch to come in. "Seein' as you're a brother and we were a little sidetracked when we brought you in, we figured your birthday was a good time to give you this."

Danny looked at the box, then at all the guys. "What is it?"

"Won't know until you open it." Jace tucked Vivienne into the crook of his arm. Based on the grin on her face, the brothers weren't the only ones in on the surprise. In fact, everyone seemed to be in the know but her and Danny.

Danny fought his way out of his lounger's deep cushions, took the box from Axel and slowly opened the lid. "Ah, man." A huge smile split his face, and he lifted a thick silver chain from inside. "I got tags." He swiveled toward Zeke, the heavy pendants made of platinum and etched in black with their custom logo dangling from his fingers. "I got tags."

Zeke dipped his chin in one quick, affirming nod. "You're a brother. You get tags."

Tossing the box to his chair, Danny pulled the chain over his head. "Fuckin' sweet."

Indeed, they were, but not nearly as awesome as the happiness on her brother's face. One by one the guys ambled to him, taking turns shaking his hand or smacking him on the back in their man-love way.

Everyone except Zeke. As if content to simply enjoy the show, he wrapped one arm around her shoulders and whispered in her ear, "I think he likes 'em."

"Oh, yeah," she said. "You just made his day."

"That's good. I like having Danny for a brother." He nuzzled her neck, running the tip of his nose along the sensitive spot behind her ear. "How do you feel about him being a brother-*in-law*?"

All around them, laughter, congratulations and birthday wishes rumbled in a happy cacophony, but in her head it was background noise. A nuisance while her mind tried to reevaluate what she'd just heard. She twisted for a better look at his face. "What?"

"I was thinking it would be nice if we made him more than just a brother by choice." Zeke grinned, clearly enjoying her stupor as he tucked her hair behind her ear. "Do you like having a big family, *gatinha*?"

A question. Her brain registered it as such, but damned if it could kick out an answer. Or, for that matter, prod her mouth to move. "Yeah, I like it," she finally muttered, though how the words actually found air she wasn't sure. It was like her mouth had developed some backup autopilot mechanism she never knew existed.

Reaching to the same table where Axel had hidden Danny's surprise, Zeke pulled a small box from under the same pile of towels. Unlike Danny's, this one was much smaller and covered in black velvet. He opened it, the hinges squeaking a tiny protest before he turned it and showed her the contents. "Then make one with me."

A beautiful ring nestled in the middle of the soft black

fabric, a big square diamond in the center and two not-so-smaller ones on either side of it. A princess cut. A fact she only knew because Viv had one similar to it, but more old-world styled than this one.

Zeke's voice cut through her shock, the tone of it low and a little hesitant. "If you don't like it, we can go pick out another one."

"I love it." She brushed one fingertip along one side of the big diamond, afraid if she moved too fast the whole moment would evaporate the way dreams did the moment she woke up. "It's beautiful."

He wiggled the ring free and slid it onto her finger. "Say yes."

Not a dream. Not short-term and so much more than just right now. "You really meant forever," she whispered, her emotions barricading her throat too efficiently to allow anything of more substance.

"Of course, I meant it. I told you, I knew it the minute I saw you." He kissed her fingers. "Now, say yes."

"Yes." It floated past her lips as easy as the evening wind slipping through their shaded corner of paradise, but it felt like it roared all the way up from her toes. She lifted her gaze from the ring to him, the love on his face as bold and beautiful as a morning sunrise. "Yes."

He smiled huge and shifted her on his lap, guiding her knees so they straddled his hips. "So, how big is our family going to be?"

"Kids?"

"A family usually implies kids." His innocent smile shifted to a deliciously wicked grin. "I'm looking forward to making them. Lots of them."

God, if he kept looking at her like that, she was looking forward to it, too. A lot. "I don't know. I never thought of it before."

"Yeah?" He swiveled in his seat and stood, guiding her legs around his waist and cupping her ass with his hands. "Well, you'd best get to figuring it out. I've got work to do."

"Right now?" She glanced around the patio, her startled commentary cutting into all the congratulatory banter going on around Danny. She lowered her voice. "But… I'm taking that shot. We can't get pregnant."

"You know me." He hefted them both toward the back door to the house. "Doesn't mean I can't get a running start."

"Hey, Zeke!" Danny's shout rang out across the pool, all the other chatter falling silent in its wake. "I take it this means she said yes?"

Zeke kept walking. "She said yes."

"Don't you think you should stay and let us offer congratulations?" Jace shouted.

"Congratulate us later." Zeke glanced over one shoulder right before he slid the glass door open. "Right now I've gotta show my woman gratitude."

The hoots and hollers from the family they'd left behind rang out long after he'd closed the door behind them. Once upon a time it would have freaked her out to be the center of attention, or made her want to curl up in a tiny ball and disappear. But today? Today, she didn't care. She might have issues and a past to bury, but with Zeke she could do anything. For the first time in her life, she couldn't wait to jump.

* * * * *

*Trevor's used to living outside the rules
in order to save lives, but this time
he's willing to risk everything to save hers.*

*Read on for a sneak preview of
CLAIM & PROTECT, the next book in
Rhenna Morgan's Men of Haven series*

Chapter One

Any bar owner in Dallas's Deep Ellum district would be tickled shitless with a light crowd on a dreary, October weeknight. But seeing more than half the tables of his own pub occupied and both bartenders knocking out nonstop drink orders—that was a thing of beauty.

Not too shabby for a college dropout. But then, if there was one thing Trevor Raines had learned from his brothers in the last ten years, it was that the right focus and a little ingenuity made anything attainable.

Beside him, Jace Kennedy leaned into the brotherhood's reserved table and motioned with Scotch in hand at Trevor's newest waitress across the room. "That one's a hustler."

Trevor followed his gaze in time to witness said hustler sidle up to one of the oversized corner booths with a drink-laden tray balanced on one palm. She was a little thing, five-foot-one at best and couldn't weigh more than a buck-twenty sopping wet, but she had a friendly face and a way with the customers. For a woman who'd never taken a drink order in her life, Natalie Jordan had acclimated to her new job a whole lot better than he'd anticipated. "Just hired her a few weeks ago. Basically told me she'd be the best waitress I ever had if I gave her a chance."

"Gotta love a woman with spunk," Jace said.

Another of their Haven brothers, Zeke Dugan, nursed

his Bohemia Weiss and studied Natalie over the rim. "She looks familiar."

"Wouldn't surprise me," Trevor said. "Since I was just hiring for a waitress, Knox only ran a cursory background check. He still turned up an expired RN license she hadn't put on her application. Was a long time ago though."

Zeke nodded. "Yeah, that's gotta be it. But she didn't work down in trauma with me. I'd remember that swagger."

Zeke's fiancée, Gabe, looked up from the wedding magazine anchored between her and Jace's wife, Viv, and smacked him on the shoulder. "You're weeks away from being a married man. You're not supposed to appreciate another woman's swagger anymore."

"Didn't say I appreciated it, *gatinha*. I said I'd have remembered it." He snatched her hand before Viv could drag her back into all things wedding dresses and cakes, kissed her knuckles, and grinned. "I'll take your leisurely strut to a power walk any day."

Trevor reclined against his seat back and reconsidered his newest hire while she worked. Defining the way Natalie moved as a power walk was a little harsh. Yeah, she got from point A to point B without a whole lot of dillydallying, but it didn't diminish the subtle sway of her hips.

Done with handing out drinks, Natalie wove through her section, eyes sharp and checking for needed refills. The soft mini lights strung across the ceiling cast her pixie features in an easy glow, and the standard-issue tank top with The Den's logo showcased one helluva of a rack. She'd just about made it back to the arched opening that led to the main bar when she slid her phone out of her back pocket, checked the screen, and hurried out of sight.

"Damn it," he murmured before he knocked back the last of his beer.

"There a problem?" Jace asked.

Probably. Though he'd really hoped his new recruit would pan out. "Fucking cell phones. I told her they're off-limits while she's working and I've busted her with the thing twice tonight."

"Could just be checking the time," Zeke said. "And if she's taking care of her people, what's the harm?"

"If you were with a patient, would you text?"

Zeke chuckled. "Point taken. But then I don't have time to text when someone's bleeding out all over the ER's floor."

"With your attention span, you'd probably try." Jace spun the toothpick anchored at the corner of his mouth with his tongue and focused on Trevor. "Don't jump the gun on your new girl too quick. Could've been a misunderstanding on her part. If she's doin' all right otherwise, talk to her first. Unless you're in a big hurry to start interviewing again?"

"Hell no." The last round had taken him three weeks to hire two girls. Natalie had ended up being the only one worth the effort.

Viv straightened from the mini wedding huddle at the end of the table and slid the two inch thick bridal magazine right in front of Gabe. "Really? You don't like that one? It'd look great on you."

Gabe dipped her chin and aimed a you've-got-to-be-kidding-me glare back at her. "I fix cars for a living and wear jeans three hundred and sixty-two days out of the year. The only thing a train is going to do for me is make sure I face-plant in front of everyone."

"I don't get it," Trev said to Zeke. "If you're not doing a big shindig, why go through all the cake and dress nonsense? Just let me fly you to Vegas like we did for Viv and Jace."

Viv scowled good-naturedly across the table. "Cake and dresses are *not* nonsense. No matter where they get hitched, every woman gets to feel pretty on her wedding day." Seemingly satisfied she'd gotten her point across, she licked her finger, flipped to the next page, and hunched closer to Gabe.

Zeke lowered his voice, obviously intent on skirting any more dirty looks from the women. "Gabe doesn't know what she wants yet. Whatever we do will be just family, but if she opts for someplace quick and fun, we'll take you up on the ride."

Trevor shrugged. He still didn't get why everyone made such a big deal out of one day when what really mattered came after. "Whatever works."

"Spoken like a man who's not yet surrendered. One of these days though…" Jace grinned and sipped his Scotch.

Trevor held up both hands. "Don't turn your matchmaking sights on me. I'm not a qualified candidate for marriage."

"Don't know why you're so against it," Zeke said. "Out of all of us, you're the one who had the best relationship role models."

"I'd hardly call my dad a role model."

Zeke's expression blanked hard and fast. "I meant Frank. You're nothing like your biological father, flesh and blood or not."

Right. Because Trevor had done so well reining in his fists growing up. Didn't mean he didn't wish Zeke was right.

Deftly dodging a chatty group of girls who weren't looking where they were going, Natalie hustled to a twelve-top full of rowdy college guys and started doling out pints. If she had any clue half of them were eyeing her sweet ass, she didn't show it. Hard to blame them for looking though. Now that Zeke had pointed out her swagger, it was all Trevor could focus on.

One of Natalie's customers reached out as she rounded the table and tried to wrap his arm around her waist.

She shifted just in time, patted the guy good-naturedly on the arm, and hurried back to the bar. She slid her phone free and checked the screen without breaking stride.

"I gotta go deal with this." He stood, snatched his empty beer bottle, and motioned to everyone's drinks. "Anyone need a refill?"

"Nah," Zeke said. "We're good."

"Zeke and Gabe are heading out to Haven with me and Viv," Jace added. "The moms keep begging for a chance to weigh in on the dress."

Trevor shook his head. "Women." He chin lifted toward Zeke. "You wanna tie the knot someplace outside of Texas, the offer stands. You takin' Gabe out in my Cessna might have made her giggle, but my G6 will make her purr."

"Got a rock on her finger, brother. Stop trying to sweet-talk my woman."

Winking at Gabe as he rounded the table, he squeezed Viv's shoulder. "Thought you knew. The ones you can't have are the best ones to chase."

Not that he'd ever chased a woman. Between his genes and no desire for a long-term relationship, there'd never been a need. He ambled through the room, eyeballing the handsy bastard who'd tried to corral Natalie. Which was stupid, really. She'd handled it fine, and his manager, Ivan, wouldn't have tolerated it for more than a nanosecond, but for some reason it pissed him off.

Inside the main room, the gleaming honey-stained bar he'd flown in from Dublin was packed with everything from Goths to post-workday businessmen. The rock and movie memorabilia he'd paid a small fortune for hung from every wall, but gave the rest of the old-world pub décor a trendy edge. Two of the other wait-resses were stationed at tables near the front but Natalie was nowhere in sight.

He sidled up to Vicky behind the bar. "Where's Nat-alie?"

Frowning, his top-notch bartender scanned the room and tucked her bottle opener in her back pocket.

A dark-headed guy with full sleeves and gauge ear-rings big enough to shoot a .44 through swiveled from his wingman. "You lookin' for the perky little waitress with the powerhouse stride?"

Great. Another one to keep an eye on. "Yep, that's the one."

The guy nodded toward the employee entrance at the back of the bar. "She ducked out there a few minutes ago."

So much for Zeke's time-checking theory. As rules went, Trevor didn't spout a long list, and he damned sure couldn't go bending the ones he had no matter how ef-ficient an employee was. "Appreciate it."

The crowd's rumble and the bass from some new alter-native rock song on the sound system faded as he strolled down the back hall. A woman leaned against the far wall with arms crossed waiting on whoever was hogging the bathroom, but otherwise the space was deserted. Maybe Jace was right and he was jumping to conclusions. Al-though, how the hell he could misread her palming that damned device all night he couldn't fathom.

Slowly, he eased the door latch open. The employee parking lot's lights buzzed overhead and the thick hu-midity walloped hard before he'd so much as put one boot heel on the asphalt.

Natalie's voice cut from the shadows on the far side of the lot. "I know you're scared, but you can't call the cops."

Stepping free of the door, Trevor found her perched on one of the more private picnic table benches his employees used for smoke breaks. Her back was to the entrance and she fisted a good chunk of her mink-colored hair on top of her head like she might pull it out in another half a second.

"Mom, if you call the cops, he's just going to haul us back to court. I can't afford any more attorney fees." She paused and sat up straighter, letting her dark hair fall free around her shoulders. "I know he's the one not following the rules, but it won't matter with the kind of friends he's got. Just keep the lights off, keep Levi quiet, and don't answer. I'll be home after the bar closes."

She glanced over her shoulder, and her eyes popped wide. Her voice dropped, but not enough to cover her words. "I gotta go, Mom. You'll be fine. Wyatt's an idiot, but not enough to break down the door." She clicked off the phone and stood, slipping the device in her back pocket with the same practiced ease she'd shown all night.

Trevor let the door swing shut. "There a problem?"

"Nope. All good." Striding his direction, she pasted a fake smile on her face and motioned toward the picnic tables. "Just needed a quick break to settle something at home."

Not budging from in front of the door, he crossed his arms and cocked his head. There were two ways his could play this—call her on what he'd overheard, or see if she'd pony up the info on her own. Considering he hated anyone poling into his own business, he opted for door number two. "Pretty sure we talked about my policy on phones during work."

She stopped just out of reach and squared her shoulders. Despite her proud stance, her gaze didn't quite reach his, focusing on his collarbone instead. "Yes, sir."

"So are you going to tell me why you'd risk your new job breaking that policy?"

"I'd rather not." The same gumption she'd shown the day she'd interviewed fired bright behind her eyes, but there was something else there tonight. A desperation she couldn't quite hide beneath her sass.

"Not gonna lie to you, Nat. You're good with the customers. Reliable. Fast. Friendly. I have a hard time finding one of those qualities in a waitress, let alone all three. I'd rather not have to cast my net for a replacement, but you're not giving me much help."

She swallowed big and pinched her lips together like it was all she could do not to rip him a new one. "My son's seven, and my mom's scared to death of my ex. I keep my phone with me so they can reach me if they need to. I promise you, I'm not letting it interfere with my service, but if that's a deal breaker for you, then I understand. I can either finish out the night, or cut bait now."

Oh, yeah. Total attitude *and* sass wrapped up with the kind of lingo he could appreciate. But then from the minute she'd first walked into his office, he'd sensed she'd be the down-home type. "Your mom got a reason to be afraid of this guy?"

She held her tongue, but her face blanched a shade or two.

"Not asking for you to tell me the sordid details," Trevor said. "I'm asking so I can gauge if I'm gonna have a rowdy asshole show up at my bar. I also need to know if this is going to be something you juggle on a daily basis."

She huffed out a tired exhale and her shoulders slumped. "I'd say her fears aren't unfounded, but it's not something you'd have to deal with here. Wyatt saves his tantrums for smaller audiences."

Every muscle in Trevor's body locked up tight, reflexes born at a young age flaring hard and fast. He knew exactly the type of tantrum she meant. Had lived under his father's tyrannical fists for seven years before fate and his mother's death had turned his whole world upside down. "Get your stuff and get home."

"You're firing me?"

"No, I'm telling you to quit jacking around here and get home to your son." He forced himself to take a solid breath and unclench his fists. "From here on, if you need to keep the phone with you, that's fine, but use it in private. I don't need other employees claiming I play favorites. And next time, don't try to handle two issues at once. Tell me or whoever's managing the club you've got an issue then get your butt home and deal with it right."

For the first time since he'd met her, her smile reached her eyes and the careful mask she kept in place slipped. "Thank you." It was barely more than a whisper, but thick with enough emotion it almost knocked him over. She reached out as though to touch his arm, but tucked her arm back against her side just as fast. "I promise. You won't regret this."

Before he could respond, she slipped around him, yanked opened the door, and hurried down the dark hall.

He caught the door in one hand before it could close and stared after her, dangerous ideas taking root in his head. Nope, making a concession for Natalie where phones were concerned wasn't a decision he'd regret, the same way he wouldn't lament beating the shit out of her ex if the bastard ever laid a hand on Natalie or her kid.

Chapter Two

No human being should be allowed to drive on a cocktail of frayed nerves, fear, and adrenaline. Especially not a mother trying to get home to her kid before her narcissistic ex scared him to death banging on the door.

Barely slowing to check oncoming traffic, Natalie whipped a right-on-red and gunned her Lexus SUV the last block to her apartment complex. Thank God her new boss was a decent human being. She'd been panicked reading her mother's texts all night, but had been equally terrified of losing her job. Once upon a time, her salary as even a starting RN would have made being the sole provider for her mom and Levi a doable proposition, but that was years and a bad decision ago, and processing health insurance claims didn't rake in the big bucks. Her tips working one of Dallas's trendiest bars definitely helped take the edge off.

Bypassing the main parking lot, she paralleled farther down the street and killed the engine. Trying to hide the gleaming white and chrome vehicle from Wyatt was probably a wasted effort. It stood out almost as strong as a neon sign on a clear night, but it was less than a year old, reliable, and paid for. Aside from the clothes she and Levi had managed to pack, it was the only asset she'd asked for in the divorce. Plus, it made for one heck of a reminder. A reflection of how much of herself she'd given up before Wyatt had literally knocked her back to her senses.

The car's locks engaged with a subtle click, but the automatic headlights stayed illuminated, painting a bold path between her and the staircase across the parking lot. Not exactly the stealthiest approach, but definitely safer in this part of town. Besides, if Wyatt was waiting for her, there'd be no getting around a confrontation.

Halfway up the staircase, she scanned the cars below. No lights glowed other than the old street lamp and no movement registered, but her heart hammered as though the hounds of hell were queued to pop out of the shadows at any moment. Fucking Wyatt. Just once she'd like to feel safe again. To actually believe she could call the cops and expect some kind of help.

She worked the old but solid deadbolt until it clunked open and forced the door open with her shoulder. Soft, white light glowed from the galley kitchen's stove, just enough to let her mom and Levi get around the two-bedroom apartment if they needed to, but not enough to clue Wyatt in to anyone being home. Her mom lay stretched out on the couch with Levi tucked up in the crook of her arm. His dirty-blond hair was tousled and had grown so long it nearly reached his eyes, but cutting it wasn't a battle she was ready to fight yet. For Levi, a haircut meant looking more like his dad than he already did, which meant he'd fight tooth and nail to avoid it.

She placed her purse onto the end table, eased to her knees beside him, and whispered, "Hey, sweetheart."

Her mom jolted awake, simultaneously squeezing Levi closer and shifting to protect him. Only when she realized it was Natalie crouched beside them, did she let out a shaky breath and relax into the cushions. Once upon a time her hair had been a lustrous dark brown, but now it was nearly all gray. While she never went out of the house without minimal makeup and her simple bob styled just so, tonight it was frazzled. She pressed the heel of her hand against her heart. "Warn an old woman next time, would you?"

"Sorry. I was in a hurry." Natalie picked up Levi's hand and squeezed it, loving the warmth and comfort the simple contact provided. One touch and her heart settled. At the first hint of his little boy scent, her lungs drew their first decent breath in hours.

Careful not to jar Levi, her mom pushed upright and squinted toward the cable box perched on top of the old box television set. 9:08 beamed back at them in neon blue. "I thought you wouldn't be home until after close?"

"Yeah, well it turns out my new boss isn't just hot enough to seduce half of Texas's female population, but has a heart of gold, too." When she'd first walked into Trevor's office for her interview, his looks had literally knocked her for a loop, leaving her as coordinated as a drunken sailor wearing clown shoes. Thick blond hair tied back in a ponytail, sigh-worthy blue eyes, and a square jaw that made her think of Vikings—he was one hundred percent, Grade-A visual goodness.

Apparently, she wasn't the only one who thought so. Every woman who walked in the bar rubbernecked the laid-back cowboy in blatant appreciation. For that reason alone, she'd vowed never to ogle him or his jean-clad ass again, even if it meant keeping her gaze locked on his chin through all their conversations.

She smoothed Levi's bangs off his forehead. "How long's he been out?"

"Since Wyatt quit banging on the door about forty-five minutes ago." Her mom frowned and double-checked to make sure Levi wasn't feigning sleep. "He's terrified of him, Nat. It took a full hour after Wyatt started knocking for him to believe me when I said I wouldn't let Wyatt have him."

And her mom wouldn't either. Maureen Dubois might be petite and almost seventy, but she'd protect Levi with her last breath. The same way she'd tried to protect Natalie by begging her not to marry a highfalutin plastic surgeon. "You know Wyatt. He only wants what he can't have. Sooner or later, he's bound to get tired and find something shiny and new."

At least that was what she hoped happened. It was a heck of a better plan than following through with her fantasies of running the bastard over with the high-priced SUV he'd bought her.

She squeezed Levi's shoulder and kissed his cheek. "Come on, kiddo. Let's get you in bed."

Levi stirred, wrinkled his little nose, and rubbed the back of his hand across his eyes. God, he deserved so much more than the father who'd sired him. Hell, he'd deserved a justice system that wouldn't turn a blind eye to an abusive man too, but in the end, Wyatt's good-old-boy network had proven stronger leverage than human decency.

Finally waking up enough to realize his mom was home, Levi's eyes sharpened and his whole body went tense. He lurched forward and wrapped his arms around her neck. "He tried to take me. It's not his turn. He can't make me go when it's not his turn."

"I know, baby." Taking him with her as she stood, she hugged him close and paced toward the room he shared with her mom, smoothing her hand down his back. "He's not going to take you yet. I promise."

A heavy knock rapped against the door.

Natalie whipped around and froze, eyes locked on her mother.

Inside her arms, Levi's once-languid body went rigid, and he whimpered.

She palmed the back of his head and whispered in his ear. "Shhh. Don't say anything. He'll go away and it'll be okay."

At least if they were lucky, he would. But then the one thing she'd learned in the most painful way possible the last eight years was that Wyatt didn't let something go once he'd set his mind on it. Ever. Once the court granted her divorce decree, what he'd decided he wanted was his wife and son back—even if he hated them both.

The knocks came harder and faster, followed by Wyatt's bellowing voice. "Open the goddamned door, Nat. I know you're home. You really think that Lexus blends with this piece of shit neighborhood?"

She kissed Levi's cheek and peeled one arm from around her neck. If she didn't defuse Wyatt quick, he'd shout the whole damned complex down. "Baby, I've gotta deal with him, but I promise you, he's not getting in, okay? Not so much as one step in the house. I'll just tell him it's not time for his visit and he'll go away." It wasn't a complete lie. More like a fervent wish that had a snowball's chance in hell of coming true, but she'd give it her best. At this point, she'd call the cops to make it happen if she had to.

Levi grappled to regain his hold, but didn't make a noise. And how sad was that? Seven years old and already versed on how best to avoid his father's wrath.

Crouching next to the couch, she sat Levi next to her mother. "It's just for a minute or two, sweetheart. You'll see." She focused on her mother. "I'll lock the door behind me. Take Levi to your room. No matter what, don't open it. I'll tell him I'm headed out and that you two are gone to a movie. If I have to, I'll take him out for coffee until he's mollified."

"Call the police, Natalie. It's safer."

Wyatt banged on the door. "I want to see my son, Nat. Open the door. Not going to play this game all night."

"Sorry, Wyatt!" she called out as chipper and innocent as she could. "I'm coming. Just give me a minute." She frowned at her mom and squeezed her knee. "No police. We tried that once, remember?" All she'd got was a shrug from the police and extra lawyer bills when Wyatt accused her of breaking custody arrangements. Funny how the onus was on her to prove she'd abided by the decree instead of the other way around.

She cupped Levi's face and smiled as big as she could manage. "Soon as this is over we'll read a book. You wanna sleep with me tonight?"

He nodded, barely appeased by the bribe.

"Deal." She stood, struggling to keeping her smile in place while Levi and her mother hustled to their room.

She could do this. For Levi, she'd relocate the damned Sierra mountain range with her bare hands. Snatching her purse off the floor, she sucked in a bracing breath and coiled her hand around the knob. *It won't last forever.* In the last nine months those words had been her mantra. The one hope that kept her sane. But tonight was here and now, and whether she liked it or not, she had an asshole to face.

As bad ideas went, snooping around Natalie's house with a bully ex-husband on the loose had to be damned close to the top of the list. Outside Trevor's driver-side window, a run-down 7-Eleven had a mini congregation of thugs huddled off to one corner. They couldn't be more than thirteen at most and were huddled into oversized hoodies to fight off the incoming cold front.

The quiet strains of Chris Stapleton's latest release disappeared, replaced with the automated feminine voice from the GPS. *"In a quarter mile, make a right turn on Mount Auburn Avenue."*

Shaking his head, Trevor gauged the distance on the onscreen map and fought the urge to cancel the program. He rarely stooped to using the feature that had come with his newest truck, but tonight speed seemed more important than feeding his pride.

He took the turn indicated and coasted another half a block, checking out both side windows for numbers on mailboxes.

"Your destination is ahead on the right."

As soon as the guidance trailed off and the music kicked back into play, Trevor pulled up to a smallish parking lot. The building behind it wasn't the worst apartment complex he'd ever seen, but it wasn't the best either. No gates or signs of security, and probably older than the ranch he'd grown up on, but the grounds were well-kept and a few antiquated streetlights cast a moderate glow.

He snatched the Post-it he'd jotted Natalie's address on and compared it to what he'd punched in on the nav.

Yep. Definitely the right place. For some reason, seeing her Lexus in the employee lot and appreciating the simple but quality clothes she'd worn for work every night, he'd expected something completely different. Then again, all he'd really had time to learn about her was that she seemed undaunted when it came to tackling new tasks, which made him seriously reconsider only doing cursory background checks on entry-level employees.

This whole thing between her and her ex wasn't his business. With his past, he was twenty shades of stupid for being here, but he just couldn't shake the fear in her voice before she'd hung up the phone with her mom.

Wyatt's an idiot, but not enough to break down the door.

How many times had he heard his mother with that same frustration? That same dread? No one had helped her, and look how that had ended up.

He swung his Silverado Dually into a wide spot at the back of the parking lot and killed the engine. Being here might be stupid, but the least he could do was be there for Natalie the way he wished someone had been there for his mom.

He'd barely put one boot on the cracked asphalt when voices sounded in the distance, one woman and one man. They weren't exactly shouting, but it wasn't a private affair either. More like a heated debate with the potential for a full-blown toe-to-toe.

Ahead, a sidewalk ran between two long buildings that faced each other. He followed it. Natalie's light Texas drawl grew clearer with each step, but with the way the voices ricocheted through the tight space he couldn't judge which apartment was hers. He'd just about neared the staircase when she and her ex came into view on the top floor standing just outside the corner unit. He ducked under the landing right beneath them.

Despite the calm delivery behind Natalie's words, her voice shook with impatience. "He was just with you four days ago, Wyatt. The court said we switch every week. This is my week."

"I don't give a fuck about the courts," Wyatt said. "He's my boy, and I'm gonna see him when I want."

"Well, you can't see him now. He's not here."

"After nine o'clock on a school night, and he's not here? Don't shit me, Nat. You keep that boy so locked to his schedule, he wipes his ass by the clock."

"Well, he's not. Mom took him to a movie."

Not a bad tactic, but not one that would work long term. Not with a dick like her ex.

"Then maybe I need to file a case for sole custody seeing as how my boy's mother doesn't have enough common sense to have her kid home on a school night." He scoffed. "Hell, looking at this place, I'm thinking I ought to file regardless."

"It's safe, and it's clean."

Movement sounded above Trevor, and Wyatt's voice dropped low and menacing. "He's in there, and I know it. Now, open the goddamned door, Natalie."

Trevor was in motion and jogging up the stairs before his mind could reassess the action. Adrenaline surged fast and furious, but he reined it in tight, reminding himself this wasn't about dealing with his past. This was about Natalie and her kid. He rounded the top landing and forced his steps into an easy amble.

Nat's eyes got bigger than a July full moon.

Wyatt, on the other hand, sneered like he'd just watched a vagrant take a shit in plain sight, and damned if that didn't give Trevor exactly the plan he needed to knock that son of a bitch off his high horse. It may not be as satisfying as pounding the fucker into next week, but he'd be damned if he let some arrogant, polo-wearing bastard get the better of him. "Hey, darlin'," he said to Natalie, still twenty feet away. "What's goin' on?"

"Um." She glanced back and forth between him and Wyatt and wiped her palms on her thighs. "My ex stopped by for a chat."

So far so good. Hopefully, she'd clue in to what he was

up to as fast as she'd learned how to wait tables. He slid up next to her, wrapped one arm around her waist, and pulled her tight to his side. "Yeah? You sounded upset." He kissed her temple and glared at Wyatt. "There a reason my woman's upset?"

Wyatt's gaze shot from Trevor's possessive grip on Nat's waist to Trevor's face. "Your what?"

"My woman. Been seein' Natalie for about a month now and don't enjoy stopping by to make sure she got home from work all right to find her trading heated words with her ex."

Wyatt scowled at Natalie. "You're fucking someone else?"

She might have been stunned stupid up until that point, but the crass comment kicked that stubborn streak he'd glimpsed earlier into high gear. Mirroring Trevor's action and wrapping her arm around his waist, she lifted her chin a fraction. "We're divorced, Wyatt. The day the judge signed the paper was the day it stopped mattering who I see or what I do with them."

"Not with my boy in there."

She fisted Trevor's shirt just above his jeans, and Trevor gave her hip a reassuring squeeze. "Trevor never stays when Levi's here," she said. "He only stops by to make sure I make it home. Those are the rules in the divorce decree, and I keep them."

"Those are the rules today." Wyatt scanned Trevor head-to-toe and cast an evil smile at Natalie. "We'll see how quick you are to jump in bed with someone else when I take your boy." He huffed and spun for the stairwell.

Muscles bunched tighter than a guy wire in straightline winds, Trevor fought the need to stride after the uppity jackass and throw a few threats of his own. Hell, he'd be content just to land a handful of punches. Though, God only knew what trouble that would cause Natalie after it was over.

Together, they waited, both of them eyeing Wyatt's progress through the parking lot to his shiny black Mercedes without saying a word.

When the door slammed shut and the engine revved, Trevor spoke. "He really gonna follow through on that claim?"

Nat sighed, and her shoulders sagged. "With him, there's no telling. He doesn't want Levi around. Hasn't since I got pregnant a year into our marriage, but he does want me. Or thinks he does." Only after Wyatt sped out of the parking lot did she drop her arm from his waist and hang her head. "Levi makes good leverage."

For three or four heartbeats his instincts grappled for what to do next. Part of him wanted to give in, chase Wyatt down, and end Natalie's problems for good, but most of him was fixated on how to get her next to him again. He hadn't noticed it until she'd stepped away, not with his focus so zeroed in on Wyatt, but without her body next to his he suddenly felt unbalanced. Awkward, like someone had forced his feet into new boots that fit all wrong.

Behind them, a metallic clink rattled from the window.

Trevor shifted in time to see the window blinds swing. "That your apartment, or a neighbor's?"

Nat closed her eyes and frowned. "That's mine." She dug in her purse and pulled out her keys, but the door swung open before she could use the lock.

An older woman about Natalie's height and build beamed at him from the threshold. Her hair was full gray, but there was no mistaking the resemblance between her and Natalie. Clinging to the woman's thigh and staring up at him with big eyes was the most adorable kid he'd ever seen. Sandy blond hair that was long enough it hung close to his hazel eyes. Definitely his daddy's genes, but on him they were pure goodness.

"Natalie, are you going to invite your friend in?" Her mother stepped forward as best she could with a kid glued to her leg. "I'm Maureen Dubois, Natalie's mom. This is her son, Levi." She patted the boy on the back. "Say hi to the man, sweetheart."

Levi swallowed big enough his head bobbed, but he released his hold on his grandmother, straightened, and stuck out one hand. "Hi."

Careful not to scare the kid, Trevor stepped forward and clasped his little palm. "Hey, bud. I'm Trevor. I work with your mom."

Levi's eyes got big like the sum of two plus two had just clicked in his head. "You're my mom's boss. I know 'cause she talked about you a lot for like three days."

"Did she?" Trevor grinned at Natalie beside him and offered his hand to Maureen. "Nice to meet you, ma'am. Sorry if I woke you up. I just wanted to make sure Natalie made it home."

"Nonsense." She stepped back and waved him through the door, not the least bit upset to be talking to a stranger in her pink and gray pajama set. Come to think of it, the outfit looked a lot like the sets his adopted mom, Bonnie, had worn around at night, only Bonnie always favored blue. "Why don't you come in and visit a bit?"

Well, this was awkward. "I appreciate the invitation, but—"

"He might come back," Levi blurted. "He's already been by four times tonight, and mom says he's persastant."

Natalie moved in quick and cupped her son's shoulder. "It's *persistent*, Levi. And Mr. Raines has already done more than I can thank him for."

Reevaluating, Trevor wasn't too sure he'd done anything but stir up trouble. Yeah, he'd stalled the dickhead for tonight, but men like Wyatt seldom gave up without some kind of grenade tossed over their shoulder. Nothing pissed a man off more than another one marking their old territory.

He nodded to Maureen. "Levi probably needs to get his sleep."

"Oh, Levi's got another thirty minutes at least." Maureen grinned huge, a happily scheming momma if he'd ever seen one. "And Levi's right. Wouldn't hurt to have you here for a little while at least."

Trevor coughed and rubbed his chin, too chicken to make eye contact with any of them. Bailing Natalie out of a bind was one thing, but spending time with a star-struck mother, an employee, and her kid was something else.

Nat smiled at him, the expression soft and mixed with gratefulness and resignation. "It's okay, Trevor. I appreciate what you did. We'll be okay."

Translation: *You staved things off for one night, but this won't be the last time we deal with it.*

Well, fuck that. She might have to deal with it on another night, but for this one at least, he could make sure the monkey stayed the hell off her back. He winked at Levi and planted his hands on his hips. "I reckon I can stay a little while."

Chapter Three

Nothing made a woman realize how tiny and run-down her place was until a six-foot-three hunk of a man ambled in and took his sweet time scanning every detail. A really good-looking, Adonis hunk of man that had scrambled her wits with nothing more than an arm around her waist. As powerful as his touch had been, it would take a week before her body stopped tingling.

Tucking her hands in her back pockets, Natalie cleared her throat and nodded toward the kitchen. "I'm not much of a drinker, but I was thinking I'd make some coffee if you're up for some."

"Oh, that's a great idea." Maureen ushered Levi toward the kitchen with one hand and waved Trevor toward the kitchen table. "Trevor, why don't you and Natalie take a load off, and Levi and I will get a pot going."

Trevor dipped his head in that polite way Natalie had come to appreciate. "Thank you, ma'am."

"You see, Levi?" Maureen said as they rounded into the galley kitchen. "I told you nice men always use good manners."

"But you said men should keep their hair cut too, and his is long. If I say *yes, ma'am*, can I grow my hair long like his?"

Trevor grinned, ducked his chin, and scratched his

jaw like he wasn't sure what to say. When he spoke, his voice was low enough Levi couldn't hear from the kitchen. "Sorry about that."

"Don't be," Natalie said. "Long hair I can deal with, but we've really been struggling with manners. If he takes a cue from you on that score, I'll be grateful." Realizing she was just standing there like a clueless teen, she hurried toward the kitchen and pulled out a chair. At least her mom had been smart enough to steer things toward the kitchen. With only a couch and an old club chair available in the living room, any kind of seating arrangement would have been awkward. "Have a seat."

Instead of following her straight away, Trevor glanced back at the window beside the front door, made quick work of opening the blinds, then strolled to the table. If he'd seemed big in comparison to her apartment before, seeing him rounding the ancient dinette put him on par with a giant. He settled in the chair beside hers with his back to the wall and a straight-on view of the window.

"Are you a real cowboy, or do you just dress like one?" Levi asked from behind her.

Natalie spun in her chair. "Levi, that's a rude question."

"No, it's not," he argued back, innocent as ever. "Bobby says lots of people dress like cowboys, but they're really not." He focused on Trevor, animated and warming up for the details that always followed with stories of his best friend. "Bobby's dad works on a ranch, so he's a real cowboy, but says most people who wear boots just wear 'em to look good. Since you have a bar instead of a ranch, I figured you wear 'em cause they're awesome."

"Levi!" Natalie shot to her feet. More than anything, she loved the guileless way her son's mind worked, but not everyone took his comments as lightly as he intended them. "How Mr. Raines dresses and why is none of your business."

"Why do you call him Mr. Raines if he's your boyfriend?" Levi glanced back up at his grandmother. "He told Dad that Mom was his woman, so doesn't that mean he's her boyfriend?"

Her mom patted Levi's shoulder and cast the same patient smile she always used on him. "I think it's rude to eavesdrop and bad form to ignore your momma when she says to still your tongue."

"But—"

"No buts." She lifted her gaze to Natalie and Trevor. "Coffee's brewing. I think Levi and I will call it a night and let the two of you talk." She held out her hand to Trevor. "Mr. Raines, it was nice to meet you."

Trevor stood and shook her hand, but it was a more polite and gentle touch than Natalie had seen him use with men at work. "Call me Trevor, ma'am. And thanks for making the coffee."

"I'm happy to do it." She herded Levi down the hall, a not so simple task considering how Levi kept craning his head around to watch Trevor with those big, adoring eyes. And damn it if that didn't break her heart a little more. That was the way a boy should look at a man. Not constantly ducking his chin and avoiding eye contact the way he did with Wyatt.

The door to their bedroom clicked shut.

"Your mom's a real nice lady," Trevor said, still standing.

Shit. Of course, he wouldn't sit until she did. Which probably explained why her son didn't have a clue on manners. Hard to teach them if she didn't follow them. She eased back into her seat, and Trevor followed suit. "I think she likes you, too." Probably more than Trevor would be comfortable with if he had any inkling what the gleam in her mom's eyes meant. On the plus side, Maureen Dubois's stamp of approval said a lot about a man. Neither her mom or her dad had cared for Wyatt, and look what ignoring their warnings had gotten her.

Angling his chair for a better angle on Natalie, Trevor reclined in his seat and rested one arm on the table. "Your ex always pull stunts like tonight?"

And there was the rub. The reason why she kept herself so isolated as far as friends or relationships went. Being reminded every day of how stupid she'd been marrying Wyatt nine years ago was bad enough. Having to own it with others was mortifying. She studied the dinette's old cherry veneer and tried to come up with some answer that wouldn't sound as bad as reality.

"You don't have to tell me anything you don't want to," he said, "but it might help me better understand what I jumped in the middle of."

He had a point. And considering he'd bought her and Levi a little wiggle room, he deserved at least the basics. "He wasn't always this way."

Trevor kept his gaze trained on her, his focus utterly undivided. Now that she thought about it, he was always like that. Focused on one thing or person at time, always giving them his full attention. While his expression stayed neutral, there was something in his eyes that silently encouraged her for more.

She swallowed, hating the truth as it fought its way out. "I got pregnant with Levi right after our one-year anniversary. Things changed after that." She shrugged and smoothed one palm along her thigh. "I tried to fix it, but nothing worked."

"Tried to fix it how?"

God, he was quick. Sharp and always focused on the smallest nuances. She'd need to remember that going forward. "To be the wife he wanted. Social events, lots of friends that weren't really friends, a housekeeper. A plastic surgeon's trophy wife." She met his stare and smiled the best she could. "That just wasn't me."

"How long have you two been split up?"

Not long enough. Every day she prayed Wyatt would find some new focus for his life, and yet the one time he'd backhanded her still felt like it happened yesterday. Like the bruise still pulsed beneath her skin. "About a year. I tried to save up before I walked out with Levi, but time ran out, and I had to make do with what I had. Mom helped. She sold her house and we used the money to cover legal bills and get set up here."

Trevor frowned. "What do you mean, time ran out?"

Oh yeah. Nothing got past Trevor Raines. She scrambled for something to say, anything to put him off course.

He tensed and narrowed his eyes. "He hit you?"

"Uh…"

"Or was it Levi?"

She clamped her lips together hard, fighting the need to run and hide away in her room like she'd always done with Wyatt.

But this wasn't Wyatt. This was Trevor. A man whose employees respected him and who ran a tight ship at work. Who'd calmly walked up beside her and taken a stand against her ex. Although, the way that he studied her now, she was beginning to think her new boss wasn't quite as laid-back as she'd thought underneath.

Trevor's gaze shot to the front door, then back to Natalie. "He got any way of getting in your apartment?"

"No. I told the people who manage the place there's history I'm trying to get away from, so they know better than to let him in. I've told Levi and my mom never to answer the door for anyone."

"So he *did* hit you."

In that second, Natalie half expected Trevor to launch out of his seat and track Wyatt all the way to his fancy Grapevine home. The idea should have terrified her. Or at least have spurred her to defuse Trevor's growing anger. Instead, all she could process was relief. A much appreciated sense of protection after months of feeling alone, no matter if the sensation was real or not.

"Should have decked the fucker like I wanted." Trevor scanned her tight posture, let out a slow breath through his nose, and unclenched his hand on the table. "Sorry. Abuse is a trigger for me."

It was? The unexpected scrap of information hit her so hard out of left field, she nearly asked him as much, but caught herself before she could let the question air. She'd already shared more with her boss than she should. Asking him personal questions would only clear the path for him to dig deeper in return. "It's okay. I understand."

Behind her, the coffeemaker gurgled and hissed as the last of the hot water emptied the reservoir. She stood and motioned for Trevor to keep his seat when he started to do the same. "Relax. I appreciate the manners in front of Levi, but it's not necessary with me. How do you take your coffee?"

"Black's fine."

Natalie shuddered and pulled out a few of her mother's oversized clay mugs. The yellow cups had been in her mother's kitchen as long as she could remember and would probably work as self-defense weapons given how heavy they were, but they brought good memories. "I don't know how anyone can drink the stuff straight. I need almost as much milk and sugar in mine as I do coffee."

"Got a sweet tooth, huh?"

She poured the coffee and slid the carafe back on the

burner. "Guilty. Pastries, cakes, or candy, it doesn't matter. I'm a glutton." Pouring milk in one cup, she huffed out a chuckle. "Makes keeping my booty a reasonable size a bit of a challenge the older I get, but if I have to choose between dessert or a small behind, then I'll take dessert, thank you very much."

She finished off stirring in her sugar, turned with both mugs in hand, and nearly stumbled mid-stride back to the table.

Trevor's smile was gone and his smoldering gaze took a long, leisurely trip up her body. "If sweets are what give you those curves, I'd say it'd be a damn shame for anything healthy to pass your lips."

Dear Lord in heaven. How any woman alive could keep from melting into a puddle of goo beneath that expression, she'd never know. It'd been years since a man had looked at her like that, and wowza, did it do a number on her girly parts.

"Thank you." It was a lame retort, but what else was she supposed to say? No matter how good the attention felt, he was still her boss. Even if he wasn't, she wasn't sure she'd ever be up for tangling with another man. Clearly, her judgement wasn't sound enough to pick healthy partners.

She set his coffee in front of him and carefully took her seat, blowing across the top of her mug and studiously avoiding his gaze.

"Your kid's a hoot." One simple, easy statement and he had them back on track.

Part of her was reluctant to let the moment go, but it was probably for the best. "He's the spitting image of his dad at that age, but they couldn't be more different in personality. Levi's got a huge heart. And he's smart. Never misses anything." Some of the moment's lightheartedness dimmed. "Especially not the struggles I was having with Wyatt. Even as a toddler, he steered clear of his dad or found creative ways to keep us apart."

"How the hell did an abusive dad end up with joint custody?"

For a moment, she thought about deflecting and keeping them in safe conversational territory, but having someone to talk to, someone willing to simply listen for once, was too tempting to pass up. "Because Wyatt is nothing if not connected. I didn't ask for anything in the divorce except for custody of Levi. So naturally, that's the one thing he wanted."

"But he hit his own kid. The judge didn't factor that in?"

She shook her head and cupped both hands around her mug on the table. "It only happened once to Levi, and once to me before that. When he hit me, it woke me up. I started planning and saving. But when it escalated to Levi, I knew I couldn't wait. I got us out as soon as Wyatt left for work the next day. Only problem was, the mark Wyatt left on Levi's cheek wasn't enough to convince the police Levi had done anything except fall off a bike. Wyatt played me up as a vengeful wife, and the judge bought it."

On the surface, Trevor seemed to keep his cool, but the air around him changed. Whatever it was that somehow tied him with abuse, it was entrenched deep.

She laid one hand on his wrist and squeezed. "Let it go. God knows that's what I'm trying to do."

"Hard to let it go when he's knocking on your door."

"True." She pulled her hand away and sipped her coffee. "Eventually, Wyatt will fixate on something or someone else, and he'll accept I'm not coming back. That's my hope anyway."

"That's what he wants? You two to reconcile?"

"No, he made it quite clear what a disappointment I was as a wife. According to him, my getting pregnant ruined our marriage. He wanted someone to attend events and travel with him when it suited, not the responsibility of a parent. Though, if you ask me, what really pissed him off was that he wasn't the center of attention anymore."

"Then why's he coming around?"

"Because he can't have me, and Wyatt always wants what he can't have." She winced and set her coffee on the counter. "That sounds really pompous doesn't it?"

"Not if it's the truth. And he wouldn't be the first man who didn't know how to take no for an answer."

"What about you?"

He cocked his head and crossed one foot over his knee. It'd been forever since she'd owned a pair of boots. Well over a decade, in fact, but she'd bet good money his black boots were top dollar Luccheses. "What about me?"

"I've spilled my guts since you got here, and all I know about you is you've got the patience of a saint and are Deep Ellum's reigning pub king."

"Pub king?"

She shrugged. "That's what Ivan calls you. He says most bar owners don't hold a following in that part of town as long as you've been able to."

He smiled and rubbed his knuckles along his chin. He didn't quite have a five-o'clock shadow yet, but she'd bet he'd have an irresistible one first thing in the morning. Clean shaven, he was dreamy, but with some stubble he'd be every daddy's worst nightmare. "I got lucky with The Den. Though my brothers know bars like a native language. They guided me into it. My real love is flying."

She raised her eyebrows, silently encouraging him for more.

"Been flying since I was eighteen. Once I met my brothers, I set out to make it my profession. Now I've got a private charter service."

"What do you mean 'you met your brothers'?"

His expression blanked. It wasn't a complete shutdown, but more of a topic he didn't quite seem ready to share. "Long story." Picking up his mug, he uncrossed his leg and stood. "It's late, and according to your application, you've got a day job tomorrow."

She nodded and stood as well, torn between begging him to sit back down, and welcoming the chance to be alone and gather her wits. She took his mug and carried it to the sink. "Thank you again for what you did. I know you didn't have to, but I'm hoping it'll get Wyatt to back off for a little while." Not to mention her baby boy would be chattering nonstop about manners and cowboy boots for days.

"You're my employee, Natalie. You don't have to thank me."

She planted a hand on one hip and leaned into the counter. "You're telling me you spend a lot of time checking up on all your waitresses after hours?"

"Nope. I'm saying I've got a vested interest in you having your head in the game at work. If that means helping you not worry about your boy by stepping in, it's a no-brainer." He grinned. "Plus, it satisfies the shit out of me for a man like Wyatt to get a little of his own medicine."

With that little quip, he winked and sauntered to the door.

Natalie followed, shamelessly enjoying the way his faded jeans molded to his very nice ass. Funny, she couldn't remember the last time she'd ogled a man, but Trevor was a prime candidate for brushing up on long-dead skills.

He opened the door, studied the parking lot beyond,

and motioned at the blinds he'd opened. "You close those up, and lock up tight, all right?"

"Yep. Got it."

For a handful of heartbeats, he just stood there, studying her. "Want you to promise me something."

She tilted her head. "What kind of promise?"

He narrowed his eyes and stepped close. The same woodsy cologne that had coiled around her when he'd tucked her tight to his side assailed her senses and sent her heart kicking in a happy rhythm. "I appreciate you've told your mom and Levi not to answer the door, but if your ex comes back, I want your promise you won't answer the door either. And I don't give a fuck what kind of beef the cops gave you in the past. He shows, you call 'em anyway."

"That's two promises."

God, he had an amazing smile. Gorgeous white teeth and a roguishness that made her insides tingle. "Yeah, it is. Now tell me you'll do what I asked."

She nodded, too muddled by his presence to do anything else.

"Good." He cupped the side her face and brushed his thumb along her cheekbone, the simple touch alighting flutters in places she really shouldn't feel for her boss. "If the cops don't treat you the way they should, you let me know." He dropped his hand and strolled out the door, but there was no missing the dark promise in his parting words. "Wyatt's not the only man with connections."

* * * * *

Don't miss the next book in the MEN OF HAVEN *series,* CLAIM & PROTECT *by Rhenna Morgan.*

Acknowledgments

Pulling off some of the suspense nuances of Zeke's book would have been a challenge without the wisdom shared by Dr. H. Dwight Hardy III. Thankfully, he seemed to get a kick out of my next hero being a trauma doc, so he invited me out to his country retreat and loaded me up with all kinds of doctorly wisdom I could wield in my dastardly plots. My utmost gratitude to him for his support, his guidance and, most important, his care throughout the years. He is simply *the best*.

I also owe Angela James more cyber hugs than I can count for not only helping me whip this story into the best shape possible, but loving Zeke and Gabe as much as I did. There's absolutely nothing better than working with someone who "gets you" and is willing to champion your stories. For her time, her patience and her support, I am supremely grateful.

Finally, much love and high fives to my tribe—Cori Deyoe, Juliette Cross, Kyra Jacobs, Audrey Carlan, Dena Garson and, of course, my family. Really, you guys are my go-to peeps in any and all situations. Navigating this world wouldn't be nearly as much fun or gratifying without you.

About the Author

Rhenna Morgan is a happily-ever-after addict—hot men, smart women and scorching chemistry required. A triple-A personality with a thing for lists and an almost frightening iPhone cover collection, Rhenna's a mom to two beautiful little girls and married to an extremely patient husband who's mastered the art of hiding the exasperated eye roll.

When she's not neck-deep in writing, she's probably driving with the windows down and the music up loud, plotting her next hero and heroine's adventure. (Though trolling online for man-candy inspiration on Pinterest comes in a close second.)

She'd love to share her antics and bizarre sense of humor with you and get to know you a little better in the process. You can sign up for her newsletter and gain access to exclusive snippets, upcoming releases, fun giveaways and social media outlets at www.rhennamorgan.com.

If you enjoyed *Wild & Sweet*, she hopes you'll share the love with a review on your favorite online bookstore.

Get 2 Free Books,
Plus 2 Free Gifts—
just for trying the Reader Service!

Get 2 Free Books,
Plus 2 Free Gifts—
just for trying the
Reader Service!

MED17R2

Get 2 Free Books,
Plus 2 Free Gifts -
just for
trying the
**Reader
Service!**

YES! Please send me 2 FREE novels from the Essential Romance or Essential Suspense Collection and my 2 FREE gifts (gifts are worth about $10 retail). After receiving them, if I don't wish to receive any more books, I can return the shipping statement marked "cancel." If I don't cancel, I will receive 4 brand-new novels every month and be billed just $6.74 each in the U.S. or $7.24 each in Canada. That's a savings of at least 16% off the cover price. It's quite a bargain! Shipping and handling is just 50¢ per book in the U.S. and 75¢ per book in Canada*. I understand that accepting the 2 free books and gifts places me under no obligation to buy anything. I can always return a shipment and cancel at any time. The free books and gifts are mine to keep no matter what I decide.

Please check one: ☐ Essential Romance   ☐ Essential Suspense
                      194/394 MDN GMWR   191/391 MDN GMWR

_____
Name   (PLEASE PRINT)

_____
Address   Apt. #

_____
City   State/Prov.   Zip/Postal Code

_____
Signature (if under 18, a parent or guardian must sign)

Mail to the **Reader Service:**
IN U.S.A.: P.O. Box 1341, Buffalo, NY 14240-8531
IN CANADA: P.O. Box 603, Fort Erie, Ontario L2A 5X3

**Want to try two free books from another line?
Call 1-800-873-8635 or visit www.ReaderService.com.**

*Terms and prices subject to change without notice. Prices do not include applicable taxes. Sales tax applicable in NY. Canadian residents will be charged applicable taxes. Offer not valid in Quebec. This offer is limited to one order per household. Books received may not be as shown. Not valid for current subscribers to the Essential Romance or Essential Suspense Collection. All orders subject to approval. Credit or debit balances in a customer's account(s) may be offset by any other outstanding balance owed by or to the customer. Please allow 4 to 6 weeks for delivery. Offer available while quantities last.

Your Privacy—The Reader Service is committed to protecting your privacy. Our Privacy Policy is available online at www.ReaderService.com or upon request from the Reader Service.

We make a portion of our mailing list available to reputable third parties that offer products we believe may interest you. If you prefer that we not exchange your name with third parties, or if you wish to clarify or modify your communication preferences, please visit us at www.ReaderService.com/consumerschoice or write to us at Reader Service Preference Service, P.O. Box 9062, Buffalo, NY 14240-9062. Include your complete name and address.

STRS17R2

READERSERVICE.COM

Manage your account online!

- Review your order history
- Manage your payments
- Update your address

We've designed the
Reader Service website
just for you.

Enjoy all the features!

- Discover new series available to you, and read excerpts from any series.
- Respond to mailings and special monthly offers.
- Browse the Bonus Bucks catalog and online-only exculsives.
- Share your feedback.

Visit us at:
ReaderService.com

RS16R